There was an archive h
gicians. Those were the
the working of magic, r

Mikk yanked on a p
The stone paving groaned but did not give way. Strange, he'd opened it easily three days ago.

(Up.)

"Who's there?" he demanded loudly.

(Look up. You must go up.)

"Who are you?" His words echoed in the high-ceilinged room as he gazed up and spied another trapdoor overhead.

(Join us above.)

Chills ran up and down his spine as dust tickled his nose.

(There is no dust in the up.)

That sounded good. But he'd been warned about enemies of the crown who would not hesitate to kill or kidnap a member of the royal family.

"I'm only second heir and a distant cousin from the female line. I'm not valuable to anyone other than my grandparents," he muttered.

(We value you. We know who and what you are.)

That was too good to be true.

Still . . . He dragged a wooden bench across the floor and placed it beneath the trapdoor. A tug on the short rope dangling from the wooden square opened the access. A ladder unfolded until the bottom rested snugly on the floor. He sprinted up until just his head cleared the opening. He found a thick layer of darkness that swallowed light and sound and, above that, long chains of bright and pulsing colored light.

(Welcome to the realm of dragons!)

Be sure to read these magnificent
DAW Fantasy Novels by
IRENE RADFORD

*Coming soon from DAW Books

THE
BROKEN
DRAGON

Children of the Dragon Nimbus #2

IRENE
RADFORD

DAW BOOKS, INC.
DONALD A. WOLLHEIM, FOUNDER
375 Hudson Street, New York, NY 10014

ELIZABETH R. WOLLHEIM
SHEILA E. GILBERT
PUBLISHERS
www.dawbooks.com

To my sister Sally
who has proven over and over that broken doesn't
mean done.

PROLOGUE

*L*IKE A SPIDER *sitting in the center of his web, I seem immobile and harmless. As I have done for decades. I have set my bait. I have only to wait for each of my prey to come forward and stumble into the far-reaching strands of my web. They do not have to step far away from their own desires to find me. I am the key to their dreams. Their dreams will give me my dreams. Mine are more encompassing, more important. Mine belong to the future and the many generations to come, and reach deep into the past. Their dreams are limited to the here and now.*

The past must be my template. It must guide the future. Restoring the past ensures the future.

Let them scheme and plot. If I can read their dreams while they sleep, surely I can find a way to speak to them through the void and make them think they form their own plans and solutions. King Darville of Coronnan thinks he has two heirs: his bastard son and his aunt's bastard grandson. I have poisoned the queen so that she can never give him the male heir he dreams of. Neither of his heirs is worthy, neither has been raised to think like a king.

The University of Magicians and its leader Jaylor think they have regained power and prestige within the govern-

ment. Also a mistake. He and his minions Marcus and Maigret—I have stolen Robb out from under their noses—tamper with the proper magical fabric of the land and will pay for their sins when I restore the land of my birth to its natural order.

I only regret that I must depend upon women to spring the traps I have set. Women have no place in proper magic. But then, men are always disgustingly vulnerable where women are concerned. I have found allies who know this truth and will give me what I need to complete my plans, my revenge. The women and my followers will serve me, and then I will discard them, as is proper. And none of the criminals, royal or magical, will know the source of their downfall. They have dismissed me as inconsequential, too conservative, not imaginative enough, too much talk and not enough action, for the last time. Everything is in place so that they must acknowledge the righteousness of my cause, pay homage to me. And then die.

CHAPTER 1

"READY OR NOT here I come!" Valeria called to her supposedly hidden siblings. Slowly she peeked through her fingers to make certain six-year-old Sharl and two-year-old Jule had found places that were not out in the open. They needed to think they played this game correctly and that they won honestly.

Ah, there was one tiny bare foot visible behind the chopping block. On the other side of the sturdy stump with the hacked surface, Val spotted her twin Lillian crouching beside their youngest brother. Her faded blue dress, the same color as her aura, didn't quite fit behind the perennial landmark in the family clearing.

A faint giggle behind Val revealed that her older brother, Lukan, had climbed an everblue tree, dragging their sister Sharl with him. Lukan always went up. His routine never failed. Lily on the other hand always sought deep contact with the ground, trusting their mother planet, Kardia Hodos, to shelter and shield her.

"I spy . . ." Val called as she deliberately ran in the wrong direction. "I spy the hoe someone didn't put away." She turned a double circle with the tool held high for all to see.

More giggles. She sensed Sharl oozing down the everblue from branch to branch, responding to her need to put everything in its proper place, even when tidying up was someone else's chore. She needed order and organization to function. Even at six, she'd be a wonderful help to Mama when Lily and Val left tomorrow to take their journeyman's journey.

They all needed this last game together before the family split in different directions, perhaps forever.

A pang touched her heart. No, she wouldn't think about that yet. She would enjoy this game *now*, as she hadn't been able to for most of her sixteen years.

Val dropped the hoe and ran toward her twin. "I spy Lily!" she crowed. "Behind the block."

"Have to tag me first," Lily called back. She jumped up and darted away, leaving Jule "hidden."

Val laughed out loud and levitated a loose handful of grass, ferns, and dirt from the forest verge. Without bothering to touch the clump, she flung it at her sister. It landed square in the middle of Lily's back with an audible thump.

"Oh!" she whoofed as she stumbled to a halt, as the game rules dictated. "No fair! Magic isn't in the rules."

"It is now." Still laughing, Val swung around and headed toward Lukan's tree. She ran for the sheer joy of feeling the wind cooling her overheated face and ruffling her hair.

"Tag you, tag you," Jule chortled in his baby mastery of two words at a time. He'd been talking his own nonsensical language almost since the moment of his birth. Nonstop. Now he finally put sounds together in something resembling words others could understand.

Val slowed a little, to give her brother a chance to catch her skirt in his grubby fist. Meanwhile she sought something suitable to fling at Lukan, still up in his tree. Something that would bring him down from his perch before suppertime.

A flusterhen squawked in mighty disapproval as Jule tripped over the bird. In protest at the indignity, the hen loosed an odiferous white stream. Val thought new dirt into covering it quickly. Then she smiled with a wicked idea. While the dirt coalesced around the blob she pushed a tendril of magic beneath it, lifted it high and pushed, keeping an image of Lukan in her mind's eye.

The damp clod plopped against something soundly within the thick branches.

"S'murghit, Val!" Lukan cursed, then repeated it three times. The sound of cracking branches followed his rapid descent from his sanctuary.

Not wanting to be on the receiving end of his temper, she whirled to run around behind the cabin. Oh, he'd stomp and storm and yell for an hour. Then when she least expected it, he'd apply suitable revenge.

A deep, wheezing cough stopped her before she moved a step. Her breath caught in the back of her throat. Pressure in her chest threatened to crush her. She bent double, forcing blood to flow into her head before she passed out from lack of air.

"Breathe, Val," Lily ordered, pressing on her spine.

A tingle of strength flowed from Lily's hand into Val. It helped her fight the restriction in her throat and lungs.

"I'm all right!" she gasped, tilting away from Lily. Her twin had done this too often, giving her strength while Val gave her magic in return.

"Val?" Lukan asked cautiously.

The two little ones clung to Lily's skirts as she backed away. Tears threatened as her jaw twitched and eyes blinked. Clearly she was disappointed that Val had rejected her once-necessary ministrations.

"The flywacket is out of me, no longer leeching me of strength. That cured me of most everything. I just need to catch my breath," she told them angrily. "I'm not an invalid anymore!"

"I guess you aren't," Lukan agreed. "But no more running for now. Mama probably has supper ready."

"Do you think Da will get home in time . . . ?" Lily asked hopefully.

"Doubtful," Lukan didn't seem to trust himself with

more than one word. He wouldn't voice his true anger toward their father, or his frustration with life in this sheltered clearing, his masters at the University, the world in general. Of being left behind while their oldest brother, Glenndon, went to the capital to be heir to King Darville, and Val and Lily went off on their own journey.

As if to change the subject he picked up Jule and held the boy against his shoulder, stroking his soft hair until he rested his head and found a thumb to suck—dirt and all.

"Da is still in the capital. He's not due home until late tonight or early morning," Val confirmed.

"Just in time to leave again with you two on some secret errand." This time Lukan's frustration shone through his voice. "He doesn't even stay around long enough to notice how sick Mama grows, by the day."

"She's pregnant again. She's not young anymore . . ." Val stated the obvious. Lily's scowl stopped her. "Is it more?"

Lily nodded. "I don't know what pains her, but this pregnancy is different from Jule and Sharl."

"With you two gone, I don't know how to help her," Lukan confessed.

Val knew this was his real fear and that he masked it with his habitual anger. "We need to talk to Maigret the potions mistress, and Linda her apprentice, and . . . and Marcus, before we go with Da tomorrow."

"Has anyone noticed how changeable Da's health is?" Lily asked. "Mama puts something in his tea every morning. But he's not always home and he won't accept medicine from anyone else. If he even knows he's taking medicine."

"His color is higher than normal," Val said, realizing for the first time just how unusual it was. "And his temper is shorter. He won't let anyone do anything for him. He has to do everything himself."

"Controlling everything and everyone to the tiniest degree," Lukan said bitterly.

"I wonder . . ." Lily said, resting her left hand on Sharl's dark red curls.

"What?" Lukan encouraged her.

"Just . . . one of those old stories. Something about Da accidentally taking an overdose of the Tambootie and . . . and getting lost in the void for a long time. Could that have damaged him in some way?"

"I don't know," Val murmured, suddenly seeing patterns. "Glenndon has a Tambootie staff, and he got lost in the void right after he went to the capital to become Crown Prince." The story of their eldest brother being the child of the king, conceived during that episode when Da was lost in the void, suddenly made sense.

"Val, you were lost in the void," Lily said, biting her lower lip. "The dragons had to rescue you."

"But I had no association with the Tambootie. And I still had the flywacket— a kind of dragon—while I drifted in the realm of dragons. I'm safe. And healthier than I have ever been."

"I think we need to warn Glenndon next time we see him," Lily continued. "If nothing else, he can keep an eye on Da."

"You can warn Glenndon if he ever deigns to receive us again," Lukan sneered. He held Jule closer and stalked toward the cabin and the welcoming smells of yampion pie. Da's favorite. That he wouldn't be home to eat.

"When we are all separated, I think we need to scry each other. Often," Val said quietly. "We need to know what's happening here with Mama, and you, Lukan, need to know what is going on elsewhere."

"If something happens to Mama . . ." He bit his lip as he blinked rapidly, forcing back tears. "Lily, you're the empathic healer in the family. I'm going to need your help and advice. Maigret and Linda are good magicians and healers but . . . they don't feel what's wrong with their patients. They just treat symptoms. You will know what is wrong."

"But . . . but my talent isn't strong. I can receive a scry, but I can't initiate one."

Val needed to reach out and reassure her twin, be the strong one for a change.

"But I can summon you," Lukan reminded her. "I'm not a great and wonderful magician like Glenndon. But I can put together most spells. It just takes me longer than it does him."

Like a full heartbeat instead of half of one, Val thought sarcastically.

"How . . . who will come get me with the transport spell? I'm not likely to be able to walk back here in time if you really need me."

"I will," Val insisted.

"You know the transport spell?" Lukan asked cautiously.

"Of course I do. And so do you. We wouldn't be Jaylor's and Brevelan's children if we hadn't eavesdropped and spied on our masters." They all grinned widely. Even Lily. She might not have enough magic to throw the spell, but she knew in theory how it worked.

"Then I need to work out a way to include all three of us in a scry, no matter how far apart we wander."

"We'll always be family," Lily reminded them. "Family is the strongest tie of all."

Above them, a nearly invisible dragon bellowed an agreement.

"Get that evil beast away from me!" a woman screeched, from behind the stout wooden door reinforced with iron bands and magic wards.

Lillian, daughter of Senior Magician Jaylor, flinched at the noise akin to a dragon in distress. Her ears hurt, but she dared not show her weakness in front of her Da and her twin, Valeria. They both possessed more magic in their little fingers than Lillian could ever hope to control.

Nor did she wish to admit that she had dreamed that

strident voice. Upon recognizing it in daylight, with her eyes and mind wide open she knew that deep-rooted fear—terror—fueled that voice.

"Kill it!" the woman yelled. A loud clank of something metal hitting the door followed.

A cat screeched in the same tones as the woman, outrage and fear battling for dominance. If it was like any other cat, outrage would win. It too hit the door, claws scrabbling for a purchase against the wooden surface.

This time both Da and Val backed up, making a warding gesture with their hands.

Lily deferred to their superior experience and skill and followed suit. There wasn't a lot of room to move on the landing, five stories up in this isolated stone tower. She might escape up or down steep spiral stairs cut into the stonework if she had to give the others more room to work.

Unless she could fly. Which she couldn't. And neither could the lady held within the tower. Her sister had dreamed of flying with dragons. That was the one experience Val had not shared with her.

The lady had tried to fly, at least twice in the last fifteen years. Fortunately her companions had stopped her in time.

Or was she truly fortunate in continuing to live? Here. A prisoner of her own insanity?

"Da, do you smell that?" Lily asked. Her nose wiggled in search of the almost sweet scent of hot coals merging with the wooden door, followed by the acrid stench of cat urine and fire clashing with the magical wards.

"Aye. Time to intervene I think. Before she kills the cat."

"This is ridiculous. Can't anyone see the terror in her mind?" Val demanded, hands on hips, chin thrust out. She stepped forward and passed her open palm across the door in the intricate rune pattern that would release the wards and negate any lingering fire from the coals.

Lillian couldn't even see the wards, let alone hope to

make them obey her. She'd studied the rituals. But she had no talent to make them work.

"We're coming in, Ariiell," Val called. She pushed gently against the door. It swung inward about half a hand-width. Out streaked a gold, black, and gray cat, eyes wide, ears laid back, and fluffy tail bristled as wide as the rest of her body.

Lillian caught a whisper of a name. Grilka. She smiled that the cat willingly shared her true name—not the one the cook and servants called her—Grilka. *A lovely name for a lovely creature,* Lily reassured the cat.

She stepped out of the cat's way rather than stoop to soothe it. In its current mood, she'd probably walk away with bloody scratches on face and hands. The poor creature disappeared down the stairs, not even trying to quiet its footfalls.

The door opened wider. "I have to kill her. Kill her and that filthy weasel that follows her. They'll steal my baby. That's all they ever wanted from me was my baby!" A skinny woman with lank and tangled honey blonde hair appeared, an open warming pan held over her shoulder like an ax, ready to chop something to shreds. She'd been pretty once. Gaunt cheeks, parched skin, wild eyes, and worry lines on her brow, around her eyes, and turning down her mouth had robbed her of her beauty.

"Mistress Ariiell, calm yourself," Da said gently. "The cat is gone. The weasel with it."

Ariiell blinked several times. Panic vanished and her pale blue eyes cleared. Understanding dawned in her gaze. Some of her crone ugliness sloughed off. "Excuse me, Lord Jaylor, for my rude inhospitality." She dropped a light curtsy. The copper warming pan interfered with her hands holding her skirts out. She stared at in incomprehension.

"Here, let me take this from you," Val said, easing the handle out of Ariiell's grip. Her eyes looked strained as she focused on the older woman.

Lily rushed to her twin's side, very familiar with the

look of fatigue and headache that followed her magical exertions. A sharp tingle of power repulsed Lily's hand as she sought to add her strength to her frailer sister.

She looked more closely into Valeria's eyes. All of her sister's focus and talent probed Ariiell. For the first time in their lives, Val had no need of Lily's help and shut her out of her mind.

Something broke inside Lillian. A barrier stood between her and her birth mate. They'd never been separated for more than an hour or two. They shared everything! Lessons, chores, thoughts and dreams: all belonged to both of them together.

Except the dream of flying with dragons.

Lillian looked to their Da for an explanation. Panic and tears threatened to choke her.

"Valeria?" Da asked. "Are you ... are you in control or her?"

"Of course she doesn't do anything more than probe me, Lord Jaylor," Ariiell said. "I am in complete control of my own mind and actions. I just have these spells ... Sometimes I forget, or remember too much. I'm not exactly sure which. But now that the cat and her weasel companion have been banished to the void where they belong, I am fine."

She backed away slightly and gestured to a comfortable seating arrangement by an arrow-slit window. The room curved around the full circumference of the tower without walls between sitting, sleeping, and bathing areas. The interior wall around the central stairwell was the only barrier in the room. Three hearths with plastered chimneys protruded inward and warmed the space where thick stone trapped winter's chill, even on this warm afternoon in early summer.

Valeria stayed two steps behind Ariiell and to her left, her eyes slightly crossed and glazed in a light trance. She was inside the older woman's mind whether Ariiell admitted it or not.

Lillian began to shake, alone in her mind and not liking it. Not knowing what to do, how to think without Val. They were twins. They'd been inside each other's thoughts from the moment of birth—and before. She slumped onto a stool beside Da's big padded chair. It looked like it had been made for his height and solid breadth.

He took Lily's hand and held it on his thigh while he addressed Ariiell. "My lady, your father, Lord Laislac of Aporia, has requested you return to his household," he said, making sure each word came out clearly.

"About time the bastard acknowledged me!" Ariiell spat. "Who's he going to pawn me off on this time? Marriage, I think, is in his plans; safer than trying to control the Coven through me. He's lucky The Simeon left him alive. He's got an alliance in mind. Otherwise he'd have no use for me. Just as he's had no use for me or for my baby these . . . Stargods! How many years have I been locked up here? It seems like . . . like last month at most that I gave my son to a wet nurse."

"Your son, Mikkette is fifteen now," Da said gently. "He attends the king at court and is considered a potential heir to the Dragon Crown. His grandmother, Lady Lynetta, has raised him gently and educated him suitably for royal kin. We call him Mikk."

Ariiell reacted with only a lifted eyebrow and a deep breath. "Fifteen years? I must be getting a bit long in the tooth for an arranged marriage."

"I do not know your father's plans, my lady. Do you consent to leave the safety of this tower for your father's household?"

Valeria blinked. She was tiring and losing focus.

Lillian desperately needed to go to her, brace her; give her the physical strength to continue. She didn't know what she could do inside Ariiell's mind to keep her calm, but she had to try.

Her twin held up her hand palm out and shook her head. Valeria had to do this alone.

Alone.

A hole gaped in Lillian's gut.

"Safety? Didn't you see the cat I evicted? You call it safe when Rejiia and Krej waltz in here anytime they wish? They are trying to steal my baby, take him back to the Coven. Use him as their next blood sacrifice! If we don't stop them now they will assassinate the king and take over the government. Then they'll evict the Council of Provinces and rule Coronnan with every cruel whim they choose. Without resistance."

"The cat that just left calls herself Grilka and inhabits the pantry, keeping it free of mice," Lily offered.

Da looked at her with something akin to approval— an emotion missing since he'd discovered she had no talent, and had relied upon Valeria to make it look as if she threw magic. "What color was the cat?" Da asked, blandly, as if Ariiell's near hysteria meant nothing.

This time Ariiell blinked. Val's eyes took on the glaze of acute concentration.

"She was . . . it was . . . calico." Ariiell's chin trembled and her eyes filmed with tears.

"Rejiia's cat body is all black except for one white ear," Da reminded her. "It looks akin to her human black hair with a white streak that ran from her right temple all the way to her hips. And there is no sign that her fa ther, Krej, in the body of a tin weasel with flaking gilt paint, was anywhere near the tower."

"Stargods, what have I done this time?" Ariiell buried her face in her hands and trembled all over.

Val shook herself free of the trance and stepped away from the troubled woman. Only then did Lily realize that her twin had kept a hand on Ariiell's shoulder the entire time.

"She'll be okay for a while," Val said softly and promptly collapsed onto the small, rocking chair on the other side of Da. Her face had leached of color except for the dark circles under her eyes. Her veins pulsed so close to the surface of her nearly translucent skin they looked purple.

Lily took a chance and moved her hand from Da's grasp to rest it on her twin's knee. "Don't," Da said, reclaiming her hand. "She has to learn to do this on her own."

Lillian glared at him and yanked her hand free, replacing it on Val's knee. Concentrating on their blood and mind bonds, she trickled reviving strength into Valeria. Just a little. Enough to keep her from falling into sick exhaustion. "She may not have good control yet, but I do," she whispered.

Valeria smiled and unlatched the door to her mind. Not a full mingling of their thoughts, but an opening if Lillian needed it.

Having that opening, she found she didn't need full contact. Just the knowledge that she could have it if needed.

"So, my lady, do you consent to return to your father?" Da asked again, returning his full attention to Ariiell.

"I suppose. At least it will be a change from these same walls all day, every day. When do we leave?"

"You cannot travel alone, my lady."

"I have a maid."

"You need a companion."

"You mean a keeper?"

Da nodded. A dreadful feeling crept out of Lillian's stomach. This was why Da had brought her and Val with him on this errand.

"Very well. Which of the three healers who regularly visit me is to keep chains on my mind?"

"Someone more gentle. Someone who will help ease you back into a less solitary life."

Lillian wanted to gag. Even with Val's help she didn't think she'd be able to manage Ariiell's "spells."

"Which of your two daughters?" Ariiell speared Lillian and Valeria with a penetrating gaze that seemed to reach all the way into the depth of Lillian's soul. "How old are they? Sixteen? Fifteen? Hardly out of the schoolroom. The same age as my son."

"How old were you when The Simeon manipulated you into joining the ranks of his Coven?"

"Fifteen," she sighed. "I'll forget that, in few hours or days. Just as I forget everything important, or trivial, when I have one of my fits. I hope life treats your girls more gently than The Simeon did me."

"The Simeon is dead, Ariiell. The Coven is broken. The last remaining members are either dead or transformed into powerless totem animals. We broke the Coven many years ago and I've seen no sign of anyone reviving it."

"Are you certain? I can sense Krej and Rejiia. They are still alive."

"But no longer in positions of power. You are safe from the Coven. I would know if anyone in Coronnan tried to organize rogue magicians against the University and the Circle of Master Magicians."

She nodded, then looked at Lillian again. "Not her." Ariiell shook her head and turned to stare at Val. "That one will do. I find her soothing. She smells of cat. A strong cat. So I presume she is capable of protecting me from Rejiia and Krej."

"I thought the same as well," Da said. "Valeria will go with you as companion. I have a separate job for Lillian."

CHAPTER 2

JAYLOR SETTLED HIS twin daughters into a small bedroom on the third floor of the tower. They at least had a decent sized window overlooking a broad meadow where plow steeds grazed. He felt safe in assuming neither of his girls would attempt to fly out of it. Unlike Ariiell.

This land belonged to Lady Lynetta, the king's aunt, and her husband Lord Andrall. Close enough to the capital city for quick summoning in an emergency, far enough away to protect troubled Ariiell and her son—until he grew enough to require education with his grandmother. The lord and lady were senior among the twelve provinces, well respected, and strong enough to fend off any interlopers who might try to manipulate an heir to the crown and his mother.

Beyond the next line of rolling hills, Jaylor knew the Coronnan River ran, broad and serene, only a few miles from the delta islands that made up Coronnan City. After three months, the water had settled back into a normal channel. He still had nightmares about the near disastrous damming by a tangle of Krakatrice seeking to turn Coronnan into a desert. When the dragons had broken the obstruction of dirt, felled trees, and other debris, a wall of water seven feet high had rushed seaward, carving new channels, obliterating small islands, and leaving new ones behind.

Jaylor and his son Glenndon ... stepson ... now Prince Glenndon ... had fought the Krakatrice matriarch, while trying to contain an eruption of pure, raw magical energy in the confined courtyard of the royal barracks. They won. Barely. But lost much.

"Da, what does this all mean?" Lily asked. She looked as pale and shaken as her twin. But color and vigor returned to Val's face, while Lily looked near to fainting. An opposite from their usual reactions.

"We'd best sit for this," Jaylor said, perching on the side of one of the two cots set up for them. The girls huddled together, arms draped about each other, on the other bed. That was normal: two halves of one whole, one never complete without the other.

Now he had to separate them for their own good. He and their mother, Brevelan, had discussed this for months. They'd sought every possible way to teach the girls how to act independently so that Valeria—never physically strong or healthy until recently—didn't exhaust herself working magic for both of them. And Lillian had to learn to act on her own, probably without magic.

"I didn't want to say anything in case Ariiell rejected this plan of her father's," he said hesitantly, propping his chin in his hands and his elbows on his knees.

"Why not?" both girls asked at the same time.

"Because life is about to change for both of you."

The girls looked at each other, mingling their thoughts, as they always did.

"You are separating us," Val said flatly. "I'm to go with the lady upstairs, keep her calm and rational."

"Your job as a journeyman magician is also to report back to me anything untoward in Lord Laislac's household," Jaylor informed them, sitting straighter.

"Journeyman?" both girls gasped.

"Both of you have journeys to take and reports to make. But still, a journey is about learning and problem solving on your own. Reports should be few and far between except in a dire emergency until you arrive at your destinations. We are returning to the old style of politics. Each lord now has a master magician in his retinue who acts as neutral adviser, scribe, and archivist. The bond between lords and their magicians often goes well beyond the political; they become friends, tied to each other and dependent upon each other. The masters are not always neutral. The lords do not know that they each will also have a journeyman infiltrating their household to keep me and the king apprised of what really goes on. What conversations they hold with outsiders, who visits and who doesn't, who are their friends, and who are their adversaries."

"How loyal they are to the king," Lillian said.

"How often do they turn a blind eye to those who cross the borders of their province," Valeria completed the thought. Aporia, where she would escort Ariiell, bordered on SeLennica, ancient enemy and sometimes uneasy ally of Coronnan. Two minor and rarely used passes through the mountains opened into Laislac's lands.

"Exactly," Jaylor agreed, proud that his girls understood their new roles so well. "Lord Laislac gratefully surrendered custody of Ariiell to the king's aunt and her husband when her insanity became unmanageable. Now he wants her back. Why?"

"You said both of us," Valeria offered. "I understand why I am to go to Aporia."

"Lady Ariiell rejected me," Lillian added. "I'm not going to Aporia, am I?"

"No, Lily. I have a separate, and possibly more important, job, for you." He took a deep breath, trying to find gentle, unalarming words. "Lady Graciella, Lord Jemmarc's new bride, is not well. She needs to return to Castle Saria to rest and breathe fresh sea air, away from the demands of the capital. You will go with her as nurse and companion. You know herbal remedies. You demonstrated a degree of healing empathy last spring."

"Saria," they both said on a deep exhale. "Lord Krej's old province." Valeria took over the thought.

"If Lord Krej and his daughter are still about, even if transformed into their totem animal bodies . . ." Lillian continued and broke off in deep thought.

"Saria is on the coast, with secret landing sites for an invasion," Valeria continued listing the variables in the situation.

"Why doesn't Lord Jemmarc return to Castle Saria with Graciella?" Lily asked. "Surely he'd be better company to an ailing wife than a . . . one of us."

"Lord Jemmarc was deeply involved in the recent rebellion. His son, Lucjemm, was its instigator," Jaylor reminded them. They'd been there during the battle for power over the Well of Life.

"Lucjemm is in a coma, at the Forest University," Lillian reminded them.

"We don't know when or if he will awaken," Valeria said.

"He was obsessed with Princess Rosselinda."

"If he awakens . . ."

"And she returns from hiding . . ."

"Lucjemm could try to use her again to rebel . . ."

"And claim the throne."

The girls thought better together, jumped ahead of Jaylor with their combined intellect.

"We don't know how trustworthy Jemmarc is, with or without his son. Politically it is expedient to keep him in the capital where we can observe him closely," Jaylor said.

"You've stripped him of much authority . . ." Valeria said.

"And influence. He could become resentful and start a new rebellion," Lillian added.

"He blames Princess Linda for his son's ailment."

"He resents the entire royal family."

"He could import mercenaries from Rossemeyer or the Big Continent to his province," Valeria said.

"Keep them secret and march on the capital before you or the king knows what he's up to," Lillian finished.

"Precisely."

"When do we go to Sacred Isle to get our staffs?" they asked together. A staff to channel and enhance magic was a life-long tool, acquired only as a reward for promotion from apprentice to journey status.

"Not yet. A staff is too overt a symbol of a Magician. I need you both to be overlooked, dismissed as unimportant."

"Like Old Maisy at court, a babble-mouth seamstress who was everywhere," Valeria said sadly. She'd been with the woman when she died last spring, helping to save the kingdom from wild, raw, and uncontrolled magical energy, unleashed and lashing out against the poison of an iron pole thrust into the middle of the Well.

"If I had a staff to ground me, I might be able to initiate a summons to you, or Val," Lillian said sullenly. "I'll need to do that if I'm a spy in a household set up for treachery. What if I have something important to tell you, Da, and I can't because I'm a failure at being a magician?"

Skeller slung the straps of his harp case over one shoulder and his smaller rucksack of essential clothing and supplies over the other. Automatically he patted Telynnia, the harp within the specially designed case, to make sure she was still in there, whole and ready to sing with him the moment he tuned her loosened strings. Quietly he watched the crowd of passengers and crew disembarking from the commercial ferry that ran regular routes between his home in Amazonia and Coronnan City. Travel between the two ports had become more regular this past decade, after centuries of isolation and mistrust, but not any shorter. He needed to stretch and walk a bit to ground himself in this new land. A loud group of dark-skinned merchants wearing flowing robes and high turbans elbowed him aside. He slipped into line behind them. Merchants always traveled ahead of diplomats, laying the groundwork for understanding and advantage.

The harried customs officer on the dock barely lifted his eyes from a parchment roll as he barked, "Customs duty, one dragini for each of you."

The head merchant grudgingly fished in his belt wallet hidden beneath the outermost layer of brightly colored robes and pulled out three coins. "Three drageen," he counted as he placed the first coin in the customs officer's open palm. "Six drageen." He placed another coin in the man's hand, then looked around as if counting heads. Skeller kept his face low, wondering if he had enough copper pennies to make a full dragini.

The merchant replaced the third coin in his wallet, making a big production of extracting a smaller metal disc. "Seven drageen," he said with some satisfaction. "Seven brother, seven drageen."

Skeller counted heads as well. He made the ninth member of the group of merchants.

The customs officer examined each coin and bit into it to make sure it was solid and untainted by baser metals. Seemingly satisfied, he dropped the coins into his own belt pouch and waved the men on. He didn't bother counting heads for an accurate taxation. Maybe he couldn't count. Skeller had heard many a strange tale about the dearth of education in Coronnan.

Skeller sidled to the far side of the group now that he was off the narrow confines of the plank, staying as far from the customs officer as he could. But the official had already turned his attention to the next passenger departing the ferry.

"That was too easy," Skeller muttered. "Nothing in my life is ever that easy."

Just to prove that the Great Mother and all her sisters laughed at him, he spotted the face of the most untrustworthy man in the world, the one person who must never recognize him in this foreign kingdom.

He was standing behind the customs officer, avidly watching the departing passengers and crew. Behind him, anonymous servants with the shoulder-length hair common in Amazonia, but too short for Coronnan, carried a box about three feet cubed toward a sledge lined in animal furs and special braces. The red and black enamel paint in cryptic slashes told Skeller all he needed to know about the cargo.

He shuddered in fear.

Skeller had no doubt the man he knew only as "Sir" had hastened to Coronnan City ahead of him in his role as spymaster, and now first ambassador in a long time, for King Lokeen of Amazonia. Lokeen, a man who ruled by his own authority and not his wife's, made Skeller gag in revulsion. Unnatural. More unnatural than the deadly cargo in the red and black box.

And Lokeen had hired an unnatural adviser and spymaster. A magician! A magician who had corrupted sacred beliefs about the sanctity of life and made them into *outdated* policies. A magician who moved between Coronnan and Amazonia often and without notice and even now checked every arriving ship for Skeller as well as that box.

Time to do the unexpected.

He searched the bustling crowds and caravans of snorting sledge steeds for inspiration. Caravans?

Hmm. He wondered which of them needed a bard and wondered if any of them traveled in the same direction he needed to go.

At the moment any direction would do, so long as he removed himself from the docks forthwith.

CHAPTER 3

GLENNDON, CROWN PRINCE of Coronnan, hastily sanded the fresh ink on the parchment. He watched the lords in the Council Chamber as they milled about, discussing trivia and local gossip. The ink still looked too wet to roll the parchment. Stargods, he should be able to be-spell the black liquid before a meeting, so that it dried rapidly without the sand. But he hadn't had time since becoming Crown Prince to do more than dash from one assignment or ceremony to another. Every day, it seemed, the king handed him new responsibilities, hastening his education into all things governmental and diplomatic.

He could whisper a few words to hasten the drying process, but not in public, with so many of the leaders of Coronnan still afraid of magic.

Master Magician Dennilley passed a hand over the chronicle of today's meeting as he followed Lord Bennallt. The lord paused beside Glenndon.

"I look forward to watching you dance with my daughter tonight at court," he said, loud enough for the entire Council of Provinces to hear. Then he moved on, taking Master Dennilley with him. The ink looked dry and solid.

Glenndon groaned as he rolled the parchment. He

liked dancing with Lady Miri, but she always, always wanted more. Usually he managed only a brief kiss behind the tapestries in an alcove. Not an unpleasant experience. But Glenndon didn't like the aura of commitment that came with a kiss.

As Crown Prince he had to think beyond pleasure. When he made a commitment to a young woman, both of his fathers, the king as well as the Senior Magician, would have more to say about the alliance than *he* would.

"Do you have time for a practice bout in the arena?" Mikk asked, frowning. Mikk also liked to dance with Lady Miri, but she never trapped *him* in a quiet corner.

Glenndon relaxed a bit. He liked his shy and bookish second cousin. They shared the chore of recording the proceedings of the Council of Provinces, then comparing notes and producing a clean and coherent report for the archives. Mikk was better at the clean and coherent part.

After three months of working together they'd formed a kind of friendship. Not quite brothers—no man would replace Glenndon's brother Lukan in his affections—but it was nice to have another male near his own age and rank within the court to talk to. He had Frank too, his bodyguard who was also the son of the king's bodyguard. But Frank was always on the job, rarely unbending enough to carry on a conversation that didn't involve escape routes and positioning so that an assassin couldn't creep up behind them.

Frank had turned his back and whistled jauntily many times when Miri shoved Glenndon into a corner.

"You sure you're up to another bit of training?" Glenndon asked. This was the first time Mikk had voluntarily asked for a bout. He hadn't the height, breadth of shoulder, or strength that Glenndon had. But there was time. Mikk was three years younger than Glenndon. He would grow.

"I need to develop skill as well as strength. Grand'Mere never allowed me to do much of anything at home. Except read. Grand'Pere always brought home new books whenever he returned from court. I think they intended me for the Temple."

"Then a bout it is. I have listened to the lords hiding subtle threats and anger beneath polite political phrases for too long today. So be prepared to succumb to my blows." Glenndon grinned and slapped his companion on the back.

Mikk didn't quite stagger, but he clasped the edge of the desk they shared face to face.

Together they set about rolling their parchments (Glenndon nodded thanks to Dennilley's back for the assistance), cleaning their quills and capping the ink-wells. By the time they finished, the lords had gathered in their cliquish groups and exited. Glenndon and his cousin shared a quick glance, noting who gathered with whom, and whom they shunned. Only Mikk's grandfather, Lord Andrall, of all the eleven lords, sought the king's company openly. Lord Jemmarc hung back, trying to ingratiate himself into the aura of power without being obvious. Besides, since his disgrace last spring, none of his peers dared talk to him lest another faction interpret politeness as rebellion.

Glenndon briefly checked his father the king—the father he hadn't known was his until last spring, when Darville needed a male heir so desperately to keep his lords in check that he finally acknowledged his son and legitimatized him. Not quite noon and the king's hands were still steady, his speech clear, and his color healthy and tanned. Three months now since he'd had a drink of beta arrack, the strong liquor imported from Rossemeyer, the queen's homeland.

Perhaps he could maintain his vow of abstinence. He didn't even take wine or small beer with his meals now. Only water that had been purified of poison and disease-bearing taints by a magician.

"I've a mind to try a slightly heavier practice sword today," Mikk said brightly.

Glenndon suppressed a groan. "Stargods only know

I'm not an expert, but I think it's easier to develop skill first with a lighter sword, then build strength," he offered.

"You use a broadsword nearly twice the weight of the one I use." Mikk didn't quite pout, but he came close.

"I'm three years older with broader shoulders. There are times I wish that General Marcelle would allow me to train with a battleax. I'd certainly have more skill and a more comfortable grip." He'd honed that skill splitting logs and chopping wood to feed his mother's hearth.

"Only peasant infantry use an ax," Mikk gasped. A look of horror opened his eyes wide and pursed his mouth into a deep frown of disapproval. "A noble, especially a prince, needs to ride a magnificent steed and carry a sword so he can be seen by all his troops and inspire leadership."

Glenndon swallowed a sneering protest that he'd been raised as a peasant magician at the Forest University with his mother and Senior Magician Jaylor, the man he had considered his father until the unwanted summons to court last spring; the man he still called Da.

And though he saw his Da most every day in the city or Council Chambers, he missed Mama with a deep and abiding ache.

"What are you wearing to court this evening?" Mikk asked, interrupting Glenndon's sad and looping thoughts.

"Hadn't thought about it." He urged Mikk out of the round Council Chamber. "Whatever someone lays out for me." He hated maintaining a fashionable wardrobe. What was wrong with his homespun, forest-colored, but serviceable tunic and trews as long as they were clean? He grabbed his staff from where it stood leaning against the wall beside the huge stained-glass window and stumped toward the door with three scrolls beneath his arm.

As they emerged from the chamber into the wide receiving room with King Darville's and Queen Rossemikka's thrones on a dais to their right, Glenndon came to a stumbling halt. Across the polished tiles, gathered into a huddle like a gabble of flusterhens, six teenage girls awaited them. Lady Miri, Princess Rosselinda's former lady-in-waiting and now attendant upon the queen and the two younger princesses, raised her head and engaged his eyes with a winsome smile.

"Stargods protect me," he whispered, pounding the staff lightly against the floor.

"What's wrong?" Mikk asked, sidling slightly behind Glenndon. He had no weapon other than a ceremonial short sword—next to useless—and his penknife.

"Girls. Always hanging on me as if I alone stand between them and a long and painful death," Glenndon grunted.

"Oh, the girls. They aren't so bad. You just have to get them talking and pretend to listen. Actually, they know more about the goings-on at court than anyone else. I've learned many interesting things from them."

"That's because they see you as a friend. I'm prize meat in the marriage market at the moment because I'm the heir. All they talk to me about is how their pretty lace, imported at great cost from SeLennica, enhances their bodice. An open invitation to stare at their cleavage."

"You don't find that enticing?" Mikk blinked rapidly in dismay.

"Of course I do. But I'll never get to act on it. As long as I stay in the capital, I can expect nothing less than an arranged marriage to a foreign princess."

"Ah, but if any these girls can bear a royal bastard before your marriage, it enhances your reputation as a virile mate and gains her family much influence with the royal family. I, on the other hand, will have something to say on the choice of my bride when the time comes."

"I won't do what my father did—beget a bastard and ignore him until he needed me."

Glenndon looked around and rapidly noticed each and every person in the room or stationed at doorways.

Frank, his bodyguard, wearing the green and gold uniform of a trusted royal attendant, peered out from behind an elaborate tapestry hanging behind the throne. He beckoned. Glenndon grabbed Mikk by the elbow and judiciously retreated through the private family passage before the girls could follow him. "Swordplay. I need to bash some heads to get the sight of all those heaving bosoms out of my mind."

"Today you ride instead," General Marcelle said, appearing out of nowhere and grabbing each young man by the elbow.

Glenndon groaned. Mikk sagged as if his thighs already ached and chafed from contact with a saddle.

"You just said, Master Mikk, that a prince must appear princely on a magnificent steed. As of yet neither of you looks anything but miserable astride an embarrassed steed, even a dainty palfrey the young princesses feel at home with." The general propelled them toward Frank's hiding place. The bodyguard held the hidden door ajar for them.

"Maybe if we started with dainty palfreys and worked our way up to magnificent stallions . . . ?" Mikk asked hopefully.

"His Grace the king told me not to coddle either of you. You have a lot to learn, in a hurry. Best we start where we hope to end up."

Mikk rolled his eyes, and Glenndon firmed his posture. Learning to speak after a lifetime of silence was easier than mastering the steeds General Marcelle considered docile.

"Lukan, where are you going?"

Lukan paused in his attempt to cross the home Clearing as rapidly as possible. He shrugged rather than answer his mother.

"You are not Glenndon. I will not allow you to dismiss me with that horrible gesture," Brevelan admonished him.

She slipped a well-worn travel sack over her shoulder—she must have had the thing since before she met Da—and stepped into the sunshine.

He watched her lift her face and welcome the light and warmth. A brief word of thanks crossed her lips. Her once bright red hair tossed glints of gray and darker shades into her aura. Tiny lines around her eyes and mouth smoothed out for that short moment. She looked as young and vibrant as his sisters.

Then she turned her attention back to him, and advancing age slid back onto her face. How old was she? Thirty-six? Not forty yet. Surely. Yet she looked as if she'd aged a decade in the last few months, ever since she had stopped ignoring her latest pregnancy and openly admitted that her seventh child was due in early autumn—or earlier judging by the size of her belly.

"Long ago, the dragons promised you six children in a dragon-dream." He cast his gaze upward, away from her. "Which of us is the unwanted seventh?" he whispered to himself, knowing that he was the unwelcome one, the odd one, the ordinary one in a family of brilliance and talent.

"I might ask you what you are doing, Mama," he said aloud, moving to her side and taking the sack from her. "Where are you going with a travel sack?" He suddenly felt protective. Brevelan, the core and center of life in the family, and in the Forest University, seemed tiny, almost shrunken beside him. The top of her head barely reached above his shoulder.

He remembered hugging her knees because that was all he could reach.

"Since when do I have to report my comings and goings to my second son?" she asked, a bit of humor returning to her voice. She reached up and caressed the partially healed weal along his cheek. "That's going to scar. Mistress Maigret has an ointment that might help."

Lukan shook off her caress. He'd earned that scar observing the Circle of Master Magicians, spying for Da

and figuring out who was going rogue before his father
or either of his sisters had a clue. Master Marcus had
sought him out and praised him for his actions. Da had
ignored him. "I ask because you never leave the Clearing
without good reason."

She heaved a sigh and rubbed the side of her belly.
"Yes, this trip is a bit out of the norm. I'm meeting your
father at the University. We are transporting to the old
University to see Lillian and Valeria off on their journeys."

Lukan dropped the sack at her feet. Anger boiled in
his stomach and heated his face. "My *younger* sisters are
to be promoted to journeymen ahead of me!"

"Lukan, it's not like that. Your Da has to have a journey suited to a young magician before promotion. I
doubt you'd deal well with either Lady Ariiell or Lady
Graciella . . ."

"That's not the point, Mama. I've passed all my tests.
I'm older and more experienced than half the apprentices he's promoted. I'll never be good enough for him."
He slammed a fist into the nearest tree trunk and instantly regretted it. A bone-jarring ache spread from his
stinging knuckles to his shoulder. Blood dripped from
the barked skin. He sucked on it, turning his back to his
mother. If he admitted how much it hurt, she'd have him
back in the cabin and soaking it in some foul mixture of
herbs and goo before bandaging the injury.

He wanted her to concentrate on him for a change.
But he wouldn't stoop to childish tricks to gain her attention.

"Lukan?" She squeezed his shoulder from behind.

"It's not you, Mama. It's him. I'll never be as talented
as the golden dragon child, Glenndon—even though he's
only just now learned to speak. I'll never be frail like Val,
requiring coddling and special foods. I'll never be as
lovely as Lily, or cute as Sharl and Jule. I'm nothing."

"You are our son."

"The second son, born eleven moons after Glenndon

because Jaylor the greatest magician of all time had to prove he could sire a child on you just like the king did."

A resounding crack startled him before he knew that Mama had slapped him. Hard. His scarred cheek burned. She jolted him into silence.

"I have never struck you before. I have no intention of ever doing so again. Unless ... unless ..."

"I'm sorry, Mama," he whispered through clenched teeth. He didn't know if his lip had split when it came into sudden contact with his teeth. He didn't want to chance shedding more blood in her presence. "I didn't mean to insult you."

"But you did mean to insult your father. Your Da. The man who loves you above all things."

"No, he doesn't. He loves Glenndon. He loves the girls. He loves you though lately he's never around to show you his feelings."

"He doesn't have to be here. I know how much he loves me, and I him. He is my life, and I his." She sighed wistfully. "Though I wish he'd linger longer when he does come home. But he will always come home."

"He'd just as soon forget me," Lukan grumbled. "I'll never have a great talent. I'm only an adequate magician, which is why he handed me off to Master Marcus for training. He'd rather forget me than admit he sired a son who is less than Glenndon."

"Lukan, you will swallow those words and escort me to the University courtyard. You will then travel with your father and me to the capital to wish your sisters good journey."

"And who's going to look after the little ones while you're gone? Or does Da wish to forget them too?"

"Sharl and Jule are with Mistress Maigret and Princess Rosselinda ..."

"That's Apprentice Linda. We agreed to forget her title and treat her like any other student."

Suddenly Mama stilled. She frowned and wrinkled

her brow in puzzlement. "Lukan, why are you so angry with the world?"

He shrugged. The source of his problems with the world was obvious to him. It should be to her too.

"Seventeen. You are seventeen and your body is maturing faster than your emotions. Nothing fits, not your clothes or your skin. That's your problem. I wish you'd hurry and grow past this." She heaved a sigh, shouldered her pack, and set off on the trail to the University.

Lukan stared after her. "It's more than that!" he shouted.

"Is it? Well, if you won't come with us, you can start in on fixing the leak in the roof above the girls' loft. And make sure you dig enough yampions to keep you fed for two days." Then she stalked off, leaving him to deal with the curdle in his stomach and his bleeding fist and lip by himself.

Always by himself. No one cared about him. They were always too busy taking care of everyone else.

CHAPTER 4

"**Y**OU KNEW THIS day would come, Mama," Valeria whispered to her mother as she hugged her tightly.

"Just not so soon. You have both just reached your sixteenth birthday." Mama didn't bother wiping away her tears. She clung to Val fiercely, her fingers digging into her back. "You've never been strong. I worry about you being gone so long, on your own."

Val shared a desperate moment of loneliness with her mother. But there was something else deep within her. Val linked her mind to Lillian on the other side of the old University courtyard. Lily had an empathic talent most magicians did not recognize as real magic. But healers treasured the ability to feel and understand what their patients endured, and thus know what to remedy.

Do we need to worry more than we already do? Should we insist on staying home until she's well? Val asked her sister.

She's hiding something. Hiding it deep. Something to do with the new babe, Lily replied. *She won't let us stay even if she needs us.*

Even from across the wide-open space filled with steeds and sledges and litters for the ladies, Val knew how her twin scrunched up her eyes and bit the tip of her tongue in concentration. Before she formed another thought, Lily ducked beneath the bobbing head of a gray steed, around three overly curious goats, and elbowed through the milling crowds of guards, handlers, cooks, and laundresses; all the people necessary on a long journey. Twice as many people, actually, since there were two caravans forming up: Val's with Lady Ariiell and Lily's with Lady Graciella. They'd follow the same road for about a week, then separate.

Mama and Da stood on the University steps, as if presiding over the whole noisy, anxious, disordered affair. Prince Glenndon stood behind Da's right shoulder holding his odd staff quite possessively. He was part of the family and needed to say his farewells too, even if he was now part of the king's household and nominal heir to the Dragon Crown. His fancy new clothes fit him now. He'd grown into his princely status. Mostly.

Val didn't like to think about him being only a half brother, sired by the king, then *Prince* Darville, before Mama married Da. He was still her brother and champion, still the one she looked to for support beyond what her twin could give her.

"Mama," Lily said, somewhat breathless after her scramble through the crowd. She reached to hug their mother and Val at the same time. "Isn't this exciting? A real journey to new places, meeting new people, seeing new things."

Through their bond of blood and magic, Val shared her twin's probe to the source of Mama's anxiety. More than just worry about her daughters. More than loneliness. More than concern about the new life growing in her belly, her seventh child. A special number, to be a seventh child. Mama should be content and basking in the glory of this pregnancy, as she had the previous two. She'd been desperately ill when Val and her twin sister were born. After that she'd taken ten years to restore her health before conceiving again. Jule and Sharl had given her no trouble.

This time Mama hid a fear. Something was wrong with the child.

Maybe you need to stay and take care of Mama, Val sent on a tight line to Lillian. So tight that Da couldn't eavesdrop.

Lily passed a negative feeling back. Nothing she could do yet. But she did push a little strength, reassurance, and well-being into Mama. A temporary patch to lessen the fear.

Does Da know? Val asked.

Lillian shrugged.

Val shifted to include her father in the hug. She needed physical contact to wiggle through Da's formidable barriers around his thoughts. She sensed little worry about Mama, just gratitude that she'd left their home in the mountains long enough to see her daughters off on their journeys and congratulate them both on their promotions from apprentice magician to journeyman.

A sharp bellow from a curved ram's horn at the head of Val's caravan signaled the caravan master's readiness to depart. Val broke free of her parents and reached to hug Glenndon. "Take care of them," she whispered with a jerk of her head toward Mama and Da.

Take care of yourself, little one, he sent to her on a tight band that couldn't be overheard, even by their fath . . . the Senior Magician. *Don't overstretch yourself. You are stronger, but your stamina is still lacking.* He returned both her hug and her thoughts. *You know how to find me, any time of day or night.*

I will watch my strength. Lady Ariiell doesn't need much magic to take care of her, little more than what I share with Lily all the time.

He kissed her cheek and gave her a little shove toward the litter where her companion awaited her. Lady Ariiell hadn't shown her face in public, except when heavily veiled, since boarding her conveyance yesterday outside her tower. She'd stopped at the port only long enough to load a few boxes, things her father required, into the compartment beneath the litter, masked by a lattice of narrow slats. Lady Graciella had a similar baggage compartment beneath her conveyance. When the steeds were removed from their traces, fore and aft, the litter would rest on those compartments, about two feet above the ground.

At last Valeria turned to Lillian. Her constant companion since birth. Her friend. More than just a sister. Her twin. The other half of her soul.

I don't know how to say goodbye, she almost wept. A huge vacancy opened in her middle while her heart seemed crushed under the pressure of tears.

"Then don't say it. We will always be only a thought apart. And we won't truly separate for another week." Already Lily's attention wavered toward the litter where Lord Jemmarc helped his wife, Lady Graciella, settle into the steed-drawn litter. The man with graying hair assisted his much younger wife with rare gentleness. His aura reached toward her, needing to envelope her in warmth and care . . . and love.

Graciella withdrew from him, severing contact with his hands and his life's energy. She kept her aura so tightly bound to her body that Val couldn't tell how she felt about anything. Only that she turned her face away from her husband when he tried to kiss her.

General Marcelle half emerged from the shadowy doorway behind Mama and Da. "A word?" he asked tentatively, nodding to Da and Glenndon in the same gesture of respect.

"Of course," Da replied, easing away from where Val and Lily still hugged Mama.

"I need your daughters to hear this, my lord," the general said firmly, his gaze searching the crowd warily. "We've had reports of Krakatrice eggs passing through the port in disguised crates."

Val shuddered. They'd helped battle the huge black snakes. A millennia or more ago, they'd mutated away from the benign dragons. They shouldn't have thrived.

Yet they had. And become evil and bloodthirsty beings bent on changing the landscape into desert and destroying humanity along the way. They'd corrupted the mind of Lucjemm and pushed him to a final rebellious battle right here in the courtyard last spring.

"I'd appreciate the girls keeping an eye out for any sign of the beasts," the general said. "His Grace the king needs to know who sends and who receives any unusual crates. Report back as soon as possible." He retreated into the shadows once more with a parting nod.

Val felt Lily sidling behind her. Any report she made would have to go through Val and then to either Glenndon or Da. She couldn't shoulder that responsibility.

Go to your lady. We'll figure this out later.

"I doubt anyone cunning enough to import the eggs would try to hide them in a caravan's luggage," Lily said.

"What better place to hide something so dangerous, and illegal?" Glenndon muttered back to them. *Keep your eyes open and sniff regularly for the presence of rotten magic.*

Lily bounded over to Lady Graciella's litter and climbed in. She relaxed against the piled pillows so that she faced her new companion. Lord Jemmarc reluctantly backed away, eyes fixed upon his wife until he bumped into a stranger carrying a harp case and satchel. Only then did the lord turn around and look where he was walking.

"Lady Ariiell has no one to love her," Mama said to Val, resigned to her daughters' leaving. "Do what you can for her, Val, even if you have to eat meat to gain enough strength for the task."

Val tried not to roll her eyes. She'd been eating meat, along with Da, Glenndon, and Lukan for years. Lily shared Mama's empathy with the animals that gave their lives to feed humans. Val and others in her family didn't. They needed the protein to help fuel their magic.

"Ariiell's life has been hard and painful. No wonder she retreated into insanity rather than remember what she has done, and what has been done to her," Mama continued, unaware, or ignoring, Val's digressing thoughts.

Val's stomach suddenly felt empty. She longed for the stash of jerked meat in her pack within Lady Ariiell's litter.

"You can help the lady, Val," Da added. "You may be the only one who can."

Then they both stepped back and away, leaving her to her journey, and maybe her destiny.

"I have a feeling we are missing something," Glenndon said quietly to his parents—Jaylor and Brevelan. Almost three months in the capital and he still couldn't bring himself to admit that the king was his father. All evidence aside, King Darville had three beautiful daughters and a lovely and gracious queen. They'd been a loving family long before Glenndon came into their household. He felt like an intruder even if he was the acknowledged heir to the Dragon Crown. He'd been a part of Jaylor and Brevelan's family since birth. The departing twins were more his sisters than the royal princesses; though Rosselinda, the oldest, and he shared a unique bond that went beyond half-blood, well into the realm of magical unity.

How fare you, Linda? He sent a quick mental probe to her at the Forest University, near Mama's home. The huge stone building behind him was the old University, abandoned near eighteen years ago, and re-inhabited by magicians only recently. Da was still sorting out which master magicians taught and resided at which edifice.

Maigret makes her potions way too complicated. I'm sure there's an easier way. . . . Linda's thoughts drifted away from him.

Satisfied that she thrived in her temporary exile, Glenndon turned back to his parents. "What are we missing, Da?"

"Besides your brother Lukan? We're always missing something. There is always a lord, or a merchant, or a foreign ambassador, or a rogue magician with a grudge against us. We can't anticipate all of them," Da said, avidly watching as the two caravans began winding their way out the gates—newly repaired after a short-lived rebellion of lords and an invasion by Krakatrice.

Glenndon didn't want to dwell on the monstrous black snakes that tried very hard to turn lush Coronnan into a desert. Maybe that was what bothered him. This place, the scene of the final battle just a few months ago. *Stargods! I thought we killed them all. Who would be so stupid as to import more. No one can control them,* he sent to his father, knowing he'd pick up the tight line of communication.

I don't know. But there has to be a magician involved at some point in the plot. The dragons are keeping an eye out for any stray and hatchling snakes. They haven't called me out to help fight any since we capped the Well with clay so that it can breathe. The Well of Life does more to control invaders than individual lords with their armies, or a dragon, or a single magician.

Glenndon couldn't help examining the entire courtyard with all of his senses, physical and magical. And then there was the Well of Life—the source of all magical energy in Coronnan—intricately linked to ley lines, Dragons, and the Tambootie trees, all three necessary to each other. Magic permeated the courtyard, because of the Well and the leftovers from centuries of magicians, journeymen, and apprentices training and practicing here. How could he tell if anything new and dangerous crept up on him? Even his bodyguard Frank—waiting by the pedestrian gate, giving him privacy with his family—would be hard put to sense what was wrong and out of place.

Glenndon needed to be elsewhere, now that Lillian's caravan followed Valeria's onto the main road heading south. They'd separate in five or seven days, Val heading west toward Aporia and the mountains with Lady Ariiell, Lillian continuing south before angling east to Saria.

As if sensing his restlessness, Jaylor looked over Mama's head to him. "I need to take your mother home. Will you visit for a few days?"

"I wish I could. King Darville—uh—Father has given me the responsibility to receive new ambassadors. There's one just come from Amazonia, the first representative we've had from them for generations. They do like their privacy and isolation. He has an appointment to present his credentials before we sit down at the negotiation table. I have obligations." Glenndon let his head drop in disappointment. He'd really rather immerse himself in chopping wood and playing with Jule and Sharl.

Mama rested her hand on Da's arm even as he wrapped his arm around her, preparing to transport out. "I miss you, Glenndon," she said quietly. "I miss all my babies grown up and flying the nest."

"I know, Mama. I miss you most of all. But I have responsibilities to . . . to my father. You and Da insisted I understand that."

She hung her head. "I know. I know. But that doesn't stop the missing. And now with your . . . with Jaylor here so much in the capital, the cabin seems too big for just me and the babies."

"And Lukan. My scatterbrained brother has to be good for something. He'll keep you too busy just trying to prevent him from blowing something up to miss me." Glenndon half-grinned in memory of some of Lukan's escapades. His own too. Barely eleven moons apart, he and his brother had done most everything together, until this last Spring Equinox.

He wondered why the boy had stayed home. Surely saying goodbye to his sisters should outweigh whatever teenage temper had sent him skulking away from Mama and Da and the transport spell.

Gently, he kissed his mother's cheek, slapped Da on the back, and strode proudly down the steps, thumping his staff against the stone with each step. He aimed for a postern door tucked into the massive stone walls of the University. He didn't look back. Couldn't look back. He had an awful feeling in the pit of his stomach that whatever he sensed was missing was going to reach up and bitc him in the ass.

CHAPTER 5

SKELLER SETTLED HIS harp case and his rucksack more comfortably on his shoulders as he took up a position near the end of the long caravan along with the baggage and supply sledges. A gelded steed nibbled at his pack, curious and annoying in the mischievous way of his breed.

"Easy, boy. I've got nothing to appease your insatiable appetite." Skeller patted the long nose, letting his fingers trace the nap of its short hair, admiring the gentle swirling pattern of growth. There was noble blood in this steed, dilute and distant, but still . . .

The steed snorted. Its breath smelled of fresh hay and grains. Skeller returned the favor, letting the beast smell his breath and acknowledge him. Then he eased away from his new friend. "When we stop to rest, I'll find you something to eat," he whispered as he set his steps to counting the paving slates that wound out of the courtyard. No sense letting the magicians on the stairs read his thoughts and stop him from finding out the truth of this expedition. He had no doubt the big man in the blue brocade robes standing by the slender woman with faded red hair was important in the arcane hierarchy of magic and politics. That convinced him of the importance of this caravan.

And the blond youth all dressed in gold tunic and brown trews with soft leather boots had to be the prince of this land. His presence also added credence to the importance of the women in the two litters. Skeller had heard the scandal, of bringing a magician out of the southern wilds to become male heir to a king with only daughters.

Only daughters! King Lokeen and his late queen would have triumphed to produce a surplus of daughters as heirs and rightful rulers of their city-state. Instead, Lokeen had ruled in his wife's name so long, while she faded away with a long and lingering illness, that when she died, few noticed her passing, and the upstart male was allowed by default to continue as king without a wife to grant him rights and authority.

Rather than spit his disgust, Skeller swished the moisture around his mouth until a note ached for release. He released it softly, followed by another and another until a spritely walking song moved his feet along with the pace of the travelers. His strong baritone voice attracted the attention of the walkers around him. And the steed. The big gelding sidled until he could rest his head on Skeller's shoulder. It heaved a sigh of adoration, eyes drooping in bliss. The weight of him dislodged the harp case and Skeller had to scramble to keep it from falling. He couldn't risk damaging Telynnia. Above all else, she was more important to him than even his mission.

"Great Mother, if these people had outgrown the Stargods' shortsighted stricture against the wheel, I'd be dragged down and left under the rolling wagon," he sighed to himself.

The sledge pulled by the adoring steed slowed everyone down, but it didn't founder in the ruts dug by the stout pole frame.

A magician strolled by, whistling off-key, and with a gesture lifted the end of the pole on the sledge ahead of Skeller out of a muddy spot; a journeyman, by his light blue tunic and trews. Magic had its purposes.

Wheels were still better.

Ahead of them, the first litter in the long line tilted as one of the steeds supporting it stepped into a deep hole that should have been filled in months ago. The load beneath it shifted. A lady screamed in surprise and fear. Then handlers and servants rushed to steady the conveyance. Three of them each checked the compartment beneath. What was so precious in there that three men had to check the entire thing, one after another?

Who knew what special treasures grand ladies needed to travel with? Ladies didn't travel far in his homeland. Peasant women did. Ladies remained in their towers, ruling the lands with a gentle and nurturing hand through the reports of lesser women.

The city-states of Mabastion, as the Big Continent was called here, went to war occasionally. But the women settled their spats quickly and returned to peaceful trade. They were a territorial bunch, keeping each to her own and rarely allowing strangers beyond the ports into the real city and supporting lands.

The blue-clad magician raced forward to the head of the caravan to set the litter back on its journey.

The steed leaned harder upon Skeller's shoulder, seemingly falling asleep. He pushed the beast away. But the animal returned to breathe his stale breath in Skeller's ear.

The steed's handler, a barrel-chested, middle-aged man with graying hair in a sloppy tail rather than tight queue, chuckled but did not correct the steed. "Just keep singing and walking, boy. Lazy Bones will follow you, and the rest of the herd will follow him. You're doing half my work," the drover chuckled.

Other drovers picked up the laughter, and the song, adding harmony and counterpoint.

Skeller tried moving faster, to get out from under the burden of the steed's adoration. Lazy Bones defied his name and increased his pace as well.

"You aren't a fleet steed," he sang, caressing the steed's long nose. "So why are you moving so fast?"

"To get to the end of the journey at last!" the drovers replied, also in song.

"If my love trotted so quick," a laundress picked up the joke in her hesitant but finely tuned alto.

Then a lilting soprano in the litter closest to Skeller in the long snaking line of travelers added a few words, "He'd be out on his ear in a tick!"

Skeller stumbled and nearly choked as the women turned his simple marching tune into a ribald round at the men's expense.

"Bring the harp to the cook fire tonight. It's the only way you'll keep control of the song," the drover said, slapping Skeller on the back.

"Thanks for the lift in getting us started, boy," another said, righting him from the force of the first's good-natured blow.

"The lady in the litter has a fine voice," Skeller said half on a query.

"Doubt it's the lady singing. Shy and sickly she be. Probably the companion. Hear tell she's the Magician's daughter. Them magic folk from the mountains sing all the time. Sorta adds something to their spells." The drover, a younger version of the tough grizzled man but with a proper three-strand queue, turned silent and thoughtful.

"Dragons don't care for our coin, 'tis gold for which they pine. But I've a dragon penny for your thoughts, just don't ask for mine," Skeller sang.

"Worth more than a copper penny," the drover replied, speaking rather than keeping the lilt of the song going. "Magic and magicians are changing. So are politics and politicians. Best keep your thoughts your own."

Skeller watched him work his way through the baggage sledges, caressing a steed here, slapping another into a brisker pace.

"Keep walking, my friend. My shoulder's not yours to lend," Skeller told his adoring steed and ducked away from him to pace behind the litter. A white mare fore and a gray one aft kept the conveyance level, if swaying gently in rhythm with the walking pace.

This one had closed red and green draperies with gold trim concealing the occupants. The one further up the line had lavender and dark rose trimmed in silver, supported by matched pale gray mares. For the first time since joining the caravan he wondered if the women traveled together at all. And which one did he need to follow if they took separate roads?

Mikk patted Lady Miri's hand where she'd placed it in the crook of his elbow. "You don't really want to come with me, Miri," he said, smiling down on her, grateful that in his latest growth spurt he now topped her by almost three inches. So much better for his image as a royal contender to be tall, like Glenndon and the king.

Besides, he liked looking down on her lovely blonde hair, even if it was twisted and twirled and glued into place. It framed her face, setting off her delicate skin and intelligent brown eyes.

A flicker of movement off to his left told him he wasn't alone. If he ever acted on his impulse to kiss the girl, it would be in full view of Geon, his servant-bodyguard-clerk. The tall, gaunt man would never speak of it. Taciturn and glowering, he rarely spoke at all.

"Oh, Mikk, it's just so boring at court with Princess Linda off in exile and Glenndon hiding from *all* social activities. You're the only one I can talk to. So why won't you show me this fabulous library?"

Mikk hesitated a moment, not certain how to address a delicate response. "Were you given the privilege of learning to read?" He tried to keep his tone casual. But in the greater scheme of things and the laws passed down by the Stargods, only those with magical talent and bound for the University or Temple were allowed to read. Something about keeping their civilization pure, or some such nonsense he didn't understand.

If that held true, how had Geon learned to read? He didn't seem to have any magical talent or . . .

"Of course I can read!" Miri stamped her foot and drew her hand away from him. Her anger set her scant bosom to heaving beneath her tightly fitted gown giving him hints of the glories beneath.

He mentally slapped himself free of the images his imagination conjured.

"I learned alongside Princess Linda and her sisters, and so did Lady Chastet, though you'd never know it to talk to her."

"Which is why she now attends the young princesses and you sit with the queen. Her Grace is very intelligent and well-read. She likes having equally educated ladies to converse with," he replied, forcing his eyes to gaze into hers and not at the curves beginning to swell above her bodice.

All concern about Geon observing every move he made vanished.

"So, I need to keep reading new material. Things that will interest the queen."

And Prince Glenndon, Mikk thought. The girls at court sought out Mikk in friendship. They panted after the Crown Prince.

"How about I bring you something. A good historical account of Battlemage Nimulan and his wife Mirilandel—for whom you are named—and how they brought about the first covenant with the dragons?" He smiled at her, wishing she'd notice this tremendous favor as more than something one friend would do for another. Something a courtier might do for his lady.

"I'd rather pick it out myself." She pouted prettily.

Did he dare kiss away the frown beginning to form?

"I know, my dear. I know the joys of winding through stacks of books and browsing titles for the perfect one," he said, patting her hand rather than indulge in a kiss that might get him slapped and banned from her company. "But it is incredibly dusty up there. You'd ruin your gown and hair. I'd hate to see something as lovely as . . . as you besmirched by mere dirt."

She twisted a bit, showing off the nip of her waist, allowing a bit more of her breast to swell above her bodice, preening for his compliments.

It was a start in getting her to notice him.

"I bet Prince Glenndon appreciates a bit of dirt now and then in his pursuit of knowledge."

Mikk's hopes crashed around his ears. Was that Geon chuckling in the shadows behind him?

"I'll bring you something to engage his conversation at court tonight." He turned his back on her and proceeded up the turret stairs. He didn't even look back to see if she watched him while he searched out the proper sequence of stones to push in order to unlock the door. He knew she'd gone off before he'd climbed halfway.

With a sigh, he pushed open the door and let the glory of books wash over him. Here he felt at home. Here he knew the power of his mind outweighed his failures in sword practice or steed racing. If the girls at court could just see him for what he truly was rather than just a small shadow behind the magnificent Glenndon.

He began searching out the books he'd truly come looking for, forgetting Miri and her need of something interesting to read. Dimly, he noted that Geon had slipped in before the door closed and headed off in the opposite direction in search of his own reading material.

"If my mother was Ariiell, the great and evil sorceress, then I should have some magical talent as well," Mikk mused. "I'd have to have at least a trace of magic if Grand'Mere intended me to study for the Temple. Every priest, monk, and prelate can at least draw flame to candle and incense. It's part of the ritual, the awe, the authority of the priesthood."

With Glenndon off doing princely things, Mikk had a

few hours to claim as his own. His cousin King Darville only seemed to want him around when he needed to show the court he had two heirs, both viable, both reliable, and both young enough to marry off to appropriate princesses or noble daughters.

In the meantime, Mikk didn't have to pretend to enjoy the princely sports of swordplay, wrestling, steed training—though chasing cross-country on a hunt was thrilling, as long as he didn't think about the blood and gore of killing an animal at the end of it, or the chafing on his thighs that left him walking bowlegged for days. For these precious few hours he could indulge in his lifelong passion: learning.

Since coming to the palace three months ago, he'd found all kinds of treasures up here in the tower, treasures that Grand'Pere would not consider proper reading for his only grandchild, or if he did then Grand'Mere wouldn't and she'd scold both of them and then cry. Grand'Mere cried a lot.

Perhaps that was why she came to court so rarely. She cried too much to be seen in public.

He ran his fingers along the edges of the bookshelves, both freestanding and along the walls, reading the runes carved into the stone through his fingertips. Mostly records of Council Meetings and official ceremonies on this level. They no longer interested him. Though the account of his grandparents' wedding and the grand celebration that followed had shown him how much they loved each other. She'd been a princess, sister to King Dracine, Darville's father. Grand'Pere had been the son of a minor lord with little wealth and less power.

No, today Mikk wanted something different, more adventurous. He headed toward the trapdoor and ladder to a sublevel with tales about magic, compiled over centuries. These were publicly acknowledged books, more about the history and personalities of the magicians who had helped shape Coronnan, but there was another archive hidden and accessible only to magicians. Those were the books he needed, books about the working of magic, not just the results. But in order to find that archive, he needed more information from this one.

Secure in his solitude—he'd notice if Geon followed him down the rickety ladder—he yanked on a pull ring embedded in the floor. The stone paving groaned but did not give way.

Strange, he'd opened it easily three days ago.

(Up.)

"Who's there?" he demanded loudly.

(Look up. You must go up.)

"Who are you?" His words echoed in the high-ceilinged room as he gazed up and spied another trapdoor overhead.

(Join us above.)

Chills ran up and down his spine as dust tickled his nose.

(There is no dust in the up.)

That sounded good. But he'd been warned about enemies of the crown who would not hesitate to kill or kidnap a member of the royal family.

"I'm only second heir and a distant cousin from the female line. I'm not valuable to anyone other than my grandparents," he muttered.

(We value you. We know who and what you are.)

That was too good to be true.

Still . . .

Fingering the ceremonial sword at his hip, he dragged a wooden bench across the floor and placed it beneath the other trapdoor. Where was Geon when Mikk needed a boost? A gentle tug on the short rope dangling from the wooden square opened the access. A ladder unfolded until the bottom rested snugly on the floor, nestling into grooves placed perfectly to steady the light contraption.

Mikk tested his weight against a rung just to make sure it was still steady, still stable enough to hold him.

Curiosity overrode any lingering fear or caution, and he near sprinted up until just his head cleared the open-

ing. He could still retreat if he had to. He'd been here
once before, and seen nothing but more rows and rows
of bookshelves.

Today he found a thick layer of darkness that swallowed light and sound and, above that, long chains of
bright and pulsing colored light.

(Welcome to the realm of dragons!)

CHAPTER 6

MIKK MISSED HIS step one rung below the top of the ladder and slid down three. He grabbed tight to the lip of the opening and flailed his feet for purchase. His fingers ached all the way to the bone before growing numb. How could he avoid falling all the way down a good twelve feet to the floor below?

Gasping for breath and heart in his throat, he found a rung and braced his feet.

The blackness faded along with the pulsing coils of light.

(You are not ready.) The voice in his head sounded disappointed.

"What must I do to be ready?" he whispered as much to himself as the voice. "I've talked to Glenndon a lot these last three months. We have become close. Friends. He doesn't hide much from me. He hinted at passage through the void. And being stuck there. I recognize this as . . ."

(You are not ready.)

"Point me toward a book that will guide me to you. Please." He added the last as an afterthought. He might be second in line to the throne, but even Glenndon and the king had to be polite to dragons. At least he hoped he was talking to dragons. Who else would speak directly into his head?

Surely an enemy magician would seek someone more important to manipulate mind-to-mind.

The voice had to come from a dragon. Had to. He wondered which one. Shayla, the matriarch, had the reputation of communicating more freely than the others. No. The voice was definitely masculine. Maybe Baamin, Shayla's favored mate. He was rumored to hold the spirit of Jaylor's predecessor as Senior Magician and Chancellor of the University. And to be a stern taskmaster, pulling the best out of recalcitrant students.

"Please help me to prepare for your lessons," he begged, pulling himself up until the lip met his waist. Three more steps up, and he'd be all the way into the upper room. For it was a room once more. He could barely see where the coils of colored light had been. Sunlight filtered through a dozen arrow-slit windows above the stacks of books.

Relief washed over him. He knew this world. The realm of dragons frightened and thrilled him at the same time. He could barely wield sword and shield; how could he think about embarking on any kind of adventure other than through books and lessons?

A distant chuckle rattled in the back of his head.

(You will need no sword for this experience, boy. Look to your books for now.)

"Which books?" Mikk replied eagerly.

(Figure it out.)

"When will I hear from you again?"

(When you are ready. When you have grown from boy to man and back to boy again.)

"*S'murghit!* What does that mean?"

No answer. Nothing but a vacant feeling at the back of his head. Vacant enough to upset his balance again. A sensation of falling washed over him while he could still feel the press of the ladder rung against the soles of his boots.

Using his forearms as a brace he crawled out of the ladder well onto the wide wooden planks of the floor. He sneezed out centuries of dust and collapsed onto his chest. The dust smeared his tunic heavily. Another curse almost escaped his lips at the mess the fabric absorbed. He needed to get himself upright. But his feet still dangled in the opening. He crawled forward again until his toes scraped wood. Only then did he attempt to rise to his knees, grabbing hold of the nearest stone bookcase and pulling himself upward. His head cleared. Dust motes sparkled in the streams of sunlight.

Maybe he'd imagined those coils of light and had seen only clouds of dust.

And maybe cats flew.

He stumbled forward, right hand on the nearest shelf. His fingers bumped into a protruding book.

(Figure it out.)

Had he truly heard that? Or remembered it? Or imagined it?

He pulled the book free of its mates—all snugged back into line. A thin book with a plain, undyed binding, frayed around the edges. If there had ever been a title and author impressed or painted on the spine or front cover it had vanished long ago.

Almost afraid to breathe and cause the pages to crumble, he opened the fly to the title page. He saw letters but did not have enough light to decipher them. He tilted the book until one of the weak shafts of light landed on the fine lettering. Written in a clear and careful hand, common to all University students, he picked out the dark brown ink atop a light brown parchment:

*Chronicles of a Pirate
Or
How I became the Magician of Coronnan
By
Kimmer Scribe of the South*

The chuckle filled the vacancy between his ears.

"Do I have permission to take this back to my room

and read in better light so that I might understand the lesson?" he called into the air.

Silence.

Skeller slung his harp case around from his back, thinking the caravan was lagging and in need of a tune. The second he loosened the flap from its buckles he knew something was different. In his view of life, different could mean very wrong and out of place or new and exciting and therefore wonderful. Like watching the girl with the red-gold braid as she gently maneuvered and manipulated the lady in her charge. Her eyes danced as she smiled. Surely this young woman enjoyed life and found merriment in all that she graced with her gentle touch.

A new tune bounced from his mind to his fingertips. It began with her smile as she peeked from between the caravan's draperies and laughed at the antics of a baby goat trying to keep up with its mother and snatch a quick drink from her udder.

He reached into the carrysack for Telynnia with eager fingers. Instead of satiny wood and crisp strings he brushed a crackling fold of parchment. Good parchment, heavy enough to scrape clean and use to write music on later.

Where did it come from? He'd brought no such obvious signs of wealth with him.

Carefully he pulled it free of the harp, holding it by his fingernails. The sea-green wax seal made him pause.

"Got yersel' a dispatch," Garg, the head drover said gleefully. "Them's rare and expensive. Only magicians can send those things so they always find who they're addressed to and only them." He came up beside Skeller, peering avidly at the document.

Sure enough, Skeller's long, pompous, legal name appeared across the front in his father's florid hand. Had he truly used royal purple ink? *Showoff,* he thought contemptuously.

"Kin you read it?" Garg asked him skeptically.

"Yes," Skeller replied. The man's awed expression told him not to add, "Can't you?"

"Must be University trained. Sure, no one but a magician could turn a simple tune into magic that Lazy Bones would follow. Only magicians got business sending and receiving dispatches." He jerked his head toward the adoring sledge steed that even now tugged his load a little faster so he could drape his head over Skeller's shoulder.

Skeller kept silent, neither admitting nor denying his education. But the old man had taught him something. A dispatch sent by a magician. His father had a magician as chief counselor and spymaster, a man who'd appeared on and off over the last several years and schemed his way into the king's good graces with too much ease to be anything but magical manipulation.

"Well, ain't you goin' t'read it?"

Skeller glanced around. Only Garg and the big steed seemed to be watching him. The contents he could keep to himself if he needed to. He slid his fingernail beneath the seal, as he'd been taught, to pry the wax loose without damaging the parchment and keep the seal intact at the same time. Never knew when you'd need proof of the sender.

"My dear son," Father began the missive. Skeller had never been dear to the man, and rarely acknowledged as a son. Father usually ignored him completely rather than admit he'd sired a *male* with no interest in politics or political power.

"Wonder what the old man wants this time." Skeller scowled at the written words. "Great Mother, he wants me to marry my cousin Bettina!" he nearly shouted.

"That a good thing?" Garg asked.

"Not really."

"Ugly as sin so she can't attract anyone but a cousin in an arranged marriage." Garg chuckled knowingly.

"She's pretty enough." His gaze strayed toward the litter with the girl he'd been watching.

"But . . . ?" Garg pressed.

"I'd have to go home and I have no interest in going home," Skeller finished. He didn't mention that Bettina had a fascination with watching huntsmen and butchers prepare meat for cooking. He wondered if her fascination would tip over to the need to kill the animal herself or possibly another human. Her father and mother, who ruled the neighboring city-state of Venez, executed criminals. Publicly. Maybe that was where her bloodthirsty interest had come from.

Violence colored Bettina's attitude daily.

Skeller's father had many faults, but at least as long as his wife lived, he'd sent people into exile, and never executed one.

But before Skeller fled the continent on his current mission, he'd watched Lokeen order the private execution of a man and his wife who'd publicly questioned a man's right to rule without a wife to grant him authority.

Violence in the streets and marketplaces became more common each year; people settling their differences with fists and cudgels. Women disputing a husband's wandering eye with heavy iron pans swung with malicious accuracy. He'd needed to escape this descent into a primitive lack of civilization.

Running away hadn't cured the situation. If anything, it got worse. In the back of his mind he recognized his duty to return to Amazonia and do *something*.

He wasn't ready.

"If'n you returned home, you'd get a pretty wife and you wouldn't have to sleep out in the open under the stars with old Lazy Bones as your only friend," Garg reminded him.

One glance at the man's swollen knuckles and stiff gait told him Garg was nearly ready to retire. He didn't have many more long journeys in him.

"I like sleeping under the stars and listening to the music of the world as I drift off to sleep," Skeller said. "I'm not ready to settle with one woman, in one place yet." But if the girl with the red-gold braid showed any interest in him, he might reconsider.

But if he pursued the girl, he failed in his duty as his mother's son.

※

"My lady, do you truly want that rosehip candy?" Lillian asked Graciella, somewhat shocked that of all the foods available to her, even sweets, she chose the one that would make her intermittent bleeding worse.

Graciella turned her vague gaze from the decorative box of treats up to her companion. "I . . . I have craved them for weeks now. I always feel better after a cup of rosehip tea, or rosehips shredded on my greens, or rosehip jam on my bread, but especially rosehips dipped in honey." She popped the confection into her mouth and smiled with eyes closed in near bliss.

"My lady," Lillian tried again. "Do you know what rosehips do to your body?" She tried narrowing her eyes and focusing her gaze above Graciella's left ear. Nothing. She caught no trace of the woman's life energy or colors surrounding her head. If only Val were here to loan her a little talent, a little skill, a little something to help her figure out what was going on in Graciella's head.

"Does it matter?" the lady asked, eyes suddenly clearing and her tone sharpening.

Lily's attention snapped back to her charge. "Yes, it does matter. You carry a new life within you. You have a responsibility to keep yourself healthy for the baby's sake. I have the responsibility to help keep you healthy." Lily reached for the pretty wooden box. A lovely golden grain swirled through the slightly darker oak. Pink and yellow rosettes of satin ribbon and costly lace had been glued to each corner of the lid. The latch gleamed in gold flourishes that spread up and down, almost the full depth of box and lid together. A costly container for a potentially deadly gift.

But did the giver know that the rosehips, which could

help cure many ailments, thinned the blood as well, thinned it until it stopped clotting and leeched strength?

"My husband gave me these as a parting gift. He knows how I crave them," Graciella said flatly and turned her face away. "A craving is a woman's body telling her she needs something in that food to help the baby grow. My husband wants what is best for our—my child."

Lillian stilled, thinking furiously. Had Lord Jemmarc given her the treats because she craved them and he truly cared for her, or did he promote the craving knowing that if she ate enough of them his wife could bleed to death, especially if she miscarried.

Then there was Lady Graciella. She looked so vague and lost, like she truly didn't care if she lived or died. Or was she trying to force a miscarriage?

Oh, Val, I need you. Less than an hour away from you and I'm already lost.

Look and listen. It's what we do best. That is why Da sent us on these separate journeys. Look and listen, Valeria returned. *Not so very far away yet*

I'll have a scrying bowl and candle set up awaiting your summons tonight. I can receive even if I can't send. Lillian touched the tiny shard of glass in her belt pouch, a true symbol of their father's trust in them as journeywomen. Only magicians carried precious glass.

Lillian breathed deeply and focused on the tiny lines around Graciella's mouth and eyes. Only a year or so older than herself, she was far too young to look so burdened. Yes, burdened, not vague and uncaring. She carried secrets behind that mask of bored listlessness.

"I hear there is a spectacular variety of cabbage rose that thrives in the brisk sea air of Castle Saria," Lillian offered. "I love roses. We don't cultivate them at home in the mountains. They require too much land and effort that is better applied to kitchen gardens. If you crave something sweet, I can make you a yampion pie. It's the best dish for restoring energy after a hard day of work."

Lillian knew she prattled, a lot like Old Maisie had. She covered probing questions in an avalanche of words.

"Not meat," Graciella spat. She shuddered in revulsion, much as Lillian and her mother did. "But yampions?" Graciella's eyes brightened. "We used to have that at home. Jemmarc never allows it to be served in his manor, or the castle. Peasant food, he calls it."

"After near three months in the palace and the old University, I think plain country food is better tasting, and better for you, than all the fluffy and fancy, but inedible, decorations the nobles eat," Lillian said, looking at Graciella sideways. She caught just a glimmer of energy and interest spiking from the lady's mind. Not a true reading of her aura, but–something.

"I've heard that Castle Saria has little in the way of gardens. Something about the brisk sea air being too windy, too cold, and too salty." Graciella turned her head to stare out of the litter into the far distance, or deep within herself.

Lillian couldn't tell the difference.

"There are ways to sweeten the soil. Ways to shelter delicate plants from the ceaseless seeking wind. I'd like to help you restore the gardens." She wanted to say something about Lady Lucinda, Graciella's predecessor, having no interest in gardening, but thought that might not be polite.

"My stepmother is Lord Jemmarc's sister. She took me to the castle once, just after . . . after Lady Lucinda left," Graciella said hesitantly, as if she'd followed Lillian's chain of thought. "She hoped that my lord would ask her to stay on as chatelaine of the castle. He didn't. Luc . . . Lucjemm didn't like her."

"Lucjemm liked very few people. I think that's why he adopted those awful black snakes as pets. He thought they were his only friends."

Graciella's mask of boredom slipped over her expression again. "I'm tired. I think I should nap." She shifted uneasily against the mass of pillows behind her and closed her eyes. Shutting out Lillian as well as the rest of the world. Within moments her breathing evened and deepened. The tight lines around her eyes and mouth relaxed.

Lillian saw her simple beauty beneath the cosmetics of her newly privileged position. A sturdy country girl thrust into the thick of complex politics at court, married off (against her wishes?) to an ambitious man with an unstable son.

Our beginnings are the same, she thought, *I pray that we both find a happier ending*.

Carefully she eased the fancy box of rosehip candy out from under Graciella's hand and dumped the sticky contents out of the litter.

CHAPTER 7

JAYLOR HELD TIGHT to Brevelan longer than he needed as solid ground materialized beneath his feet.

"That never gets easier," Brevelan said on a heavy exhale. She kept her eyes scrunched closed, as if in pain, while she clung to him.

He sensed that her legs weren't quite stable enough to support her yet. Common enough reaction from people who didn't experience the transport spell often.

"You'll think differently next time you sense one of your chicks in danger or I have to be gone for more than a few days. Then you'll fly off to where you think you need to be before you can consider the transport dangerous and uncomfortable." He kissed the top of her head and gently eased away from her, still keeping his hands on her waist to make sure she didn't stumble.

She squeezed his shoulders and stood straight on her own. As straight as she was wont to these days, anyway, a little hunched over her belly, protectively. "How long can you stay home this time?" she asked, finally looking up at him.

"'Til dawn at least." He kissed her lightly, thought better of it and kissed her again, deeply, passionately, thoroughly. "Then again, perhaps I ought to leave Glenndon alone for a few days to see how he copes on his own."

The glass disc in his tunic pocket began vibrating. Both he and his wife sighed. "The responsibilities of being Senior Magician, Chancellor of the University, and councillor to the king. Someone always needs my attention."

"And your wife is always last to get it." Brevelan moved away from him toward her cabin. Always her cabin, never theirs, as it was before they met.

He swallowed the chill of her leaving and removed the palm-sized glass from his tunic. Without a scrying bowl and candle flame he saw only a swirl of red and yellow curlicues. He wet his fingertip on his tongue and tapped it against the glass three times. "I'm coming, Marcus. I'm coming." He set his footsteps on the half-mile path to the Forest University buildings.

Life was easier in the old days when there was only one University in the capital. But in those days magicians didn't keep wives, never acknowledged their children, and were a lot lonelier. Somehow his connection to his fellow magicians while in a magical circle, their talents building and compounding into far more than the sum of their individual parts, that complete unity of mind and purpose, paled in comparison to holding a newborn babe in his arms and knowing that out of his life had come another, and another. Or the joy of loving Brevelan, totally and completely, even when she was pissed at him.

The scent of fresh, raw yampion tubers being peeled and sliced enticed him back toward the cabin. Hours yet before the sweet, rich pie finished baking. He plowed on through the forest to his responsibilities, knowing a hot meal, a warm hearth, and a loving family awaited him at the end of the day.

"What demands my attention so urgently," he demanded of Marcus the moment he cleared the doorway into the master magician's office. He'd given over his place here at the Forest University when he reopened the old University in the capital several months ago. Still, the changes his former apprentice had made shocked him. Different books lining the shelves, a smaller and more upright chair than his own—which now graced his office in Coronnan City—a long smooth wooden pen and bronze inkwell instead of Jaylor's pile of quills and silver inkwell, all made him feel as if he had walked into a stranger's private parlor.

He stopped in the doorway, needing permission to enter, though Marcus was never one to stand on ceremony, unlike his former partner Robb.

"I may have a general location for Robb, his three journeymen, and two apprentices," Marcus said, waving Jaylor closer to his desk where he peered through a large master's glass, a smooth slice of clear glass in a gold frame. From a distance, and without joining the other man's spell through physical contact and a sharing of talent, he saw only a candle flame shimmering behind the glass.

But Marcus had no candle or scrying bowl before him.

"Thank the Stargods they didn't get lost in the void during a hasty transport!" Jaylor shouted, leaning over Marcus with hands on the desk and his chin atop the younger man's head—a position he often took when teaching apprentices, including Marcus and Robb when they were much younger.

"What do you see?" Jaylor asked more quietly. "Aside from the flame."

"Dirt and stone, a sense of confinement. Solitude. Only a single candle for company, a new one each day, brought with a meal."

"Prison," Jaylor said on a sigh. "Where? Who *could* kidnap a master in the middle of a transport spell?"

"Another master," Marcus returned. "A rogue."

"Or an exiled and disgruntled master."

"Neither Samlan nor any of his followers had enough skill to do that."

"On that I agree. But if they are somewhere they can still gather dragon magic, they could, with patience, possibly join together and grab one of the journeymen without any finesse. They were all linked so that they'd arrive at the same point at the same time." Jaylor began pacing, mulling over possibilities. He'd never thought of kidnapping a person out of transport. Never needed to. Or wanted to. Transports were dangerous enough without interference.

He'd been lost in the void once. Lost in the wonder of having no body to feel with, no eyes to see with. Only his mind perceived the dozens of bright, pulsing umbilicals of life. Each one carried the color of a person's essence. He'd seen his own blue and red braid for the first time, a pattern echoed in the twists of his staff. Brevelan's green, yellow, and bronze had coiled around him with love and concern. King, then-Prince, Darville's green and gold had twined through both of them. Somehow, the love the three of them shared had reached through the void to find him and brought him back to reality.

He didn't know if the bonds of love and friendship among Robb, his wife Maigret, Marcus, and his wife Vareena were strong enough to snatch Robb back.

"How do we find the location of his prison?" Jaylor asked, before he lost his thoughts in an endless loop of memories and despair.

"I don't know," Marcus replied softly. "I've tried everything I could think of, and this is the first glimmer of success in three months."

A hesitant knock on the door roused them from sinking into depression. "Yes?" they both answered at the same time.

Heat flushed Jaylor's cheeks, and he deferred to Marcus with a gesture. This was no longer his office, though technically, as Senior Magician he outranked Marcus, even here.

"Sir," came a young voice that deepened from adolescent squeaks to an even tenor but still held the variability of youth.

Jaylor looked up to find himself staring at his second

son, Lukan. Actually his first son, since Glenndon had been sired by Darville on that night long ago when Jaylor had lost himself in the void, too enthralled with an abundance of Tambootie hallucinations to know where he was.

"Da?" The boy stared back in surprise. He tossed his dark auburn hair out of his eyes with a flick of his head that reminded Jaylor of Brevelan. As usual, his three-strand queue had loosened to the near nonexistence typical of Jaylor when distracted. The burning slash across Lukan's cheek, left by a stray spark of magic, still looked angry and raw. It would scar rather than heal clean. "I didn't know you'd return, sir." Lukan looked away, concentrating on Marcus, his master and tutor instead of his father, whom he hadn't seen in weeks. "I thought about finding Master Robb while I was studying the maps of Coronnan's coastline."

"And?" Marcus asked.

"What if we did a scrying spell with the bowl and candle placed atop the map?"

"I've tried that," Marcus said sadly. "I saw only this candle flame illuminating a dry prison cell." He gestured to the paraphernalia on the desk.

Jaylor noticed the map for the first time. He'd been so interested in the vision within the glass he hadn't noticed anything else.

"But you don't have a candle and bowl of water . . ." Lukan protested.

"Not this time." Marcus heaved a sigh. "Thank you for sharing your thoughts, Lukan. This matter concerns us all. If you think of anything else . . ."

"Have you tried a crystal pendulum?" Jaylor interjected, happy that his mind finally worked. He smiled at his son and beckoned him forward.

Lukan remained rooted to his position in the doorway, pointedly ignoring his father.

Jaylor lifted his eyebrow in question. Lukan kept his gaze level with his master.

"A crystal, hmm. Vareena suggested the same thing," he mused. "My wife uses old hedge witch practices. I dismissed it, thinking gathered magic was stronger, more accurate."

"Never dismiss the gentle magic of a hedge witch," Jaylor laughed, thinking of Brevelan's subtle powers that outlasted and worked with finer detail than many a master spell.

"Lukan, can you please fetch me a crystal and a . . . an uncut crystal and a leather thong, I think. A silver chain and jeweler's tools might taint the primitive intention of the quest," Marcus said while peering at the map spread out on his desk.

"Like this, sir?" Lukan pulled a piece of opaque quartz from his pocket. It dangled from a thin strip of blonde leather knotted around the center of the vague lump. "I thought that if he's underground, maybe we'd need something raw, like it was just dug out of the ground."

"Good thinking, boy," Jaylor smiled at his son, almost surprised at his logic. The boy had run so wild, with little concentration on anything but his own whims that Jaylor tended to dismiss his intelligence and talent. Then too, Glenndon so outshone everyone as a person and a magician that Lukan kind of faded into the background.

"Marcus, you're closer to Robb than I," Jaylor said. "Perhaps you should hold the pendulum."

Lukan snorted.

"What?" Jaylor demanded, anger heating his face and tightening his fist.

"If closeness is your criterion, then maybe you should have Robb's wife Maigret, or one of his children hold the leather." Lukan threw the crystal at his father, turned sharply, and near ran out of the room.

"What?" Jaylor asked, totally bewildered.

"He's seventeen and *still* an apprentice because no one thought to promote him to journeyman until after his older brother made the same step. He's not the miracle worker Glenndon is, so everyone presumes he has no talent or intelligence at all," Marcus said quietly. "And you promoted his two younger sisters, barely out of the schoolroom, passing him over once again."

"I know that! I needed the girls and their keen observation. Their journey takes them into realms where a boy, no matter how skilled or senior, would not suit."

"Does he know that?"

"Um. I think the operative word in your castigation of me is that Lukan is seventeen. I forgot how I felt at that age when I was passed over for promotion because I couldn't explain how I threw my spells, which is important when working in concert with others. I was too full of my success in knowing the spells worked, and worked well."

"He feels forgotten by both his tutors and his family. Let him sulk for a while. I'll bring him into a circle of magicians to work this old and primitive search for my friend. I had already planned to promote him tonight. And I will bring in Robb's two sons, young though they are, they can still gather magic and join with the circle to increase the power of the spell."

"May I join your circle?" Jaylor asked meekly. His former student had just proved to him how well-suited he was to this office.

"I don't want to take you away from precious time with your family, sir."

"All of you are my family. Especially you and Robb. You were always my favorite students. And I now realize that teaching my own family is not always the best idea." His gaze strayed to the doorway, which still seemed to hold Lukan's shadow. "I'm too close to the boy, and lacking patience when I know he must learn, but want him to be my equal from the beginning."

CHAPTER 8

GLENNDON SHRUGGED AND rotated his shoulders to ease the binding of his fine golden brocade tunic. He'd spotted General Marcelle lurking in the shadows of an interior buttress, slapping a riding crop across his palm and waiting to ambush Glenndon or Mikk for another lesson. Quickly, he darted into the illusory refuge of a different alcove. If he stood absolutely still and willed himself to blend with the stone wall, then maybe, just maybe, the general would give up and go away.

Then too, Glenndon needed to be wary of the gaggle of teenage girls milling around the hall. He ardently wished they'd turn and go the other way. *You don't see me, I'm invisible. I'm not here.* He threw a hint of magic into his unspoken words, willing them to be true. Sometimes he liked having all of the female attention. Not now. They just got in the way of his work. And they never gave him any privacy.

Besides, they broadcast their lustful, greedy thoughts without a hint of a barrier. He barely needed any magical talent to read them. He didn't want to try. He was a prince without a princess and old enough to begin looking for one: a valuable prize. Nothing more.

None of them saw him for what and who he really was. None of them eased his loneliness.

So far, he'd only approached a sense of belonging with his cousin Mikk and his bodyguard Frank. Mikk reminded him a lot of Lukan, half-forgotten, lost in an adult world, and trying desperately to fit in. But Mikk didn't have Lukan's anger and stubbornness. That made him all the more loveable and attractive to the girls. As a friend. Lukan attracted girls because of his rebellion against authority and the anger he used to justify it. The bad boy, always in trouble and forbidden to the girls by their cautious fathers. At the University they fluttered around him like moths drawn to a flame.

He shrugged his shoulders again and heard a tiny rip. Regretfully he returned his posture to the original, uncomfortable Court Slouch. Old Maisy knew how to make clothes fit. Now that she was gone, the other royal seamstresses seemed to have forgotten everything about measuring and fitting and allowing a man to move beneath the cloth.

"Nothing serious, Highness," Frank whispered from behind his right shoulder. "If you allow your queue to drape over your left shoulder, no one will notice the separation in the seam."

Glenndon grumbled something impolite. *Stargods*, he wished he had his staff with him. But Father had suggested he leave it behind at official meetings. Coronnan hadn't yet discarded their deep distrust of magicians.

Then he looked up at the berobed clerk, a minor magician by his vague orange aura, wringing his hands beside the doorway into an official greeting parlor.

"Has the new ambassador arrived?" Glenndon asked the anxious messenger.

"Not yet, Highness." He looked around, worry pulling his mouth into a deep frown, making him look older. "I arranged the seating beside the cold hearth and had the housekeeper fill the grate with fresh flowers, as you requested."

Frank snorted. He didn't approve of flowers for anything but presenting to a lady he courted. The idea of their perfume masking the scent of men recently returned from the practice arena didn't occur to him. Glenndon had grown up with the rare luxury of soaking in a hot-spring pool with a dragon for a companion after heavy exercise. City folk settled for sluicing off with cold water when necessary and bathing only on rest day before Temple services.

Glenndon watched the messenger's eyes. "Do I know you?"

"Not really, Highness. We were in first-year apprentice classes together, briefly. I was a late bloomer and so untalented your father assigned me to clerical duties. Quite an honor for my poor family to have a son allowed to learn to read and write." Some of the tension bled out of his voice.

"I'm sorry, I forgot your name."

"No need to remember it, Highness."

Glenndon waited out an embarrassed silence.

"Keerkin, Highness."

"Thank you, Keerkin. Tell your master I'd like you to be assigned to me henceforth. I find I need someone to keep track of all my appointments and the masses of parchment I am required to read and sign. And it wouldn't hurt to have you transcribe my scribbled notes from Council sessions. I can barely read them and Mikk—um—Prince Mikkette has other duties as well. Anyone searching out laws and precedents would find my notes useless."

"Yes, Highness. Thank you, Highness." Keerkin bowed repeatedly in his gratitude.

"He prefers to be called 'sir,'" Frank whispered conspiratorially. "This Highness thing is still new to him."

"Very good, High . . . sir." He bowed again.

"Please announce the ambassador when he arrives and then join us to take notes." Glenndon nodded to his new scribe and strode into the parlor, easing his shoulders and not caring when the fabric shredded a bit more.

Frank followed him and took up his post, behind and

to the right of Glenndon's high-backed chair. He rested his right hand on the pommel of his sword, leaving Glenndon's dominant left hand free to draw his own near-useless ceremonial sword. The blasted decoration was supposed to make him look strong and virile. It was more often in the way when he wanted to sit, or move in a hurry. S'murghit, he wished again he had his staff, a tool and a weapon better suited to his skills.

Bright summer sunshine filled the room with warmth, despite the chill trapped within the stone walls of the palace. Sweet floral scents rose from the grate until they cloyed at Glenndon's senses. His legs cramped from sitting straight in a chair meant for a shorter man. His fine linen shirt beneath the decorative tunic scratched his damp skin.

He stretched and slumped. Then he rose and paced. Frank prowled the room, poking his nose into every bit of furniture, scuffing at the green and gold carpet, peeking behind tapestries that depicted great moments of battle in the history of Coronnan.

Outside the Temple bells rang the noon hour. "He's late," Glenndon growled.

"Yes, sir," Frank replied absently, finding the image of a red-haired Stargod hovering in silent observation and blessing of a victory more intriguing than the missing ambassador. The first ambassador from Amazonia in generations.

"My father sent me to greet the man, an honor, and then escort him to the king's presence. Where the hell is he?"

"Unknown, High . . . sir." Keerkin appeared in the doorway, looking over his shoulder along the long corridor leading toward the Great Hall. "Ah, sir, I see a messenger. One of the City lads, not a private servant."

A scurry of footsteps on the polished wooden floor accompanied that announcement. Then a plainly dressed boy in brown wool slid to a stop before Keerkin, handed him a folded missive, tipped his cap, and dashed off again.

"Well?" Glenndon asked impatiently as Keerkin slid a finger beneath a black wax seal and unfolded the parchment.

"Ambassador Amazonia, they never give their real names over there on the Big Continent, just title and city-state of origin, sends his regrets and apologies. He has been unavoidably detained by a problem at Customs with a shipment of rare wine from his home."

Glenndon fumed a moment in furious thought. Then he smiled. "Inform the ambassador that when he is ready to open trade negotiations and possible marriage alliances with one of my sisters, he may apply for an appointment. My father will consider if it is worth the time of one of his servants to serve him a cup of our finest wine while he awaits our pleasure."

He stalked off, shedding tunic and ceremonial sword as he headed for the barracks and training arena. "I need to bash some heads, Frank. Quarterstaff practice today."

S'murghit! I had everything set to lure in the king, make him vulnerable to my cause and thus plant the instrument of his destruction. The crate with my other instrument of restoration is already on its way to my colleague in the rebellion I invoke. A necessary rebellion to bring the Circle of Master Magicians back to the proper path. The distance of my instrument's journey is the only reason for delay.

Except His Grace is too busy to meet with me. Me! The ambassador of his newest ally. No he can't be bothered to rule his land. He'd rather lock himself away and drown himself in hard drink. Oh, the nobles say he has given up liquor. But I know the lure, the craving, the demands of a body once used to it. 'Tis similar to the effects of the Tambootie. I've seen that often enough among magicians. But I've never been tempted by either. I am stronger than an addiction. King Darville is not. He just drinks in private now. I'm certain of it.

The people no longer know their king, or his ailing queen. They do not trust him.

So he sends his bastard son. Not only a bastard but a magician in a land that only recently allowed—by independent royal decree—members of the royal family to be magicians.

I could not chance that Prince Glenndon would recognize me. He can't be allowed to report back to the Senior Magician that I am here in the capital working to bring him down, to end his tyrannical rule over the University and the king.

Lord Jaylor could not trust his closest comrades with the truth, that Glenndon is not his son, but the king's. If he'd trusted us, we would have worked with him. Instead he kept silent and ruled the University alone. Now he will die alone, left with nothing. Not even his honor, or his son. I can turn this to my advantage.

"Can't you remember anything?" General Marcelle yelled at Mikk in exasperation.

Mikk hung his head, wishing he could squeeze his throbbing and swelling right hand under his armpit to ease the bruising from the general's vicious slap with the flat of his sword.

He glanced across the arena to a separate practice yard where Prince Glenndon angrily thrashed three opponents at once with a quarterstaff. His weapon looked suspiciously gnarled. It might be his magician staff, except it lacked the telltale white bone embedded along the top. If he used the staff, he might be tempted to fell his comrades with magic instead of physical prowess and skill.

Mikk wished he knew enough about magic to use just a little to lessen the general's blows.

And there was Geon, hunkered in a corner with his nose in a book, only half-watching the arena for threats to Mikk. The slim volume looked suspiciously like the one Mikk had retrieved from the upper archives.

"I . . . I'm sorry, sir. My mind wandered," he tried to excuse himself. Truth was, phrases from the book he'd found in the archives kept swimming through his head.

Transmission of energy from the mind. Or more enticing: *Fluctuations in the magnetic field.* He sort of thought he knew what Kimmer, Scribe of the South, was talking about, but not really. He needed to study the words and phrasing in context to glean the meaning and then execute it as magic.

He wondered if Geon understood the words and if they talked about it together, maybe Mikk could understand them better.

Not a dragon's chance Geon would talk about anything. In three months barely three words a day had crossed his lips.

"A wandering mind will get you killed, boy," Marcelle reminded him, less angrily than before.

"I'm . . . I never thought I'd have to train as a warrior, sir," Mikk said. "Grand'Mere intended me for the Temple."

"Did she now?" The general shifted his grip on the broadsword. "She'd know better than me if that's what would suit you best. But fate has made you a prince. The Temple isn't good enough for you, boy. Let's hope you never have to lead men into battle. But if the worst ever happens, I intend to make sure you can." He frowned at Mikk's hands. "Who taught you to hold your sword like that? It isn't one of those harps the music master uses."

Mikk looked at his fingers curled around the fat grip. "Um, Prince Glenndon showed me a few things."

"Hmmf," Marcelle snorted. "Prince Glenndon is many things, but only slightly better-trained than you. He can wield an ax or a staff better than a sword." The general sheathed his own weapon and grabbed Mikk's blade by the crosspiece in one hand. "Flat of your palm on the fattest part of the grip, pommel resting along the inside of your wrist."

Mikk slid his hand down until the metal made him straighten his wrist and forearm into one long line.

"Good, good. Now three fingers around the grip, thumb and pointing finger up under the crosspiece."

Mikk put all of his strength into his fingers.

"No, no. Not so fierce. Control your blade with the thumb and first finger. The other three just balance."

"But I'll drop it," Mikk protested.

"Less likely. A soft grip gives you control. A fierce grip takes away your control. This is a light blade. You can do tricky things with it you can't do with a broadsword."

"Light?" Mikk's arm trembled from the weight of it.

"Yes, Light. We'll build you up so that this one feels like a feather. Then we'll move you into heavy weapons that you have to hold with two hands. No finesse with those, just brute force."

"Like yours?" Mikk asked in admiration.

"Spent a lifetime doing this. My broadsword is like an extension of my hand. Doubt we'll get you that far. But I'll train you so that you don't embarrass me in the arena, or out on maneuvers. Might even save your life if we have to go into battle."

Mikk wanted to sneer at that statement. He didn't think he'd ever be as comfortable with a sword as he was with a book. "I'll do my best, sir. For you."

The general smiled. "That's the first lesson. Now, *en garde*. Keep your elbow tight and your feet spread."

Mikk obeyed without words, more eager to endure this private lesson and learn something now that he had a glimmer of the elusive control over his blade.

Thank you, sir, he thought. The general smiled back with evil mischief in his eye.

CHAPTER 9

"WE'RE STOPPING, MY lady," Val said quietly. Ariiell twisted in her doze, turning her head away from the harsh voices and snorting animal sounds coming from her right.

Val leaned over and parted the heavy curtains a bit. Cool evening air slipped between her fingers, lightening the damp heat within the litter. "My lady," she said a little louder. "We are stopping for the evening. We'll have fresh water and a meal shortly."

"Nnnnooo," Ariiell mumbled, flicking her head right and left in agitation. "Stop. Now. You're hurting me." She thrashed her legs and arms, fighting dream restraints. "Let me go. Please, please stop. You're killing me!"

Instinctively, Val pressed back against the pile of pillows behind her, putting as much distance as possible between her and the evil memories that plagued Ariiell.

You are my charge. I can't let you suffer this way, she reminded herself. She sat straighter, folding her legs and tucking her feet close. "My lady, you must awaken from this dream." She pushed a mental probe into Ariiell's mind.

Chaos pushed her out again. Making contact with Lillian had never been this difficult, even when Valeria had been trapped within the body of a flywacket, a large black cat with iridescently feathered wings.

Val reached forward tentatively with gentle fingers on
a thrashing ankle and concentrated on a slender thread
of magic, worming her way around and under the churning miasma of emotional and physical pain. Overwhelm-
ing grief, guilt, and regret looping back upon itself and
intensifying with each whorl and swish of memory nearly
swallowed her whole.

She remembered eavesdropping on the Circle of Master Magicians as they worked one of their spells in the
courtyard of the Forest University. To avoid detection,
she'd had to bury her consciousness in the soil, like a
worm pushing its way along, oblivious to anything except
to keep moving and eating. Like that little worm, she
pushed aside this tiny tendril, bent around that deeply
rooted rock. Black, clinging vines, covered in piercing
thorns, twined around and around a huge knot of ugliness.

Ah! That was the core of the problem; she'd have to
work on breaking it up later. Only when it had become
small bites, easily digested, would it dissipate and allow
Ariiell to live with her memories without lapsing into
insanity.

Around the next bend, hiding in the shadow of
dreams, Val found what she sought. Slowly but surely she
opened The Forget and spread it over the hard rock, like
a soothing blanket.

A new idea brightened her mind. The Forget slipped
often, exposing raw and ugly memories. What if . . .
Slowly carefully, Val slipped one of her own memories
beneath The Forget; a pleasant memory. One of Val's
best. For a brief time while wearing the flywacket body
she had flown. Flown like a dragon across the skies. Light
and air holding her up and dazzling her mind.

Then she eased back out of Ariiell's mind the way
she'd come. Before she'd completely withdrawn, the lady
opened her eyes and looked around. "We've stopped for
the night. I smell fresh water. Have we reached Lake
Apor already? Can you get that irritating box out from
under me?"

"There is nothing between you and the bottom of the litter but a down mattress and pillows."

"Oh. I must have dreamed about creatures of magic breaking free of their eggs. I think I'm supposed to do something with them. Have we reached Lake Apor?"

Eggs? Had General Marcelle said something about eggs? She hadn't paid close enough attention. But she'd searched the entire caravan and smelled nothing wrong. She would have to push into Lady Ariiell's dream later.

"Not yet, my lady." Val swallowed the bitter taste in her mouth left over from Ariiell's memories. "We'll be on the road another two weeks at least before we reach your father's lands." She rolled and pushed through the heavy drapes that had hidden them from prying eyes all day. She spotted a tall, lean, uniformed guard lifting a waterskin from the lake four yards away. The treated leather dripped, the drops sparkling like fine jewels in the westering sunlight.

Valeria dashed toward the soldier wearing the royal colors of green and gold. "Please, sir, may I have a drink?" she pleaded, looking up at him shyly from beneath her lowered lashes.

"Aye, lady. 'Tis been a long and dusty road." He handed her the cool leather by its carry rope.

Val grabbed it with both hands and drank greedily, all the while scanning the long chain of sledges and people in search of the other gaily draped litter for sign of her twin. The moment she spotted the bright colors Lord Jemmarc claimed as his own and for his lady, she thrust the skin back at the soldier with barely a thank you.

Desperately, she needed to talk to Lily, share her experience and gather some ideas for a cleansing ritual. A shedding ritual. Either that, or take a magical hammer and chisel to that ugly writhing knot in Ariiell's mind.

"This would be better outside," Lukan said quietly to Jaylor as they joined Marcus, three other master magicians and Robb's two sons, Stevie, aged five, and Robby, aged seven, in a circle around Marcus' desk. Marcus unrolled a large and detailed map of Coronnan, anchoring the four corners with specially chosen rocks. A tiny beeswax candle, smaller than Jalyor's little finger and with a virgin linen wick, sat in a tiny clay cup, anchored by a drip of more melted beeswax over the section of the Southern Mountains that Forest University called home. Another clay cup containing fresh spring water sat atop a blue splotch on the map that represented Lake Apor, near the Western Mountains.

"Arranged to your liking?" Jaylor asked his son.

"Needs to be outside," the boy muttered again, looking over his shoulder toward the window. Marcus had partially closed the shutters, giving the crowded room privacy with only a little fresh air—and not enough of a breeze to disturb their tools or the spell.

"It's late and raining. The ink on the map would run and confuse the spell," Marcus murmured gently.

"We know where everything on the map is. The magic will too." Lukan set his chin in a combative mood. His usual of late.

"Hush, time to breathe deeply and center yourself. Left hand on my shoulder. Right on . . ." Jaylor clenched his fingers around his staff, momentarily forgetting that Lukan did not yet have a staff to anchor and channel his magic.

"I know." Lukan ground his teeth together.

Jaylor wanted to tell his son that after tonight he would have a staff. But that was Marcus' privilege.

Maigret, the potions mistress and Robb's wife, ushered her two young sons to stand between Jaylor and Marcus. The boys couldn't reach hands as high as the shoulders of the tall men flanking them. They had to settle for grabbing hold of an elbow or hand. The little ones joined their free hands and held the leather strip supporting the crystal pendulum.

"Now breathe deep, just like we practice every morning," Maigret said softly to her sons, from outside the circle. A woman could not gather dragon magic and thus her presence inside would disrupt the flow of power.

Jaylor didn't think he'd ever heard a gentle word from the headstrong, determined adventuress he'd sent as a spy to the palace when Darville and Mikka had first married. But then he'd never thought she would willingly cease journeying and settle in one place long enough to learn to love and nurture children.

Her sons mimicked her, matching each inhalation to each other. The masters and Lukan had more training and control—they had to find the boys' natural rhythm and make it their own.

Jaylor closed his eyes and listened with his mind as well as his ears. Consciously, he increased the pace of his breathing to match the youngest among them. His heartbeat followed and felt like it raced.

"Not natural!" his body tried to tell him. He shut down the impulse. Heat rose into his face. A headache threatened to pound behind his eyes with the effort to follow rather than lead in this critical part of the spell.

The other masters seemed to have as much trouble as he. Only Lukan, a natural mimic who could copy anything but initiate little, fell into the rhythm easily.

At last, after much longer than usual, they all settled into the pattern, odd though it was. Jaylor's left hand tingled where it rested atop a child's head. The energy stretched across his arms and shoulders into his staff and beneath Lukan's touch on the other side.

The magic grew.

In the back of his mind he saw colors shooting up from the top of each staff, colors that matched the signature of each magician in the circle. The strands blended and twined with each other, spreading outward and upward. He caught the barest whiff of aromatic tree bark. The Tambootie. Marcus burned a single leaf in the candle flame to aid Lukan and the two youngsters in joining.

With a nearly audible snap, the varied colors met and

closed a dome above them, completely enveloping them and their spell.

Only then did Jaylor fully open his eyes. The candle burned brighter, flame, wick, and wax each separate unto themselves and yet combined to complete their functions. The water did not quite meet the edges of the bowl, a separate element from its container. So too did the men, their staffs, and their magic sharpen in detail rather than blur together as they should.

Alarm began to spread through Jaylor.

He tamped it down while widening his senses. He noted the boys' auras blending and encompassing the pendulum as it swung in wide circles, seeking.

Like to like, Jaylor projected to every individual mind. The bonds of friendship and camaraderie stretched far. The bond of blood between the boys and their father defined the search, narrowing the circle of the crystal.

The pendulum's path stretched into an oblong, narrowing until it swung back and forth between the lake and the sea, pausing at each end but settling nowhere.

Marcus opened his eyes and stared at the map.

Jaylor felt a dip in the magical energy. The dome lowered and cracked.

Lukan gasped, gargling dry choking sounds from the back of his throat. He yanked his hand away for contact with his father's shoulder to clutch his temples. He dropped to his knees keening in pain. "Get out of my head!" he screamed over and over. "I'm not dreaming. You have no right to my thoughts."

Jaylor broke his contact, reaching for his son.

Magical energy released too soon without grounding whipped and snapped about, lashing faces and hands, any exposed skin, leaving all present burned and bloody.

CHAPTER 10

"LUKAN!" JAYLOR SCREAMED with mind and voice, through his own blinding pain between his temples and behind his eyes. He groped forward and dodged the lashing magic that burned as it passed and shredded his formal blue robe, even though it did not touch his skin. Yet.

Lukan! Where are you? He ducked and crawled toward where his son had collapsed. He wasn't there! How could he have moved away from his spot in the circle in only two heartbeats?

He heard Maigret wailing and calling her boys to her side. She'd been outside the circle. Perhaps . . .

"Maigret, ground the magic. Do it now, before it kills us all!" he yelled over the cacophony of men crying out in pain and the whir and slash as the magic tendrils turned into vicious whips.

He sensed her twisting her fingers, weaving the magic strands into a pattern, giving it purpose. Every time she managed to bring three whips together, one would fray and break free.

She tried again while sheltering her two sons in her lap. They cried and clung to her, too frightened to help in the game she'd invented for them.

A chuckle of amused triumph tried to sound in the back

of Jaylor's mind. He almost recognized it. Another slash of migraine blindness threw the voice out of his head.

Then his hands found the trembling form of his son. Lukan still knelt with his hands pressing against his temples, eyes buried in the crooks of his crossed arms. "Not my fault. Not my fault," he whimpered pitifully. "He invades my dreams and now my spells. Not my fault. I can't keep him out. I'm not trained. I don't have a staff. *Get out of my head!*"

Jaylor sat and pulled the boy close, letting Lukan bury his face against his father's chest as he did when a child. Child no longer. Jaylor rocked back and forth, back and forth, with his face pressed tight against his son's dark auburn hair, so like his own. His son. His own true son and he didn't know how to help him. How to help himself when every movement tore at his eyes and his sanity.

(Focus,) a friendly feminine voice whispered from far away. *(Focus on the Kardia, the land that nurtures you. Let the land take you. Feel the land within your heart.)*

Jaylor breathed deeply, the first lesson of a magician; learn to breathe. *Focus your breath and heartbeat until they become one. Feel the pulse and rhythm of Kardia Hodos, the world, his home. The path of the heart. Merge with it. Blend with it. Let the magnetic pole to the south orient your senses and give you direction.*

He followed the litany of his youth. Whispered the words as he obeyed the rules of the lesson. Slowly, carefully he found his sense of self buried in the land beneath the wooden floor of the wooden building of the Forest University he had helped build with his own hands.

The wild magic around him slowed, straightened, lashed with less energy.

(Draw the magic into you and drag it deep, deep into the heart of Karidia Hodos where it belongs. Forge a path for it to find its way home.)

"Home," he said aloud, still rocking his son. "Go home." He nearly cried out as the untamed energy shot through his heart, down through his body, down, down,

down into the depths of the world. Each time he thought he'd sent the last of it on its way home, another long strand jerked away from Maigret's careful weaving and burned a hole in Jaylor's heart, his gut, or his brain while it sought to follow its fellows back to the Kardia.

The pain was too much. He screamed and released Lukan so he could try and hold his head together with the strength of his hands.

(Focus!)

Shayla, matriarch of the dragons and longtime friend, turned that one word into a scathing condemnation of his pitiful attempts to accept her nurturing. Jaylor had never heard a curse from that gentle dragon voice. Didn't know if Shayla could curse. That one word came too close for him to dare defy her.

He opened his mind one more time, found the last four whipping strands of blue and red. His colors. With a deep breath he commanded them to braid together, just like his queue when it went wild, taming it into order. Magic resisted. He pushed. Blackness covered his eyes. He welcomed the cessation of blinding light that stabbed his mind from all directions, inward and outward.

At the first sign of obedience from the magic he fumbled for his staff, always nearby, even when he dropped it. Someone pushed the wooden tool into his hands.

(Focus!)

"Come!" he commanded with mind and magic and voice. The blue and red braid twined around the staff, accepting a like pattern as part of itself.

With a mighty effort he slammed the butt end of the staff against the floor, dislodging the raw magic and sending it shooting straight into the Kardia below.

"Lord Jaylor, you did it," Marcus gasped.

"And that is why he is Senior Magician," Maigret affirmed.

"Not much longer," Jaylor sighed. "I think I'm quite blind." He passed a hand in front of his face and saw nothing. No shapes, no outlines, only streaks of colored light, akin to the lashing magic. Or the umbilicals of life pulsing through the void between here and there, now and then.

"Stargods, it's all my fault!" Lukan screamed. Running footsteps followed by the slamming of a door signaled he had run away from responsibility once again.

"My own son ran away from me!"

People are so naked in their dreams. All of their hopes and fears reveal themselves to the careful watcher. That little nap Jaylor took this afternoon may have rested his body, but his mind remains in turmoil. He barely noticed as I latched a piece of my mind to his. In fact he welcomed the tiny bit of calm that surrounds my presence.

He and I are one now. What he knows, I know.

I could not allow him to find my prisoner. When the crystal changed its circle to a straight line between the two points of interest, I had to break the circle. I am not yet ready to release Robb. My prisoner is strong in mind and body. He commands the respect and obedience of his journeymen. If I cannot break the master, I must separate him from his juniors. His belief in their betrayal is the strongest weapon I have.

But I have absorbed the wild magic at the same time as Jaylor. I have endured the same pain as he. I knelt in the center of my own circle wailing in pain, trying to pluck the searing lightning from my eyes. I came close to embarrassing myself before my followers.

Mind links have their dangers. If I sever my connection I may regain my sight quicker than he.

But then I lose a great advantage.

What to do? I have never been indecisive before. I have always known my path.

What to do?

I can endure this pain no longer. I give it all back to Jaylor.

But I found the boy. I dismissed his dreams as too easy

to read. He is too transparent and harbors few secrets. Worthless. I had no hold over him. But he is vulnerable because he is so young and so very angry with the world. I can manipulate him through his anger.

Lukan climbed. The fastest path away from Da's temper was to move upward, faster than his father could follow.

First he ran. Blindly. A tree root tripped him just beyond the University steps. He flailed to stay upright, moving forward with each awkward step. When his head and feet knew up from down, right from left, he ran on until his knees connected with a boulder as high as his waist. Pain jolted from the bruised joints down to his feet and up his spine. His head wanted to disconnect as shadows within shadows spiraled around him. He flew forward with a gush of air exiting his body. Smooth granite scraped his palms.

He wanted nothing more than to crumple to the ground and let the cool drizzle wash away his hurts, inside and out.

"Lukan!" Da called from inside the building.

Clumsily, Lukan braced himself on the boulder and pushed upright.

"Lukan, come back here," Da commanded on one of his trademarked roars.

Lukan hastened around the solid rock, his feet finding the well-worn path uphill. Sixteen long strides and he sensed an opening among the trees. An apprentice meditation circle. Straight across the small clearing he found another path and continued. Thirty strides and he heard the chuckle of the creek above the first fall. Then one hundred strides until he found his tree. *His* tree. The stunted everblue with sturdy limbs that stretched close to the ground. He could crawl up against the trunk and remain as hidden as if in a cave.

He'd done that often enough when hiding from Glenndon in childish games. But Glenndon always found him.

So he climbed, finding handholds and foot grips by memory. The rough bark oozed soothing sap over the scrapes on his palms. "Thank you, my friend," he whispered with mind and voice. Tree responded with a ruffle of long needle tufts and a sense of enfolding Lukan within his shadows.

Lukan's tree might not be as tall as his fellows but his limbs were stout and solid ten feet up before they spindled into a fluffy top. Clinging to the trunk he edged around until he settled his butt into a convenient fork that always fit his body as he grew and allowed him to lean back to rest his head against a soft splotch of moss.

He heaved a sigh and listened to the wind. The gentle breeze carried only its own gossip, not the turmoil he knew must roil through the University at this moment.

"What's happening to me?" he asked both the tree and the wind.

They answered by releasing the sharp scent of the sap and . . . and something more. Something exotic that had picked up the weight of salt water, grain-filled plains, and a spice that tantalized and burned his nose at the same time.

"Foreign," he guessed. "Something from far away." That wasn't quite right. "*Someone* far away."

Wind and tree quieted in agreement.

"Someone invades my dreams, trying to learn what I know. But I don't know anything. I'm just an apprentice and no one trusts me."

He thought back to the scrying spell that had gone all wrong. Such a simple spell. A basic spell with crude tools.

Simple tools, the tree reminded him.

"Simple?" That was the key. Nothing complicated. A simple path from mind to magic to answer. Anyone with half a mind and cunning could step onto that path, probably in his own shadow and watch all. And then . . . and then just as the answer seemed obvious that shadow person from his dreams had twisted the path, hidden the answer, and wreaked havoc with the spell.

"Not my fault!" he cried to the wind. "But I will be blamed. Just as I am always blamed. Even when I am innocent. Though I'm usually not. But this time I am."

Satisfied that there was nothing he could have done to prevent the chaos, he wrapped himself in the warmth radiating from the tree's sun-warmed bark and slept.

Slept for the first time in weeks without troubling dreams with strange whispers and images awakening him every hour.

CHAPTER 11

SKELLER PLUCKED A string on Telynnia. It twanged a hint sharper than the middle C he needed. A touch to the string key sweetened the tone to match his voice. The D sounded true.

All the bouncing and changes in temperature during the day's march hadn't affected his old friend much. She just needed a bit of tender loving care to remind her he'd not forgotten her.

The young woman with the sun-streak red-gold hair from the bright litter turned her head away from ladling up a bowl of stew—the one without meat—for the pale and vague woman who paced around and around the litter that now rested at knee height on four boxes instead of at chest height when supported by two steeds.

He smiled at the girl. A slender young woman in the way of girls passed into the middle of their teens, but sturdy and well-rounded in the right places.

She returned the smile, giving him only half her attention. Partly she watched her charge. She also kept her head tilted, tuned toward her sister. He guessed the scrawny girl with barely any curves at all who'd come running in search of them the moment the caravan stuttered to a stop was a younger sister. Younger by a year, more likely two. Other than that little bit of maturity in her figure, the two girls were very alike in height, in features, in coloring, and posture.

He played a chord, testing how each string blended with its fellows. The rose-gold blonde picked out the top note and sang it lightly. He took up the challenge, matching his light baritone to the bottom note of the major chord, letting the harp hold her own with the middle.

One bowl of stew delivered to the vague lady, the girl with the sunset hair carried two more as she joined him on a convenient rock beside his own. Still no meat. Oh, well, he'd grab a more substantial bowl with chicken after a song or two.

"Lillian here," she said shyly. Her speaking voice sounded as lyrical and melodic as her singing.

Odd phrasing though.

"Skeller here," he replied.

She raised both eyebrows in surprise.

"What?" he asked.

"I thought my family was the only one that spoke to dragons."

"Huh?"

"Oh, you were just mimicking me." Her face fell out of the smile.

An ache of disappointment tightened his chest. Not knowing how to bring back that smile he played a complex set of scaling patterns to loosen up his fingers.

Behind him, the steeds stamped restlessly.

"They love you," Lillian whispered. And the smile came back.

His chest lightened. "It's a curse. Every time I sing, one of them decides I'm the herd's newest best friend. They think I'm one of them and not human at all. They'll follow me anywhere." He sighed dramatically at the burden of his life.

"Do cats and dogs do the same thing?" She spooned up a bite of the luscious smelling meal. Even devoid of meat it carried the subtle aroma of skillfully blended herbs.

"Stray dogs do, not the ones who have a master to look to. Cats not so much." He set aside his harp in favor of the stew, deciding he'd sing better on a half-full stomach. He wouldn't truly be satisfied until he'd had some real meat. "I sing in a different key from cats. Or maybe it's the catgut strings on Telynnia." He patted the harp at the same time he grinned hugely to show he was only kidding.

Her look of horror changed to a gentle smile as she realized his joke.

"Cats do view the world as their own private universe and humans as obnoxious aliens," she replied quietly. "They sing their own songs and work their own magic in ways that have nothing to do with our perceptions."

"You should work on that. If you could herd cats, the world would worship you."

They both laughed.

"You know cats then?"

"Mama has a few that keep down the rodent population in the kitchen garden. Sometimes they listen to her." She lowered her eyes to her bowl and refused to lift them to his face.

They ate in companionable silence for a time. He scanned the assorted personalities in the caravan, seeking a suitable song to fit the end of a long day of walking. The caravan master prowled the long line, mindful of his duties. He scowled deeply at Skeller, reminding him of *his* duties.

"Time to sing for my supper," he said when he felt his spoon scrape the bottom of the bowl. Too soon. He wasn't sure if he needed more stew or more conversation with Lillian.

She took the bowl from him and went in search of the vague lady's for general washing up. The spoon he wiped clean with a handful of grass, wrapped it in a linen serviette, and tucked both away in his pack.

Then he held Telynnia, his song mistress, in his arms and strolled about, strumming this and that, waiting for a reaction. When a group turned toward him with their bits of cleaning and mending, willing to listen, he plucked a joyful chord and sang the opening phrase of a rousing drinking song.

At the back of a sledge someone opened a cask of ale. Skeller heard the pop of the bung and smelled the yeasty froth of liquid. He repeated the chorus urging his companions to join him.

Lillian gave him a sip of ale, keeping the wooden cup nearby so he had both hands free for the harp.

Whimsically he kissed her cheek in thanks and turned the song to the soaring delights of a barmaid.

She laughed and blushed. The crowd joined him on the first chorus.

A rush of wind and screeching roar overhead drowned him out. All and sundry travelers ducked their heads beneath their arms or upflung aprons.

Except Lillian and her sister. They looked up, searching the twilit skies with big smiles on their faces.

"What was that?" he asked when the noise passed on.

"Magic," Lillian breathed.

"A dragon," her younger sister said with the same sense of awe.

They looked toward each other in silent communication he could not fathom.

"Sing us a dragon song," Lillian finally said as the camp returned to normal.

"I don't think I know any."

"Where are you from that a bard knows no dragon songs?" the younger sister asked in disgust.

"Play this," Lillian hummed a tune that sounded like a joyful hymn.

He repeated it, feeling the harp come to life with a vibrant joy he'd never felt before. And then Lillian sang in her bright soprano of the pure joy of soaring among the stars on dragon wings.

The crowd swayed in unison, humming along.

Almost, for a moment, he felt as if he and the music

soared with the great beasts of legend; that his harp and the dragon sang to each other.

"Magic," he whispered. "The stuff of magic."

Magic. The one thing he'd come to discredit, along with the magician who so unwisely counseled Lokeen, unrightful king of Amazonia.

Then he looked more closely at the sisters who had spawned this magical moment. Sisters, much alike in face and form. Each sister rode with a great lady in a litter.

Which one was the pawn of Lokeen and his magician counselor?

Glenndon watched his father, King Darville, tap the feathered end of his quill against a small square of parchment laying flat on his massive desk.

The king read the missive again, eyes flicking back and forth rapidly. A frown tugged his mouth into deeper and deeper disapproval.

Glenndon fidgeted, shifting his weight from foot to foot, rotating his shoulders, fingering the pommel of his useless ceremonial sword, missing his staff, trying to stand respectfully before the man with graying gold hair who held his future in his hands.

The king's bodyguard Fred, father of Frank, hovered in a corner, unobtrusive and constantly wary, as he should. General Marcelle lounged in a chair beside the cold hearth, one of the few allowed such familiarity in the presence of the king. He'd earned the right over the years, loyal, constant, giving cautious counsel when needed—both when asked and when needed but not asked.

Finally King Darville leaned back in his massive wooden chair and glared at Glenndon, as many a teaching master had glared at him over the years of study at the Forest University, trying to force him to speak when he had no need to speak. "Do you know how important our new alliance with Amazonia is?" the king growled, no sign of the affectionate and proud father in his voice or posture.

Both the general and Fred leaned forward with interest.

Glenndon flashed a glance at General Marcelle. The older man frowned at him. His loyalty clearly aligned with the king first and the king's family second.

Glenndon nodded to his father once, sharply, retreating into the safety of silence. As he had always done.

"Then why did you dismiss the ambassador without even seeing him?"

Glenndon's eyes narrowed in suspicion as he reached for the parchment that had been sealed with deep, sea-blue wax.

The king placed his hands atop the letter, blocking Glenndon's view of the damning words.

"Tell me what happened, yesterday noon that prompted the ambassador to send me a scathing reprimand this morning," King Darville demanded.

Glenndon turned his head away, finding his old defense of silence inadequate and yet . . . yet. . . .

"Talk, son. Talk to me. I know you can speak. My daughter Linda taught you how. There was a time when words poured forth from you as easily as they did her."

But Linda was gone. A thousand miles away, studying at the Forest University. She was safe there. Safe from prejudice and assassins and treaties that assigned her a husband. She used that precious gift of time to learn control of the gift of magic Glenndon had given her. In return she had given him the gift of words during a healing spell. Once again he lived the moment of marvelous blending of their minds and souls encased in a bubble of magic. The half sister he'd not known existed had truly become his sister in those moments while she removed magically burning acid from his hand, along with the blockage of scar tissue from his throat. While they both resided in the capital she was closer to him than either Valeria or Lillian, whom he'd grown up with.

Now that she was so far away, he wasn't sure their perpetual mind link was as strong as before.

He swallowed deeply, trying to ease the dryness in his throat.

"The ambassador threatens to pack up the entire diplomatic delegation and return home, ending all of our trade and talk of mutual defense treaties," the king said, bringing him back to the immediate problem.

"He . . . he never arrived," Glenndon said, surprised his voice rang true without a trace of cracking or croaking.

Darville raised a single eyebrow in question. "His letter says he was turned away at the palace doors, under your orders."

"He lies."

Again that single raised eyebrow. Waves of orange distrust roiled through his gold and green aura. General Marcelle reached for his ever-present sword pommel, ready to defend his king and rid him of those he could not trust implicitly.

Distrust of Glenndon, the king's son and heir, or distrust of an unknown ambassador from far away?

Glenndon's natural defenses suspected the distrust was aimed at him. Why should his father be any different from his tutors and masters? They trusted words more than they trusted him.

He reminded himself that an adult would trust another adult before believing Glenndon, not quite eighteen and new to court and politics. Had he earned trust from a father he'd known only a few months?

He thought he'd earned General Marcelle's trust through countless hours of arms practice and steed training. If he had, he also knew the general would not speak to the king until Glenndon left the room.

"Keerkin, my clerk, brought the apology the ambassador wrote. The hastily scrawled message said the ambassador's presence was required to supervise the unloading of a rare wine." Glenndon stood tall and defiant, eyes steady on the king. His father!

Darville stilled a moment. He returned Glenndon's steady gaze, then broke contact, looking around his private office for something . . . probably a cup of betta arrack, the distilled liquor from Rossemeyer, the queen's homeland.

But he'd given up the bracing alcohol sometime ago after it dulled his senses enough for a juvenile Krackatrice to attack him and infect him with deadly venom. If the black snake had been more than a year old, the king would not have survived the speed or the strength of the venom.

Even now he gave in to bouts of physical weakness unknown in him before. He'd lost a lot of blood in removing the toxin from his system. The queen had made sure all of the poison flowed out before it paralyzed his heart and lungs.

But he had not resorted to drink to dull the ongoing pain.

"I want to believe you, son. But such an unimportant errand . . . a cask of wine more important than presenting his credentials to the palace? It sounds contrived by a boy inexperienced in the ways of politics." Darville returned his gaze to Glenndon, holding it, begging to read the truth.

"I swear to you that I tell the truth. I was so angry I tore the letter in half and told Keerkin to scrape the parchment clean and reuse it. Now I have no chance to analyze it for forgery or magical manipulation." Glenndon leaned forward, hands braced on the desktop, putting him at eye level with his father.

"What did you glean from first glance, Glenndon. Your Da, my best friend, taught me long ago to trust first instincts."

"An elegant hand, University trained in language and script," Glenndon blurted out without thinking.

"Keerkin is University trained. As are you."

This time Glenndon stilled. Disappointment and disbelief thickened in his throat, making it hard to swallow. He'd thought, perhaps he and the clerk could become friends, having shared bits and pieces of their lives in apprentice classes. He had more in common with the barely talented Keerkin than anyone else in the palace.

"Frank, my bodyguard, Fred's son, was there, he will bear witness."

"I have never known Fred, my bodyguard, to lie to me. I expect he raised his son to the same standard. Call Frank and Keerkin. I will question them, one after the other, one hour after noon. Perhaps the queen can raise the ink back into the torn pieces of the letter." Darville pulled a different letter atop the diplomatic complaint and bent his head to study it, clearly dismissing Glenndon. Still not fully trusting him.

"I could raise the ink . . ."

The king did not look up.

General Marcelle jerked his head toward the door. Good advice to retreat and gather his resources. Evidence. The truth, obvious and hidden.

CHAPTER 12

FROM HIS WARM nest within the thatch of the cabin's roof near the central chimney, Lukan checked the wheel of stars overhead. Another hour before dawn dimmed the blazing points of light. A waning moon sank toward the tree line. He couldn't call the circle of everblue tops a horizon. They were too close, enclosing only about five acres of land around his home.

His stomach growled, reminding him why he lay wakeful at this hour when all, even night hunting predators, drowsed. Sounds inside the cabin had drifted to silence hours ago. His father no longer whimpered in pain from the lashing magical storm. For a time he did not cry in his sleep for the loss of his precious eyesight.

A rustling disturbance of the ivy growing on the south wall of the house made him stiffen.

Who? He sent out a subtle query.

"Just me," Master Marcus said quietly. He sounded weary and out of breath. "Ooof," he grunted as he transitioned from the wall to the roof.

"Master?" Lukan sat up, trying to untangle his blanket—stolen from the University cupboard.

"Rest easy, boy. I'm not here to scold you. We need to talk and this is about as private as it gets around here."

"Yes, sir." Lukan continued sitting, bracing his back against the warm chimney.

"Nice view of the stars. I can see why you like this place rather than your snug bed that is sheltered from the rain."

Lukan shrugged rather than reply. That kind of response always worked for Glenndon.

"You had the right idea for the spell tonight," Marcus said, easing down to sit beside Lukan, careful not to slide down the slope of the roof. He wore casual tunic and trews, like any other prosperous farmer. Not a trace of magician robes or even blue journey leathers.

"It should have worked," Lukan admitted. "I don't know what went wrong. I researched everything . . ."

"The plan was right. But something went wrong with the working. I wonder if it was too simple when we expected complicated and did something extra that twisted . . ."

"It wasn't the working," Lukan said quietly. Almost hoping his master didn't hear him.

"Then what?"

S'murghit, Marcus had heard him.

"What went wrong? You shouted something about 'Get out of my head.' I'm wondering if the same thing went wrong with the transport spell that Robb and his boys never emerged from. Someone got into his head and diverted him elsewhere."

"Um . . ."

"Talk to me, Lukan. I can't promote you until I know what happened."

"Promote?"

"We'll talk about that later. Right now we talk about who is talking to you, listening to every word and thought you have."

"It's my dreams mostly. Someone seems to listen in and then add ideas."

"Like?"

"Like . . ." Anger began to boil along with frustration.

Lukan clamped down on it. This was Marcus who had sought him out, not Da demanding he attend him in his office and then lecture and pronounce rather than listen. "Like I should give up trying to find Master Robb. Like I should abandon the University. Like Da is a traitor to all magicians."

"Hmmm."

"What does that mean?" Lukan demanded sharply.

"It means I need to think a bit. I have an idea about what is happening to you. And to Vareena." He mentioned his wife. She didn't have much talent other than being able to see and talk to the dead. Her job was presiding over the transition from life to death and making sure the spirit of the passing moved on to whatever came after life.

"Why would someone try to twist Mistress Vareena's dreams?" Lukan blurted out.

"That I cannot tell you. Only that someone is working from within, manipulating those who have not yet mastered all their skills, or are vulnerable, weaker magicians. I think I know who, but I can't confront them or even protect against them until I have proof."

Guilt stabbed Lukan's gut, banishing his hunger. If he'd held on a little longer ... If he'd studied harder and been a stronger magician and banished the lurking presence left over from his dreams ... If he hadn't had a bright idea that *might* find his missing master ...

"We'll talk more in a day or two," Marcus said and placed a reassuring hand on Lukan's shoulder. "Think hard about who invades your thoughts and ways to build walls to keep him out, or banish him if he breaks through." Slowly the master magician eased to the caves and swung his legs over the edge. He twisted around to face Lukan as he sought footholds in the greenery. "I can remember doing this many years ago. I think I'm getting too old for climbing trees and walls." With a sigh he lowered himself and disappeared.

Failure kept pushing toward the surface of Lukan's

emotions. "Enough," he whispered to the uncaring stars. "I can't change all the what ifs in the world."

Slowly he unwound the rough blanket and folded it neatly. A quick rearrangement of some loose thatch hid the blanket from casual view. Of course that loose thatch meant he'd need to patch the roof before the autumnal rains began.

He eased himself toward the gutter, reached up toward an overhanging branch. From there he scrambled into the tree and slid down the thick trunk to the ground. He wondered that the ivy had supported Marcus. Lukan hadn't trusted it for months now. But the tree had always offered him easy access. He preferred trees. Even Glenndon the magnificent didn't think to look upward when they played games of hide and seek.

Or if he did, he granted Lukan the illusion of success in the game.

His brother was like that.

For the first time in months, Lukan felt no jealousy of his brother. "I miss you, G. Terribly. But we've grown up and our lives are different now."

He stood for a moment staring north, toward the city and his brother, his closest companion and friend. "If you'd stayed here, maybe you could help me banish the slithering eavesdropper. I haven't allowed myself to sleep much of late. I'm afraid, G. I'm afraid of what he might learn from me. What he might make me do while I think I'm dreaming but I'm not."

Lukan knew the person on the other end of his dreams was male. He wasn't sure how he knew, just that no female he knew would have the thrust, the power, the viciousness to break down sleep shields to invade his dreams.

That kind of power came from combined dragon magic, not solitary ley line magic, and women couldn't gather dragon magic.

No answer came to his mind from his brother. Of course not. If Glenndon was awake he had more important things on his mind than answering his very lonely little brother.

Lukan shrugged off his loneliness and slipped silently into the cabin. Mama had left him bread and cheese and a slice of yampion pie. It was cold, but tasted just as good as hot right out of the hearth pot.

"Thank you, Mama," he whispered to the only person he knew loved him. Then he retreated to another hiding place overlooking the University courtyard. If he dozed, the noise of his fellow students waking and preparing for the day would rouse him with plenty of time to get to class.

The boy is smarter than I thought. He has shut me out of his dreams. His guilt and anger combined to make him an easy participant in my plans. He hates his father almost as much as I do.

But now he is useless to me. He sleeps little and fights his dreams. The barriers he has erected against me are strong because they are instinctive instead of deliberate.

I must find another willing mind to merge with.

Hmm. One of the ladies or their companions, I think. Ariiell is vulnerable because of The Forget imposed upon her mind by the healers. She does not remember her dreams, only that they are troublesome. She is in a position to inflict damage upon the daughters Jaylor loves.

But the weaker twin? Perhaps my revenge will be to turn one of those daughters against her father.

Oh what joy I will find when my enemy discovers his own child bringing about his downfall, possibly even his death.

"Do you ail, my lady?" Valeria asked Ariiell, watching how the woman sat upon a folding stool, hunched over, elbows on knees, peering away from the morning camp-fires. She looked west, away from the dawn light, into gray upon gray dimness.

"Hush, they are out there. Watching me. Waiting for a moment of inattention."

"Who, my lady?" Valeria shifted her feet until the thin soles of her shoes throbbed with the power of the Kardia. She brought her hands up level with her heart, palms outward, fingers curved slightly to catch whatever information the wind might part with in passing.

"The black cat with one white ear and the weasel the color of weathered tin with flaking gilt paint," Ariiell whispered, never taking her eyes off the shrubs and grasses of the open plains.

That old imaginary danger.

Still, just in case the lady could be right (stranger things had happened when sorcery was fueled by pain and fear), Valeria focused her senses on the nearest clump of miggenberry bushes, their round fruit still shiny green in the growing light. By late summer they'd turn a rich blue-black, each as large as her thumb. Good eating for people, livestock, and browsing creatures of the wild. They stained hands and clothes a deep purple-blue, her favorite color. The same color as Indigo, the juvenile dragon she'd grown up with and shared . . . much.

The long, narrow leaves with barbs in the notches rustled in the light breeze.

"There, see that!" Ariiell proclaimed in triumph, her words still hushed.

"I see all of the bushes and grasses moving in the breeze rising from the creek that feeds the lake," Valeria said soothingly.

"And I was told you have a strong magical talent!" Ariiell snorted in disgust. She rose from her rock and sought her litter, anxious to be away from this place and her illusory fears.

No one believed Ariiell's fancies. She'd killed at least one cat, a gray tabby, and attacked the calico who called herself Grilka, thinking they were her old enemy Rejiia.

Something fueled those fears. Valeria hoped Ariiell's damaged mind, with that huge, ugly knot of memories and guilt, conjured her frequent visions of Rejiia, mistress of The Simeon and daughter of Krej. All of them members of the dreaded Coven. What horrors had the Coven inflicted upon Ariiell? She'd been an honored member as well as victim.

Valeria knew the story well, having heard it told and sung on many a dark winter night. Near twenty years ago, Lord Krej threw a spell to enscorcel King Darville into a statue of his totem animal, a great golden wolf. The magic had backlashed from the Coraurlia, the magical glass dragon crown, and changed Krej himself into his own totem statue, the tin weasel with flaking gilt paint.

Rejiia had carted the statue around the country for nigh on five years before another spell backlashed, animating Krej into a live weasel and transforming Rejiia into her own totem animal, the black cat with one white ear.

Normally neither a cat nor a weasel would live fifteen years in the wild. Still, those two animals had begun as people. People with huge, if twisted, magical talents.

On the off chance that Ariiell might perceive the truth through the veil of forgetfulness imposed on her, Valeria paused a moment, centered her mind and body with the Kardia, letting the rhythm of the land, the cool morning air, the fiery sun, and the rapidly disappearing dew, absorb her essence. She felt herself sinking into the elements. They sustained her, became one with her.

When her skin became no different from crumbling dirt, her blood flowed with the timeless chuckle of the creek, her lungs moved air hither and thither, and the fire within her mind basked in the added heat from the sun, she sent her senses outward. A probe here, a quest there, all one, learning who trod nearby, who splashed water, who sang while stirring porridge, which branches burned to heat the cereal. She cast further afield.

A mouse here, a bird there, an inchworm, a gray rabbit, and . . . and a cat crouching as still as still could be, waiting for the mouse or bird to come closer. Was that a weasel waiting, equally patient, for the bird to forget the dangers all around in its need to grab and eat the worm?

"Val!" Lillian called from the other end of the caravan. "Val, where are you? I can't find you."

Valeria jerked back into her own body and solitary mind with a jolt that made her bones ache and stabbed pain behind her eyes. She blinked rapidly in the too-bright sunlight and fought her roiling stomach for control. Not quite solitary. Lillian was in her head, as she always was, just a thought away. Letting that presence grow soothed her aches and comforted her appetite. But a hunk of jerked meat would certainly taste wonderful right now.

"Ah, there you are, Val." Lillian bounced toward her, all smiles and bounding energy.

"Lily, we have to talk. Alone. Where Lady Ariiell cannot listen in with either her ears or her mind," Val said beneath her breath, knowing Lillian would hear no matter how far away.

"Oh?" Lillian paused, hand to her mouth in surprise.

"I need your help. I need you to observe what happens at your end of the caravan."

"Observe? Oh, *observe*." She took Valeria's arm and led her away from the wagons and shouting people who stacked boxes and trunks atop resting sledges preparing for the day's journey. Their steps took them toward the line of steeds amiably grazing on the meadow grasses a quarter the way around the small lake.

Val noted that the bard stroked the noses of two sledge steeds that listed on one foot, half dozing under his caresses. She checked over her shoulder for Ariiell's presence. She'd moved her stool closer to the campfire, half turned to keep an eye on the miggenberry bushes. Her aura looked tightly closed, keeping stray magic out, and her own in. Lady Graciella stretched her legs, wandering aimlessly between her litter and the nearest fire while she spooned tiny bites of cereal toward her mouth.

If she ate any of it, Val couldn't tell, as she didn't seem to swallow.

"We're safe here," Val said, tugging on her twin's arm to keep her from getting closer to the bard. His sea-blue aura tinged with a bit of green didn't seem to quest outward in search of stray conversations. From this distance she couldn't tell if any magic hid within the gentle waves of color.

Lillian cast a lingering glance toward the bard.

"You can talk to him while we travel. Ask him to sing to Graciella. Maybe music will ease her craving for rosehips."

"Oh." Her face sank into a disappointed frown. "Oh!" She brightened and turned her attention back to Val.

"Now listen carefully. I need you to watch beyond the people and sledges. I need you to note any animals that seem to be following us and alert me the moment you think you see something."

Valeria flooded her sister's mind with her earlier encounter with Ariiell and what she had observed while in a near trance.

A half-smile quirked up on Lillian's face. "What if I ask Skeller to sing something that will entice the enemy out of the shadow, into the light of day? That way we know who and what we are dealing with."

"No!" Val nearly shouted. "You are not to involve the bard in this. If you see something, let me know and I'll alert Da. It's too dangerous to do more."

"Oh. But we aren't supposed to contact Da at all on journey, unless what we find endangers all of Coronnan."

"The cat and the weasel do endanger all of Coronnan. You can't let your interest in the bard overshadow your interest in your mission."

"You don't understand . . ."

"I think I do. Your thoughts are mine and mine are yours. But he comes from elsewhere, his hair is short and loose, his accent more clipped and nasal than ours. We don't know him. We can't trust him."

Valeria watched as the young man lifted his head from the attention of the steeds and stared right at her, as if acknowledging every word she had said.

"We can't trust anyone then." Lillian frowned in deep disappointment.

"No one but ourselves. And Lukan. But he hasn't summoned us in several days. I think . . . I think I should try to reach him tonight." Val steered her sister back toward camp, keeping a bit of her attention on the bard who watched their every step.

CHAPTER 13

S KELLER WATCHED the sisters walk away from him. They stayed at an angle so that the little one could watch him through narrowed eyes. She'd kept her side to him the whole time they talked so that he couldn't read their lips—a skill common to bards.

Deep dislike and distrust rose in him like burning gall from his empty stomach. As much as he enjoyed Lillian, her sister seemed the exact opposite in disposition.

He stroked the long nose of the adoring steed one more time. "Do you have a name?" he asked the beast idly.

The steed responded with a snort and a nibble on his loose, shoulder-length hair. He'd have to let his muddy brown curls grow if he stayed in Coronnan longer than the length of the journey. He'd like to find a land that did not accept violence as a natural part of every day. That attitude was becoming too common in Amazonia after a millennium of striving for peace and harmony among governments as well as individuals. Heated arguments rarely stood long after a public debate. When violence did erupt, the perpetrators were sentenced to exile in the desert interior of the Mabastion, the Big Continent. When faced with a dire struggle to survive, disputes became trivial.

He'd become a bard as much for the freedom of escaping home and the increasing violence, both political and personal. Confining his hair in the cage of a braid, like the locals, seemed a symbol of all that he'd run away from.

Champion, came into his head from nowhere, along with an image of a sleek, white, fleet steed rearing proudly to defend his herd of mares.

"Is your name Champion?" Not at all fitting for the steed Garg called Lazy Bones. He ducked out from under the steed's burly neck and held the chin with both hands so he could look into its eyes. The image in his head was of a smaller-boned animal without this one's bulk or height at the shoulder. A fleet steed, intelligent and nimble, suitable for riding, not a sledge steed that moved at a plodding gait suitable only for hauling heavy loads and answering to simple directions.

It was also intact, not gelded.

A sense of affirmation flooded him as Champion lifted his head and jerked it down again. Then he began nibbling at the curls atop Skeller's head, not minding at all that he left it loose.

"You're impossible."

"You got that right," Garg muttered, approaching the herd with steed collars and harnesses. "Dreamy-eyed lout. He's strong but lazy. Keep singing to him and we might keep him awake long enough to get where we're going."

Skeller wanted to ask where they were going but knew that would raise questions. Anyone who attached themselves to a caravan should know the destination ahead of time. His tutors, when he still lived at home and his father had hopes higher for him than becoming a lowly bard, had taught him to approach an issue sideways when he didn't want to be obvious.

"Do you know anything about the lady in the brightly colored litter? She looks very young." Not much older than Lillian, but drawn and pale and . . . sad.

"Only that we're diverting to Castle Saria to deliver her. Normally wouldn't climb that dangerously narrow ridge to the cliff top. Bloody awful trek it be. To the ugliest and dreariest castle in all of Coronnan. Built right into the mountain face, of rock quarried out of the cliff to make room for it. Heard tell the main gate is only a false front. The living portion is actually in caves deep within the mountain. Impregnable with a view across the sea nigh onto the Big Continent."

The Big Continent. *Mabastion.* Where Amazonia presided over the largest deep-water harbor on the entire coastline, with good roads deep into the grain fields of the interior. Amazonia where Lokeen looked for a new young wife among the noble daughters of Coronnan.

"And the lady herself?" Skeller prodded. "She's quite pretty."

"If you like 'em vague and obedient."

The way Lokeen liked his mistresses as well as his wife.

"Give me a gal with some meat on her bones and some fire in her eyes. Like that cute little sunrise blonde hired to companion the lady." Garg nudged Skeller with an elbow and a wink.

"Yes," Skeller replied. He liked Lillian well enough, happy to have found a voice that could match his in song. "About that girl ... she seems familiar with country ways and dresses quite plainly for a lady's companion." She also claimed to talk to dragons.

The drover shrugged and draped the harness and collar around Champion. "Overheard Lord Jaylor, the head magician, telling caravan master that the two girls companioning the ladies were to be respected and their requests treated as orders from him. Figure they spent some time at the University up in the mountains, away from civilization."

Skeller wanted to scuttle away from contact with magicians and magic. Until his father's spymaster brought magic to Amazonia, they'd done well enough without it.

Why wait for a servant to fetch a magician to light a candle when he could do the same with flint and steel in a matter of moments?

Champion sidled, nearly pushing Skeller off his feet.

"Easy, Champion. Easy," Skeller soothed him, half singing the words. "Yes you have to put up with the collar. You have to earn all that expensive grain you gobble down." He added a few chin scratches. "Is there a raw spot right about . . . ?" Skeller felt for the spot between the shoulder blades that matched the itch in his own. "Here!"

"Well, I'll be . . ." The drover immediately removed the collar and fished in his belt pouch for a clay pot full of aromatic salve. He rubbed a generous portion into the sore spot.

Champion sighed and let his knees relax, dropping his head back onto Skeller's shoulder.

"Get off me, you great, heavy brute," Skeller admonished on a laugh. "No more lullabies for you, Lazy Bones. Bright and lively marching songs only."

Champion sighed and supported his own weight while the drover made adjustments to the tack so it wouldn't rub the wrong way.

"Go get you some breakfast, boy. I'll deal with the team. Champion you called him? Then Champ he be. Appreciate you walkin' nearby to keep this lazy lout putting one foot in front of the other just to follow you."

"I will." But he'd keep the same position in today's march to watch the lady in the litter.

And her companion Lillian. Maybe over the campfire tonight he could glean a bit more information about the lady headed toward Castle Saria with its protected landings and view across the ocean toward Amazonia.

And maybe a bit more about Lillian. If her sister left her alone long enough.

He'd ask questions about the sister and her lady later. For the moment Lillian's lady seemed the best candidate for his father's plots. Plots that must be thwarted.

❧

"Come, my lady, you need to walk about a bit," Lillian said, offering her arm to Graciella before she could climb into the litter. The drovers hadn't even harnessed the steeds to the poles yet.

"But we are leaving," Graciella protested, hands clutching her skirts and one foot lifted to rest on the mounting box.

"Not yet, my lady. See, the lead sledge is delayed." Lillian pointed toward the head of the caravan where a steed reared and fought the heavy collar meant to ease the load he carried away from his neck and onto his shoulders and back.

"Oh," Graciella put her right foot back on the ground. "I'm tired. I did not sleep well last night," she added sullenly.

"You'll be in the litter all day, dozing. Same as yesterday. You need to stir yourself. Come walk with me. I'll hold your arm to steady you." Lillian offered her crooked arm to the lady.

Graciella heaved a great sigh. "If I must. But my Lord Jemmarc would not force me to walk. It might stir the bleeding again."

"A walk might balance your blood so it is not so thin." Lillian tugged at her charge to move her away from the impatient drovers and stamping steeds. Even Master Lazy Bones, the steed that loved to rest his head on Skeller's shoulders, seemed eager to move forward rather than stand still and adore the bard.

She aimed Graciella along the lake edge. A fish jumped toward a flying insect and plopped back into the water. Lillian paused to admire the silvery sheen of the scales in the morning light. Graciella jumped at the noise and edged behind Lillian, away from the water.

"Water frightens you?" she asked, moving again, parallel to the water's edge, where it lapped the sandy shore in gentle movements.

"Have you ever seen the waves crashing ashore among the rocks and shoals beneath Castle Saria?" Graciella looked a little paler than usual.

Lillian shook her head. "The closest I've been to the sea is the bay shore near Coronnan City. A storm was sweeping in from the east and some of those waves were tall and impressive."

"Not like the ocean meeting sharp rocks, crushing you between the water and the knife-sharp edges that will slice you to ribbons." Graciella shuddered and took two steps farther away from the water's edge.

"I promise you, my lady, this little lake is not dangerous. 'Tis not even very deep. You'd have to work at drowning in it."

Graciella kept shaking her head and aiming their steps up toward the uneven, but solid ground above the sandy shore.

Lily felt the same great weight and trembling within her chest and mind that Graciella did. Her empathy reached out, needing to share the manifestation of the fear if not the cause.

But she had to understand the fear to banish it.

What frightened this girl who'd been removed from the protection of her family home very young and thrust into the role of wife, stepmother, and lady of a great estate? There was something more in her fear than the uncertainty of rapidly changing circumstances.

Lillian wished, not for the first time, for her twin's talent of reaching into a mind and soothing fears. She had to settle for gentle words to ease this girl's troubles.

"Did you get caught beneath such a wave?" she asked, barely above a whisper, allowing a bit of awe and fear to tinge her voice.

"No. Not me."

"But you saw someone?"

"Lord Jemmarc's son, Lucjemm, told me how in the old days Lord Krej would chain criminals to one of those rocks so tightly their backs bled, and then wait and watch while the tide rushed in. Even without a storm pushing them, the waves were huge. Reaching halfway up the cliff, lashing everything in their path. Drowning anyone caught in the water even with a boat. But he was cruelest when he weakened and loosened the chains, knowing the prisoner had a chance to escape. But if he broke free, the waves would toss him about until the rocks shredded him. . . ." She buried her face in her hands and retreated farther away from the water.

"From what I've heard about Lucjemm, he threatened you with that punishment if you did not obey him," Lillian whispered.

Either Graciella did not hear or ignored her.

A new thought, a horrible one, landed right beside that one. What had Lucjemm demanded of his new stepmother that warranted such punishment if she did not obey?

Lillian fortified herself with a deep lungful of air as she sought to center herself and anchor her awareness in the Kardia. Her senses remained right where they were. Val's would expand until she merged first with the land then stretched out as far as the stars, possibly allowing her mind to soar with dragons. Steady breathing helped Lillian sort her thoughts even though she didn't touch a dragon mind.

"Look, my lady, a dwarf flusterfoot plant." She pointed toward a cluster of broad reddish leaves with strong green spine and veins. "Don't see them often in the wild. Mama grows them in a corner of her kitchen garden."

"The greens will be good alongside whatever inedible stew the drovers prepare for our supper," Graciella said, peering curiously at the plant, her fears momentarily forgotten.

"The roots in the stew as well. Thick chunks will satisfy much better than any meat the cooks might throw in," Lillian said. She drew her utility knife from her belt pack and began loosening the soil around the leaf crown.

The roots would also help thicken Graciella's blood, balance her from the excess of rosehips. Red meat might help too, but she couldn't contemplate the loss of a life just to feed the lady when plants did just as well.

"I don't like flusterfoot roots," Graciella announced proudly and strode back toward the litter with her head held high, as if born to the semiroyal line she'd married into.

"Don't you want to save your baby?" Lillian almost shouted at her.

Every word of their conversation seemed to etch into her mind with hot acid.

Maybe Graciella did want to lose her baby, because she didn't know for certain if her husband Jemmarc or her stepson Lucjemm had fathered it. Maybe reaching for rosehips all day every day was her way of shaking it loose, before it got too close to her heart, too big to discard safely.

"Maybe I should let you continue on this self-destructive course," she whispered. "But if I do, you'll likely bleed to death in the process."

She returned to digging the big red root free of its grip on the soil, whispering apologies to the spirit of the plant for disrupting its growth cycle. "You're getting flusterfoot tonight and every night, Lady Graciella, until I know for certain you will not die, even if you do lose the baby."

CHAPTER 14

G LENNDON KICKED THE door to his room. It remained sturdily closed. A judicial bit of magic into the lock . . .

"I wouldn't advise it, Your Highness," General Marcelle said from behind him

Glenndon stared at his stretched fingers as he withdrew the energy from them that wanted to scream forth and fry something, anything, to dust. By will alone he evened his breathing and centered himself, pushing the heat and light of magic back into the wooden floor beneath his light, indoor boots.

"What can I do for you, General?" Glenndon asked, keeping his back to the man and his voice artificially po lite.

"We are going hunting." The slap of a riding crop across a palm emphasized his words.

Glenndon groaned. Audibly.

"Best way to learn to ride is to spend as much time steed-back as possible. Hunting is necessary to put meat on the table and to practice any number of useful skills, like shooting a bow at a moving target while guiding your mount with your knees."

"But . . ."

"No buts about it. We are going hunting. It will also

give you a chance to vent your frustration in private to a sympathetic ear."

"You believe me?" Glenndon whirled to face the general, one of his father's most trusted companions and advisors.

"Of course I do. So does the king. But His Grace has other things troubling him and keeping the trade agreements with Amazonia intact is only one of them."

"Why would the ambassador lie?"

"The same reason he took ship half an hour before his letter of complaint was delivered. To gain something in those treaties he doesn't think he'll get without coercion?" The general cocked his head and widened his eyes, an expression Glenndon had learned meant for him to think it through.

"What do we have that he doesn't?"

"A princess nearing marriageable age."

Glenndon's gut turned cold. "Linda is too young . . ."

"Princess Rosselinda is royal. If you listen to the gossip on the wharfs, the ferry crew and merchants alike, you'd know that King Lokeen sits on a shaky throne. He needs a strong alliance to keep it. Something about tracing their lineage through the women. His wife has died. He has two sons. No daughters."

"Why haven't I heard this before?"

"Because official representatives of Amazonia don't talk. At all. What we know officially about their city-state wouldn't fill a thimble. What your father's spies learn on the docks is enough to disturb us. Lokeen should have relinquished his wife's throne and crown to *her* cousin on the day of her funeral. He didn't. One son has tried repeatedly to take Temple vows. The other son has disappeared. The queen's relatives are restless. His only hope is to remarry and produce a daughter. Who he courts is still an open question."

"They have the opposite problem of Coronnan, requiring a legitimate male heir. Both Mikk and I are illegitimate."

"You'll look more legitimate if the people see you acting like a prince. We're going hunting."

"Can't you take Mikk?"

"Oh, he's coming too. He just doesn't know it yet. Now change into serviceable leathers and decent boots. Your presence is required in the forecourt in a quarter hour." General Marcelle stalked around the landing to Mikk's suite and pounded on the door, most emphatically.

Glenndon sighed and opened his own door with a mundane twist of the latch. If he had to put up with the discomfort of riding, he'd take his staff, let it rest in the spear holster on the saddle.

But first, he'd scry Linda to warn her of this newest threat to her independence.

Skeller grabbed Telynnia out of her carrysack and ran his hands along the wood, testing her for any signs of swelling or bubbling in the rapidly changing humidity—walking through liquid air one day, then air sere enough to give him a sore throat the next. He ran through his mind lively tunes he could play without singing, rather than strain his voice. Presuming Telynnia held up to the changes.

He plucked a chord on the loosened strings. No more out of tune than the slackening of tension would produce. His most prized possession, his livelihood, his friend remained alive and ready to quicken beneath his loving touch.

"We're safe for now," he whispered to her as he watched Lily settle Lady Graciella into her litter with a cup of wine cooled in the creek while they had eaten a noon meal—the stop was more to rest the livestock than for the refreshment of the travelers.

Soon, another two days at most, they would reach the crossroad and divide into two caravans. He needed to check on Lily as often as he did his harp in the coming trauma. She relied upon her younger sister for her own mental health. As smart as Valeria, and more vibrant of personality, he would expect the relationship to run the other way.

Briefly he wondered what secrets they harbored. Certainly they had normal sisterly secrets, but this unbalanced dependence harbored a bigger secret. A much bigger one.

For Lily's sake he needed to find out what.

Then he needed to decide if his mission would force him to follow the westbound caravan with Lady Ariiell, or stay southbound with Lily and Lady Graciella. Which one was King Lokeen manipulating into aiding and abetting his latest plot to keep his throne?

His back itched with odd familiarity, but he couldn't find the notes in his memory that would trigger full memory. Maybe it was just a storm brewing. He'd weathered bad storms before, traveling with trade caravans in Amazonia. A big continent generated big weather. Coronnan was tiny in comparison, the open stretches cradled and protected by mountains. Anything they'd encounter out here was nothing compared to the tornado he'd seen last year that hopped, skipped, and jumped across a thousand miles, demolishing crops, livestock, houses, and towns wherever it touched down.

He turned to hang Telynnia's carrysack across his back, not trusting the hooks on the sledge's back frame to hold his precious friend, but he stumbled.

"Merrow!" a cat protested, more plaintive than outraged. He'd never known a cat to endure gracefully the insult of someone stepping on them, even when they'd put themselves directly in the path of the stepper.

He looked down to find a large black cat with one white ear stropping his ankles. Her fur was matted across her shoulders, behind her hind legs and along the extra-long length of her skinny tail.

She broadcast her need to be picked up long and loud. He didn't need to worry about his cumbersome harp she informed him with posture, expression, and more stropping. He could discard it. Her need to be held and petted was greater.

"I've met your kind before, cat," he said, stooping to scratch her chin and ears. Telynnia settled between his shoulders quite comfortably, allowing him full freedom of both arms. "You will survive another ten seconds while I take care of Telynnia." He shrugged and twisted, making sure his harp nestled snugly against his hip and ribs. Where she belonged.

"Now I can give you some attention too, little lady," he said gently as he began scratching one ear then extended his hand along her spine and around her slender middle. "You've been through a rough patch," he continued talking to the feral cat as he examined her with knowing hands. "Those feet look tired and sore."

A loud rumble erupted from the cat's throat. His hand tingled with the affection she exuded.

"Mind if I pick you up?" She pressed her head deeper into his cupped hand. "I'll take that as agreement." He squeezed her middle in preparation for picking her up.

She didn't protest the pressure so he lifted her in both hands as he stood up. The cat reached for his neck, claws politely withdrawn. He held her against his chest and she nuzzled him, front legs wrapped around his neck in a strangely intimate embrace from a feral. Judging by the prominence of her ribs, he guessed she was hungry. Had been hungry for a long time.

"Let's see if Cook has any fish left for you." Cat's purr grew louder. He cradled her lightly with one arm and took steps closer to the campfire. He smelled the pot that Cook hadn't managed to clean just yet. Fish stew. He'd eaten two plates full of the savory meal.

Lily hadn't touched it. She never ate the stews with meat, even fish, settling for piles of cooked and raw vegetables. Her sister ate anything and everything.

A shadow skittered across his peripheral vision. He peered into the shrubbery lining the creek. The only movement he saw was a fern frond waving back and worth as it dipped in and out of the rushing water.

He shook his head and headed toward the campfire, Cat wiggling to take the best advantage of his hold on her.

"Skeller?" Lillian asked. She sounded hesitant, almost suspicious.

"Yes?" He turned to face her. Cat stiffened and bristled. "It's okay, Lily's a friend," he reassured the animal with extra strokes along her spine.

Cat did not believe him.

"Um . . . Skeller . . . uh . . . do you know what you have there?" Lily remained on the step beside the litter. Odd. She usually took every opportunity to stand close to him. As he did with her.

"It's a feral cat," he said back to her. "A hungry and footsore one at that."

"That's . . . that's not just a cat."

"What do you mean? I've nursed a lot of cats back to health. They follow me quite readily. Dogs are more likely to let me pet them though. Sort of like Champion over there." He tilted his head toward where the drovers harnessed the steeds for the afternoon's journey south.

"Skeller, put the cat down," Lillian said firmly, carefully avoiding making eye contact with him or the cat.

He looked deeply into Cat's blue eyes, ringed in pale green around a *round* pupil. Unusual, but not unknown eyes. Unusual cat.

Cat purred louder, her sides visibly vibrating.

"It's just a cat. I'll let her ride on the sledge full of food supplies. She'll keep the mouse population down." He grabbed a wooden spoon with his free hand and dished out a morsel of fish from the stew pot. Cat nibbled at it daintily, directly from the spoon, still keeping her front legs on his shoulders. Nice manners for a feral.

"If she's just a cat, then what is that tin-colored weasel

with gold-tipped fur doing lurking beneath the saber ferns?" Lillian asked haughtily.

"Huh?" The conjunction of the cat and the weasel made no sense to him.

Lily cocked her head in the peculiar way as if watching the sky for the appearance of a dragon, and listening for them as well. She clung to the litter as a lifeline, or protection from some unseen menace. Maybe weasels in this part of the world carried some horrible disease. Had it infected the cat as well?

He looked more closely into those mesmerizing blue and green eyes; clear and bright, no trace of film over the moist iris or crust at the corners. Though skinny and paw sore she wasn't starving, and he'd found no ulcers or weeping sores.

Cat purred some more and rubbed the top of her head on his scraggly chin. Reassurance flooded him, as well as affection. He gave her some more fish. She still ate carefully, not gobbling as he'd expected. Hungry and thin, but not starving.

That should tell him something.

Lily's fear puzzled him more.

"You're just a cat, aren't you?"

"No she's not!" Valeria proclaimed from beside Lily. Where had she come from? And so quickly.

"Put the cat down," she insisted. "Then walk away very slowly, and very carefully."

"This is ridiculous."

"Please, Skeller, do as Val says. This is important," Lily added her pleas.

"If you insist. But I'd really, really like an explanation." He stooped and released his hold on Cat. She clung to him a moment longer, extending her claws into his leather jerkin.

"Come to me tonight," he whispered in that special chanting voice he reserved for the animals who seemed to adore his singing. Champion understood most every word when he used that voice. The cat should too.

She caught his gaze with her own and passed reassurance to him before scampering off toward the head of the caravan. Toward Lady Ariiell's litter.

The direction Skeller didn't want to take. When the caravan separated at the crossroad he wanted to stay with Lily. He was sure that his quest needed him with Lily and Lady Graciella. Lady Ariiell couldn't possibly hold any value for King Lokeen and his magician counselor.

Or could she?

Suddenly he doubted his own judgment.

Lily slipped her hand in his. "Thank you. Getting rid of the cat is important."

He nodded as he watched Valeria stalk off after the cat, glowering in anger and determination.

"She'd better not hurt the cat," Skeller said, still bewildered.

"It's not a cat. Not really," Lily said softly, as if afraid someone other than Skeller might hear her.

"Magic?" he asked in disgust. "Useless and violent."

"Evil magic. Magic so evil we're better off not even thinking about it."

CHAPTER 15

VALERIA MARCHED THE length of the caravan cursing beneath her breath. "Lady Ariiell was right all along." She slammed her fist into her thigh to release some of the emotions roiling within her. "If Rejiia is flirting with Skeller, then he is doubly untrustworthy." She honestly didn't know if she should send Da a summons or not. A journey was about learning to solve problems on her own. The living presence of Krej and Rejiia endangered all of Coronnan. But not until they found a way to transform back to their human bodies.

Just then the cat scampered past her toward the muted draperies hanging from the litter.

"No, you don't. You are not going to corrupt my lady again!" Val dashed after the cat. Ariiell might have enough magical talent to reverse the transformation spell. Fifteen years ago she was probably the only magician alive interested in restoring them.

Now?

In the way of a normal cat, Rejiia did not run in a straight line. She arched her hind end and skittered half sideways until she nearly tangled with the restless feet of a steed succumbing to the control of a harness. Then the black cat locked her front legs and bullied through the crowd of people readying sledges for the afternoon march.

Val headed directly for the litter, intending to block entrance to the cat. But just as she slowed to control a stop, the cat dug her claws into the ground and swung her tail around to take her away from the litter, almost tipping her nose into the dust. The moment she had her balance again, she was off, toward the front of the caravan. Two sledges forward she ducked beneath the raised end of the conveyance and disappeared into the undergrowth of the rolling grasslands.

That moment of redirection allowed Val to shorten the distance between them. She didn't have Lily's strong empathy but this beast had no controls over her thoughts and feelings; neither fully human or fully feline. Val drew closer, close enough for her to encounter the wall of heightened emotion and cunning that described Rejiia in any form. Elation gave way to disappointment and frustration. So close to Ariiell. So close and yet not close enough. A wall of subtle magic that smelled of poison and sorrow blocked her.

Now I'll have to find a new time and place to convince Ariiell to change Cat back into Rejjia. The cat's thoughts spread wide and clear, fully understandable to anyone who might know how to listen.

Val stumbled to a halt right where Rejiia had made her about turn. "Just as I thought, Ariiell is the only magician strong enough to reverse the transformation spell who might be willing to do it," she muttered as she examined the litter with all of her senses. Something in or around it had stopped a relentless sorceress. What?

All she could filter through the persistent smell of steed and trampled grass, the sense of impatience to get moving again, the bloating from eating too much not-quite-cooked-through flatbread, and nervous checks of the sky for signs of a storm, was the usual sense of isolation surrounding the litter. It didn't smell any different than it had twenty minutes ago.

Val shrugged and opened the draperies.

"I need to write a letter of apology to Lady Lynetta," Ariiell greeted Val without preamble. "She treated me with kindness, raised my child into a normal, healthy young man, and all I did to her was attack her cats without reason."

Val paused a moment. So, her attempts to flake off bits of guilt from the knot of ugliness in the lady's mind were working. Lukan had given her some help in finding a wedge to insert into the knot to begin breaking it up. She smiled to herself. A mentally healthy Ariiell was the best defense against Rejiia's manipulations.

"If you would rather offer your apology more personally, I can summon her household magician and bring the lady into the spell," Val offered.

At the look of horror on Ariiell's face, Val knew she'd pushed the healing too far, too fast. "Very well, we can compose the letter this afternoon and I'll dispatch it to the lady this evening."

Then I'll summon Lukan. I might not ethically report to Da or the masters, but I can talk to my brother. I can warn him about Rejiia. And where that cat runs, Krej cannot be far behind.

Jaylor winced as a candle flame passed before his eyes. He slammed them shut before the blinding light could stab deeper into his brain. His head ached all the time. He hated making it worse.

"Well that's an improvement," Brevelan said blandly.

"Improvement?" he asked around a dry mouth.

Sharl, his six-year-old daughter, passed him a mug that sloshed with water. He took it from her with a smile, wishing he could see her sweet face with tousled red-gold curls, cheeks just losing baby fat, and big blue eyes that saw a lot more than he wanted her too. Like his shaking hand.

"If you can perceive light, then the blindness is fading,

albeit slowly," Brevelan said. She sounded worried, even though he knew she put on a bright face for the children.

Children. Once the cabin had been full to overflowing with six children and a seventh on the way. With only Sharl and two-year-old Jule left in the house—Lukan should be here too, but he slept elsewhere, creeping in silently in the middle of the night to take the food Brevelan left for him and eat it somewhere else—this home seemed eerily silent.

And dark. If all he could see was a blur of light, and that stabbed him with knife-sharp pain, how could he throw a spell? So much magic depended upon layering images one atop the other and timing by the angle of the sun. Without those markers he was helpless, defenseless.

Useless.

His insides withered into a tight knot centered in his belly.

"You'll figure it out," Brevelan said. Her voice moved away from him. Her skirt rustled against her bare legs and feet. The metal pot hook creaked as she pulled it out of the hearth. Then he heard a slight click as she hung a pot on the hook. His nose detected fresh-cut onion, garlic, and sliced carrot before he heard them sizzle in hot fat.

A lessening of warmth on his other side told him that Sharl moved away from him to help her mother. Then the tug of a tiny hand against his knee and he reached to pull Jule into his lap, knowing the little boy still sucked his thumb in uncertainty.

These things he knew. He could even walk to the bedroom he shared with Brevelan at the back of the cabin and only bump into three pieces of furniture. The chair, the chest, and a worktable helped him mark his location.

But how could he throw a spell?

"It's just backlash from the ungrounded spell," Brevelan continued. Her utility knife sliced through a yampion, the thick tuber flesh sounded crisp and only half-willing to separate under the pressure of the blade.

Then the plop as the bit of vegetable landed in the pot with the other sizzling components of their midday meal. "It will pass, in time."

"Will it?" He sounded petulant to his own ears.

"If you give it time and don't go hurrying off to manage the entire world all on your own."

"I don't . . ."

"You do."

"I have delegated . . ."

"An illusion only. You are wearing yourself to skin and bone bouncing back and forth between home and Coronnan City. You stand at the king's side, you run the old University, you check on Marcus here and have to approve every decision he makes. You have no time left for us, your family."

He held his breath at the venom in her words.

"You haven't complained before."

"I had you home every night before you returned magicians to the Council of Provinces. You were busy. But you ate the food I put in front of you and you slept by my side. Every night. You talked to me. Shared everything with me. Now you talk to the king, to Marcus, and to Glenndon. Everyone but me."

"Dear heart, I. . . ." What could he say in the face of the truth. "I've missed you."

"Have you?"

"Yes, my love. You are the light of my life and the anchor for my soul. And if I never see again, the one image I will treasure in my memory is your face."

"Oh, Jaylor!" She dropped things, the knife clattering against the clay bricks before the hearth, the tuber splatting in the same region. Then she cupped his face with both hands and kissed him long and hard.

But her lips felt more desperate than passionate. After nineteen years and many adventures together, he knew the difference.

He shifted Jule to one knee and tugged Brevelan onto his other, holding her tight around her swelling waist.

"We'll get through this, my love," she reassured him, resting her head on his shoulder. "And while you learn patience and how to rely on your other senses, you will allow Marcus, the king, and Glenndon to succeed or fail on their own. And when you are well, you can charge in and correct all of their mistakes roaring in displeasure and secretly triumphant that you know best after all."

"I don't do that."

"Yes you do. Especially the roaring. I miss hearing you yelling at everyone and everything in your path. That is what worries me most. You sit and brood. Or pace and brood. One would think you are Darville and not yourself."

"You could bring a few apprentices to me so that I can find fault with their technique in the loudest voice possible."

"That I may do." She shifted away from him, returning to her place before the cook pot. "If you will allow them to help you too."

He heard her retrieve the knife and realized he could see her silhouette bend to pick it up. She clenched a fist against her lower back as she straightened up. Not a good sign for her to feel this much discomfort only five months into the pregnancy.

Before he could voice his concern she spoke. "In the meantime, think about where Lukan might be sleeping and how we can bring him back to us."

"I fear he won't come home with less enticement than a journeyman's staff. He's due for one. But I can't just give him one. He needs a journey and at the moment I need him here."

"Then tell him that. Make his work here his journey."

"How can I talk to him, when he isn't here?"

"Figure it out. For now let Jule lead you outside to the garden. I need more carrots. Surely you can figure out how to uproot a few without damaging them."

He considered rejecting that order as impossible. How could a blind man dig vegetables?

"With your hands," she replied contemptuously before he voiced his complaint. "Trust me, you'll figure it out. But you have to learn patience."

❋

"Skeller," Lily touched his arm tentatively as they walked behind the litter. Deep within the curtained dimness, Lady Graciella composed a new recipe for banishing a prickly heat rash. Lily didn't understand how she could finalize the ingredients without actually mixing and mashing them together, but working it out with pen and ink first seemed to work for her. Perhaps the lady understood the soul of each plant better than Lily.

Skeller flinched his arm away from Lily, masking his rejection in a need to fuss with his harp case.

"The black cat with one white ear is a piece of legend out of our history," Lily said, as if he listened to her closely. She knew he did. He just couldn't let her know that. Not yet.

"I need to make you understand what you are dealing with in accepting her and offering her affection along with food."

"There are lots of black cats with one white ear," he said softly, still keeping his gaze and hands on the harp.

"Many years ago, when King Darville first assumed the crown—the Coraurlia, it's this huge glass artifact gifted to our royal line by the dragons . . ."

He snorted, not quite trusting the importance of the magic-infused crown.

"The Coraurlia protects the wearer from magical attack, sends it back to the magician who threw the spell. We call it backlash. The magic compounds and gets really ugly. By the same token, no one who isn't of the royal line and blessed by the dragons can touch the crown without burning to ash."

Skeller made no noise, but he still wouldn't look at her.

"The king's cousin, Lord Krej, was a secret magician.

In those days, neither the king nor a lord could legally possess a full magical talent. Krej wanted to be king. But he couldn't do that without killing Darville. He devised a spell that would turn a living being into a statue. He turned Shayla, the dragon matriarch, into a life-sized glass sculpture. Inside the prison of glass she was alive and aware of all that was going on around her."

Skeller blanched as he thought about that peculiar kind of torture. Then his fingers began to pluck and drum against the harp case. She knew he was composing an epic ballad of this adventure. He wasn't the first.

"When Krej turned the spell on a human, his victim turned into the animal that reflected his personality. The king had spent several months in the form of a golden wolf. My mother, with the help of Shayla, rescued him from a blinding blizzard, nursed him back to health and helped my father return him to normal."

A new light came into Skeller's eyes, the kind of light she'd seen only when he sang. He was born to sing and compose music. She loved that about him.

"When King Darville finally confronted Krej, Krej needed to turn him into a statue, not a living animal. My father knew how to reverse that spell. But neither he, nor Krej had counted on the king actually wearing his crown, the real one, not the small replica he uses for daily appearances. The spell backlashed and Lord Krej became a statue."

"What was Krej's totem animal?" Skeller finally spoke. His fingers kept working out chords and melody lines on the case.

"A tin weasel with flaking gilt paint."

"That explains the shadow in the bushes. But how did he become animate, and what does that have to do with the cat?"

She had him now, he was fully interested. She could almost hear the tune rampaging through his mind down to his fingers. It would be better than any of the other ballads she'd heard. She wanted to sing it with him, harmonizing her light soprano to his more confident baritone.

"That happened some years later," Val said. "Krej's province, Saria, passed to his cousin Jemmarc who is now married to Lady Graciella. He has absolutely no trace of magic in his life. The Council of Provinces bypassed Krej's daughters, especially his eldest Rejiia, who turned out to be a very powerful sorceress connected to a coven bent on the destruction of Coronnan."

"Your people do not value women as leaders. They do in Amazonia."

Lily nodded. She hadn't heard this little tidbit about the lands across the sea.

"Wait, Jemmarc. Lady Graciella's husband? She's married to the lord, not lady in her own right!"

"Yes. He's much older than she and was already married with a son when he became Lord. Then . . . he . . . his wife passed and he remarried rather quickly. Lady Graciella conceived almost immediately."

"There are an awful lot of magicians floating around this country. In Amazonia, magicians are few and far between, not valued."

She giggled at the image of her entire family floating around Coronnan. Everyone of them except her. She banished that last thought and continued her story. Maybe she belonged in Amazonia where women had value as leaders and her lack of talent might be appreciated.

"Fifteen or sixteen years ago, around the time that Val and I were born, there was a big dustup in Aporia to our far west—that's where Lady Ariiell's father rules. I don't know all the details, but Lady Ariiell was there, working for the same coven as Rejiia, and some ghosts and other things happened. In the aftermath straightening out old spells, and freeing people of curses and such, Krej was brought back to life as that ugly weasel and his daughter became a black cat with one white ear. They were last seen chasing each other the length of the kingdom. I'm told that in real life she had shining, straight black hair down to her hips with a white streak that ran from her left temple the full length of her hair. She was said to be the most beautiful woman in the kingdom."

This time he snorted again. "I doubt that she was that beautiful. Beauty brings its own power. Truly beautiful women don't need magic. Or a less attractive woman uses magic to make her seem more beautiful."

"Ariiell is deathly afraid Krej and Rejiia are coming for her, to manipulate her, and work more evil upon her. Her nightmares are very violent."

He looked her straight in the eye. "I find your story interesting material for a teaching ballad. Nothing more. Such violence should be repressed. People need to overcome it. As you have."

She stopped short, mouth agape. "How . . . how can you say that?"

"Because I have no need of magic even if it were readily available. From what I've heard, magic is more evil than good. It . . . it tempts people to do evil things just because they can, not because it is needed or beautiful, or even right. It needs to be banished."

CHAPTER 16

MIKK LOCKED THE door to his room with a firm click. He didn't need Geon sticking his long and overly curious nose into his business right now—especially not into the books Mikk borrowed from the library. Hopefully the tall, thin, sour-faced man had enough to do cleaning Mikk's riding leathers to keep him elsewhere for an hour or so.

With careful steps, Mikk assembled his tools, then eased into the straight-backed chair at his writing table. General Marcelle had eased up on arms practice to concentrate on riding and shooting arrows from steedback. Mikk couldn't remember hurting so much. Ever. Even Grand'Mere's occasional reprimand with the flat of her hand on his bum hadn't hurt this much. Absently he rubbed his chafed thighs as he concentrated on the candlewick in front of him.

His gaze ran down the list of preparations in the tiny book by Kimmer, Scribe of the South.

One: breathe in slowly on a count of three.

Two: hold the breath on the same count.

Three: release the air held in your lungs completely.

Four: remain still for a count of three.

Five: repeat the above as many times as necessary to feel at peace with the world and find a connection to the

Kardia. The magnetic South Pole should tug at your back.

Oh. He faced east where the narrow window on that wall offered a little extra light on his tasks.

Reluctantly he grasped the seat edges of his chair, braced with his legs and shifted one quarter until he faced north and his back was to the all-essential south.

He groaned as his legs protested any movement. Then he had to lunge to keep the candle from tipping and rolling away. Learning magic in stolen moments of privacy was hard work. But he had to do it. The dragons had spoken to him, led him to the book, and insisted he learn.

"I can do this," he affirmed to himself. "Breathe in on three, hold three, out on three, hold three." He followed his own instructions, concentrating on filling and emptying his lungs.

Repeat. And repeat. And repeat. Nothing. No peace. No grounding. No connection to the magnetic pole. Nothing.

(Repeat!) The word sound loud in the back of his head. The masculine voice of a stern teacher commanded him.

Startled, he gasped out an extra morsel of air. The top of his head lightened and threatened to float free of his body.

(Repeat. Breathe long and deep.)

He did so without thinking.

(Again.)

And again; five times he filled and emptied his lungs, lengthening his count until the air flowed in and out, in and out. His vision glazed into tiny squares of color. Outlines became abstract suggestions of the objects in his room, the bed, the tapestries, the thick and comfortable chair by the hearth, the cloudy sky through the window.

On the sixth breath his back itched. He couldn't reach the tiny spot between his shoulder blades. He squirmed and almost lost the strange lightness of head and heart.

(Turn.)

He could not disobey. The compulsion to shift his chair once more overrode any concerns of aching muscles and raw skin. Keeping his eyes half-crossed and his attention on his breathing he lifted the chair once more and turned to face south, staring into the empty hearth.

The itch disappeared and his feet felt as if they melted into the plank flooring, apart from the building . . . no, he was a part of the land, the wood and stone were merely an extension of the Kardia.

A blast of air into his face ruffled his tightly bound hair and added to the filling of his lungs. He breathed it out, completely, until he thought he'd have to plant his face against his knees because nothing inside him supported his spine.

The world snapped into focus. Too sharp. Too bright. He breathed again long and full. His mind accepted the new reality his vision found.

(*Now, think of the candle. Separate the wick from the wax in your mind.*)

A fuzzy memory of how the candle on the desk looked flashed before his inner vision. He needed to turn around to see it.

(*Do not move. You do not need to look to see the candle.*)

Mikk concentrated on his last memory of a stout column of beeswax, a creamy yellow in color. The ribbed texture made it easier to hold in his hand without having it slide out of his palm. It fit nicely into his hand, needing his entire hand to enclose it. He had to stretch his fingers wide to measure the candle from top to bottom. A scholar's candle designed to burn long into the night while he studied or wrote.

(*The wick?*)

"Braided linen. Nearly beige next to the yellowish wax. It stands one fingernail above the well of wax," he replied, keeping the image firmly in his mind. He could almost see the candle within his hand rather than on the desk behind him.

(Light the candle.)

"How."

(See it lit!) the voice demanded, almost angry at his dimwittedness.

Mikk imagined a flame topping the illusory candle in his hand . . .

(No. You must see the fire leaping from your heart to the wick and finding a new home there.) A new voice whispered to him, still masculine, but younger, gentler, and friendlier. An almost-chuckle escaped from this new personality.

(The fire must come from his mind,) the older voice snorted in derision.

(But he thinks with his heart.)

(That's his problem. He doesn't use his mind, his logic. He reacts before he thinks.)

(He thinks with his heart. Mikk, the fire you need is deep within you, waiting for you to allow it to exit. Let the flame leap to the wick. Don't think about it. Just let it flow.)

Mikk sighed. Just like home. Grand'Mere and his tutors always argued about what was best for him, what he needed to learn. No one thought to ask him what he *wanted*.

(What do you want?) the older voice asked, no longer irascible or demanding. Just asking.

"I want to light this candle with magic."

(Then do it.)

Mikk closed his eyes, keeping the image of the candle firmly in mind, and watched a tiny spark jump from his heart to the wick.

It burst into flame like a flower opening its blossom all at once.

(Now look at the real candle,) the younger voice giggled.

Slowly, fearful of undoing what he'd just done, Mikk turned his head to look over his shoulder. Sure enough, the candle burned brightly.

Triumph blossomed in his gut and his mind.

"Master Mikk?" Geon asked loudly as he rattled the latch. "Master Mikk, the queen has requested your presence in her private parlor. Master Mikk, you must come now."

The flame blinked out, leaving an uncharred wick, as if it had never known fire.

Lukan nestled tighter in the fork of two branches of his everblue tree. The linear ridges of the bark irritated his back as they never had before. He shifted his butt, twisted his shoulders, then leaned forward

Nothing helped. He still felt as if the ungrounded magical whips from the abortive spell had flayed him.

But it wasn't *that* magic rubbing his skin raw. Something else. Something not right, but controlled.

And therefore dangerous.

He watched the stars emerge in the darkening sky. They looked frail and dim compared to his usual observations. He'd seen no clouds. And yet . . . the color of the sky was off too.

He needed to figure out how and why.

Inside his tunic pocket, his apprentice glass tingled against his skin, warm and comforting, a gentle massage rather than the annoyance of alien magic. He knew without looking at the violet swirl of color that Val summoned him. She did most every evening if he didn't make the time to scry for her.

"Not tonight, little sis. I have more important things to think about than your recounting of the day's march across the prairie." He wiped a dry finger across the glass, terminating the spell without even looking at the caller's identifying colors.

"Now what, or rather who, is tampering with the weather?"

"What is magic?" Skeller asked the steeds as they plodded forward. Almost like wading across a sluggish river in the thick, humid air. "My tutors told me that all magic could be explained by logic if we just look deep enough for another explanation." No one in Amazonia wanted to become a slave to magic, so they denied its existence, even in the face of incontestable evidence.

He puzzled over Lily's tale of cats and weasels, ghosts and curses, speaking to dragons. "Stuff and nonsense." His spoken words no longer held the ring of truth. He wasn't in Amazonia anymore. Magic ruled in Coronnan. He'd seen it. He'd heard a dragon.

Lily knew and loved magic.

"No one employs magicians or magic at home." Though King Lokeen had employed one for years. "Until I came here, I'd only ever seen one *true* magician and I do not trust him at all, Champion."

Skeller remembered entering his father's office without knocking. He hadn't expected the king to be working there. He should have been at his wife's bedside, holding her hand as she passed.

Instead he'd found the King of Amazonia staring blankly into a bowl of water. A candle flame reflected light upon a tiny shard of glass in the bowl. Lokeen mumbled strange words in an oddly accented spate, then paused as if listening to a reply from within the depths of water . . .

Three months later, Lokeen's magician adviser moved permanently to Amazonia and began taking on more and more royal duties. The same nameless magician who had come to Coronnan City as ambassador.

Champion snorted and sidled, trying to come close enough to Skeller to rest his heavy head on an inviting shoulder.

Skeller had an impression of tiny whips filling the air, lashing steed hide with stinging barbs.

"You too, my friend?" His own skin felt as if rubbed raw by wind-driven sand. How long had the irritation crept up on him until he could no longer ignore it?

Champion didn't answer. He didn't need to. Skeller knew what the massive gray beast thought and felt . . .

How did he know?

He'd never questioned it before, assuming everyone communicated with beasts. But they didn't. On six caravans over the past three years, Skeller had grown into the role of speaker for the steeds and their needs to the drovers who should have known.

"How did I know where the harness and collar were rubbing you wrong, Champion?"

"You knew because he told you," Lily replied for the steed. She slipped into the rhythm of his stride.

"Does Lady Graciella sleep?" he asked, knowing that was the only time Lily could sneak away from her.

"Aye. Restlessly though. The litter is hot and stuffy. But she won't let me open the curtains. Not even a little bit for some fresh air."

"Not that the air is so fresh," Skeller grumbled, wiping sweat off his brow with a kerchief. He lifted his lank hair off his neck, suddenly understanding why the local men braided their hair.

"There's a storm brewing," Lily replied.

"Not today. Our sky is blue, even if it is slightly off color, enough sulfurous yellow blending in to push it toward an unnatural green."

"As green as a campfire. Did you know that our natural flames are green because of the heavy concentration of copper in the wood?" she asked. Her face tried to brighten, and failed, as she deliberately looked away from the gray smudge on the northwest horizon.

"No. I did not know that. What color should it burn?" Logic. He was comfortable with logic, but wondered how Lily knew such esoteric things.

"If you leech out all the copper . . . my da could tell you how to do it, I don't understand it all . . . the flames burn shades of red, orange, and yellow. The same colors as the sun."

"If you look closely at the heart of a green fire, a normal fire, you can sometimes see the red heart of the flames. I'd never wondered why before."

"Maybe that's why you don't understand magic or its place in the world. You've never looked for it."

"I've never needed magic before," he mused, wondering if basking in the glory of her smile, or feeling the tingle of her nearness before she reached to hold his hand was magic of a sort.

"The black cat with one white ear and the large, tin-colored weasel with flaking gold on the tips of its pelt are still following the caravan," she said quietly, peering into the undergrowth on the other side of the caravan.

"I know."

"Ask yourself why."

"They're hungry."

"They are natural enemies to each other." She looked at him, sternly, with a bit of contempt in her eyes. "And yet they are always together. Close together." Anger began to swell in her chest, replacing softer emotions.

He'd never seen her anything but gentle and caring. Nurturing, fitting to any proper woman from Amazonia. She'd said she didn't eat meat because she felt the life passing out of the creature . . .

"I think you are a thing of magic. You've brought magic into my life. The magic of love," he blurted out before he could think twice.

She stopped, eyes wide with wonder.

He had to stop too, even though it meant Champion would plod into moving in place rather than leave him behind.

"Lily, I . . ."

She nodded with a tiny smile as she pulled his hand up to entwine their fingers.

"Falling in love was not part of my plans right now. Eventually . . . but . . ."

She stood on tiptoe to brush his cheek with her lips.

At the last second he turned his head and captured her caress with his mouth. Gently he gave in to the wonder of kissing her, tasting her warmth, blending his mouth into hers.

Slowly she drew away.

"Thank you," she whispered.

They stood there, silent and still for a long moment. Then energy seemed to fill her. "Now think about magic and the way your music changes the world around you. Think about ways to make your songs banish Rejiia and Krej and the smell of rotten magic that surrounds them." She loosened her grip on his hand, ready to bounce back to the litter.

"It isn't the cat and the weasel that smell rotten. The steeds tell me it is something in or around Lady Ariiell's litter." How did he know that? He just knew it. The moment she'd said rotten, he'd known where and what it smelled off.

"Then we need to sweeten it with music and herbs and a thorough cleansing ritual. I know just what to do!" She skipped up the line of the caravan in the direction of her sister.

"I still don't know what magic is, Champion," he said resuming his march. The silent steed followed him, content to be beside him as long as he could rest his head on a willing shoulder.

CHAPTER 17

GLENNDON'S EARS RANG with fullness that wouldn't pop, and the air in his suite seemed to carry devil's vine thorns that made his skin itch.

Whatever was wrong with him was worse than the buzzing in his head whenever the girls hung around him, pressing too closely, touching his arm, trying desperately to get him to notice them.

Oh, he noticed them alright. But then the shallowness and the greed in their thoughts penetrated his mind, even when he tried to block them out. The daughters of the court didn't want him. They wanted his position and prestige.

Miri and Chastet were the worst, the highest ranking in their generation. Somehow they both thought he belonged to them by right of title. Like a rich piece of brocade or fine lace. More like a prime steed ready to take to stud.

So he hid in his suite whenever he didn't have something specific to do for his father. And to ease the ache and chafing after the latest hunt that had lasted most of the morning. He'd liberally applied a salve Mistress Maigret had sent him. It soothed the burning skin and smelled sweetly of mint. But the ease didn't last. Within an hour or two he longed for more. More each time.

Something was wrong with the formula. He needed to talk to Linda to see if she could fix it.

Mostly he needed to talk to Linda. She always put his problems in perspective and gave him insights into court personalities to laugh about.

Don't fret. I'll see about using a different mint, more alcohol, and less bean oil, she said across the miles without him having to work a scry or summons spell.

"The air in the city wants to smother me almost as much as the girls do," he grumbled in response.

It's almost perfect here in the mountains, if a little too dry. The south wind is picking up but it carries no clouds with it. We need rain. Come for a visit.

Keerkin rummaging through hundreds of pieces of parchment disturbed Glenndon's reverie.

"I wish," he whispered to her. "But I can't."

The connection faded.

"I . . . I'm sorry, sir. I can't find the original missive from Ambassador Amazonia," Keerkin apologized. "I know I put it here in this pile, ready to scrape clean and use for notes later. I know it!"

The calm Linda brought to Glenndon's mind evaporated and anger rushed back in to replace it, like a wave returning to an empty shore.

"Three S'murghin days! We've looked for that letter for three days. I'm beginning to think we imagined it." He snarled as he paced his suite, bedroom: right seven steps, left ten steps, left again four paces to the bed, thirteen paces around the monster piece of furniture that required three wooden steps to climb into and near fifty yards of brocade to drape the four posters and canopy— he still slept on the floor before the hearth with a woolen blanket as he did at home in the Clearing   then another four long strides to the corner, back along the tapestry-covered interior wall to the doorway into his sitting room.

"Is it possible, sir, that the missive was removed by magic?" Frank asked from his customary post beside Glenndon's desk in the parlor.

That made Glenndon pause a moment. "Magic?"

"I distinctly remember receiving the parchment," Keerkin said, coming alert.

"And I remember watching you read it, sir," Frank added.

"Therefore, I did not imagine it," Glenndon concluded. "I received it. I read it and tore it in half."

"I took the pieces from your hand and folded them neatly. When we returned here, I put the pieces in this cubbyhole, atop three other pieces awaiting time to scrape them clean."

"What's in the cubby now?" Frank asked, stretching his legs and tilting the chair back onto two legs.

"The three pieces that were already there, but not the torn missive."

"Removed by magic? Or stolen by mundane hands?" Glenndon sank into his desk chair; an uncomfortable straight thing not designed to ease anything. He rarely sat there, except to transcribe Council proceedings into a neat hand.

A neat hand.

"Ambassador Amazonia writes a neat hand. A too-neat hand. One that has had much practice at the arcane art of writing. Where did he learn?" he asked the air as much as his companions.

He thought about General Marcelle's network of wharf rat spies. Would they know if Amazonia had a university? Did they honor reading and writing for all, or reserve it for the elite?

Did they honor or respect magic?

He didn't know enough to plan a strategy for countering the ambassador's accusations.

If he could just breathe fresh mountain air for a few moments he could clear his head of the pressure that robbed him of thought while filling him with anger.

Did Amazonia have clearer air?

Long ago the Stargods had commanded that in Coronnan, Rossemeyer, and SeLennica the wheel was forbidden as was reading and writing. Those skills were reserved for magicians.

Glenndon did not know if Amazonia even worshiped the Stargods—they spoke the same language, basically, but it sounded strange to his ear, oddly accented with cultural references he didn't understand. They might adhere to a different religion and allow everyone to learn reading and writing. And the use of the wheel.

He knew nothing about the country or their rude, lying, cheating ambassador.

"Three days since I wrote an apology. Are you certain you delivered it into his hands?" Glenndon demand of Keerkin, who laboriously transcribed Glenndon's hastily written notes about the latest decisions from the Council of Provinces.

He wanted to break the pen in half to make Keerkin cease the endless scratching against parchment.

"Yes, Your Highness. As I have repeated every hour for the last three days, I placed the scroll directly into the hands of his secretary. He read it, smiled, handed it to a page, and dismissed me without a word," Keerkin replied, putting a final flourish on the ending words.

His complaint was delivered an hour after the ambassador departed the embassy, and he hasn't been seen since, General Marcelle had said.

"The ambassador never read it. He left the city before presenting his credentials to be the ambassador. It is my *job* to receive him and accept those credentials before presenting him and those credentials to the king. He left before his note was delivered by a street messenger." Glenndon fought to unclench his fists.

"Perhaps he hopes to push your father, the king, into a high state of anxiety over a potential war in order to win better trade concessions." Keerkin shrugged and attacked the next sheaf of papers that required organization and neatness. *S'murghit* he was calm. Too calm. Irritatingly calm.

The pressure inside Glenndon's head wanted to explode. Couldn't Keerkin feel it?

"Perhaps he's angling for a betrothal between you, sir, and one of the royal daughters," Frank added, juggling a long dagger and a shorter utility knife, gripping the blade tip of one, tossing it into the air, retrieving the other by the grip and tossing it up while catching the first. Over and over, always knowing precisely where each one was and how it spun.

Today the knives spun faster than usual. Frank tossed them higher with more aggression, as if he absorbed some of Glenndon's mood, but not the deepening pressure in the air that made it hard to breathe and more difficult to think.

A good skill to practice. Glenndon hadn't bothered to master it, begrudging the time and patience. Like today. He had a rudimentary knowledge of swordplay which worked out much of his frustrations. Still, he preferred to defend himself with magic.

Magic.

"Keerkin, did you notice anything unusual in the aura around the ambassador's household?"

"Unusual how? I'm not very skilled at reading auras. I can detect their presence on individuals but the colors all blend together."

"If anyone in the household had worked magic recently, could you sense it or smell it?" An elegant, University-trained style of writing. A disappearing missive. An unwillingness to show himself to . . . to someone who might recognize him.

Keerkin shrugged again. "Unlikely."

Glenndon began pacing again, winding his way around stray pieces of furniture. He'd tried to eject most of it as unnecessary, but servants kept returning it. Why did he need a dozen stiff and simple wooden chairs, five intricately carved chests, three worktables, four dainty serving tables and three high-backed, over-stuffed armchairs?

"I need more information," Glenndon said. Maybe he should talk to Mikk—if he could pry the boy out of the archives. Mikk did seem a keen observer and his blue and yellow aura held tight to his body, as if suppressing a talent that wanted to explode in glorious magical colors, like the queen did. She needed to hide her magic from prejudiced mind-blind courtiers who would rather condemn her as a witch than accept any form of magic.

"Shall I recruit a spy to place in the diplomatic household? That might be hard. I heard the ambassador brought all his own servants and retainers, not hiring anyone local," Frank said, catching his knives and sheathing them in one smooth movement.

"Amazonian ships won't hire local sailors even when short of crew. What are they afraid of?" Glenndon puzzled over the problems of remote observation, cursing his limitations. A simple scrying spell wouldn't work without a designated recipient, and then he could only see what was reflected in a bowl of water illuminated by a flame.

He might be able to ride a dragon's mind. Indigo was usually willing to help, but then, he'd only be able to see what the dragon could see, outside.

He needed a talisman to plant in the household. Something receptive of an observation spell. Something the ambassador would touch and then place in the center of his most frequented room, like his desk in an office.

"I need to send the ambassador a gift," he told his companions. His ears popped and his mind cleared. For a moment.

Keerkin looked up from his work. "The apology should have been enough. If you were indeed at fault, which you weren't. Why should you send the man a gift?" He flipped the quill back and forth, back and forth, back and forth.

Glenndon grabbed it from him and set it flat on the desk.

"Something costly?" Frank asked, cocking his head, as if thinking, or listening to a dragon.

Glenndon wondered just how much magical talent his bodyguard possessed. Both he and his father were supposed to be mind-blind. That didn't mean they hadn't hidden their gifts from the sight of the court.

Frank needed enough talent to sense someone creeping up behind them, or a covered pit before their steeds stepped into it. Maybe the dragons did advise him occasionally.

"Something special, that the ambassador will treasure and use often," Glenndon said a little too loudly as his ears filled again.

"Ah, something useful as well as expensive," Frank agreed. He half closed his eyes in thought.

Silence filled the room, except for the continuous scratching of Keerkin's quill pen. The man could copy words endlessly without thinking, often mimicking another's handwriting so closely only another magician could tell the difference.

Stargods! He could have forged the note from the ambassador.

But he didn't. I trust him. He wouldn't do such a thing. I'd see the lie in his aura.

The bobbing of the feather tip caught Glenndon's attention. It made odd little circles and lines back and forth, up and down, drawing him into a meditative state. A welcome relief from the scratchiness of the air and heavy pressure in his ears.

"A pen," he whispered. "Any man who writes as neatly as does the ambassador must write often and long. He needs an endless supply of pens."

"Quills do wear out," Keerkin acknowledged, pausing to examine the nib and reach for his penknife to sharpen it. Tiny shavings of quill drifted onto the desktop.

A pen made from a dragon bone would hold a spying spell and never need sharpening.

"I have an idea." Glenndon grabbed his feathered

cap, the green one with a fluffy squawk-drake plume pinned to it with a costly emerald-studded brooch. He yanked out the annoying feather and cast it onto the cold hearth.

Frank checked his weapons for readiness, and stepped behind Glenndon.

"I have to do this alone."

"No, Your Highness. My orders from my father and yours are to stay at your side at all costs."

"I appreciate your duty and responsibility. But you cannot go where I have to go."

"And where is that, Your Highness? I know this city better than you, having grown up here. I can keep you from getting lost among the tangle of islands and streets and wharves." He waved vaguely at a tapestry depicting the Stargods descending from the skies on a cloud of silver flame to the myriad islands in the river delta that became the capital city. The pictures were more interested in reverence for the three celestial brothers than the accuracy of the map.

"Only magicians and priests can go to Sacred Isle." Glenndon pointed to the small island on the west end of the delta, near the middle of the River Coronnan, as depicted metaphorically in the tapestry. Legend claimed the Stargods had landed in the clearing at the center of the island, burning away the trees in a perfect circle. Later, a pond had filled in the depression left by their silver cloud. No bridges connected it to the rest of the city isles.

"So, I can row you over and stay with the boat until you finish your errand. Whatever it is," Frank insisted, sounding very much like his father.

"And what precisely is your errand?" Keerkin asked. He put away his writing materials, sanding the ink on the latest scroll. He looked prepared to come with them.

"There is a Tambootie tree that owes me a favor. Or I owe it a favor, I'm not exactly sure of the relationship of obligations . . ."

"Then you'd best take your staff." Keerkin pointed toward the length of Tambootie wood standing against the corner where a cloak tree met the wall beside the door.

No one but Glenndon dared touch the piece, not even another magician. Added to the respect for the bond between a magician and his staff was the rarity of the sacred and magical Tambootie wood that had already begun to flow into a new pattern of knots and swirls representative of Glenndon's magical signature. Glowing faintly along the top of the shaft, a fragment of dragon bone had embedded itself into the wood. It alone remained straight and true along the original wood grain.

Glenndon's eyes concentrated on that precious bone.

"We need to arrive at Sacred Isle about sunset," he whispered.

"When else would you go there?" Keerkin asked. He knew the tradition of a journeyman spending a night alone on the island before being granted a staff by a living tree willing to give up a branch.

"Should I bring food and water, prepared to stay all night?" Frank asked.

"Always prepare for the worst and the worst won't happen. But I don't expect to remain more than an hour."

CHAPTER 18

VALERIA GRATEFULLY ABSORBED the damp warmth of the evening air. For the first time in ages her joints did not ache with cold. The lack of discomfort added to her concentration as she carefully watched the copse that lined the rushing creek. For three days now she'd sensed someone, something, following close beside the line of sledges. It . . . they . . . were Rejiia and Krej. She knew them by sight now that Rejiia had tried drawing Skeller into her web of control.

The caravan had passed beyond the open farms and grassland into more frequent clumpings of trees. Tomorrow, at about noon, the caravan would split. She and Lady Ariiell and half the sledges would take the western fork of the road inland to Lake Apor. Lillian and Lady Graciella would continue south, climbing the foothills into the rocky ridges and sheer cliffs of the Sarian Peninsula.

Krej and Rejiia, father and daughter, sorcerers both, were always closest to Lady Ariiell's litter, as if iron drawn to a lodestone. The lady leaked her magic. The litter was permeated with it. Valeria could smell little but Ariiell's musky perfume tainted by rotting magic.

That was the only way to describe it.

Krej and Rejiia needed that rotten magic to regain

their human bodies. They'd haunted Ariiell's tower for fifteen years, waiting for her to waken into sanity enough so she could throw the spell, but not enough to question the consequences.

Now, thanks to Valeria, Ariiell managed to stay coherent and sane more and more. Val had no doubt her charge could control her magic enough to reverse the curse.

But was she sane enough to know what she was doing?

Sixteen letters of apology had fluttered away. The tight knot of guilt and ugliness in Ariiell's mind was smaller but still in need of a blanket of The Forget and an occasional memory/dream of Val flying with dragons.

Val didn't trust Ariiell, or Rejiia, or Skeller. The bard walked closer to Ariiell's litter than Graciella's these last three days since he'd brought Rejiia to camp and fed her. What was he up to? And why was he here?

She was certain his attention to Lily was just a distraction, a disguise for his actual purpose. A dalliance that would wound Lily to the core when he dismissed her without a backward glance. And he would.

Val had dreamed it.

But he'd given up eating meat and turned his back when Cook slaughtered flusterhens or a goat to feed the caravan. Was that only part of the disguise?

Today, the cat and the weasel matched pace with the plodding steeds. They kept enough distance to remain invisible to the casual eye. Or small enough to hide in the trees and shrubs alongside the road. Val couldn't smell the stalkers. But she knew they were there. If they used magic, Ariiell's scent masked it.

Skeller walked on the opposite side of the caravan, away from Rejiia. He plucked his harp and sang easy marching songs to keep the caravan on pace and on schedule, but not so fast as to exhaust them all. He must have experience with caravans to know so many lively — but not too lively — tunes.

Valeria felt hemmed in, suffocated by the stalking animals on one side and Skeller on the other. She cherished the first few moments after stopping for the day as her rare chance to be alone, or to soak up Lily's comforting presence; opportunities to escape the confines of her enemies.

She narrowed her eyes against the glare of sun creeping beneath smoke-colored clouds to the west. Then she dredged a small amount of talent up from the Kardia through her feet and legs into her vision. The leafy fronds of a saber fern became transparent to her sight. Thick groundcover parted, revealing the softly churned dirt beneath. And nothing else. The two shadows that had drawn her to this clump of greenery had vanished. Even if the creatures she sought cloaked themselves in look-the-other-way-you-can't-see-me spells, which she had mastered long before anyone thought to teach them to her, she would see a distortion, or something.

Annoyed at herself she slapped her thigh to shake loose her concentration before she fell into a trance and thus became oblivious to all else around her. The sound of her palm striking flesh irritated her ears and made her cringe away from the strange light just before sunset. The light and air should be soft not glaring, sulfurous, and harsh.

A faint rustle among the ferns taunted her. Like someone shook the individual fronds in a different direction, just to mock her inability to find them.

Deliberately, she shrugged her shoulders back into balance and set her chin level as she walked, not trudged, through the thick air. She needed fresh, cool water to soothe Lady Ariiell's furrowed brow. She'd cried most of the day, seized with yet another piece of her guilt.

Val knew that they would compose a seventeenth letter this evening. One more step toward the lady's journey toward sanity. One more piece of armor against Rejiia and Krej.

"I really should summon Lukan again, make him listen

so that he knows what I know," she sighed as she scooped water from the creek to refresh her face and sweating neck. "Krej and Rejiia are still neutralized by their animal bodies. A journey is about learning to cope with difficulty and strangeness without help. We have a bit of time. If Lukan would just come out of his self-absorbed anger long enough to listen and help me plan."

As she thought that, her breathing became more labored, as if she battled a lung infection that filled her body with liquid illness.

They were far enough from the Great Bay's influence that the air no longer smelled of salt, and it should dry during the long days of early summer. Not today. The air was heavy and damp. She could almost see tiny droplets suspended in the air. The weight of it sat on and in her chest like . . . like it did after a long magic session hiding Lillian's inability to throw even simple spells, and her strength ran out long before she'd finished and grounded the spell.

She needed to talk to Lily, find out if the air felt unusual to her too, or if it was a return of Val's childhood illnesses. She'd tried, really tried, to keep her magic to the minimum so she didn't exhaust herself. But she had to do more and more to keep The Forget in place over Ariiell's eroding knot of guilt. The ugliness had to seep out bit by bit. All at once would send Ariiell back into her semitrance of incoherence. Or to suicide.

Val missed Lillian, her strength and comfort, the constant presence of her mind, her understanding. Her physical strength. Knowing her twin would soon be separated from her by hundreds of miles made Val's lungs catch and her heart beat too rapidly.

"Val?" Lillian whispered excitedly from nearby as if Valeria had conjured her.

She stood up from her crouch among tall miggenberry bushes bordered by saber ferns at the creek side. As she focused on her sister she felt Lily droop from excited happiness to more sober reality.

Something had happened. Something Lily thought wonderful. Something to do with the bard probably.

Lily kept her thoughts close inside her, unwilling to share just now.

"Val, do you see them?"

That was what had sobered Lily so suddenly. "Just a glimpse, barely an understanding of what I saw." Valeria said on a whisper. As her sister drew closer they wrapped arms around each other's shoulders and stared in comfortable silence at the joyful plunge of water over and around rocks and stumps in its eager rush toward a larger river, and on into the Bay.

"I tried to tell Skeller the danger of befriending them," Lily said. "We talked. We kis . . . we found metaphors I think he understood, but I don't think he truly accepts magic yet. He wants to control everything with his own hands, without magic."

Val knew without being told that the bard rejected the tale as just another legend to make into a song. He'd probably kissed Lily to distract her from the subject.

I sense them, close, closer than before. Val touched Lily's mind with images of rustling branches and bouncing fern fronds. Better to keep her sister from thinking about the bard. *Whispers of a dark shadow creeping beside them, or a paler shadow slithering in the wake of something leading it.*

Me too. Nothing definite.

We separate tomorrow. Who will they follow? Val asked, already knowing the answer.

You, I think. Skellar says the steeds can smell rotten magic under Ariiell's litter. Besides, Lady Graciella interests no one but her husband. She is but a pale ghost of herself with only a little plant magic.

Lady Ariiell had a great talent at one time. I see it writhing in her mind every time I chip a fragment from the ugly knot of her memories, or refresh the blanket of Forget. But The Forget seems to cover her access to magic as well as block memories too awful to keep her sane.

"Have you seen her memories?" Lily asked. Her curiosity overrode her caution and she spoke with her voice instead of her mind.

Not fully. Just hints of fire, flashing knives, naked dancing, and pain. Pain so great she had to draw on every scrap of magical reserves to make it stop.

The Coven? Lily reverted to the privacy of silent communication when speaking the forbidden name of the old enemy of both Coronnan and University magicians.

Val nodded, unable to fully confirm her suspicions.

"What do we do? I won't be close enough to help you if you get into trouble," Lily gripped Val's shoulder more tightly. "I won't have you to block the thorns in the air as a storm builds in the ocean waiting to crash into Coronnan."

So, that was what made Valeria's skin crawl. Lily might not be able to throw a spell, but her magic was born of the Kardia and growing things. Weather affected crops and the patterns of browsers, so she was sensitive to changes in the air as well, knowing the source and the timing without knowing how she knew.

"I'm stronger now," Val said, leaning into her twin's warmth; the other half of her.

"You have more color in your face, but you are still too skinny," Lily admonished.

"And you are fair to blooming. I suspect the attention of the foreign bard has something to do with that." Val couldn't help nearly spitting the word "foreign."

"He's nice. Funny. Interesting. Except that he doesn't like magic. He's read a lot and seen so many places we never thought of. Did you know he's actually been to the Big Continent? They call it Mabastion."

That would explain the clipped accent and the lack of knowledge about dragons, the refusal of magic. Even if the people of Coronnan didn't appreciate or trust the dragons, they were schooled in dragon lore.

"Lily, stop and think. Why would a bard from . . . from over there be traveling through Coronnan?"

"Broadening his experiences, gathering new songs to take home. . . ."

"Spying for his lord? Or is he running away from something . . . like he's a criminal?" Val could go on and on about bad reasons for him following this caravan and becoming vulnerable to Rejiia. "Maybe he's the one following Lady Ariicll. Maybe he works for the Coven." She whispered the last word, afraid. Da said the Coven was broken, no longer able to work their evil magic.

But some of the members had escaped. Like Rejiia and Krej. And . . . wasn't there a soldier who joined the Rovers?

They could be recruiting new members, waiting to come to full strength with thirteen. Were they following Ariiell, trying to bring her back within their circle? Needing numbers, as much as talent for their perverted form of magic—though no one had ever told her the form of their magic that made it evil.

Ariiell's memories had given her ideas. Pain was a large part of their rituals, inflicting it and receiving it.

"Don't trust the bard, Lily," Val admonished her twin. "Don't trust anyone. Lady Graciella seems like a good candidate to be tempted by the power the Coven offers."

"Her magic is trifling," Lily dismissed the idea. "She knows how to bring out the magic intrinsic to plants but not much more."

"Ariiell said her magic was minor, hardly worth noting until The Simeon needed her placement in a noble household for political reasons. He brought it out, made her use it at full strength." Was that the reason for the torture Ariiell needed to forget? She needed to be suffering so much she had to either will herself to die, or force her magic to surge to the surface in order to make it stop.

Val grew cold at the thought.

Lily held her tighter, feeding her warmth and strength. And love. No one had ever given Ariiell love, except perhaps Mardoll, the idiot son of Lord Andrall and his wife Lynetta, the king's aunt. He'd loved Ariiell and given her a child, even if he didn't know what he was doing. That child, Mikette, was now at court, a potential heir to the throne, along with Glenndon. What kind of talent did he have? No one had ever said. Few had seen him before his recent arrival at the palace.

"She needs me so much," Val said quietly, thinking of Ariiell. "She needs me to protect her, to help her remain sane, and to comfort her. All her life she's been used or locked away in a tower. That's all she knows. This imperative summons from her father sounds like another opportunity to use her again." Maybe she should summon Lord Laislac's magician and find out.

"Graciella is the same," Lily admitted. "Her stepmother is Lord Jemmarc's sister. They arranged the marriage, without consulting Graciella. Jemmarc needs a son that no one can question the legitimacy of. His sister wants political power and is willing to use her stepdaughter any way she can. I think they threw her into the household with no preparation, no instructions, nothing but her wispy beauty and a marginal talent. She's said some things that make me think she was used by Jemmarc's son, Lucjemm. Possibly raped by him with threats of death. A horrible death. Maybe to become food for his hideous pet Krakatrice."

Val shuddered at the secondhand images in Lillian's mind. Secondhand they made her choke with fear. How bad were they in reality? As bad as Ariiell's time with the Coven?

"Don't let her go the same route as Ariiell," Val begged. "Help her find her own way, her own strength. Don't let the Coven recruit her!"

"The same to you, Val."

"I'll miss you, Lily. I miss you already, but there is no way we can stay together until we know both our ladies are safe. We are the only ones they can trust."

A large clump of ferns between her and the creek waved and wiggled as something burrowed into their deep and hidden center.

A gray shadow watched them. The strange evening light gilded the long, thin silhouette.

Lillian noticed the movement as well. Without a word they shifted their grip on each other from shoulder to hand and ran back to the safety of the caravan.

Better to know and see who eavesdropped on their last conversation together than wonder who listened from the darkness of the forest.

Tonight they would break the rules of journey and summon Da. They had to.

The young prince is up to something. My spies tell me through my glass that he has left the palace with his body-guard and his clerk. He carries his staff. A staff he has not earned. In the unified new order I will bring to fruition, he will be stripped of his powers and his tools for his crime of arrogance. I may have to have him killed if he stands in my way much longer. My apprentice is in place, ready and willing to slip a knife into the prince's heart when he least expects it. I will not tolerate a magician on the throne of Coronnan. On any throne among my territories.

Magicians advise a king. We rule through a mind-blind mouthpiece. The dragons and the Stargods made it so.

And Glenndon's sisters! Those two brats thwart me at every turn. They trust only themselves and say nothing to my spy. They close their dreams to all but each other. They even reach out and surround their ladies' dreams with a barricade that I cannot penetrate. Graciella and Ariiell cannot remember their dreams in the morning. Neither can they relate the substance to me. I need their dreams to bring all my plans together.

I need their dreams to know that my weapons are still in place, dormant but ready to awaken when I tell them to and not before.

I need to remove the twins. My tools for their demise are in place and remain undetected.

The king and his queen have not the familiarity with

their people to organize them and lead them in overcoming the disaster I throw at them.

My plans and spells come together. I must watch and manipulate from a distance for my own safety.

And when all three children of the current Senior Magician are gone, Jaylor will know the grief I have known. Glenndon will go sometime tomorrow I expect; and the twins when they reach their destinations. Jaylor will suffer as I have suffered. His blindness is just the beginning of the pain he will endure for his crimes against me, against the world. Against magic itself.

CHAPTER 19

JAYLOR FINGERED HIS quill in dismay. The feathered edge brushed the side of his hand and wrist reassuringly. This was his favorite pen. He used it often, fitting new metal nibs on the tip every few months.

"I can do this," he whispered to himself, smoothing a square-cut piece of parchment with this left hand and marking with his index finger a spot on the left-hand side about an inch from the top.

Then he reached to dip the nib into the inkwell that was always, precisely six inches to the right of the parchment edge.

"Habit," he continued to reassure himself. "Writing is the habit of lifetime. I don't need to see more than the outline of my paper. I'll know if I form the letters correctly. I just need to slow down so I don't make mistakes I can't correct. Presuming I can figure out what I need to say."

Brevelan had gone to the University to help Maigret teach an advanced class in gathering plants and minerals for potions. She'd taken Jule and Sharl with her, leaving Jaylor alone with his thoughts. Alone with the knot of uneasiness that gnawed at his gut.

"I know I can mend whatever is wrong between Lukan and me, if I can just find the right words." A thought occurred to him. He needed to start the letter with affection; reaffirm his love for all of his children.

Somehow he misjudged the distance and knocked the pewter inkwell off his desk onto the floor. It thudded, bounced and then glugged as the black fluid emptied into the rush-covered dirt.

"S'murghit!" he roared at the top of his voice. "Who put my inkwell in the wrong place?"

"Did you call for me, Master?" a young voice, probably female, just firming into maturity, asked from the doorway across the cabin's main room.

"Who the hell are you?" He could just make out an outline, backlit by sunlight in the Clearing beyond. She wore a pale robe. He could tell nothing about her coloring as a pale scarf covered her hair, and only a few darker tendrils escaped to frame her blurry face. Pale robe and scarf, an apprentice. By her height he guessed she'd reached adult proportions, and therefore had some experience.

"I'm Linda, sir. Master Marcus sent me to assist you."

"Linda." He rolled the name around his brain seeking familiarity. "Linda?" he roared. "Princess Rosselinda?"

"Just Linda now, sir. Mistress Maigret had it from Mistress Brevelan that you needed an apprentice to bully. Master Marcus sent me."

"I can't bully you."

"Mistress Brevelan said you need to try. And that I need to accept that I can learn from you, but not be so accepting that I let you bully me." She stood firm and straight. From the tilt of her head, he guessed that she leveled a steady gaze at him.

"I . . . I don't need anyone. Least of all a pampered princess who has only been here a few months." He stood and faced her, fists on hips and chin jutting forward.

"Yes, you do need me. I have clerical skills, diplomatic training. My control of my talent may be borrowed from

Glenndon, but I can help you with all of your adminis-trative duties better than anyone at the University."

He knew without looking just how her stubborn chin lifted. Her father and her mother were just as stubborn. More stubborn than he.

He didn't need stubborn, he needed a student he could teach ...

(*You're over-thinking again. Just like you did when you were her age,*) Baamin reminded him with his usual dragon humor. The old man hadn't laughed as much or as often when he was Senior Magician and Chancellor of the University. Nor had he dismissed inadequacy with a joke. Maybe there was something about assuming a dragon body that mended an overly serious mind and personality. He could learn from that.

(*Of course you can. We all need to continue learning. Every day of our lives. Our princess knows that, so why don't you?*)

"What kind of quill do you prefer, Linda?" Jaylor asked mildly, not ready to roar at her yet. He'd learned roaring as a teaching technique from Baamin. Maybe it was time to amend his methods.

(*About time you figured it out. Not everyone loves your roar because they love you as Brevelan does.*)

Jaylor humphed.

"I like a brass tip fitted over a flight feather from a flusterdrake, sir," Linda replied proudly. "And I like my ink mixed with alcohol, not water. It dries quicker and cleaner."

"You know how to write formal letters. Can I trust you with personal correspondence?"

"Yes, sir. But my spelling is archaic, more useful in formal settings where I must observe rituals of address," she replied, assessing the interior of the cabin with quick jerks of her head, right and left.

"Cloaking true meaning in the codes of formality I can do. Finding the right words to mend an argument ..."

"Difficult for everyone, sir. We can only try."

"You'll do."

He pushed her in the direction he thought the desk lay, indicating the fallen inkwell. She stooped to retrieve it, brushing off bits of straw from the graceful cylinder, smaller at the top and solidly broad at the base.

"There's not much left, sir."

"I'll grate charcoal for more while you use that up."

"What do you need written, sir?"

That "sir" was getting on his nerves. Proper for an apprentice addressing a master, but from Linda . . . she was the daughter of his best friend, half sister to Glenndon, his near equal in social rank. Surely they could compromise on something less . . . less. . . .

No, they couldn't compromise on respect for their new positions. When she returned to her home and family, then they'd discuss proper forms of address.

"How shall I address the letter?" she asked again, sweeping the skirt of her robe smooth to sit straight on his chair without wrinkling it.

"A letter to my son."

"Which son, sir?" she asked, fidgeting for a comfortable position in his oversized chair. She had to stretch to peer over the top of his desk. Her feet dangled, not reaching the floor.

"Um, maybe you should sit over there." He waved vaguely toward a smaller worktable with a Brevelan-sized stool.

She shifted to the more comfortable seat, taking parchment, quill, and inkwell with her. "Which son, sir," Linda asked again, pen poised over the parchment.

He paused a moment. Maybe he should shift his plans. Lukan had not showed his face at home while the family was awake since . . . since the accident that had near-blinded Jaylor. Brevelan knew he'd been in the cabin by the missing food she left out for him each night. They guessed he slept in a dormitory at the University. Jaylor hadn't the courage to ask Marcus, or maybe Maigret, for confirmation.

He'd planned to leave a letter of explanation and love for Lukan.

No, that was far too personal a message for a stranger to compose. Linda wasn't exactly a stranger, but that communication touched raw nerves around Jaylor's heart he was not willing to share with anyone except Lukan.

His relationship with Glenndon, however, was already the stuff of legend, a part of the history of the country. Linda shared a special bond with Glenndon. In one intimate healing spell they had shared and absorbed all of each other's knowledge, memories, and secrets. She'd taught him to speak in two heartbeats. He'd taught her every bit of magic he knew. The words Jaylor needed to send to his golden child weren't as personal as what she already knew directly from Glenndon.

"Your oath of secrecy, Linda," he demanded. He knew she could be discreet. But he needed formal affirmation.

He watched her spine bristle with indignation. At least he hoped that was what his broken eyes told him.

"Of course, sir."

"Your oath," he insisted upon the ritual.

"My oath as a magician, I promise never to reveal the contents of this letter to anyone, not even a dragon, on pain of imposed magical silence."

He wanted to chuckle as the words suddenly took on new meaning for him. "The dragons will know even without telling them."

"Sir?"

"They live as much in my mind as they do in their lair up the mountain."

"Have you been there, sir?" Awe tinged her voice.

"Yes, Linda. I have. And if we both live long enough, I'll tell you that tale. For now, write this: Dear Glenndon, son of my heart. I apologize profusely for not revealing the truth of your origins to you earlier. You deserved to know . . ."

❦

"So, I'm not good enough to receive a letter of apology," Lukan snarled from his listening post beside the chimney on the roof. He heard every word spoken inside the cabin. Every *S'murghin* word. Not one of them concerning him.

"Nor am I good enough to become your scribe, Father." Anger twisted inside his gut, turning his breakfast to acid that wanted to burn itself out and up.

"Of all the apprentices in the University who know how to write a fine hand, I'm the last one to be considered for the job. I'm not good enough for anything. So why am I still here?"

(Your mama needs you,) Indigo said sadly.

Lukan looked up for some sign of where the young dragon might fly. Nothing. Not even the flash of sunlight on an iridescent wing. The entire sky looked as dull as his heart felt.

"Mama only needs Da. Her children are always second in her affections," he replied, justifying his anger and hurt.

(Is that so?)

"Of course it is."

A void opened in Lukan's mind where the dragon voice had been.

"I know, I know, that means I should think about it."

(Agreed.) Another long moment of silence followed. *(Have you thought about it?)*

"Yeah," Lukan replied reluctantly. "Mama loves us all. Equally." He hated that the dragon was right. The dragons were always right.

(And?)

"And, I don't think Mama is well. The new babe weighs heavily in her belly and in her heart. She turns to Da because he has always protected her."

(The little ones are too little to help her. She needs you to lift and carry. She needs to lean on you when she walks.)

"Is she going to be all right?" Worry replaced anger but still roiled in his gut.

Indigo did not answer. He was still inside Lukan's mind, but didn't have an answer.

"I have to stay here and help Mama. Da can't. Jule and Sharl can't. There's no one left but me, and I'm an inconsequential second best."

(You are what she needs.)

"But not what my father needs."

A flap of huge wings rising from the bathing pool answered him. Indigo flew away, deserting Lukan as everyone else had.

⚘

"I need to write a letter to my father," Lady Ariiell said flatly the moment Valeria returned to the litter.

"Directly after we eat," Val replied. She'd given up calling the evening meal dinner. Dinner implied something more substantial and interesting than the inevitable stew made with dried meat, tubers, and whatever the cooks could glean along the road for greenery. She expected grass to begin showing up in the pot before too long.

"I don't know that I can wait that long," Ariiell confessed around a trembling lower lip.

Val paused a moment, as much to gather her courage as for effect.

Ariiell grew impatient and fidgeted nervously.

"Are you ready to try a summons?" Val asked tentatively.

"My father is as mind-blind as those flusterhens going into the cook pot."

Val raised her eyebrows; in some ways the birds were more closely in touch with the magic in the land, the air, the rain, and the ax that would end their existence, than most humans. But she understood Ariiell's assessment.

"From whom did you inherit your magic?" Val knew the answer, but she needed Ariiell to say it, acknowledge it, and put it behind her, not forgotten, just accepted.

"My mother." Ariiell turned her head away. "No one gave her training to control her talent. It drove her insane and she threw herself off the highest tower of Father's castle in Aporia." Again the flat intonation, no emotional involvement. As if she denied guilt in the event.

"What did she hear telepathically that she wasn't supposed to that drove her to such desperate straits?" Valeria settled into her cushions facing Ariiell. This could take awhile. They'd been through a similar routine before they composed letters to King Darville and Da—Lord Jaylor.

"I . . . I don't know." Ariiell looked up with that thought. Bewilderment clouded her eyes. "I was very young and alone. She didn't love me enough to stay, to help me learn magic properly, to explain *anything* to me. No one loves me . . ."

"Was she trying to hide her talent?" Val prodded.

"I guess. I was young, not quite eight when she . . . when it happened."

"Did she try to teach you anything about controlling your talent?"

"No. I remember her saying that revealing that I could light candles and levitate food from the kitchens with only a thought would brand me a witch and I'd be burned for it. She did tell me to find a way to block out people's random thoughts."

"Wise woman. Women possessing talent is more accepted now. But according to my history lessons, at the time, any woman who could do those things was considered evil, traitorous, in league with Simurgh." She named the red-tipped dragon from before the time of the Stargods. The beast had developed a taste for human meat, not bothering to cook it with his natural fire or to wait until his prey was fully dead before eating. The Dragon Nimbus had outlawed Simurgh. Ever since then, his name had been used as a curse.

"But I continued playing with my little tricks and Mother killed herself because of it."

"No, she didn't."

"What?" Ariiell opened her eyes wide. A brief glimmer of hope crossed her face then died aborning.

"Think about it," Val advised.

"I have and I know I'm responsible. I have to apologize to my father for killing my mother."

"No, you don't. He needs to apologize to you for blaming you, for using your guilt to control you."

"He wouldn't . . ."

"He did. And he sold you to the Coven."

"But . . ."

"You were only fifteen. You could not have met The Simeon unless your father introduced you. You did not run away with a charming man on your own. Your father sent you with him."

"I don't remember . . ."

"You have buried that memory along with many other horrible ones. Both your father and The Simeon needed you guilty and submissive, blaming yourself for all that happened afterward. They used you."

"Why? What could the Coven offer my father? He's a powerful lord. He controls a wealthy province and has the ear of the king."

"King Darville was recently married at the time. He consulted his wife, Queen Rossemikka, more than his lords. Your father's grip on power at court was slipping. Your brother was lost at sea. You were all he had left. A girl who couldn't inherit."

"A girl with a magical talent," Ariiell finished the thought. "I was his tool of alliance with the Coven. But what could they offer him?"

"Regency for your son. Mardall has royal blood, but a malformed mind. His child, your child, carries that same royal blood as the king's aunt, Lady Lynetta. King Darville has only daughters, who can't inherit either. Kill the king and who is next in line? A grandson of the king's aunt? Lord Laislac was promised regency, with the Coven as his chief advisers." Val was guessing at this. She knew bits and pieces of it based on lessons and morality tales. But it was the only logical explanation that combined all those elements.

"They promised me the regency. All I had to do was seduce an idiot who didn't know what he was doing."

"It must have been terribly embarrassing to you. To have others tell you what to do with your body."

"After what The Simeon did to me, in full view and participation of the Coven, Mardall was sweet and gentle. I did it because my body, my life, and my soul, were no longer mine. I was a slave to the Coven."

"Bought and paid for."

"Yes!" Anger flushed Ariiell's face for the first time. An honest emotion generated by herself, not what others expected of her. "I want to talk to my father. Set up the summons."

"What are you going to ask him?" Val grabbed a fine white porcelain bowl to fill with water for the spell.

"I need to know why he summoned me home after leaving me to rot in that tower for fifteen years. I need to know who he has sold me to this time."

In ten minutes they had their answer. Through the medium of water in a silver bowl and a fine beeswax candle set up by his magician adviser, Lord Laislac nearly bounced in his enthusiasm. "I've arranged a marriage between you, my beloved daughter, and King Lokeen of the city-state Amazonia," he chortled.

CHAPTER 20

LILLIAN LOOKED AT the juncture in the road with dismay. The path to the west forked gently to the right, staying wide, straight, and easy across the gently undulating prairie. Val's path. Lily certainly hoped her twin's journey remained easy and free of obstacles. The South Road, however, the one Lily must take, narrowed and began to wander around hills and boulders the size of a house. A long ridgeline stretched east to west. Once past it, she would be fully out of sight of Val's half of the caravan. Would she be out of mind as well as out of sight? Was this road merely a reflection of the changing landscape? Or ominous portent?

Maybe Lily's imagination made the worst of the situation.

Within hours Valeria would travel farther away from Lillian than just across the Clearing, or the city, or the other end of the long caravan.

Would their telepathic connection stretch that far? Was Lily's magical talent truly strong enough to receive a summons through her tiny shard of copper-banded glass, a bowl of water, and a candle flame? Even from Val?

Valeria wrapped her arms around Lillian, clutching her back with fingers that dug deep into her flesh, almost like a raptor's talons. Or a cat's.

"I'll scry for you as soon as the sun sets," Val said on a gulp.

"I'll be waiting," Lillian said, barely choking the words out.

"Remember to keep watch for the cat and the weasel. I have to report them to Da. Eventually. If they do more than follow us."

"Of course. What . . . what are we to do with them? We can't just let them run free."

"I expect Da will tell me to kill them. Especially if they show signs of transforming."

Lillian almost choked at the thought. "We don't have the right to kill anything, not animals, not anything!" Mama had drilled that into them over and over. Mama hadn't eaten meat, not even fish, since before she met Da. She said she couldn't bear the thought of eating something that had lived, even if someone else took the life. "Krej and Rejiia were once humans with minds and souls." They still had the essence of life and intelligence.

"They are evil. They can't be allowed to endanger anyone again. Not ever. If you knew . . ."

Suddenly Lily's mind filled with the horrific images of Ariiell's initiation into the Coven. Rejiia had been there. Had taken a burning brand from the fire and applied it to Ariiell's naked skin with delight!

More images.

"Stargods, why did they make her suffer so?" Lily shuddered and buried her face in her twin's shoulder to block out any more secondhand pain.

"They needed to use her to gain political power, to exploit this land and our people through terror for their own pleasure. No one would benefit from their rule except themselves. They knew if they hurt her enough she would either will herself into death or release her magic full force. They found the torture and rape of an innocent more pleasant than we would . . . find petting a kitten." Val clung tighter.

(They will kill the dragons. All of the dragons, for they

know we would block their attempts to rule,) the sad voice of Shayla, the dragon matriarch, whispered into the back of Lily's mind. Shayla had been a victim of Krej when he ensorcelled her into a glass statue.

"We can't allow the Coven to gain power. Ever again. And if that means killing a cat and a weasel, we have to do it."

"I don't think I can." Lily imagined a black field of nothingness to blot out the persistent images.

"You'll have to if they approach you or Skeller again."

Lily nodded mutely. She couldn't, she wouldn't think about it. But she had to protect Skeller. And Graciella. Both were vulnerable. . . .

"Watch your back, Lily. And be careful." Val's last words took on a desperate tearfulness.

"You too. I think our enemies are more likely to follow you than me," Lillian said. With something outside her own misery to focus on she could speak while her tears slowed. By naming them enemy she could contemplate their demise. But not by her hand.

A blaring of horns and snorting of steeds signaled the beginning of the end of their . . . closeness.

Lillian vowed they would always be together, little more than a thought away. She should look on their separation as the beginning of an opportunity to learn to be herself. To seek out friendships, and perhaps even to flirt more openly with Skeller, to playfully bring him to the conclusion that magic was beautiful and natural, was useful. And important. Without Val's constant disapproval, maybe she had a chance to let that tentative liking grow into something more.

Maybe Skellar would kiss her again.

"Remember to chip away at Lady Ariiell's knot in her head. She's healed a lot already. But there is more locked up in there. I know it. She's not strong enough yet to know what it means to be herself," she advised Val for lack of other words to fill the impending gap between them.

"And you remember to find Lady Graciella's biggest

fear and help her face it before she goes crazy and gets locked in a tower," Val said into Lily's ear as they clung together a moment more.

Other travelers flowed around them, impatient with their overlong leave-taking. A drover snorted in disapproval as he urged the team supporting Lady Graciella's litter forward on the South Road.

Lillian stiffened her spine and sniffed back a new spate of tears. "Your lady is already half a mile along the West Road," she whispered to Val. "You'll have to run to catch up."

"At the speed of these lazy steeds I need only walk a little faster than normal. But Lady Ariiell will miss me. She's grown quite dependent upon me, afraid of those who stalk her, and of herself."

"Lady Graciella seems quite friendly when we talk about restoring the gardens and teaching the castle cook how to use better herbs in his recipes. But any time I try to get her talk about herself, she feigns sleep."

"Is it feigned? Or does she escape from her memories?" Val asked, pulling away but still holding Lillian's hand.

"That remains to be seen. Take care of yourself, Val. Remember to sleep. And to eat, even when nothing tastes good or you think you are too tired to eat."

"The same to you. And be cautious of the bard. He can't be trusted. He's foreign. He knows nothing of magic or dragons. He's too pretty." With grim determination she turned her back on her twin and headed toward her lady.

Lillian did the same.

"Now you can learn to be yourself and not a reflection of her," Skeller said, coming up beside her.

"It will be nice to travel at the head of the caravan and not have to eat the dust of the other half," she replied, putting an extra arm's-length between them and moving a bit faster toward Lady Graciella's litter. Maybe Val was right. Maybe she shouldn't trust this man who disapproved of her twin. Her other half.

A flash of agreement crossed her mind from Val.

"It's only the truth," Skeller said louder, more defensive. He made up the distance between them in two long strides.

"How can you say that! Val is my twin. We are the same person stretched between two bodies." She stopped and stamped her foot, anger at him replacing the deep emptiness in her belly.

"Twins?" He stared at her, mouth gaping.

"Of course. It's obvious to everyone else."

"No, it's not. She looks a lot like you, but you are ..." He paused to scan her figure with a faint grin of approval. "You're more mature in mind and body. She's a wispy teenager where you are a woman."

"I am?" A pleasing warmth tamed the roil in her middle. "But ... but she's smarter and...." How could she admit that Val had more than enough magical talent for both of them? In the eyes of her family, that meant Lily was as broken in mind as Val was in body. Together they were one whole person. Apart ... "She's been ill. A lot," she added, a lame excuse, not admitting any of her own fears and inadequacies.

"But she still forces you to walk in her shadow. The same shadow she casts under Lady Ariiell's litter."

"She told me not to trust you. Now I see why. You ... you're trying to subvert us, to break our family apart!"

"No I'm not. I'm trying to get to know you better. Trying to harmonize my song with yours. That's the only way I can understand the weirdness going on here."

"Is that what you call it?" She raised her eyebrows in skepticism, wishing she could lift just one in that sarcastic look Glenndon and the king had perfected.

"For now."

"Learn to sing with dragons and then we'll talk." She flounced off to join Lady Graciella, her charge and her responsibility.

Secretly, she smiled.

❦

Mikk rotated his shoulders trying to ease the itch in the center of his back. He felt as if someone followed him as he crept through the dusty and cobwebby stacks of books seeking a lesson in magic. He now knew the story of how the Stargods had found energy within the Kardia and in the air. Gradually they had invented ways to heighten their concentration, with repeated words — Kimmer of the South called them mantras, University-trained magicians called them spells. Mikk needed to figure out how to harness the energy and create magic with it.

Lighting a candle with only his mind was still difficult, but becoming easier and more reliable.

He'd practiced staring into a candle flame for hours on end; felt the tingle of power in his toes and fingertips; visualized lifting a quill with only his mind. But he hadn't been able to connect the tingle to the quill, or seen beyond the flame into the distance outside the four walls of his room.

None of the books leaped into his hands or even nudged his fingertips as the first one had. And yet the pervasive irritation along his spine, through his nape and into his popping ears told him he was missing something. Something important.

Perhaps the dragons were telling his restless feet and eyes to seek help. Glenndon. He needed to find Glenndon and start asking questions.

He dusted off his tunic as best he could after leaving the archives. No sense in attempting to correct his dishevelment until he was free of the debris from neglect that filled the air.

Fortunately Lady Miri did not await him at the foot of the stairs, ready to pounce and manipulate him into disclosing secrets about Prince Glenndon. He could proceed to his room without risking his image as a dashing and elegant courtier.

Something more than dust, mold, and cobwebs filled the air today. The tip of his tongue tasted metallic, and the light, barely visible beyond the arrow-slit windows of the tower, had a strange coppery tint to it. And he couldn't stop wiggling his fingers in an arcane pattern that tried to weave the air into a brighter and lighter tapestry.

Glenndon would know what was going on. Glenndon knew everything.

Mikk did pause in his room long enough to change his plain linen tunic to a more formal blue and gold brocade. He couldn't bring himself to call upon the Crown Prince in anything less, no matter how casual the visit.

"Geon," he called his servant, clerk, and bodyguard away from his moody stare out the parlor window toward the eastern horizon and the Bay. Glenndon had a different man for each function, but then he was a step closer to the throne than Mikk.

Geon shook himself free of his brooding thoughts and turned slowly, stiffly, to face Mikk. His gaunt face remained pale and bland, but his eyes almost glowed with fervent excitement. Then he blinked and returned to his normal impassivity.

Must be a trick of the strange coppery light.

"Geon, would you please knock on Price Glenndon's door and request an appointment for me, as soon as possible?" Mikk tried imitating the authoritative voice that came naturally to the king while maintaining an air of politeness. As if Geon actually had a choice in obeying the order.

The tall and slender man with prematurely gray, receding hair bowed and retreated out the door without a word. Geon never said much. Sometimes Mikk wondered if his cheeks had collapsed from continuously biting back rude retorts.

"Well?" Mikk demanded when Geon returned scarcely one hundred breaths later. He knew because he'd counted them during his frequent practice of deep, controlled breathing. Geon's blank countenance hadn't changed.

"Forgive me, sir, but His Highness seems to have quitted the palace some time ago." Geon bowed again and took the first step toward the window.

"Where did he go?" Mikk asked.

Geon stopped in mid-stride, opened his mouth, closed it, then breathed deeply before speaking again. "I am sorry, sir. I do not know." Nor did he care, obviously, or he might show some emotion.

"Do you know when he left?" Mikk prodded.

"No, sir. He took his cap and cloak." This time Geon made it to his silent observation post before Mikk could think up another question.

Something was different about the man today. He seemed outlined in a copper-colored glow. Maybe it was the strange light beneath gathering storm clouds. Or maybe Mikk could finally see an aura. An aura that spiked and expanded as he watched.

Mikk tapped his foot in indecision. The air seemed heavier than before, making it difficult to draw a full breath. His mind wanted to shut down. Maybe he should take his boots off and . . .

No. He would not succumb to his grandmother's solution to all problems. A nap never gave him answers. Books did that.

The light outside dimmed, as if the clouds had moved between him and the sun. Geon's visible aura retreated but did not disappear. The metallic taste moved from the tip of Mikk's tongue to the back of his throat. He wanted to gag.

Something was very different about the approaching storm. Fisherfolk down on the wharves would understand the changes in the air. But he hated to trudge all the way down there and have to decipher the thick patois of their private language. He was sure they'd mutated their words and meanings to keep their tight-knit community private from the rest of the world.

Books sometimes cloaked meaning in convoluted mazes of words. But they had always given him answers.

Books. He'd found no inspiration or answers in the archives. Who else had books about weather and magic?

"Geon, I think I need to consult someone at the University. Lord Jaylor if he's in residence."

"Very good, sir. Do you need your cloak?" He continued looking out the window and frowned.

"It's too warm for a cloak. Perhaps a diffcrent tunic. One that will not stain when it starts raining."

"Yes, sir. The leather jerkin you use for sword practice would be best. And your heavier boots." Geon sighed as if he shouldered all the burdens of the world.

CHAPTER 21

DANGER PULSES FROM the heavy stone artifact. Bone turned to stone. All the magic of the ancient creature captured within, ready for me to tap into it. A dragon of sorts, long and sturdy. Heavy from the transformation of life into a part of the Kardia.

Power accompanies the danger. I know how to handle it, how to parcel out the danger among my followers. One more magician would help steady and balance the power. But my apprentice is elsewhere, keeping me informed of what transpires in the city.

The danger inherent in the stone bone thrills me and awakens my senses. Danger. All power is dangerous when used incorrectly. I know how to use it. I will use it for good, for the return of proper order and proper magic to my beloved Coronnan. My good intent helps me control the power. I am master of this stone bone, and therefore I am master of my followers and the elements.

Come to me Kardia, Air, Water, and Fire. Come to me and cleanse the land.

Restore Coronnan to its former order!

Glenndon listened to the steady creak of oars plowing against the river current as he watched the sun drift lower and lower toward the horizon. Clouds showed dark and menacing, streaked with crimson fire to the east across the bay, darkening the sky in that direction. But the west remained clear, blue and cheerful with the sun still an hour above the horizon. He hoped the coming storm would hold off a little longer. He should need only an hour of dryness after dark to complete his mission and then let Frank row him back to the palace. The tide should be running slack by then and the trip downstream easier.

He and his two companions continued in agreeable silence while following the winding path of the river around the delta islands, big and small, permanent and temporary. Glenndon was grateful the two men had learned his moods, knew when to talk him out of his brooding silence and when to leave him to it.

Tonight he needed to think and think hard. His nose itched as if a dragon followed them, exuding magic in thick waves. Waves that beat at something else in the air.

Lightning flashed in the first warning of the war of the winds generated out at sea.

He reached out with his extra sense to bring some of the magical power into his body and store it for use later.

Nothing happened.

He lifted his staff a few inches so that the dragon bone in the top might channel some of the energy. It remained inert, dull. When he first found the bone, on Sacred Isle, where dragons went to die sometimes (though that was a secret known only to him, to Da, and to the dragons), it had glowed softly with power and added extra fuel to his spells. But he'd used it all up.

Another slice of lightning seared down from the sky toward his staff, then veered away a finger-width from the knob and grounded into an uprooted tree drifting toward the sea.

The magic was there. He knew it! But it avoided him. Why?

He sensed no dragon presence. No dragon mind

touched his with wisdom, or warning, or even humor. It was as if someone had gathered all of the available magical energy and held it in reserve, still in the air rather than in his body. Not an easy task for more than a few minutes.

Or were the dragons flying overhead, too high for him to sense them, making their energy readily available to him because they knew he'd need it? Only, someone else had beat him to the gathering.

He opened his mind, hoping to contact a dragon; any dragon. *Indigo?* he whispered into the air.

A thought brushed his mind, too distant or distracted to pay him much attention, just letting him know that his friend was available if Glenndon really needed him. But not now. Something else occupied his concern.

Lukan? he called.

Either his brother was brooding, again, or was preoccupied and needed a full summoning spell to break through his perpetual anger.

Linda? Surely you can receive me! Again nothing. His telepathic sending didn't bounce back at him. More like it just ... evaporated, or got absorbed by someone else.

Glenndon released the tentative connection to dragons and family reluctantly. He trusted the dragons to be available when he needed them. He was learning to trust his human companions to watch his back.

"What is that I smell?" Keerkin whispered through the growing dusk.

Glenndon didn't think his clerk had enough magic to sense the thick blanket of strange energies warring with each other. That was why he was a clerk and not attached to the University in any capacity. Did he still have ties to the University? If so, who did he report to? If not, where was his true allegiance? To the king or Glenndon?

Or himself.

Or someone else?

Clouds roiled across the sky, bringing a premature twilight to the east. Fires sparked and snapped within the churning mass.

"It's just the storm," Glenndon said, hopefully. He wanted to believe that more than lose his trust in the man.

"Something isn't natural about the storm," Frank grunted, putting his back into the oars. "Moving too fast."

"How do you know that?" Glenndon asked.

"Been rowing this river since I was a tot," Frank grunted.

"I've been here five years and never seen anything like that," Keerkin agreed, pointing at the mass of black clouds the color of rain-slick basalt cliffs with fire burning off any clinging vegetation, covering the entire horizon from north to south.

"No, it does not look, or smell natural," Glenndon said, tasting acrid air that carried a taint of ley lines as well as dragon magic. Only a powerful magician could have called up that storm. Or an entire Circle of Master Magicians. He knew of no Circles outside the two Universities. And neither one of them would do such a thing.

Except . . . rogues attracted disgruntled outcasts. He knew of only one rogue. Had Samlan built an entire circle of magicians?

No. Surely he couldn't have in just a few months since his exile from the Forest University. Surely not . . .

Wind roared above them, trumpeting the arrival of its parent storm with raucous glee that would have drowned out a dragon screech.

Suddenly suspicious of everyone and everything around him, Glenndon checked the men's auras.

Frank's remained a normal white afterglow with tiny orange-tinged spikes of alarm. Keerkin's too showed the layer of white next to his skull topped by another narrow layer of sea green that suggested a minor magical talent. Then . . . then nothing. Some of his emotions should show through. Blue calm, red anger, yellow happiness, shades of orange concern. Something.

"Um . . . Keerkin, just how much magic do you have?" Glenndon asked.

"Do you have a plan for stalling the storm? I can support your talent with whatever dragon magic I can gather, but not much more. Weather is more a ley line talent and I can't find those, let alone tap them," he replied a little too eager. "I haven't worked more magic than lighting a candle or keeping a quill sharp since I left the University five years ago."

"I'm not sure I can do much either without a dragon's presence," Glenndon admitted. "Mama and Lily are the storm watchers in my family." He watched Keerkin carefully while he spoke. The man was hiding something. Perhaps instinctively. Blocking his aura from the sight of another magician required more talent than the clerk admitted to.

(Spy,) another mind whispered into his own.

Spy?

He chuckled silently to himself. Da had spies all over the capital. A habit he developed right after the Leaving. Why would Jaylor, the Senior Magician, withdraw his spies just because magic and magicians had returned to everyday life and politics in Coronnan?

Glenndon turned his mind back to the more immediate problem. "How far to Sacred Isle?" he asked. The one time he'd come here, by himself to acquire his staff, he'd taken a longer route around the outermost islands because he didn't know the river as Frank did, afraid he'd get lost and end up in the middle of the Bay.

"About five minutes. I'm fighting the outgoing tide as well as the current. Still a lot of snow coming off the mountains, running the river higher than normal this time of year."

That didn't sound right either. Last spring the Krakatrice had caused a drought with warmer than normal temperatures. Even if all the rain and snow that had been blocked from falling on Coronnan returned in gushes these last three moons, the river should still be lower than normal. The rain and snow had drenched SeLennica instead.

"Frank, slide into the lee of that temporary ait," Glenndon directed, pointing to a lump of a sandbar that had no more than two years' worth of grass and saplings clinging to it. The coming storm looked strong enough to wipe it out, as happened so often within the delta.

"Gladly," Frank panted.

"What are you thinking, Your Highness?" Keerkin asked while Frank rested, using the oars only enough to keep them in place.

"I'm thinking someone with strong magical ties to weather wants to keep us from Sacred Isle tonight, or at least delay us. I'm not going to let that happen. Shift places with me, Frank." They made the tricky maneuver without overturning the little boat.

With fresh energy, and shoulders made strong from chopping wood and lately sword practice, Glenndon channeled some of his magic into the oars as he dipped them deep into the water and pushed them out into the current. He concentrated on the water, letting his mind blend with it; understand its need to move faster and faster to its destiny out in the Bay.

He'd learned that trick from Valeria. She merged with the soil, plants, and burrowing insects or worms to hide from others while observing them. He needed to do much the same with the water.

"Um . . . Highness?" Frank stammered. "Why are you fading into nothing? You look more like a dragon than a human."

Glenndon ignored him. He'd deal with the consequences of fatigue, hunger, and headache later.

They sped upriver, barely skimming the water's surface.

CHAPTER 22

T HE LADIES SEEMED to have disappeared from the public rooms in the palace. Mikk overheard a maid whisper something about the heavy air making her lady's hair frizzy and unmanageable. He was almost grateful to avoid Miri's and Chastet's interference.

Though he did think he looked rather dashing in a roguish way wearing leather instead of brocade.

A quarter hour later, Mikk led Geon across the bridge to University Isle and up to the postern gate. An apprentice magician, clad in wrinkled and stained pale blue tunic and trews, yawned as he waved the royal visitor into the walled complex.

"Excuse me, Apprentice," Mikk addressed the young man, near his own age with thick dark hair drawn back into a three-strand queue that looked as if it hadn't been refreshed in several days. Unconsciously, he maintained a clear distance of three arm's-lengths. "I wish to consult with your librarian."

"Huh?" the boy asked around another yawn. The red rimming his eyes suggested at least one sleepless night. Perhaps he had an excuse for his yawns and unkempt appearance.

"Yes, I have some questions."

"Um, Master Aggelard isn't feeling well today. Something about shifting air pressure playing havoc with his arthritic hands. He's not taking visitors."

Alarm bells seemed to clang inside Mikk's mind. Almost as clear as the city bells that signaled invasion or flood or fire.

"The shifting air pressure is precisely what I need to consult with him about," Mikk said.

"But . . ."

"It's important."

"Well, maybe Master Bommhet can decide if it's important enough to disturb the old guy." The magician ran his fingers along the edge of the pedestrian portal.

Mikk saw a series of scratches in the stone. Then the apprentice's fingers paused and the series of straight and crossed marks glowed green. Mikk guessed this was some kind of magical communication. A flash of pure lust seared from his groin to his head and back again. He wanted, no needed, to know how to do that. Geon too seemed fascinated, leaning his head closer to the portal, almost blocking Mikk's view.

He bet Glenndon could tap into those markings and know where every master in the University was at any time.

Deep loneliness followed the want. Mikk had been left out of this exclusive group of men. Even if he'd followed his grandmother's wishes and joined the Temple, he wouldn't fully belong in this University, with real magicians.

"Master will see you. Down the long hall, third door on the left. He's in the gallery around the library." He waved again for Mikk and Geon to proceed.

Mikk followed the directions, noting how the central courtyard, for all its ancientness, was swept clean of litter and everyday dust. The mortar between the massive building stones gleamed without a trace of mold or mildew—hard to do with the constant moisture from the river and the bay. The interior smelled just like any other very old stone building, slightly musty from hundreds of men living and working here for centuries.

His nose itched as something else filtered through his senses, something he associated with . . . with Glenndon. Not Glenndon specifically, his staff. His magical staff made from a branch of the Tambootie, the tree of magic that dragons fed upon.

So much dragon magic had been thrown within these walls that the scent of it permeated the stones themselves. If Mikk squinted in the dim light—glow balls hovered near the ceiling where it met the walls—he could almost see the sparkle of magic within the stones themselves: tiny shards of many different colors and variations on those colors. Each color and combination of colors represented the magical signature of a specific magician. A talented person could meet them all just by touching those stones.

He wanted to be that talented person.

"Sir." Geon prodded him toward the doorway they sought. The servant cast an eager glance toward the massive double doors that marked the entrance to the library.

Mikk shook off his reverie and pushed open one side of the iron-banded oaken doors, cautiously, almost reverently, hoping he entered a temple full of books, worthy of respect and awe.

He was not disappointed. Rows and rows of shelves, freestanding and affixed to the walls, flowed around him and upward for three stories. Bigger than the tower archives in the palace, this library must contain a copy of every tome ever penned. He stood for a long moment, mouth agape, staring and needing to read every word of every book there. For the first time in his life he felt as if he'd come home. This was where he belonged.

"Not that one, boy," a querulous voice came from Mikk's left.

Mikk started, wondering what he'd done wrong.

He heard a soft, quickly stifled chuckle from behind him. Geon found amusement in his embarrassment! Then his servant nudged his elbow and pointed to a huge circular desk at the center of the room.

An old man, shrunken and frail, wispy hair nearly nonexistent on top but spilling down to his dark-blue-clad shoulders from an untrimmed half circle around his skull, bent over the desk peering into a bowl of water. A lit candle stood in its stick, nearly guttering, behind the bowl.

So that was how one worked a scrying spell! Mikk had read about it but never mastered the positioning of the bowl and candle. The circle of glass must be floating on the water.

"To your right, boy!" the old man admonished, never taking his eyes off the bowl. "Yes, that one. It has a record of the flood five hundred years ago."

Above them, the sound of shuffling feet alerted Mikk to the presence of another person. "The title is wrong. This one is a record of harvests transported downriver fifty years ago," came a disgusted voice from the shadows of the gallery.

A flood? A flood five hundred years ago?

"Excuse me, Master Aggelard?" Mikk ventured, taking five steps closer to the old man. He had a long way to go to consider himself within conversing range.

"Not now. Can't you see the master is busy?" the other voice said.

"Excuse me, the apprentice at the gate said I might speak to Master Bommhet with questions about the storm I sense brewing east of the bay." Mikk looked up. Way up.

A male figure came into view wearing a blue robe almost the mate to the one enshrouding the old man. He bent over the railing that looked too low to keep him on the gallery if he bent forward too far. "Ah, you'd be the one from the palace. What's your question? Ask it quickly, then leave us to our important work." He seemed almost as old as Mikk's grandfather. Surely too old to be called boy. But then Master Aggelard looked ancient. In comparison a man of sixty would be a boy.

"Sir, the storm does not seem normal."

"Of course it's not normal," replied Aggelard. "Sensed it did you? You haven't been trained in magic though. So you can't be the boy wonder Glenndon. Which one of the royal brats are you?"

"Mikkette, sir." Mikk doffed his cockaded leather cap and bowed as deeply as he would to the king. "The family call me Mikk."

"Ah, the get of that sorceress. Must have inherited the talent from her. Go talk to Lord Jaylor and get yourself enrolled before your senses get you in trouble." He barely looked up before returning to his bowl. "Bommhet, that book is too new. I need the one to the right of it!"

"That's not it either!"

"Well, then, look further. Or get yourself a new set of eyes to read the title."

"Master Aggelard, perhaps I can help find the reference you need," Mikk offered hesitantly.

"Can you read?"

"Yes, sir. My grandmother intended me for the Temple."

"Your first test, boy," Bommhet called from above. "Is to read faded titles on books too low for me to bend and see properly."

"I have some talent in finding books by feel," Mikk replied, looking around for a way up to the third level.

"So do I. So does every apprentice in the University. But the storm is interfering, and we've worked all the boys so long and hard trying to shore up dikes along the riverfront they're useless. I need intelligent eyes, not necessarily talent."

Geon pointed to a circular iron staircase behind Master Aggelard and nodded. Then he retreated to an obscure spot behind a freestanding bookcase where he could observe in silence and obscurity.

As Mikk watched, Geon's fingers caressed a book spine and eased it free of its fellows. How much observing could the man do if he was reading a text?

"That man of yours can fetch me fresh candles," Aggelard reproached all of them. "Best make use of anyone who can help while real magicians are out preparing for the worst. I know I've read an account of a battlemage raising a storm that flooded the entire river all the way to the headwaters. I know it. I just have to see the spell to know if we can counter it."

"Food," Glenndon gasped as he grounded the little boat on the narrowing beach of Sacred Isle. He'd not been this tired or hungry since he got lost in the void after an unplanned transport spell that had no timing or destination, just escape. He'd felt like he'd been lost in the sensory deprivation for days. Da and Indigo had snatched him back after only an hour, but when he landed in the University courtyard, at the center of the working circle, his stomach felt like it was gnawing his backbone.

This was worse. He'd expended too much energy skimming over the water ahead of the storm. The storm itself seemed to have sucked him dry of magic reserves as well.

Only dragon magic had left him. He still had access to ley lines to replenish him, if he had enough strength to find one.

Frank handed him a hunk of yellow cheese, the salty kind he liked best, though the palace chef considered it peasant food and beneath his dignity to use. A fat raindrop plopped on the delicacy halfway to Glenndon's mouth. More precursors to the storm turned a heel of day-old bread soggy.

Glenndon nearly swallowed them whole. And the now-swelling-with-moisture jerked journey meat Frank pulled from his inner pockets.

"We've got to get the boat higher!" Frank yelled over the roaring wind. He leaped free and began tugging fruitlessly at the bow. Keerkin joined him. His narrow shoulders barely carried enough muscle to lift three sheets of parchment.

Grudgingly, Glenndon pocketed the remains of his

hasty meal and crawled free of the boat. He landed on his knees beside it, the river lapping at his boots.

"This is weird," Keerkin said, able to help Frank now that the boat had lost Glenndon's extra weight. "Floods come after the storm, on high tide and water upstream trying to get downstream."

"Tell that to the storm." Glenndon half-rose, waddling beside them and into the tree line fifty feet away. Surely the river wouldn't rise that far in the few short hours he needed to be here.

"Help me turn the boat over so it doesn't fill," Frank grunted, placing one hand on the edge and the other on the hull.

Glenndon knew Keerkin would be useless at the task. He pulled the last of the bread from his pocket and thrust it into his mouth and chewed while he helped Frank. Together they managed to pull the boat another few feet deeper into the forest and turn it over. If worst came to worst, they could take shelter beneath it.

Then he finished the cheese and looked for more in Frank's knapsack.

"Hey, leave some for us!" Frank demanded, grabbing the stash of food away from his prince.

"Sorry." Glenndon's cheeks burned with shame.

Lightning flashed right over them, near-blinding him. Afterimages of a tall everblue tree splitting down the middle lingered as thunder clapped like boulders slamming into each other during a massive avalanche.

Instinctively, Glenndon reached out with his magic to divert the half tree that broke free and fell directly toward them.

Before he realized he had no magic left to fight the storm or the tree his head exploded in pain, and darkness laced with giant stars crashed around him.

"Mama, I can't find Glenndon," Lukan shouted, running into the garden toward his mother. "He tried to summon me, but by the time I could withdraw from my lessons, he was gone. No trace of him. And the dragons won't answer a call either."

She straightened from picking red fruit—juicy orbs with thin skin that made the driest of stews succulent. Her face blanched and she clutched her belly. "Not again," she moaned.

"Mama?"

She waved at him to assist her. He hastened to take her elbow and escort her back toward the cabin. When he placed the flat of his hand across her waist to support her back he felt the knobs of her spine nearly cutting through her bodice. Alarm over her condition banished his concern for his older brother.

"What do you mean not again?" He was afraid she meant something was wrong with her and the baby. She seemed to wash her personal linen more often than usual. Sometimes when she hung it out to dry she hadn't managed to wash away all of the blood spots.

"I mean Glenndon has this habit of wandering into situations that block his magic. Mostly exploring underground, which he hasn't done for awhile. When he needed to run away, he always sought the dragons and they masked his presence. At least you explore the tops of trees and cliffs. I can always find you." She patted his hand and turned her face up to smile at him. The smile quickly twisted into a grimace.

Lukan scooped her into his arms and carried her the rest of the way into the cabin. All the while his mind screamed for Mistress Maigret to come to his aid. Quickly.

CHAPTER 23

SKELLER LISTENED CLOSELY to Telynnia. Her strings swelled and responded sluggishly to his fingers and the tuning pegs. Her carved wooden frame felt damp. She should be light and joyous now that the shadows surrounding the other half of the caravan were gone.

He certainly felt freer in mind and spirit, except for the heavy air that made his head ache and his sinuses throb.

"I know I didn't drop you in a creek or spill ale on you," he muttered. "What's wrong?"

The caravan master had stopped before sunset, having moved south only a few miles from the crossroads. In the far distance to the west, a dark line at the base of the ridge identified the other half of the caravan, also stopped early. Everyone seemed listless and sad at the separation. Why, he didn't know. Moving away from the stinking shadow beneath Lady Ariiell's litter was a relief. His need to be alone with his music, and his harp had never seemed this strong before.

So he did what he did best: prepared to lighten hearts with a song and put some verve into setting up camp. Only Telynnia wasn't cooperating and his voice felt thick, as if he were coming down with a sore throat.

The harp responded to his ministrations with a discordant twang.

He was about to twist the peg hard enough to break a string when Lillian peeked out of Lady Graciella's litter. His heart lightened despite the oppressive air and his unease about her dependence upon magic.

She looked distressed. He knew she missed her sister. Twins. No wonder they bent their heads together so often, faces moving in reaction to silent communication. He'd known twins in Amazonia who could do that. The closeness of these two seemed stronger. Almost magical.

There was that uncomfortable thought again. Everything in his education and wandering experience had taught him that magic had no value. The effort of doing things with his own hands gave value to a chore.

Lillian smiled hesitantly at him. A soggy grin beneath tear-reddened eyes. He smiled back, trying to reassure her that all was well.

But it wasn't and couldn't be until he managed to fix Telynnia's problem.

He thought he heard a roar overhead that could be wind, or could be a dragon. But the trees near the ground stood upright, branches still, not a hint of a breeze, let alone the raging storm his mind heard.

Carefully he slipped Telynnia back into her case and tightened the strap across his shoulder to secure her. Then and only then did he dare sniff the air.

His nose dried instantly, all moisture evaporated, and banished everything but the scent of dust. Heavy dust. Sharp and coppery dust.

Telynnia should be just as dry, in need of oil on her frame and clear water on her strings. But she wasn't.

His head and sinuses still felt as if smothered in a thorny blanket even though the cloying damp disappeared. Instantly.

He looked up, squinting against the weird glare of sunlight trapped behind a pall of clouds. His heart nearly stopped beating.

Champion pawed the ground and snorted in impatience. The laziest steed in the world impatient? More likely irritated. His eyes showed more white than dark gray and he rolled them in ... fear!

A quick scan of the other sledge steeds, oxen, and milk goats showed them all sidling sideways and braying their alarm. Up ahead the lead stallion reared in his traces. The caravan master was hard put to keep the animal calm.

He'd seen something similar before. On the wide plains inland from Amazonia. The copper-yellow cast to the underbelly of the thickening sky; the sudden flash of lightning setting fire to something within the clouds; the strange taste to the air. And the animals knowing something was wrong long before the humans did.

"We have to circle up now!" Skeller yelled, using every bit of his musical training to pull volume, clarity, and authority from his gut to his words. "Make a circle. Lash down everything. Every tiny pot or length of rope. Lash it down! Now!" His head nearly exploded with the force of his voice.

Frantically he gestured for Lily to obey him. She paused halfway out of the litter, eyes nearly crossed in concentration, facing west. The direction her sister—her twin—had gone. Was she warning them?

He hoped so. This storm was big. Bigger than the horizon on an open plain.

Garg and the other drovers nearby stared at him. At least they'd stopped moving forward.

"Circle up. This storm will kill us all."

Garg looked up at the sky, then assessed the state of the animals. "Ye heard the boy. Circle up or get blown all the way to Hanassa!"

A clod of grass and shrub twigs, ripped up by a sudden gust from somewhere else hit Skeller square in the face, knocking him backward. His last thought was a faint hope that the winds would not begin to rotate, at least not until the caravan was circled, lashed, and secure.

Four masters, three journeymen, and two barely-trained apprentices are hardly enough to conjure the storm. If I had not subverted Master Robb's students, I would not have this many. My place of exile does not value magic. Dragons rarely fly there, granting us their power.

But I have secret ways of entering dreams and robbing other masters of their control, their strength, and the formulae of their spells. I will conquer Coronnan by way of my own power. Return the mighty country to the way it was.

Power may not be enough. Air, water, fire, and the Kardia rage at my control over them. They wish to destroy me.

I need to force that destructive power against my enemies and not allow it to backlash to those who have sheltered us, the Master Circle in Exile.

This storm takes on a life of its own, pulling air and water from the land as well as the sea. The storm spreads north and south of its own accord.

It endangers my magical tools on their journey to the far west.

Only my circle of magicians keeps the storm from breaking east to find more water in the ocean and add that fuel to its fury. I must rely on the talisman my new king granted me. Fitting that the one tool I will use came from Lokeen. This spell, controlled by this ancient relic, will give him the opportunity to increase his political power tenfold.

And I will restore the world to the way it should be, free of the taint of Jaylor and his perverted magic.

I need to break Coronnan, its king, and those who control the two Universities. What will I do if my conjuring destroys everything?

What if it wipes Coronnan clean of all that is good as well as evil?

I will have nothing left to rule over.

I must gather more power, more strength, more control.

I will have to partake of the Tambootie, though it is dangerous. Not as dangerous as allowing this storm free to run rampant where it will. It must go where I will it.

"No, Brevelan, you may not get up!" Mistress Maigret admonished, holding her patient flat on the big bed with one finger.

Lukan moved around to the head of the bed and fluffed some pillows. He didn't know what else to do.

He had no idea where Da had gone, and he didn't truly care to find him.

"But I have a meal to prepare, and laundry, and the hearth needs sweeping . . ." Mama protested. She looked as if she might cry.

"You need to stay in bed or lose this baby," Maigret returned.

"But . . ."

"This is my apprentice, Souska." The potions mistress gestured to a girl near Linda's age to come forward.

Lukan had barely noticed her, other than as another body in the too crowded room. Linda had bustled about, fetching and mixing things at Maigret's direction. He wasn't sure what the girl with bouncing brown curls and round cheeks did.

"Souska comes from a family that expected her to cook and clean and tend little ones." Maigret glared at Linda accusingly. Certainly the former princess had never learned such mundane chores, though she might have tended her younger sisters under the supervision of a governess.

"Nice to meet you, ma'am." Souska dipped a polite curtsy, eyes wide at the honor done to her.

Lukan surveyed the girl as curiously as his mother did. She looked sturdy and middle height under her pale blue robe. Pink tinged those round cheeks and full lips. Mama's gaze strayed to the girl's hands, strong and roughened with many calluses.

Linda hid her hands behind her, but Lukan remembered that her long fingers and slender wrists looked far too fragile to lift more than a decorative ribbon or piece of lace.

"She'll do for you as long as necessary," Maigret continued. "Probably until the babe comes, and I'm guessing he'll come early by the size of him."

Mama's hands fluttered over her belly. Then she looked straight up, as if she could see through the ceiling, loft, and roof to the bilious blue sky above. "The dragons are uneasy. So is the babe," she said, barely loud enough for Lukan to hear.

"Lukan," she firmed her voice and breathed more deeply. "Lukan, go to your master and have the FarSeers look toward the capital. Shayla and Baamin are ... are afraid."

"I've never heard of a dragon being afraid," Maigret said, mouth turned down in puzzlement.

"I have," Mama said. Fear caught in her voice. "The day that Krej ensorcelled Darville into the body of a golden wolf, then left him to die at the base of a cliff in the middle of a snowstorm. Darville was the last living royal link to the dragons, bound to them by tradition, blood, and magic. He almost died. Shayla was afraid that day."

Master Marcus! Lukan screamed in his mind. Then he took off at a run, all approving thoughts of Souska banished, all concern for his beloved mother overcome by the looming threat he sensed in the air and in the silence of the dragons.

"Sir," Mikk whispered to Master Bommhet. They were both on their knees pulling out each book in order, feeling the spine and reading the cover title. Sometimes they had to open a book to find text to know if it was the one they sought. They'd already searched three stacks of books top to bottom, moving deasil around the gallery.

Hours had passed. No light filtered in from the outside; they relied entirely upon glow balls. "Sir, I think the book we seek has been removed from the library."

"If that were so, young man, then I would not see it so clearly in my scrying spell!" old Master Aggelard yelled from his desk below them.

"Perhaps, sir," Bommhet wheezed and spat out some dust, "the book has been moved and cloaked from our view?"

"Nonsense. No master of the Circle would do that. And none of the apprentices and journeymen, either here or at the mountains has the skill and power . . ." He sat in silence for a moment, staring into the distance rather than at his glass within the water. He'd burned through three more candles while they searched and was in need of another.

"What?" Mikk mouthed to Bommhet, knowing now that the gallery was designed to carry the faintest of whispers back to that central desk.

"Politics." Bommhet mouthed back, then set his jaw firmly closed. No more words would explain that.

Mikk had heard enough ranting and slimy manipulating in the Council Chamber over the past three months to know that politics carried a number of connotations, some of them quite vile, others merely the triumph of compromise. He guessed that magical politics were just as convoluted and this particular issue was sensitive. Possibly volatile. He'd get no other answer even if he could read minds like Glenndon could.

"Sir?" Mikk swallowed his curiosity long enough to ask one burning question. "Could the person who conjures this storm have stolen the book and cloaked its absence with a spell?"

"No!" Aggelard shouted. He waved his hand over the bowl of water, mumbled something and peered deeply again.

"Yes," Bommhet said more quietly.

"But . . ." Mikk protested, looking back and forth between them.

Bommhet waved away his protest. "Help me up. My knees don't like squatting so long." He stuck out a long arm for Mikk to grab.

Mikk had done this many times for both his grandparents. He locked his grip around the master's elbow and braced his own arm with his other hand. Bommhet mimicked his action as if he too had had to request assistance many times in the past. Mikk braced himself with a wide stance as he heaved and the magician levered himself upward with a grunt and a wince. When he was on his feet again, he bent double, rubbing his offended knees and brushing away some grit at the same time.

Together they made their way down the spiral staircase, Bommhet stepping sideways and gripping the railing with both hands. Mikk moved slowly, staying two steps ahead of the master, ready to catch him if he fell.

When they stood over Master Aggelard at the center of the ground floor, Bommhet braced his hands on the round desk and leaned forward until he was eye-level with the shrunken form of the ancient librarian. "Master Aggelard, our rival has four masters with him. Almost enough for a full circle. He may have added journeymen to his cause. I suspect they conjure this storm from exile."

"But how could he get the book?"

"He was here before the Leaving." Bommhet slapped the desk vehemently. "He knows this library. Undoubtedly he read the same chronicle you did and remembered it."

"But . . . but . . . how did he get the book now, since our return to the old building and resurrecting the library from all its hidden places?"

"He could not have entered the building unannounced," Bommhet agreed.

"A disguise? Or an accomplice?" Mikk offered, intrigued by the possibilities. No one outside the University spoke of these squabbles. Magicians always, *always*, presented a united front to the outside world.

Mikk had believed, like so many others, that the magical ability to read minds meant that magicians settled their differences easily and reached compromises amicably. Apparently he was wrong. Magicians were just like any other family or group. They fought each other as much as the Council of Provinces did. The recent, but short-lived, civil war among the lords echoed a split in the Circle of Master Magicians.

What other echoes would he find hidden inside this enclave?

"We have to accept that the book is not here. You, sir, have to remember as much of it as possible so that we can counter the spell," Bommhet insisted.

"The city needs to prepare." Master Aggelard's voice quavered. "Even if we break apart the eye within the circular winds, the storm surge already building will flood the city halfway up the palace walls."

"Boy," Bommhet said in his most commanding voice; there might have been a bit of compulsion behind it.

Mikk found himself straightening to show his attention.

"Run to the king and warn him. Set the temple bells ringing. We are out of time!"

CHAPTER 24

THE SMALL CIRCLE of glass, framed in gold, buzzed and nearly bounced out of Taylor's pocket. The noise and smell of fear in the inner room of the cabin had quieted. Thank the Stargods. He wanted desperately to be in there, holding Brevelan's hand, soothing her brow, fetching and carrying for her.

He hadn't been here when she'd collapsed. He'd been closeted with Marcus at the University, just talking about everything and nothing. Wasted time. Wasted energy. He should have stayed home.

And now he needed nothing more than to be beside his wife.

But he couldn't. Maigret had banished him until Brevelan had slept and eaten and slept again. She still slept with Souska sitting at her side. He could give his attention to the summons instead of biting his cheeks in worry over Brevelan.

Maybe he needed something to take his mind off his ailing wife. His *wife!* His companion, lover, friend, helper. The mother of his children. Their lives had been so intricately twined since that long ago day when they'd first met ... here in the Clearing. She with a song of joy in her heart, and he with a mission that lost importance the moment he caught a glimpse of her bright red hair shining like fiery gold in the sunlight . . .

He turned away from the bedroom, holding the frame as if his fingers alone kept it upright, and fished the annoying glass into view. He had to squint and hold the thing up to his nose to pick out a complex twist and knot of five strands of light in varying shades of gray.

Though his sight had improved a bit, he still had trouble making out colors. Magical patterns tended to carry vivid hues akin to the magician's personality. The pattern belonged to . . . no one he could think of offhand, and he couldn't get any clues from the colors.

He had to pause and think who might be summoning him so urgently.

If only Linda had stayed to help instead of returning to Mairgret's lessons. She'd be able to interpret what came through the glass, even if she couldn't receive the message.

Souska? She murmured quietly to Brevelan, urging her to rest some more. No he wouldn't bother her with so trivial a task.

Absently he carried the glass over to the bowl of water and unlit candle he kept on the small worktable by the bedroom door that had become his office while trapped in the Clearing, nearly blind. He snapped his fingers. A spark leaped to the candlewick. When he could discern that the flame had caught and burned steadily he dropped the glass into the water, murmuring a few words that triggered a spell in his mind and carried it to the glass.

These rudimentary skills he could manage. Any second-year apprentice could.

"Master Jaylor?" an uncertain voice came through the spell, weak and unfocused. And yet the signature twist and knot had been solid and strong, if colorless.

"Here," he replied, more curious at the caller's identity than alarmed at the seeming urgency of the rapid buzz that still irritated his physical ears and his mental hearing.

"Boy, we've got problems here in the city!" A face began to emerge through the water and the glass, still not much more than an outline framed in white.

But he knew the voice now. He'd heard it admonishing him on his first day as an apprentice at the University. And there was only one man left among the ranks of master magicians who dared call him "boy." But then Master Aggelard called everyone under the age of seventy "boy."

"Master Aggelard, what sort of problems?" Jaylor replied, relaxing a bit. This he could do, sort out problems and delegate others to implement his solutions. But he hated delegating. Hated sitting on his arse while others went out and did.

"Remember that traitorous bastard Samlan?" The voice came through stronger now, the old librarian's age no longer coloring the tone.

"How could I forget?" Jaylor said, his sense of achievement vanishing, turning him once more into an inadequate student.

"He's conjuring a storm that could destroy the city. Flood it above the five hundred year mark."

(Do something!) jumbled dragon voices yelled in the back of Jaylor's mind. *(Before this storm destroys everything we have built.)*

(Save Glenndon,) a calmer but saddened dragon pleaded. *(You have to save our boy.)*

"Glenndon!" Jaylor wailed. The son of his heart, if not his body, was in danger and he could do nothing.

And the twins! Were Valeria and Lillian far enough away from the city to avoid the storm? He needed to do something.

He couldn't leave Brevelan.

But if any of her children were in trouble she'd not rest and heal as she needed to.

(We can't get through the wall of air!) the dragons wailed.

Jaylor sank onto a tall stool in despair. If the dragons

could not get through the wall of air, then Jaylor doubted he could with a transport spell. Even if he could see well enough to build up the layers of visualization to determine his destination and the tricky timing of sunlight angles and shadows.

He couldn't leave Brevelan.

"Glenndon?" Aggelard asked. He obviously hadn't heard Jaylor's silent communication with the dragons. "Nothing wrong with the boy that I know of. He's a magician. A strong one. He can take care of himself. It's the city that's in danger. We're facing a massive storm surge and flooding. It may wipe out everything. Even the islands grounded on bedrock."

Jaylor gulped, forcing himself to think beyond his personal anguish. "A big storm," he said as much to himself as Aggelard. "How big?"

"Don't know. Clouds too thick to see a horizon. And those damn clouds are soaking up every bit of dragon magic I can gather."

"An unnatural storm."

"That's what I just said, boy. Are your brains addled?"

Jaylor didn't dare tell the old man the truth, that without his sight he felt stupid, sluggish, old, and useless. With Brevelan ailing he was lost and uncertain.

"Keep me apprised of what is happening. I'll get you help. Gather a circle, even a small one, and try breaking up that storm." Jaylor rose and bent to blow out the candle, thus ending the communication.

"That's what I'm trying to tell you. Samlan has a circle. By the look of things, a big one. And he's drawing every scrap of dragon magic into his circle and forcing it into the storm. We don't have any magic left."

"Can anyone in your university tap a ley line?" Ley line magic didn't compound exponentially like dragon magic did. But if enough magicians fought the storm with the same spell in different directions, they might catch Samlan off guard. Might whittle away at his power.

"This is worse than anything planned by the Coven,"

Aggelard said tightly. "They at least wanted the land intact. Samlan will wipe away all trace of humanity and civilization."

"Alert the king, I will do what I can from here." This time he didn't await a reply and blew out the candle as he began gathering tools and plans into a carrysack.

Where was Linda? He needed help. Now.

As he reached to pull the glass from the water, it bounced up and down and shimmied with another urgent summons. Violet. The colors in the glass showed a chaotic swirl of lavender, violet, and bright purple.

Valeria.

Why could he see her colors but not old Aggelard's?

(Because you love her. Because she carries your blood,) Baamin reminded him.

Stargods! Had the storm grown so wild that it threatened the caravan, nearly a week outside of the capital?

He relit the candle, desperate to know what was happening. They'd talked late last night. Had Krej and Rejiia threatened her in any way?

The colors disappeared from the glass and the water. Just vanished as if swallowed.

And why were the dragons so worried about Glenndon. Val and Lily were of more immediate concern. S'murghit he needed his eyes to sort all the tangled threads.

"Jaylor?" Brevelan called from the bedroom, weakly. Anxious. "What's happening?"

"Nothing you can help with, dear heart," he said, leaning on the doorjamb. "I'm needed at the University. May I borrow Souska for a few moments to guide me there?"

"You are lying, dearest. I always know when you are lying. Tell me. Now. Tell me why the dragons are afraid."

Souska seemed to fade into the woodwork and scuttle into the big room at the same time.

Resigned, he apprised Brevelan of the two summons.

"Val and Lily!" Brevelan gasped as she collapsed back into the pillow that propped her up, little more than

an outline beneath the sheets. What little color was left
in her cheeks leached into the bedding until it was
brighter than she. Her hands cupped her belly protectively. They clenched as if the baby twisted and fought
confinement in her womb.

"Glenndon too," he admitted, beginning to worry in
his gut about their children. If the dragons were afraid,
then something dire plagued all of Coronnan. The storm.
An unnatural storm conjured by magicians.

A storm bigger and more dangerous than anything in
their history.

Brevelan reached for him. He eased beside the bed,
knelt on the floor and clasped her hand against his lips.
"Dear heart." He kissed her fingers, letting her know
how much he cherished her, needing to lend her whatever physical and emotional strength she needed. She
clung to him desperately with fingers that felt like claws.

"Our children will be alright. They have to be. All of
them. They are strong and resourceful. If nothing else,
they know how to hunker down and protect themselves
and then deal with the aftermath," he reassured her. And
himself.

"It's just . . . just that . . ." She swallowed deeply and
buried her face in his shoulder. "They are all my babies.
And the dragons are afraid."

"I know. I know." He rested his chin on her hair, surprised to find the dark red silk brittle and dulled, partly
by gray but also . . . something else.

He rubbed her back. Her ribs and shoulder blades
made sharp ridges beneath his hands.

"Brevelan, my love, something is wrong with the babe.
With you. Maigret wouldn't say, only that you needed
rest," he said, tightening his hold on her.

"Yes . . . maybe . . . I don't know. That is no concern of
the moment. You are needed. You have to go to the University. Do what you can to save the world. And save our
children if you have a moment to spare for them. It is
what you do. What you need to do." She pushed him

away and flopped back onto the bed. "I'll ... Souska will have a meal waiting for you when you come home. I have a feeling you're going to need it."

Valeria hunched over a goblet, barely big enough around to allow her shard of glass to float on the scant inch of liquid. Wind rocked the litter so violently she dared not light a candle and had to rely on a tiny flamelet on the palm of her hand to send the summons skittering away across the plains to the foothills, along a rapid river and up several waterfalls, through the forest to the fishing village on the bay and then uphill along a twisting path to the Clearing.

"Da!" she shouted, barely hearing herself over the howling wind. She should be able to smell the clean scent of everblue sap. All her nose detected was dust and rotting magic. "Da, I need your help."

The glass bounced and hummed in the water, setting a buzzing along her veins and in her head.

The spell shouldn't do that. It should move silently until Lord Jaylor acknowledged it. Then she'd hear his words, see his beloved face, and he'd hear her plea for help.

She pushed her magic through the glass again, knowing that she channeled too much of her strength into the spell. She might not have enough left over to survive the storm. Not enough to make contact with Lillian and hold on for dear life.

"Can I help?" Lady Ariiell asked hesitantly. "I know the forms even if I haven't worked such a spell in ... in many years."

Valeria looked up at her companion, barely sparing her enough attention to raise her eyebrows in question. "This spell is basic. One of the first we learn. Surely you could have used it to speak to friends and family outside your tower." She concentrated on the glass, willing her own violet colors to shift into Da's brighter blue and red neatly braided through the reflection of the flame.

"I didn't dare." Ariiell's voice quavered as she gripped the frame of the litter with both hands. One heartbeat later the entire structure wobbled under the force of a particularly strong gust. Something beneath them splintered. The litter listed and dropped with a shudder that bent the frame. A wave of noxious odors rose from the crates upon which the litter had rested. She wrinkled her nose, not bothering to sort out the too-sweet, too-sour, sharp and acidic odors that burned her nose and made her eyes water. She'd smelled that before, but different. A flash of heightened smell and hearing when she had assumed the form of a flywacket—a cat so black her fur took on purple highlights and her feathered wings shimmered with iridescence. For half a heartbeat she was back in that body, able to separate and discern each component of every scent.

Then it was gone before she could identify it. She only knew it made her gag. So much so the flamelet on her palm flattened and nearly guttered.

Her will and fierce concentration kept the fire alive with the essence of its primary element.

"Rejiia and Krej could easily eavesdrop on the conversation if I tried to summon someone. Or interfere and make me do things they wanted but I didn't while I thought I talked to my father," Ariiell admitted, also wrinkling her nose at the disgusting odor.

"Now I'm glad I never spoke to him. He'd have only sold me to someone else earlier ... before ... before I had your help. Remind me to thank you when this is over."

Val stored that bit of information, not having the time or attention it deserved. Right now she needed to get through to Da.

At last the colors in the glass swirled, folding her purple tones in with Da's braid until they were all mixed up, indistinguishable one from the other. That shouldn't happen.

Then the colors dissolved, bleeding out of the glass into the water that supported them.

Surprise at this oddity overcame her cautious routine. The magic broke loose from the spell and backlashed while she was still pushing new power into the summons.

Lightning ripped across the skies, grabbing hold of her magic and sending it flashing through the enclosed litter, burning and savaging everything in its path.

Light and pain penetrated her mind through her temples, all the colors swirled into one white blinding flash of lightning.

"Valeria!" Lady Ariiell screamed. "Don't you dare pass out and leave me to the mercy of this storm and my enemies."

CHAPTER 25

(SAVE OUR BOY!) old Baamin's dragon voice echoed again and again in Jaylor's mind.

"When did he become your boy?" he shouted back. Slowly, he swept his staff before him in search of obstacles that might stand between him and the path to the University. Souska had insisted she couldn't leave Brevelan, even for a few moments, let alone long enough to walk the half mile to the University and back again.

(You know,) replied the man who had commanded the University from Jaylor's earliest days as an apprentice. The man who had personally handed Jaylor the position of Chancellor of the University and Senior Magician upon his deathbed, and then sent his spirit off to become a dragon, to live out his destiny. A destiny foreseen only by dragons.

The words beat a path inside Jaylor's mind, much as his feet beat one through the underbrush of the forest. "Glenndon was conceived in the void."

A sense of agreement in the back of his head.

He flew back in memory to the night he'd experimented for the first time with leaves of the Tambootie tree. No one had written about the essential oil in the leaves that boosted one's perceptions, one's magical talent, and one's sense of invulnerability. He'd eaten too much and crossed into the void, the true realm of dragons, without knowing how or where, or anything more than the wonder of finding hundreds of colored umbilicals that represented the life spirit of everyone he'd ever known, alive and dead.

Darville and Brevelan had thought him dead and sought comfort together. Their love for each other and for Jaylor had reached out into the void and found him, returned him to his body.

In the wondrous aftermath, none of them, except perhaps the dragons, knew who had fathered the child Brevelan carried. At the time they didn't need to know. As the baby grew it became obvious. His coloring, his build, even his speech patterns, telepathic as they were, mimicked his true father.

But his magical talent surpassed all expectations. That had always given Jaylor hope that some small piece of himself had become a part of the boy. Brevelan had a strong talent rooted in the Kardia. Her affinity with plants and animals was often overlooked as a magical gift. King Darville, Jaylor's best friend and comrade in mischief, had a touch of talent, but only a touch, just enough to allow the Coraurlia, the glass crown given by the dragons to the rightful kings of Coronnan, to recognize him.

Where had Glenndon's talent come from?

"The void. The dragons gave him what he would need at the moment of conception," he whispered. Yes, Glenndon was as much their boy as Darville's. Or Jaylor's. They all claimed a piece of him.

(You finally figured it out,) Baamin admonished him, much as he had when Jaylor finally threw a spell correctly during his apprentice years. *(About time. Now what are we going to do about our boy?)*

"Whatever we have to." Jaylor set his steps more firmly and promptly stumbled over a stump. He wasn't on the path. "Linda!" he roared. "Linda, I need your help." He hated admitting it. He felt small and useless needing a child to guide him.

Then he remembered Linda had returned to the University for her scheduled classes.

"Lukan!" Maybe the boy was lurking around home. He'd taken off again the moment Maigret had proclaimed Brevelan stable and in need of sleep. No one had seen much of him since . . . since Jaylor had gone blind. "Lukan, I need you," he said more softly. Contritely. He really needed to reconcile with the boy.

"Lukan's gone," a small voice said to his left. "Let me help." Sharl slipped her tiny hand into his and nudged him half a step the right.

Amazing that she sounded so calm with her mother ill and in bed. Had anyone looked after her and Jule since Brevelan collapsed?

"Mistress Maigret told me to take Jule to play with her boys. She didn't say I shouldn't come back to help you," she said. A little uncertainty crept into her voice. Jaylor held her hand tight.

He shouldn't be surprised that she had understood his thoughts, even though he hadn't spoken. She was his daughter after all. "Thank you, Sharl. You are a big help." He moved another step in the direction she indicated.

Immediately he felt the difference in the ground through the soles of his boots. The dirt on the path had been packed hard and solid by the passage of feet over the years. Off the path he felt only the softness of broken saber ferns and composted leaf litter. He tapped his staff on the path, memorizing the vibration through the wood to his hand. Then he tapped off the path and felt the tip sink in a bit.

"Thank you, Sharl," he repeated. He allowed his little girl to guide him even though he now felt more confident that he could manage on his own.

Like combining and throwing dragon magic, he had more power to negotiate the forest with help.

In that instant he understood the source of the storm that caused the dragons so much agitation, felt the wall of clouds, permeated with magic and every drop of moisture they could gather. The rogue magician who manipulated air and water like child's toys had a dragon bone, like the one in Glenndon's staff. Only it was a big bone, possibly a shoulder or thigh, or an entire leg bone, and he used it to hold all the magic he and his circle— probably standing in a half circle to contain the back edge of the storm—could gather. With a storage place for the power, the rogue and his companions could do much, much more than just throw wind and rain.

The enemy controlled all four elements, combined them, and inflicted massive destruction well beyond his reach.

"Stargods! Lily and Val are in as much danger as Glenndon."

He paused to gulp back his trepidation.

"It's okay, Da. You'll figure it out," Sharl reassured him.

The faith of a child. Her faith in him strengthened his wavering courage. He couldn't fail. He had to save the twins and Glenndon for their own sakes, his own, and their mother's. But he also couldn't fail because a six-year-old had faith in him.

"Baamin, I'm going to need some help. Bring every dragon to the University."

(Not enough room.)

"Then perch on the roofs and in the trees. We've got work to do. A lot of hard work."

Wet. Soaking wet. Wet running off his face, down his neck ...

Glenndon blinked to clear his eyes. Gloom lay thick among the shadowed trees. Silhouettes wavered and blurred. He took a cautious breath to make sure he wasn't underwater.

Memories of Lucjemm trying to drown him in a pit on Sacred Isle pressed against the logic of knowing he'd survived that incident with the help of a Tambootie tree and his staff.

"My staff?" he croaked out.

"Beside . . . you . . . sir," Frank said gruffly, back to him. He drew a deep breath between each word.

The wet continued to soak Glenndon to the skin, chilling him to the bone. His teeth began to chatter.

"Almost there, sir," Keerkin reassured him. He too seemed to be working very hard to breathe around his words.

Glenndon remembered to look for his staff. Beside him. Where was he and . . . His hand found the rain-slick knob at the top of the length of twisting wood. He found the three smooth circles that had been the anchor point of twigs. Then his fingers reached down and around. The straight dragon bone embedded in the wood felt warm and reassuring and . . . dry.

Dry? In all this wet? The swaying edges of the trees began to make a little sense. If his men carried him. But he swayed, rather than bounced.

"Found it!" Keerkin crowed. "Fox den in an old tree, burned nearly hollow at the base." He jerked his head to the right.

Frank angled that way. In five heartbeats—Glenndon counted them, not able to decide what else to do—he found himself lowered to the ground and rolled up against a tree trunk, facedown. His right arm stretched farther than it should if he was against a solid tree.

Wiggling his fingers, he found a crumbling edge to a triangular opening. A fast-moving fire, long ago, must have damaged the tree, scorching the bark. Over the years the tree rotted behind the damage but continued to grow upward, healing and compensating for the hole.

"Anybody home in there?" Frank yelled, beating against the trunk with a rock.

Something small and furry scurried over Glenndon's fingers and exited. A small rodent had taken up lodging. Nothing as big as a fox.

"Can you get inside, sir?" Keerkin asked, neatly folding a blanket. The blanket the men must have carried Glenndon on.

"Where did you get a blanket?" Glenndon's mind was still as fuzzy as his eyesight.

"I've gotten to know you, sir, over these past few months. When you say your errands will take a couple of hours at most, something always happens and we're gone most of a day. Or night. Never fails. My da says your father was the same way. Your da . . . um . . . Lord Jaylor too, for that matter. I always have extra food, water, blankets, and bandages in my pack."

"Always?"

"Always. Even for a trip to Market Isle. Now crawl in there and feel around. Should be big enough to shelter all of us if you don't mind rather close quarters."

"If it will get us out of this rain, I don't mind." Glenndon reached around the opening. At least four feet high and five across. Must have been a bad fire. Then he leveraged himself to his knees and crawled forward. His shoulders cleared the edges. Three more cautious knee-steps forward before his head brushed something semi-solid. A shift of balance and his left hand was free of the soft nest of rotting wood, shed fur, and decaying leaves. Stretching it forward, he encountered a layer of spider-webs before reaching solid wood. The tree was huge. Not unusual on Sacred Isle, where the trees were considered holy and no one dared disturb them, except journeymen magicians on quest for a staff or priests performing arcane rituals.

He turned and sat with his back against the charred wood. Only a faint hint of smoke reached his nose. He brushed away a layer of wet from his face and banished the smell. Only an echo of memory from the tree.

"Come on in. Nice and cozy," he called, drawing his knees up to his chest to make room for his companions.

His head ached and his eyes didn't want to focus. Something about a tree splitting after a lightning strike . . .

He felt around the back of his head. His skull ached before he encountered a thick knot. His hair seemed stuck in the mess. Just touching his barely retained queue sent needle pricks all over his scalp.

"Um . . . Frank? About those bandages . . ." He felt the two men crawling in beside him, one on each side. He didn't care which was where, only that their combined body heat lessened the chill threatening to invade his bones.

"Later. We need to figure this out, sir."

"Figure what out? It's a storm. A bad one," Glenndon dismissed it. That didn't sound quite right. If only his eyes would focus properly.

The inside of the tree was darker than the gloom outside. He could barely see outlines and the opening in the tree.

"A storm fueled by magic, sir," Keerkin said quietly, as if afraid to venture an opinion.

Memories flooded back into Glenndon. He gasped as he relived the oppressive weight to the air, the irritation of every sensitive spot on his body, and the ugly copper color of the cloud underbelly. Copper shaded with sulfur.

"How bad is it?" he asked, wondering how long he'd been unconscious.

"The river is receding," Frank said flatly.

"That's good."

"There's an awful lot of water coming down." Keerkin's voice sounded as if he'd turned his head away from the conversation.

"And the tide was still coming in . . ." Frank sounded as if he wanted to say more but something held him . back.

"The river was rising when we beached," Glenndon countered them.

"Now it's not."

"What does that mean?" He wasn't sure he wanted to know.

"Storm surge," Frank said. He sounded firm, as if

there were no other explanation. He knew the river better than Glenndon or Keerkin. He'd grown up in the city with all its tales and lore.

"Explain," Glenndon demanded.

"The eye of the storm is still offshore, gathering energy."

"Gathering water," Glenndon finished for him. "Pulling water from the Bay and the river."

"Aye."

"And when it has gathered enough and moves toward us?"

"It will release that extra water in one gush."

Glenndon closed his eyes and gulped. He did not want to visualize a wall of water engulfing the city, drowning the islands. Washing away thousands of people. The king and queen, his half sisters. His family!

"How big?" he finally whispered.

"Don't know, sir. Stories tell of a time before the covenant with dragons and Quinnault became king with his foreign wife, Katie. A battlemage had lost a battle he should have won. He was angry. Wanted revenge. He conjured a storm."

"Like this one?"

"Maybe. No one knows for sure. The rain fell for days and days. People moved to the mainland or the bigger islands with some height to them. It wasn't enough. When the surge came it wiped out everything. People, buildings, animals, everything. When the water receded—in almost as big a gush as it came in—the only things left standing were the old keep and the monastery that became the University."

"That's a lot of water," Keerkin breathed.

"We have to get back to the city. We have to warn everyone to evacuate, or climb higher." Glenndon rocked forward, shifting to crawl out of their refuge. He ignored his aching head and the new trickle of warm blood from the wound.

"Can't do that, sir." Frank held him back with one

hand. "Nothing can cross the river now. Not without magic. And with that knot on your head, I doubt you can even give us a bit of flame to light this hole."

"How high are we?" Keerkin asked into the darkness.

"This tree is older than the stories. If it stood through the last storm, it'll stand now. It's got big roots that spread far and tangle deep. Land might wash out from around it, but foxes know the best trees to nest under. We'll be safe."

"It's a Tambootie tree," Glenndon said. Maybe even the same tree that had sacrificed a branch to become his staff. He held his instrument up, anchoring the tip in the soft ground and willing the dragon bone to glow with enough light to show him the truth of his statement. An eerie green light shone upward, almost high enough for him to stand upright at the center, sloping to a short ceiling on the sides. The cave had ample room for them to fold their legs under them and sit comfortably, shoulders touching.

"We'll be safe." He knew it in his soul. But would anyone in the city survive?

And who would dare conjure such a storm?

He'd worry about that later. First he had to warn the city. No tools for a summoning spell, or a scry. He had more than enough water and could probably find a puddle just by sticking his head out the opening. But flame? It probably wouldn't stay lit outside and he wouldn't insult this wonderful tree with another fire.

He drew in a deep breath on a count of three, released it on the same count. Again. And a third time. His headache lessened. His companions and the confines of the shelter faded from his awareness. He accepted the welcoming embrace of the spirit of the tree; let his mind mingle with its memories. He knew everything the tree had endured, from the drying up of the ley lines that fed its magic, to the welcome of the dragons nibbling on upper leaves, to the long cold of winter and triumphant burst of spring. And the fire. The pain that continued even after the flames had moved on, consuming underbrush and wildlife and leaf litter in a hungry dash, moving before the wind that drove it.

He lifted his mind through the tree and beyond. He let the magic essence contained within its sap fuel his quest for a receptive mind. "Queen Rossemikka? Stepmother?" he whispered across the miles, knowing her mind could receive him.

His words drifted away, dispersed within the clouds. More magic adding fuel to the storm's rage against confinement by a mage. It needed to move, surge in one direction or another, but the mage kept it in place, forcing it to gain more energy. Destructive energy the storm didn't want.

A very powerful mage with a determined circle behind him controlled the storm. No solitary magician could have that kind of power unless standing within the Well of Life. The liquid energy of the source of all ley lines would fry a magician, burn him to ashes in a moment.

Glenndon knew only one master magician with the audacity to try conjuring such a storm.

Samlan. In exile with a few other masters and journeymen. Not enough for a full circle.

Or was it?

With the right spell, the same spell, and a way of tapping both ley lines and dragon magic, he might be able to do it.

"Da!" he called. "Da, you have to do something. You must gather every master you can to fight this thing," he called into the air, hoping that somehow, someone would be able to pick his thoughts out of that pall of clouds laden with as much magic as rain.

CHAPTER 26

THE STORM HAS wrenched control from me and my circle. It has become a living entity whole unto itself. A greedy being, never satisfied. The eye has become a great maw, opening bigger and bigger with each passing moment. It pulls in air and water across a much broader expanse than I had planned. Even with a full circle and the artifact gifted to me by my sponsor in Amazonia I cannot control this monster.

The ancient bone drapes across our arms, connecting us far more efficiently than staffs and hands upon shoulders. The tool allows us to open into a half circle mimicking the back edge of the swirling mass of air.

I fear that the magic the storm has sucked up will damage my other weapons, the ones entrusted to my ally deep in Coronnan.

I must leave it all in the hands of the Stargods. Perhaps even they cannot control this thing.

Perhaps the Amazonians have it right. The Stargods are new to the pantheon of Kardia Hodos. My protector and his people believe in the Great Mother who created this world. She and her magical creatures were here long before people. Long before the dragons. Long before the Stargods.

I will offer this magnificent tool of magic to her in sac-

rifice. We will release our spell and cast the tool over the side of our ship. It will float and circle within a whirlpool, gathering energy from the churning waves. Then it will sink reluctantly, taking the maelstrom with it. The Great Mother must grant my petitions and tame the fury of the storm. It is no longer mine. Even the magic I gathered is no longer mine. It is all in the artifact. Savage, untamable, waiting for another mage to find it at the bottom of the ocean. And use it. For the bone's purpose. Never at the whim of a mere human.

The destruction and havoc this storm wreaks is the will of the Great Mother. Not mine, not the dragons', and definitely not the Stargods'.

The litter draperies billowed inward on the side facing away from the caravan circle. Lillian grabbed hold of them to keep her balance as the entire conveyance tilted again, threatening to tip into the circle of sledges.

Lady Graciella screamed and clutched her belly.

"The babe?" Lily called anxiously, over the roar of the wind. She dropped her death grip on the fine tapestry to lay her palm flat over her companion's stomach.

The rapid, steady throb of a heartbeat tingled against her hand. Graciella's neck pulse, however, fluttered arrhythmically against her skin. Too fast. Too light. The woman's panic radiated from her in thick waves that nearly infected Lillian.

She closed her eyes and willed her own heartbeat to a strong and steady rate. Just as she had so often with Valeria. Giving strength and soothing the panic of one too weak and spent to breathe normally was her only magical talent. She'd practiced it a lot over the years.

Soon she could no longer hear the thud within her, only the roar of the wind above, below and around them. When she looked toward her companion, Graciella had visibly calmed as well.

"We need to get the curtains open," she said matter-of-factly. "They act as sails. We may find ourselves flying away like dandelion fluff."

"Did ... did you grow up around boats?" Lillian asked grabbing a big handful of brocade and dragging the inside drapery to one corner, securing it quickly with a thick strap meant for that purpose.

"Yes." Graciella tugged fruitlessly at the outside curtain. The assault from the wind came strongest from that side. At the moment. Lillian rocked to her knees for better leverage and reached to help her. Their hands touched.

A jolt of magic burned through Lillian's fingers and up her blood to her shoulder and down the other arm.

A frightful image of Lucjemm, with the hideous black snake draped around his neck filled her mind on the heels of that energy transfer. Gaciella's fear became Lillian's. Something about that snake ... A Krakatrice, she knew now. Her father and brother had killed the female—obvious from the six wings sprouting from her spine, too tiny to help her fly at the time. But they would have matured along with her. The distant cousin and strongest enemy of the dragons.

"We killed the matriarch." She sank back on her heels, nearly overwhelmed by her companion's emotions.

"Did you?" Graciella asked, blandly.

Lillian knew in that moment that the lady had spent so much time hiding her memories and her fears that she couldn't react to her own emotions.

"Yes. I watched Da and Glenndon blast the beast with more magic than I thought existed in all of Kardia Hodos. She burned to ashes. There weren't even any bones left."

"Was she the only matriarch?"

"I ... I don't know. King Darville banned the importation of any more of their eggs."

"Easy enough to smuggle in a cargo. One box of eggs could start a whole new tangle."

Lillian gulped, smelling again the taint of foul magic gone awry, the burning flesh and blood, and ... and she didn't know what else, only that it made her nose crinkle in disgust and a need to run far, far away from it. "Can't worry about that right now. We've got to secure that drapery and get into the middle of the circle, or under the litter. We aren't safe here."

With renewed purpose she helped Graciella with the brocade. The second it opened even a small slit, the wind found its way to them, billowing the remaining fabric inward. Folds and folds of the heavy stuff covered and wrapped around Lillian's head. It squeezed her neck, much like the chokehold of a snake. Or a Krakatrice.

She couldn't breathe. The brocade carried the hideous scent of the black snakes.

Gasping and choking she clawed at the material.

Graciella screamed.

Lillian fought for calm as well as a reprieve from the smothering brocade. A ragged fingernail caught on a loose thread, ripping both. Not caring about the burning pain around her bleeding quick, she pulled and pulled again until the tear in the fabric gave her room to breathe, enough air to think.

Quickly she found the edge and unwrapped the clinging folds before they took on a life of their own.

"There's magic in that storm," she said.

The growling wind seemed to agree.

She ripped faster until she could wrestle free. The rotten odor of Krakatrice filled the air and her head: too sweet, like fermenting apples, with an overlay of intoxicated skunk, sulfur and sorrow.

She reached to grab Graciella and exit as fast as they could.

The lady was nowhere inside the litter.

Mikk pelted down the stairs from the rear courtyard to the narrow postern door of the palace. No time for formality. No time to think. No time to worry. He had no idea if Geon had followed him or not. If the tall servant had pocketed the book from the library or returned it.

That didn't matter. Getting the palace organized and safe did.

He skirted scullery boys with their dirty pots and kitchen maids with armloads of vegetables. "Gather food for a week and get it to the top level of the palace and the old keep. Water too!" he shouted in passing.

The kitchen grew silent and still. Dozens of gazes landed on him. "Do it! The flood of the millennium is coming."

Immediately a busy bustle began as people scurried and ordered and organized. They knew about floods. They knew what to do.

"Sh . . . shall I ring the bell?" a boy of about twelve stammered.

"Yes."

"Not before the king orders!" returned a senior cook.

"Wait and you'll drown. By my authority as cousin and second heir to the king, I order you to sound the alarm!" He turned and dashed upward toward the formal rooms on the ground floor. Before he'd touched the first step, a solemn, deep-throated gong sounded from the old keep. The lighter and sharper Temple bell from the palace compound picked up the series of long and short peals and spread them to the next tower and the next.

The scullery boy was still rooted in place near the exit.

Good. Someone else in the palace knew about the flood.

That didn't slow his steps. He continued upward, thankful for the hard exercise General Marcelle had forced upon him to build up his wind.

He didn't bother pausing on the first landing and darted across the carpeted minor hall between this servant stair and the formal staircase, which rose broad and proud toward the semiprivate offices and suites on the next story.

In his hurry he grabbed the knob on the railing and used it as a lever to swing around the bottom step and up in one smooth motion.

Except ...

He barreled into Lady Miri as she descended.

He grabbed her about the waist. They teetered a moment, staggering and clinging for balance.

"What is all this fuss?" Lady Miri asked imperiously, as if he were a mere servant. She smoothed her skirts and patted her hair to make sure her tiny cap and veil were in place.

"Not now." Mikk wanted to scream at her. The urgency of his mission pulled his attention upward, toward the king. "The alarm bells. A massive flood is coming."

"The river is receding, a bit rapidly, but heading out to the Bay," she replied, still holding her nose in the air, and not just to look at him on the step above her.

"Receding?" He felt the blood drain from his face, leaving him slightly dizzy. "That makes it all worse. The storm is pulling all that water outward, as fuel for its fury. Then it will push it all back, at once. Master Aggelard said we haven't seen anything this bad in five hundred years. I wonder if there has ever been a storm and flood like this before." He grabbed her shoulder as the nearest solid object to hang onto.

"What? What can we do?" She looked pale. A trace of panic crossed her beautiful brown eyes. But she mastered it and held firm.

"Gather the princesses and their ladies and anyone else. Take food and water, medicine, bandages, whatever, and get to the top level of the keep. Get up there and stay up there until the king says it's safe to come down." He gathered his energy and pushed himself to separate from her. He had to rely his own balance.

"Can I trust you to do this?" he asked quietly, not yet certain of his ability to climb.

"Yes." She whirled around decisively, grabbed his hand, and pulled him upward. "This is what I was born and bred to do. Take control in an emergency and see that as many people as possible get to safety."

She left him outside the king's office and continued upward to the private suites and the two young princesses. "She'll make a grand queen someday," he whispered, then pushed his way into the king's presence.

"Where is everyone?" he asked empty air.

"Mounting steeds in the forecourt," Lady Chastet said, coming up behind him, breathless but attempting to remain calm.

Mikk sighed in relief. He should have known the king and queen knew about the storm, and the impending crisis. But . . .

"They don't have time to get to higher ground on the mainland." He turned and dashed back the way he'd come.

At the bottom of the grand staircase he skidded across the floor toward the wide double doors, left ajar in someone's haste.

"Your Grace!" he called, gasping for breath on the edge of the landing. His boot toes tipped over and downward. He willed himself to stop even as he prepared his balance to keep moving forward if he had to.

King Darville glanced his way as he boosted Queen Rossemikka into her saddle. She looked so frail and pale sitting astride the tall chestnut steed that almost matched her bright, multicolored hair, undulled by the pelting rain. He realized in that instant that in the last few months she had regained some of her youthful vibrancy, but not all. Never all of it. Age and illness had taken its toll.

But she still cut an awesome and majestic figure when she needed to.

The king looked almost as magnificent. His loose four-strand queue leaked strands of wet hair and his crown—the heavy Coraurlia that protected him from magic, not the little replica he used for day-to-day appearances—sat a bit awkwardly and atilt upon his head. But his tunic was clean and unwrinkled though wet from the deluge pouring from the sky.

"Your Grace, Master Aggelard sent me," Mikk gasped, ignoring how wet and uncomfortable he was from his run across the islands and now standing in the open.

"The flood?" Queen Rossemikka demanded.

"Yes, Your Grace."

"It's worse than we thought," King Darville said as he prepared to swing into his own saddle on the white steed—a very visible and commanding animal. The right steed for a king who demanded attention.

"Yes," Mikk admitted. "Nothing like it in five hundred years. That storm and resulting flood was also mage-born. The chronicle of the spell used is missing. That one was conjured by a single rogue magician. This one is commanded by a circle of magicians," he blurted out. No time to make it sound nice and polite, within royal protocols and formality.

The queen blanched and the king looked up toward a dirty line across the middle of the old keep tower. The last remnants of the old flood, one hundred feet up.

"We have no more time, my dear. We must get as many people clear of the city as possible." King Darville swung his leg over the steed's back and kicked it into motion in one smooth movement. The queen followed him out the gate; at the last moment she leaned over and grabbed trumpets from awaiting heralds.

"Do you need me?" Mikk called after them, not knowing quite what to do now that he'd delivered his message.

"Look after my daughters!" the king called back. "Their safety is your responsibility. Live up to your potential as a leader," the king added, his words fading as he put distance between himself and the safety of the palace.

CHAPTER 27

"EASY, CHAMPION," SKELLER sang to the huge sledge steed, more a hum beneath his breath than an actual song, but music of a sort. Music that would force the beast to listen to him.

Dried grass, small branches, feathers ripped from flusterhens' hides, fabric, and anything else not tied down, lifted free of the Kardia, spun, and gave in to the relentless pull of the air. Skeller's eyes burned from the dust pelting him. Every inch of exposed skin felt scraped raw at the constant assault.

"Easy. I need you to listen to me and not your instincts. I know you want to run. Be smart just once in your life."

Champion rolled his eyes showing more white than dark gray iris. He pulled against Skeller, nearly ripping the bridle from his hands.

"Don't you dare rear and bolt!" Skeller forced into his song every bit of authority he'd ever heard his father yell. "I promise you there are no spotted saber cats hiding within that wind." He didn't know what else might be using the wind as a mask. The spotted saber was supposed to be the only predator big enough and mean enough to take down a steed of this size shod with heavy iron.

At last the steed began to calm. He still shied and shifted his weight right and left, forward and back, but he seemed to listen to Skeller. Accepting him as leader of the herd.

"Good, boy. Now, down on your knees. Down, down." Skeller tugged on the bridle, just so, to ease Champion onto the ground. Champion resisted, knowing that up was safe. Up gave him the opportunity to run from a predator. Up offered options. Down did not.

"Listen to me. You cannot run from the wind. Especially this wind. You need to be down. I need you down to shelter me. Together we are safe. Listen to me!"

Reluctantly Champion dropped lower, first onto his front knees, then his rear legs folded. Finally he settled his body upon the ground and he tucked his head around to the side away from the relentless wind.

Skeller crouched on the lee side of the beast and took a deep breath, temporarily free of the wind. His lungs stopped straining and his chest eased enough to let his heart slow to a more natural rhythm.

Then he chanced a look over the steed's back. Drovers right and left were urging their animals to follow Champion's example and taking refuge from the storm on the inside of the circle. A few managed to drag goats and caged flusterhens with them. He knew the animals, large and small bleated, cackled, neighed, and threw out a deafening ruckus. He saw their mouths working and heads bobbing in their distress.

He heard nothing over the malicious roar of the wind.

Then he saw Lily flailing with the smothering curtains of the litter. Lady Graciella didn't seem to have stayed to help her companion.

"Stay!" he ordered Champion.

The steed sort of bobbed his head in compliance. Skeller couldn't be sure how long he would obey. Hopefully long enough.

He left his harp within her case beside Champion. With a little luck the steed would accept her presence as a minor substitute for Skeller himself, and the wind could not grab it from his back and use it to strangle him.

He drew a deep breath and dashed toward the litter. Only a few feet away. He bent double, battling the wind for every inch of ground.

He persevered, gaining one step forward for every three he took.

The wind fought back, pushing him sideways and back, driving him away from his objective. He had to close his eyes to barely a slit and drape his sleeve across his mouth and nose to keep the dust from smothering him.

Using every bit of strength he'd built up from years of working caravans around Amazonia and her territories, he gained ground and reached the litter at the same moment Lily stumbled out, smacking the ground with her face.

He braced himself on the flimsy litter frame—meant to support curtains, not withstand a storm a quarter of this magnitude—grabbed hold of Lily's collar, and pulled her to her feet.

She clung to him, frantically turning her head right and left in search of Lady Graciella.

"Have to find her!" Lily screamed into his ear while holding onto his leather jerkin with both hands in a death grip.

"Not safe," he screamed back. Then he whipped around putting his back to the wind and dragged her to his shelter behind Champion.

Just in time. The steed's hide quivered with fear. He rocked forward, trying to get his feet beneath him.

Skeller did his best to calm the animal with touch and hum while shoving Lily to safety.

"She'll be killed," Lily sobbed the moment he dropped beside her.

With one arm stretched along the steed's side and the other wrapped around Lily's shoulders, he fought for control. Breathe in, breathe out. Steady the chest and throat as if preparing to sing his heart out.

He draped Telynnia's case strap around his neck and under his arm, shoving it between his back and Champion's side. They might crush the fragile wood and strings, but the wind could not steal her away from him.

"Lily, listen to me. We might all be killed before this storm blows itself out. We have to save who we can. For the moment, that's us. And Champion."

A mighty cackling screech made them both duck their heads into their knees tucked tight against their chests. Overhead a crate containing a brace of hens and a rooster flew into the wall of spinning compressed air.

Cautiously he looked up to see a sky full of yellow-brown dust to the south and a sharp edge of black, water-sodden clouds to the north. As he watched, the dust merged with the black and curled east and north.

A curling edge began to form, pulling the air into a wide rotation.

"Great Mother, no!" he breathed. Numbing cold ran from his belly outward.

"What?" Lily demanded around trembling lips.

"A giant tornado, ten times bigger than any I've ever seen. And it's merging with a ... with a monster storm from the sea; a storm so big no one has seen the like. Ever. This land is doomed."

Lily's arms tightened around his waist as she buried her face in his chest. "Hurricanes I've heard of. Even little ones can be deadly. But a tornado?"

"A dry hurricane, moves faster, pulls everything in its path up and up and up and then spits it out miles away." He shivered all over.

"What? How? Val! I can't find Val! She's never more than a thought away."

"Great Mother, protect us." He dropped his face to capture her mouth with his own. "If we die in this moment, let us die together with the taste of each other in our minds and hearts." He kissed her long and deep, yearning to hold her even closer in an act affirming life rather than accepting death.

Mikk stood on the open parapet of the highest tower of the palace. Even up here in the open he was not alone. Refugees from the city had poured in, all day. They did not all fit inside the palace above the second floor. The ground floor was too vulnerable to the storm surge. A full dozen city dwellers shared his lookout. Every other tower, many long abandoned and only today reopened, also contained wet and wailing people driven from their homes. Many came with words of praise that the king and queen had personally saved them from the coming flood, or curses that the king and queen had rousted them from their homes and places of business without reason, or forced them to leave their most precious possessions behind, bringing with them only food, medicines, and vessels for collecting water.

"Eighteen jugs," he muttered. "Not enough." Each vessel resting on the uppermost stones collected rainwater. They ranged in size from twenty cups to three.

Below in the courtyard, Mikk made out a mixed team of citizens and soldiers pumping more buckets and tubs full of water from the well. From the bits and pieces he'd gathered from Master Aggelard's rambling account, he knew that the flood, when it came, would rush into the city with dirty, brackish seawater in less than an hour. The tides and flow of the river would need weeks to push it *all* out again. But the inward rush would be followed quickly by an outward surge just as damaging.

There would be no more fresh water than what they gathered once the wall of water drove across the Bay and crashed over them.

He already smelled the dying fish, rotting seaweed, and varying amounts of salt as the river retreated, mixing with the bay and ocean, churning together in a giant maelstrom.

The cistern was the key to survival. Something was wrong with that, a distant memory, something he'd read, or something else. . . .

He suddenly remembered a time when he was still a small child and a spring freshet had undermined the cistern at the home of his grandparents north and west of here on the mainland, but still within sight of the river. The cistern had flooded with dirty, unfiltered water. Grandfather had to order the entire system flushed and a new catchment basin dug ...

General Marcelle, the king's commander-in-chief, dragged himself into the palace courtyard, urging a new line of citizens forward and upward toward safety. He was as wet and bedraggled as any of them, exhausted as well, but he still stood straight and tall and authoritative. Except ...

Except that he limped, barely putting any weight on his right leg. He used an upended spear for support.

"General!" Mikk called down to the man. The wind whipped away his words. The drumming rain on the stone absorbed any sound.

King Darville and Queen Rossemikka were still out in the city. They'd left Mikk in charge. He was tired and uncertain he'd done everything he could. He knew he'd not done enough. What had begun as a point of pride had quickly wound down to desperate searches for what to do next. He wished for paper and pen to make lists. He wished for a sense of organization and accomplishment.

Desperately he needed older and broader shoulders to take some of the burden from him.

Mikk ran down the slippery spiral stairs, barely keeping a hand on the rail for balance. Round after round he pelted downward, as fast as the rain. Not fast enough. When he finally reached the formal entryway he found it crowded with milling refugees, bewildered, frightened, and without direction.

"Up!" he shouted, pushing them toward the broad marble staircase. "Up above the flood line." He cleared the final steps and urged more people up.

The moment he spotted a clear space, he sprinted

through the crowd outside. General Marcelle had just placed one weary foot on the bottom step and paused, gathering his energy to put weight on the damaged right leg while he lifted the other.

Mikk saw a ragged tear on the general's trews, a mat of blood and badly bruised flesh. Something about the shape of the kneecap . . . *Stargods!* he'd either broken or dislocated his knee. 'Twas a wonder he'd managed to walk this far.

No time to commiserate or wonder. Later. When all were safe Mikk would tend to that wound himself if he had to.

"Sir, is there a way to block the cistern so it doesn't flood with seawater?" he asked, not certain he'd chosen the right words, or even the right question.

The general frowned as questions, brighter than the pain haze, flashed across his eyes. "Oh, shit!"

Then Mikk saw panic in the man's mind. He'd asked the right question. And knew he would not like the answer.

CHAPTER 28

GLENNDON FORCED HIMSELF to think. Hard. Very hard to do, what with the wind howling in circles above him. The rain pelted every hard surface as if it were a tightly strung drum, adding a strange and off-rhythm counterpoint. And thunder. Rolls and rolls of thunder that sounded like every dragon bugling at the same time!

He cringed with each peal, imagining dragons fighting the wind and bellowing their discontent and pain.

And then there were the walls of near-blinding lightning that revealed the white and frightened faces of his companions.

What could they do but hunker down and wait out the storm. Wait for the wild clash of magics to resolve on their own.

If only his head didn't hurt so much.

If only . . .

The staff at his feet began to pulse with power. It had been inert since the storm began, as if the storm sucked all the magic from the land, the dragons, and him. What was the white dragon bone doing pulsing red in time with his heartbeat? Why was his heart returning to a normal rhythm after the excitement and fear of enduring the hours of being battered by this unnatural storm?

He drew a deep breath and winced as his head ached with new pain. Something was changing. He didn't need to think to know that. But why?

And why was he so sensitive to that change?

He had this massive, living tree sheltering them against the storm. With that much wood between him and the elements he should have a solid barrier protecting his awareness as well as his body.

He took a deep breath, measuring the steady in, hold, out, hold. Two more to center himself and ground his magic in the Kardia. The tree hollow seemed to smooth out and curve to the shape of his spine and the back of his head. He rested easily, letting the life within the tree merge with his consciousness. Part of him dug deep with the roots, tangling with the land and the rocks, reaching deeper and deeper, anchoring against the onslaught of wind and rain, repulsing the burning lightning. This tree had learned long ago the pain and loss of becoming victim to the living fire that shot from the sky.

Then he sent his awareness upward along the trunk, feeling the way its skin rippled as the wind threw pebbles and branches torn from other trees at it. They bounced against the resilient bark. Its own branches bent and flowed with the ceaseless and relentless wind.

It had learned from experience, this magnificent tree. It had learned not to stand rigid and defiant, for that presented a solid wall for the wind to push against. Now it channeled the air around it. The roots too shifted a little bit here, a little bit there as water creeping up from below ate away at the dirt that held it in place.

Rising water. Vanishing dirt.

Glenndon brought his mind back into his own body trying to assess if their den remained safe. If this tree toppled when the water completely undermined the root system would they be safer outside or in.

A gentle reassurance washed around him. His staff gave off a whiff of The Tambootie, its parent tree. This tree had sacrificed a branch to Glenndon for a staff. It would not let him down now. It had needs that only Glenndon could fulfill. It needed Glenndon as much as Glenndon and his companions needed the tree's shelter.

He checked his staff. The bone continued to pulse red, as if stained with blood, or blood red light. Or. . . .

He shifted the staff so that the tip pointed toward the opening of the den, an opening that no longer faced the lee of the storm, but remained open to the grinding destruction that pelted them from all directions at once.

Yet none of the rain or lightning penetrated an invisible wall across that opening. None of the water creeping up from below reached the soft nest of leaf litter, crumbling wood, and clumps of animal fur and feathers.

The staff shot away from him toward the entrance, stopping abruptly when it reached the opening.

Like to like, it seemed to say to him; demanding that he release it so that the bone could join its like.

"Tell me I did not just see that," Keerkin said on a violent shudder. "Or hear that. Staffs are tools. They do not have minds of their own. No other magician can steal it from its master. It has to be surrendered voluntarily." He spoke as if reassuring himself rather than informing the others.

Glenndon chuckled, despite the danger in their predicament. He trusted the tree to protect them as long as it could, but even trees this formidable had limitations. Limitations he needed to be aware of.

Still, the tree was Tambootie, the channel between the magic within the ley lines and the dragons. The staff was the child of this tree.

What were they trying to tell him?

A tree of magic. The tree could give him magic while the storm sucked the dragon magic out of him.

Before he could move to the next thought a shaft of burning crimson light shot from the dragon bone at the top of the staff out into the chaotic wind, driving a path upward into the sodden clouds and met a bolt of lightning. Fire to fire. Magic to magic.

The two forces met and exploded into a blinding starburst.

Release me! it demanded.

Glenndon held on to the base of his staff though it bucked and fought his grip. The magic within it twisted and fought his hands with heat.

He cried out, but still he clung. Keerkin placed his hands over Glenndon's, adding his strength and minor talent. Desperately they sought to contain the magic.

Another pulse of light near-blinded Glenndon. He had to let go. He couldn't. His hands felt as if they had melted and merged with the staff, never to be parted again. Together forever, for good or ill.

Right now he felt very ill. Very ill indeed.

And frightened.

"Do you smell that?" Lillian shouted over the howling wind, neighing steeds, screeching flusterhens, and bleating goats. Noise all around her. The sounds of terrified creatures and humans. The odor must be especially noxious to penetrate her thoughts above the mind-consuming racket.

Skeller wrinkled his nose and sneezed out dust. He shook his head. "Too dry to smell," he called directly into her ear. Then he tightened his arm around her, pulling her down until she kissed her knees as they ducked for the fifth time in as many minutes to avoid flying debris. This time it looked like a fish pulled out of the dry stream, or maybe just a waterlogged branch.

The storm had wicked all the moisture from the creek, from the air, and from the land.

Champion, the solid sledge steed, writhed and tried to rise and bolt. Skeller soothed him with a caress and a firm word. Champion still quivered with the need to run away from this very nasty predator. Reluctantly Skeller wiggled his jerkin off from beneath the harp straps and fashioned it into a blindfold for Champion. Instantly the steed settled, though his nostrils twitched and his skin still rippled.

Around them, the other drovers did the same for their own frightened steeds.

"There is definitely something rotten in the air that wasn't there before," Lillian insisted the moment he settled back beside her, not certain if Skeller heard more than every other syllable.

He shrugged and encouraged her to rest her head on his shoulder, his shirt cool and wet beneath her cheek. They watched the circling air another moment, crying inwardly as trees, rocks, and more animals succumbed to the sucking power of the wind. Darkness began to fall, discernible only by a shift in the density of the clouds that covered the sky from horizon to horizon.

"Fermenting apples and a skunk getting drunk on them," she said, trying to separate out the scents within the malodorous air. A renewed gust of wind wrapping around the continent so that it could reach the Bay and the center of the chaos brought the smell more intensely. She nearly gagged.

It came from the west. The same direction Val had taken with Ariiell.

"Val!" she gasped. "Val, where are you?" Lillian turned her head toward the source of the foulness. Her heart lodged in her throat. She shifted to get to her knees and send her thoughts to her twin.

Skeller yanked her down again. "You can't do anything now! Even if you can get to your feet without being blown over, you can't walk into the wind. It's too strong. You have to wait. Think and wait. You are not a steed too frightened to know what is safest!"

Lillian blinked tears out of her eyes, as much in fear for Val as from the dust and the sharply acrid smell. "There's magic underneath the rot." She wasn't sure if she said that or merely thought it. The raging wind yanked her breath out of her body faster than she could draw new dust-laden air into her lungs.

Magic. Rot. Her mind jerked back to the dreadful battle in the middle of the University courtyard. Jaylor and Glenndon had joined their magic and their staffs to control the geyser of pure energy shooting up from the Well of Life. Val was still in her flywacket form in order to heal, while a large black snake with six leathery wings along her spine advanced with her cohort of mates, killing all that stood in her path. She aimed for anyone with magical talent to feed upon their blood. Queen Rossemikka and Princess Rosselinda looked particularly enticing with their dragon-blessed royal blood and magical talents.

Lillian and Val had done their best to help two elderly magicians uproot the iron pole sunk into the Well. The iron poisoned the magic in the raw energy and drove it into eruption.

But those snakes? Krakatrice. Enemies of dragons. They thrived in arid climes and actively worked to build dirt dams that channeled rivers away from their territory, turning vast acres into sere desert. A thousand years after their destruction by the Stargods, the Big Continent was just recovering fertility beyond the damp coastline.

Last spring the matriarch Krakatrice—not fully matured but still nearly ten feet long and as thick as a twenty-year-old tree—had smelled like the air that assailed Lillian from every direction at once.

"Stargods! Those damnable snakes are invading Coronnan. Who would dare?"

Surely Skeller must have heard about them in the lore of his homeland.

"What?" Skeller demanded. He grabbed her by both shoulders, digging his fingers into her flesh with frightful urgency. "What about snakes?"

"Krakatrice," she breathed. "They smell just like that." She pointed west, toward where her silent sister had traveled.

"Great Mother. He wouldn't dare." Skeller dropped his head, resting his chin on his chest.

Lillian reached to smooth his tangled hair, darkened by sweat. It wasn't long enough to pull back into a proper queue, not that the wind wouldn't rip it free of any restraints. Her own braids and stray strands whipped into her mouth and eyes anytime she tried to peer around the solid bulk of Champion.

"Who? Who wouldn't dare?" Instinctively she knew she needed this information and had to pass it on to Da. But how could she do that with Valeria so far away and unable to penetrate the magic that permeated the dust clouds? And Lukan? Where was her brother when she most needed him? He'd been silent for days, neither sending nor receiving calls from his sisters.

Never mind, she'd find a way. When the storm was over. For even a Krakatrice could not move through this unnatural storm. Unless they were the source of the storm, creating a desert here as they had done across the ocean.

"My father's chief adviser, a magician from Coronnan. He seeks to destroy your king and his magicians. I don't know why, only that he advises the King of Amazonia with subtle smirks and prods to break the alliance and build his army for invasion," Skeller confessed. "They have offered a bounty for any dormant eggs found in the desert. They are using the snakes to subdue their enemies—make them cower in terror before an invading army."

"Your . . . your father is a king?" Lillian gulped, barely hearing anything other than that.

Skeller nodded.

"And you're a prince?" Her daydreams of finding a future with him withered into dust as dry as the stuff pelting them. The untalented daughter of a magician and a woods witch could never aspire to linking with a foreign prince. He had other, higher-born ladies awaiting him. Eagerly.

"Not really. In Amazonia—actually all of Mabastion— men aren't supposed to rule, except through their wives.

Father usurped the throne from Mother when she passed. I have no sisters. He'll have to give up the throne to my cousins sooner or later. But until then he rules in his own perverse way, and now he listens to a magician bent on revenge. We don't have much use for magicians. Early queens banished them to solitary towers and never listened to them. And . . . and King Lokeen plots to marry a highborn woman who will give him a daughter so that he can continue as her regent."

"Samlan," Lillian said flatly.

"Who?"

"A rogue magician who defied my father in a circle of magicians and left with a small cohort of masters and journeymen. We didn't know where he went. Now I know. I have to tell my Da." She looked around again, anxious to find a bowl and a flame to join with her tiny shard of glass. But there was no water left anywhere and the wind would extinguish any form of fire in a heartbeat, if she could manage to light one.

"If your Samlan was banished a few months ago, he can't be Lokeen's adviser. That magician has been in and out for years. He'll stay a week, or a month, then disappear, and come back again just when we think he's gone for good."

"A few months ago he moved to Amazonia permanently?" Lily asked. "Could Samlan have been working against Da all those years, and not just recently?"

A long silence grew between them as the truth registered in her mind.

"We can't just sit here. We have to do something," she finally insisted, gnawing at her lower lip as she discarded plan after plan.

"We can only wait. Later . . . Great Mother . . ." He blanched.

The putrid smell of the Krakatrice took on the added flavor of burning flesh. A slithering line of black approached from the west and south along the ridgeline.

CHAPTER 29

LUKAN WAITED OUTSIDE the changing room until all the apprentices had left, chatting excitedly, their pale blue robes swishing as they walked rapidly toward the courtyard.

They all seemed so young. And naïve.

Well, they were young. Younger than he. All of them.

When the last of them scurried after the pack, a boy of about twelve, holding the skirts of his too-long robe bunched into both hands (boys always grew into their uniforms, usually within a few months of arriving), Lukan sidled into the long, low room, lined with racks for hanging robes wrinkle-free. Three robes per apprentice—two sturdy but roughly woven ones for everyday, since one of them was usually in the laundry, and a formal one of finer weave and brighter color—took up a lot of space. Neat bronze plaques with names etched onto them marked the area reserved for each apprentice.

Lukan had started using this changing room, along with the other students who lived in attached dormitories, two years ago. Having his robes hanging with the others, rather than in his attic bedroom in the cabin, made him feel like he belonged here.

Today he wasn't certain where he belonged. Mama was ill. He needed to be with her. But Marcus, his master, had called every apprentice, journeyman, and master in residence to the courtyard, in formal robes for an important working. Girls along with boys. That meant ley line magic, since girls couldn't gather dragon magic. Or both. He wasn't certain.

Perhaps he didn't belong at the University at all. But Mama needed him here.

Da certainly didn't.

"I can do this," a faint, feminine voice whispered.

Lukan froze, one hand stretched to grab the fine cloth of his robe—it was getting too short and narrow in the shoulders for him. He'd have to petition for a new one soon.

If he stayed here beyond Mama getting well.

Cautiously he peered around his rack to find the lingerer.

Souska sat on the floor, nervously picking loose stitches from the hem of her robe.

"Of course you can do this," Lukan said gently, not certain when concern for the girl had overridden his constant anger.

She looked up at him with frightened eyes. "No, I can't." A tear leaked out of the corner of one blue-green eye.

"What are you afraid of?" he asked, crossing his legs and lowering himself to the floor in front of her in one slow movement.

"I . . . I can read and write, and mix potions and ointments. I can wash and cook, but I can't really work magic," she cried.

"Can't you? Why were you sent here then?"

"Because . . . because I sing while I cook and wash clothes and tend the garden, and my stews are always more savory, my bread lighter, my clothes cleaner, and my yampions bigger than anyone else's," she said quietly, almost afraid to admit it.

"That's what my mother does," Lukan reassured her on a chuckle.

"Lady Brevelan?" She turned those blue-green eyes up to him in amazement. The film of tears across them made her looker younger, and more innocent than she should be at this age.

"Yes. Lady Brevelan, my mother. That's the only kind of magic I've ever seen her throw. Kitchen magic. She's a woods witch, according to University records."

"But she's so much more! I've learned more about healing magic from her than from Mistress Maigret, even though she only comes to our classes once a week rather than every day."

"Yes, Mama is much, much more than a woods witch. You can be too. You'll have something to add to the spell, or. they wouldn't have called you away from Mama's side. Who is with Mama by the way?"

"Two of the newest girls who *really* have no talent, but their villages wanted to get rid of them," she said sadly, dropping her chin and those lustrous eyes once more.

In the long corridor outside this room, he heard the orderly tramp of many feet, heavier feet than the entire herd of apprentices. The journeymen were moving into place.

"Come on. We have to get going." He stood and offered her his hand as assistance in rising.

"What . . . what if I can't do it?"

"Then sing. That's what Mama does."

"Sing what?"

"Whatever comes to mind."

"You should be a teacher here." She took his hand and rose gracefully, more graceful than he.

"Not likely to happen."

"But you are good at finding what I need to know and how to go about it."

"Perhaps." Lukan stalled by grabbing his fine robe and slithering into it. "But I sincerely doubt my place is here much longer." In that moment he knew he'd leave soon, with a journey or without. He'd only stay as long as Mama needed him.

With both hands, Mikk grabbed hold of the end of a slimy rope as thick as his wrist. Three men-at-arms took up positions before and behind him. He no longer cared that they dismissed his slighter frame and lesser strength in this odious, but necessary chore. The weight of responsibility rested on his shoulders, not theirs. He had to help any way he could.

To his left another line of soldiers readied a duplicate rope. Ahead of them two metal doors sagged open into the overflow tunnel, five feet above the cavern floor and sloping upward. It ran between the river and this giant hole in the ground, carved out of bedrock—or maybe a natural cavern enlarged by men—lined with gravel, that normally held half of the city's water supply. Now it contained only enough water to slosh miserably at his ankles and impede his solid stance.

Even as he watched, natural seepage through the purifying limestone around them began refilling the cistern.

An eerie silence filled the cavern. The breaths of seven men echoed against the limestone.

"Ready?" General Marcelle asked from his position between the two lines of men. He held firm to his spear grounded in the muck to prop him up. Lines of pain etched his face, but didn't affect his straight shoulders or the firmness of his voice.

"Ready," replied the two men at the head of each line, the men closest to the doors and the counterweights that would allow the doors to close inward and then drop their panels into the cavern. The press of water from the outside would keep them closed. The panels would prevent most seepage of contaminated water into the fresh cistern.

"On my count." They all drew deep breaths and anchored their feet. "One, two, three, heave!"

Together, all six men handling the ropes leaned backward, feet dug in, arms and shoulders straining to haul the heavy counterweight stones out of their semipermanent embedment in the gravel and muck.

The rope shifted beneath Mikk's hands, ancient fibers shredding and burning his palms. Months of sword practice hadn't built enough calluses. He wanted to cry out and let go.

He couldn't. This was too important. He counted in his head all the people in the palace and keep depending upon him and these few men to get those damn doors closed before the rush of water, filthy and brackish, poisoned the city's water supply.

He prayed with all of his heart that Master Aggelard had directed his magicians to do the same with their cistern. They had magic. Mikk had only these few men and their physical strength.

"Heave!" General Marcelle called again. "Come on, lads, I can see the stones wiggling free. Just a little more. Put your backs into it. And heave."

Mikk's vision closed to a single bright circle centered on the lime-encrusted stones. All else turned black. Starbursts appeared between him and the stones. Still he hung on, adding whatever strength and weight he could. His hands burned. His shoulders ached. His feet wanted to slip. And still he held on, concentrating. Willing those stones to move so the doors could slide shut.

"Heave," the general grunted.

The rope moved. The men stepped back cautiously.

The doors inched toward each other. One foot. Two feet. Six feet each. Only a few more inches to go and they would meet in a firm join. The moment metal touched metal, a series of crossbars would clear to drop in place to hold the doors against the onslaught of water. Those bars would save the city.

A scream from the front of the line.

The rope went slack. Then whipped and whirred through his hands, taking two layers of skin with it. At least.

A heavy plunking sound and the counterweights sank back into their familiar resting place.

Mikk dropped to his knees, cradling his hands beneath his arms; pressing against them to ease the pain. He saw other men, hardened soldiers all, doing the same.

The rope floated in the water in many pieces. All of them frayed and rotten.

The doors remained stubbornly open. Less than a foot gaped between them, stuck and out of alignment. The crossbars and panels couldn't drop. Any minute now, the storm surge would hit them . . .

Mikk's ears popped, filled, and popped again. Something was changing up above.

"All of you out now. Up the ladder. Don't waste any time. Get yourselves to safety!" General Marcelle yelled, fixing a stern gaze on each of them.

"You first, sir," Mikk croaked. "You need help with that knee."

"Precisely. I'll hold you all up. Don't argue with me. Get. Out. Of. Here. Now!"

The men scrambled to obey.

Mikk oozed to his feet, reluctant to infect his hands with the water rising around his knees. He knew what he had to do. "It's my responsibility," he whispered. His belly went numb even as his mind focused clearly on what he had to do.

"Leave, General Marcelle," he said, more firmly than he thought possible. "I can slip through the opening and push the doors closed so the crossbars can fall into place."

"No." The general gave him a level stare. "I can't climb. Doubt I can walk more than three steps. But I can push. You are needed up there." He gestured toward the metal ladder with his spear, looking every bit as authoritative as Lord Jaylor wielding his magical staff.

"Sir, it's my responsibility . . ."

"Your responsibility is to the people up there. I'm old and useless with this knee. You are young and hale. Now get out of here."

"Sir, at least . . ."

"Now." The older man turned away from Mikk and heaved himself onto the ledge of the tunnel, then twisted sideways to inch his way through the narrow gap.

Mikk couldn't hold him if he tried.

"Thank you, sir, on behalf of Coronnan City and King Darville, I thank you for your years of loyal service and your sacrifice."

"Remember what I taught you, boy. And when you get into trouble, take half a heartbeat to think 'What would the old general do?' Do that and you complete my legacy. That's all I ask."

"I can do that, sir. And I'll make sure Glenndon does too."

"Good idea."

Tears streaming down his face, Mikk jumped to the ladder and scrambled upward as fast as his tortured hands and weary legs could take him.

The last thing he heard as he pulled himself up the ladder was the crossbars sliding into place on the inside of the cistern.

CHAPTER 30

JAYLOR TOOK a deep breath to steady himself. In the bright light of midafternoon he could see more details surrounding the University courtyard than he thought possible—even if they still lacked color. Eleven other master magicians stepped onto paving stones, each etched with a rune that echoed the pattern of their magic and the twisting or curling of their staffs.

Journeymen and apprentices grouped behind their masters in the grassy spaces beyond the formal working area, closing a second circle. He noted the silhouette of his son, Lukan, hiding directly behind Marcus, visible only by his aura. That was the one bit of energy that showed clearly to Jaylor in full color. Why?

No time to puzzle that out right now. They had work to do.

Taking another deep breath, praying for grounding and the steadying of his heart and his magic he took one ritual step forward onto his own stone. The pattern of a twisted and knotted braid tingled against his bare feet, welcoming him. He tapped the stone with his staff as an announcement that he was ready.

"Dragons, we await you!" he called into the air, pulling magic and strength from his gut into his mind and mouth.

Immediately the constant howling wind from the south and east that tossed the tree canopy shifted, quieted and reawakened in a new pattern of up and down drafts.

Jaylor, Senior Magician and Chancellor of the University, fought the urge to cringe and duck. "Nothing to fear," he whispered to himself.

(Or so you want to believe,) old Baamin chuckled as he dropped gracefully onto the roof ridge of the main building, more alive than an elegant statue but fitting, as if he belonged there. Forever. Fitting, as Baamin had once ruled the University and the Circle of Master Magicians. Jaylor saw only the darker wing veins, tips, and spinal horns as a darker gray than the slate roofing tiles. Comforting to know that his old master and mentor joined him in this critical spell.

Another flurry of wings disrupted the flow of air that wanted very much to continue pushing north and east around the eye of the storm. Shayla, the magnificent all color/no color iridescent matriarch of the nimbus settled beside Baamin. He knew she was there more from the pulsating air around her than actually seeing her crystal fur that reflected light and sent his gaze around her. She almost glowed.

She twined her long neck with her mate affectionately. With all of his dealings with dragons over the last twenty years, Jaylor had never seen such intimate interaction between his friends. Perhaps, at long last, the land and the Tambootie trees were healing enough that the dragons considered mating again.

Later. He needed to get on with the work of the day.

Six more dragons sent the air scurrying around them as they descended to treetops, hilltops, and boulder tops. Eight dragons. Was that enough to counter the magic sucking wind?

"We have gathered in company with the dragon nimbus to balance the elements that have been disrupted by rogue magic with arcane tools. To counter this disruptive force we need all of the members of the Circle and their students. Are you all here?" he called in his most formal manner to those present.

"Aye!" Marcus replied in ritual fashion by pounding his staff against his paving stone, anchoring it with his right hand and reaching with his left to connect to the next man.

Each master in turn replied in the same way until Jaylor was the only one left to respond. He anchored his staff on the stone and placed his left hand on Marcus' shoulder. The beginning stages of a trance grabbed his mind and opened his mind's eye. For the first time in days (weeks?) his vision cleared. Colors popped into view with startling clarity. Without looking, he sensed his fellow master magicians doing the same.

When they finished, the journeymen tapped their staffs to the ground and joined left hands to shoulders in a wider circle. The apprentices standing between the two circles touched each other and their master's back. Then the journeymen edged closer so that the base of their staffs touched the heels of an apprentice.

Only three other times in Jaylor's tenure as Senior Magician had so large a Circle been called together to work Great Magic. Wonderful Magic. Necessary-to-save-Coronnan-Magic.

"Dragons, are you all here?" he continued the ritual, relieved and hopeful that this might work.

(Not yet,) Shayla replied, nearly startling Jaylor out of the spell's unity.

Another flurry of wings, much louder and more disturbing than any one dragon, no matter how large, could cause.

A quick peek with his real eyes revealed the outlines of a dozen more dragons in all sizes, from a small pony to massive sledge steeds, descending from above. They settled here and there on rooflines, atop boulders, or on the ground.

Jaylor breathed deeply, the magic in the air thickened,

tasted strongly of the Tambootie. He felt almost as if he were drowning in the stuff. He stored as much as he could in the special place behind his heart. He filled his lungs and his brain with the palpable energy. And still there was more, and more. His fellows around the Circle drew in as much as they could. And still there was more magic, ready for them to tap.

And then the world seemed to pause for a deep breath. When all within the Circle had exhaled, another dragon appeared. A little one, silvery baby fur still shining within crystal strands. Dark, dark blue, with hints of purple refracted from his tips.

"Indigo," Jaylor breathed. "A purple dragon, rarest of all, most prized by both nimbus and Circle. We welcome you."

Indigo lifted his wings straight up, changing his control of the thick air, and dropped into the center of the Circle with a ruffle of feathers and fur. He'd matured and learned more grace than the last time Jaylor had seen him, when the juvenile dragon had whisked Princess Rosselinda away from a blood-maddened mob in the city to the safety of the University.

As he thought of the princess, he was saddened that none of the women had joined the Circle of Masters. They could not gather dragon magic.

Except . . . except Maigret now led a line of twelve women, three master magicians and their journeywomen and apprentices. All of the women currently in residence. All except Brevelan. His heart lurched a moment in worry. Then he forced himself back into his ritual role. Brevelan had commanded him to save the world. Therefore he must. For her. She alone could command him away from her side.

Maigret ducked beneath the massive circle of men and boys, followed by her entourage, to form their own circle around Indigo. The young dragon preened as each female took hold of one of his spinal horns and then reached out to also hold the staff of a master. Lastly,

Princess Rosselinda, just Apprentice Linda now, with her mane of multihued hair bound tightly at her nape and covered with a light blue scarf to match her robe, caressed Indigo's nose with sincere affection and reached out to clasp Jaylor's staff.

"By my bond with Glenndon, through blood and magic, I greet you." She nodded her head formally to Jaylor. "With your permission, I join my magic to yours and thus to all gathered here." She tilted her head to include the dragons as well as the quadruple circle of magicians.

With those few words she had ritually cast off her former life as a favored royal child and accepted life in the University.

(Anyone can gather magic from a purple dragon,) Indigo reminded them all proudly, but also with mature formality.

(Now we are complete!) Shayla trumpeted vocally and mentally.

"To work, my friends," Jaylor ordered, feeling immense satisfaction. This was why Nimbulan of old had formed the first Circle of Masters. A long chain of history had led Jaylor to this role. He was honored and humbled by the intricate connections. A part of him reached across the distance to connect to Brevelan and bring her awareness here. She was as important to the circle as he.

When a slender thread attached him to her mind, he sent a small shield wall of magic upward and outward until he touched a similar wall raised by Marcus. Tricky. They had to take it upward into a dome as they always did, but also back behind them to include the junior circles. Strangely, he felt an assist, almost a lubricant, emanating from behind Marcus.

Lukan! his mind shouted with joy as he recognized the boy's aura melding with his own. No time to congratulate the boy. No concentration to spare as he accepted the merging of each master and journeyman around and within. A complex lattice grew and grew, encasing each worker individually and as a whole, bringing the dragons within as well.

"We seek the eye that commands wind and sea to flow around it, as magic flows around our circle. We seek to know and understand the force that directs the eye. The powerful eye that does not work on its own. The eye that pulls all the elements out of balance," Jaylor chanted, near-singing the words he had formed in his head.

The masters repeated his words with him. The younger magicians chanted them on the third round. The dragons joined in the fourth, and then once again all the voices and minds in the compound circled with the magic to confirm their goal.

Power built with each repetition. A spear of light grew above the lattice, drifting aimlessly, turning this way and that, seeking direction. It swirled energy of all colors and patterns around its immense shaft, growing tighter and tighter until it nearly shot off under its own volition. Then Jaylor led one final shout: "Seek the eye."

The spear shot up, trailing multihued sparkles that remained in the air, marking its path.

Images at the tip flew back into Jaylor's mind. He pulled details of forest, meadow, and river from the arrow back into the minds of each of the participants. The path descended from the foothills, out across the plains and cultivated land, out and out, past the outcropping from the sea that formed one boundary of the Great Bay. Out further across the surging and seething water.

Raging winds tugged at the arrow, seeking to absorb its energy as it gathered all else by command of the eye. Jaylor pushed with all the combined magic of dragons and magicians. Pushed with a power far beyond what any one of them could command, more than the simple addition of one magician to another. A multiplication and compounding of all their magic. Power greater than the wind circling around the eye at ever-increasing speeds at the outer edges of the storm. Air moved faster and faster closer to the eye. At the edge of the eye the wind covered tens of miles every minute. It hovered, waiting at the wide mouth of the Bay where lighter water mingled with the heavier and saltier water of the ocean.

Jaylor dared not breathe lest he and the spear lose control and come within the power of the eye.

With a mighty effort of his wide shoulders, barrel chest, and keen mind, he forced the spear east. East beyond the reach of the storm that pulled all air and water with it, sucking up the water within the Bay, drawing down the mighty River Coronnan. East to the spot where a boat writhed against its anchor, beyond the reach of the storm, but not by much.

A half circle of men gathered on the deck of the big, deep-keeled boat. They held something that glowed a malevolent, pulsating black with red flashes of lightning within it.

He'd found the eye. Not the eye of the storm, the eye of magic.

Five men. Five masters by the colors that formed around them. Masters by their black robes trimmed in blood red. Three journeymen positioned between them, they wore red robes trimmed in streaks of black lightning. And two apprentices in gray trimmed with black and red.

None of them held a staff.

Instead they cradled a bone. A long bone, or series of bones that looked like a spine.

Shayla gasped in shock. Baamin echoed her. They tried to flee the circle.

Jaylor yanked the two dragons back before their children could flee in fright as well. He held them as firmly with his mind as he held his own staff and the massive magical spell created by his circle.

(Krakatrice!) Baamin gasped, as if he found breathing difficult.

We have fought the live beasts before and killed them.

We can do it again, Jaylor proclaimed to one and all assembled.

(You do not understand the power of death and the bone,) Shayla said weakly. *(A bone turned to stone by time. Ancient beyond ancient. It holds all the power of the centuries.)*

Jaylor understood her need to disconnect from that formidable bone.

I understand. I know the power within the gift of a bone from one of your own kind that you gave to my son Glenndon. I know what we fight. But we are more. We are together in numbers and will. We are more than that circle and the artifact they wield without thought.

As he watched, the men on that flimsy boat at the edge of the storm juggled the bone as if it burned their hands. He watched as their control slipped away from their minds into the bone. Watched as the bone began to throb and writhe within the confines of their feeble, frightened grasp. It shed the matrix of stone that bound it. Bits of glaring white bone began to show through.

He knew the moment it wrenched free and dropped toward the ocean depths.

Time slowed. He observed in finest detail each inch of its plunge toward the water.

Steam rose in massive clouds as the bone approached the living water. Fish fled. The boat rocked from the gush of waves seeking the shore, nearly capsizing.

(Wait for it,) Baamin cautioned.

"Wait," Jaylor commanded his troops.

(Wait!)

"Now!" Jaylor commanded all within his hearing.

The first tip of the bone touched water. Steam hissed and rose in a cloud, obscuring clear sight of the artifact.

The arrow of dragon magic dove fast and deep from its observation point into the center of the long spine.

Red light exploded. Sparks and streaks of lightning shot in every direction. The very air screeched in pain and insult at the invasion.

A shock wave of energy rocked the magic circle, driving them all to their knees.

Jaylor fought the backlash with everything in his power, desperately holding the lattice together, forbidding another ungrounded backlash.

His heart pounded loudly in his ears, his peripheral vision grew dark. And still he pulled his own magic, strand by strand, back into his staff and thence back into the Kardia.

Lukan backed Jaylor with his own power, untangling the strands so that his Da could handle them. *Good lad,* Jaylor whispered.

His breath caught in his throat. His heart threatened to beat through his chest. His arms grew weak and numb. One more strand and the others could take over. One more strand and he'd quit.

Just one more strand . . .

CHAPTER 31

"NOW LOOKS LIKE a good time to get out of here."

Valeria blinked rapidly several times, trying to make sense of Ariiell's words and the way she placed her hands under Val's armpits and hoisted her upward.

"What . . . ?"

"The wind is easing. We've got to move before those . . . those black things decide they want fresh blood," Ariiell commanded, bracing Val's back until she stopped swaying.

"Blood. Black things. Blood and black things!" Val's brain cleared and she looked south, beyond the little vale where the caravan had hunkered down. In the dim twilight—made darker by the receding clouds and the amount of dust in the air—she needed a moment to figure out what her eyes were telling her. Sure enough, the top of the little hill, streaked with crimson from the setting sun, writhed with a mass of black things swarming over dead flusterhens, goats, and cows. A steed with a broken leg struggled to stand and limp away from them.

The smell of sulfur and skunk made her gag.

All around her the caravan people began to come to life, struggling up from wherever they'd taken refuge. They too placed hands over their mouths and noses, scrunched up their eyes and turned away from the carnage.

"I think the eggs were in one of the crates beneath the litter," Ariiell whispered. "Father ordered a bunch of stuff from the Big Continent, wine and crockery. He smuggled the eggs in with them."

"The unwitting tool of someone from Amazonia," Val stated flatly. Someone like Skeller?

Val turned to look at the collapsed litter. Swaths of shredded fabric lay strewn over a half mile, all in the direction of the tangle of Krakatrice. Mixed in with the pastel draperies were shards of vivid red and black eggs.

"They'll bloat soon and need to sleep off the meal," Val whispered to Ariiell. "They're diurnal, awake with the sun, and sleep at full dark. But the males will take turns circling the tangle all night so that none may attack them while asleep. We've got to be elsewhere before they hunt again. The more they eat, the bigger they grow. Last spring Lucjemm only controlled his tangle by limiting the amount of fresh blood he fed them. They'll eat meat, but they grow with blood."

The drover captain seemed to come to the same conclusion as he jerked his attention away from the mass of black. "Move, move, move!" he yelled at anyone and everyone. "Gather what you can carry and move. Orderly, double file along the creek bed. Keep as close to the water as you can. Catch any steed you find wandering— them that's not insane or so spooked they're grazing in SeLenicca about now. Get a move on. You don't want to be dinner for them snakes."

"The one with the broken leg!" Val called to him.

He looked across the rolling hills. Sadness nearly crumpled his face. Resolutely he marched over to it, caressed the nose and murmured a few words to the hapless beast. Then, without warning, he whipped out a sleek knife and slit the steed's throat. It dropped to its knees with a brief scream, then rolled to its side, barely breathing.

No one met the drover captain's eyes as he returned to the scattered camp and ordered everyone to prepare for a nightlong march.

Val turned away, tears streaming down her face. The animal's spirit flowed back into the Kardia along with the blood. She knew its death was necessary, accepted that the drover had shown it mercy rather than leaving it to the ravenous and savage Krakatrice. Knew it. And hated it.

Though she ate meat, she resolutely stayed away during the butchering.

She turned her back on the scene and looked for something useful to gather up. Something like a cook pot or waterskin they might need on the long march west.

Ariiell shook her head. "We need to return to the other caravan and warn them."

Val looked at her in surprise: coherence and compassion from Lady Ariiell, the mad sorceress? What had happened to the woman during the course of the storm?

"Don't look at me like that. I have something to focus on so I'm thinking straight," Ariiell said, turning her attention to gathering her comb, a spare gown, shoes, and a bottle of wine.

"What is your focus?" Val replied as she stuffed dried tubers into a pot and slung a waterskin over her shoulder. She ignored the stash of dried meat, unable to think about eating any of it, ever again. The steed . . .

"Getting away from my father. Rejoining your sister seems the wisest course of action. Besides, we need to warn them about that." She jerked her head toward the writhing tangle of snakes that seemed to grow by the minute as they covered the fallen steed.

Val tried not to gag as she sought to pick out details, looking for telltale wings along the spines. Krakatrice followed a female—like their distant cousins the dragons. Females were the most bloodthirsty and dangerous of the pack.

If they could kill the female . . .

No time, they'd not get close to her, had no ensorcelled obsidian spear tips to penetrate the magic bubble of protection around the monsters.

"I've got to tell Da," she whispered, feeling for her shard of glass in her pocket.

"Last time you tried that you passed out."

Val raised the tiny circle and held it toward the dying sun, letting the sluggish water of the creek merge with her vision. Not a true or proper summons spell, but journeymen needed to improvise sometimes. Da had said so. He'd related some of his own bright ideas when he told tall tales of his own journey.

Just then the glass vibrated and glowed with blue and brown, an unformed swath of color swirling in agitation and urgency.

"Lukan?" she called into the whirlpool of emotion, focusing her magic into making the colors more coherent than the tangle of Krakatrice on the hill.

"Da's dying," her older brother wailed and vanished.

The sky exploded beyond Coronnan City, in the center of the Bay, infecting the wall of clouds with shards of crimson light.

Thunder crackled right on top of the forks of glaring light that chased each other all around the clouds. The high-pitched anger of clashing magics broke apart. Sparks glanced off the rivers of water within the gray pall of clouds. Thunder took on deeper, disgruntled tones, rolling and echoing from treetop to hilltop and back again.

Glenndon fell backward into his companions. They lay together breathing hard, sweating, and dazed. They still held the staff. It stopped vibrating, ceased pulling him outward, dropped to the ground, an inert stick once more.

The slash of bone embedded in the top faded to bleached white. Deep striations ran its full length. Rose gold and green tinged the grooves. His color with something added.

(The colors of the dragon who once lived around that bone.)

"You're back?"

Emptiness in the back of his head. Was that his thought or a dragon's? He didn't know at the moment. The wail of the wind lessened. His ears rang in the unnatural silence.

Too silent.

What was happening outside? He needed to find out and make the next decision for their safety.

He looked to where his hands and those of his companions were joined over the base of the staff, wondering if their skin was melted together and inseparable, as he felt molded to the staff.

Frank withdrew his grip first, easing back against the wall of their foxhole. He sighed and closed his eyes.

Keerkin had to jerk his hands loose. Slick sweat from his palms had become a sort of glue. He too leaned away, giving Glenndon room to maneuver the staff. Make a decision.

"I can't hear the river," Frank murmured.

"How can you hear or not hear anything?" Keerkin replied, shaking his head and slapping his ears. "The thunder makes my ears ring."

Glenndon's hearing popped at the same time. He swallowed and heard the displacement inside his head. Sort of like when a person emerged from a transport spell. The air in the place where he landed had to go somewhere, just as air had to rush in to fill the vacancy of where he'd been.

A change in air pressure. A big one.

"Stargods! What are we in for now?" He crawled forward on his elbows, toward the top of his staff. It remained silent and still. Unlike his heart, which felt like it had climbed into his throat and would spit itself out. Either that, or tear his vocal cords to shreds with its fierce pounding.

He took a deep breath, held it, and let it go. And another. And a third. Simple, routine. The Kardia beneath his hands, the tree around him, and the air he breathed became one, woven together into a pattern of life that included him, his companions, and the fox that had once lived here.

But not the storm. The storm remained outside of him; a separate entity. Unnatural.

He breathed again and focused his eyes on the quiet auras around every drenched and lashed plant outside. They'd all hunkered down, drawing their energy deep within, giving the storm nothing to latch onto. Just as Glenndon, Frank, and Keerkin had.

With his head finally outside the tree, and his staff next to his cheek, he looked at the broader landscape.

That unnatural stillness chafed at his skin, his thoughts, and his magic. The magnetic pole tugged at his feet. His connection to the planet completed and grounded, he tucked his knees under him, ready to emerge and stand straight and tall and sure of his place once more.

Mud seeped into his boots. The sky still leaked and dripped down the back of his tunic. He was wet, cold, and miserable, but he knew where he was, who he was, and what he was.

His magic still scratched at something inside him. It was back, no longer drained out of him.

He brought a small flame to his palm. It glowed bright and true in the rapidly darkening twilight. He still had that itch in the back of his mind.

"I have my magic back. But not all is returned to normal."

"I can't hear the river!" Frank reminded him.

"The river is the least of our worries . . ."

"No, it is the biggest of our worries. If all of the river is out there, in the Bay . . ." Frank pointed east, knowing the direction more than Glenndon did. "Where is all that water going to go when the storm releases it?"

Aiyyeeee! The magic contained within the Krakatrice spine is too much. Too much. I relied on it too much. I released it too late. The moment it touched the water—bane to the Krakatrice—all the magic trapped within the fossilized bone broke forth in a single shower of deep red flames. They shot upward and outward, burning all within reach, boiling the water, adding steam to the thick cloud layer I had built.

The waves backlashing against my control toss our sturdy boat as if a splinter of flotsam. They swamp our decks and cabins. We roll sideways and dip fore and aft. I fear we must sink, or be washed overboard.

Instinctively I throw a magic shield around myself, a shield like the ones the Krakatrice possess naturally. The memory of the dead snake embedded in the bone taught me how to do that.

In releasing the bone, I released the storm as well. My heart tells me this all came too soon. Too soon to exact my revenge upon an ungrateful king and a vicious Senior Magician. Too soon. But my head tells me that I sent the storm back into the Bay just in time. If I allowed the wind and waves to gather any more power all of Coronnan would have been destroyed. This way, they will be devastated. But they will survive and rebuild.

I shall rebuild Coronnan as it should be. As it was long ago. That was the core of my storm spell. A restoration: to put back what magic has distorted, to right what has gone wrong. The destruction is a temporary side effect. I must wash away the new corruption to restore the rightful order.

My followers cringe and hide from the steam and boiling water. They hunker down, hoping the boat will shelter them. But already their exposed skin cooks and sloughs off. Their clothing comes close to igniting, melting into their bodies. The boat cannot protect them.

It will succumb. The deep keel gives the rampaging water something to bite into.

Now I must seize a tiny rowboat that I can make skim over the top of the waves and escape the dangers of this bigger boat and the keening panic of my associates. I must flee quickly, before the steam scorches my lungs. Alone I can persevere for a time. For I must survive. If I succumb to the storm of my own creation, I cannot rebuild Coronnan and bring my country back to its preeminent and rightful place on Kardia Hodos. My colleagues and the ship's crew must fend for themselves. They have served me well. If their sacrifice is the cost of this magnificent magic, so be it. The Stargods or the Great Mother must decide their fate. That is no longer in my hands.

I must see to my own survival. I send a thought to my waiting apprentice in his own boat. He escaped the city before the storm could brutalize all of the Bay. He will fetch me to safety near the headlands to the South. I will be safe there, ready to rebuild from the ancient citadel of Saria.

CHAPTER 32

"KEERKIN, COME. NOW. We have to get out of here," Glenndon ordered.

"Is it safe?" Keerkin asked, not quite daring to stick his head all of the way outside the tree's shelter.

"Not for long." Frank grabbed Keerkin's hand and dragged him upright.

Glenndon sought an image. Someplace safe, warm, and dry. A clear spot in the palace cellar, a storeroom next to the kitchen. It was where both he and Da transported to and from when they needed privacy. Slowly he built the image in his mind, layer by layer, dust mote by dust mote, the way he'd seen it last . . .

"Make sure you land us someplace high. The entire city will be flooding, any minute." Frank grabbed his arm, disrupting Glenndon's trance.

"The palace will be packed with refugees, all above the second floor," Keerkin added.

"A parapet or roof would be best," Frank agreed.

"Your rooms, sir?" Keerkin asked.

"Probably seething with people. I can't risk materializing inside someone else." Glenndon shifted memories. The semisecret room above the archives. Too difficult to find and get to for just anyone to wander in or seek refuge there.

"Hold tight, my friends. Don't let go of me no matter what you see or think you see. Just hang on to me and try not to think of anything."

With a destination image firmly in his mind, he checked the light angles and shadows. Then he reached out with his mind to find a ley line. The place was riddled with them, all thin and spidery. But he didn't need much. Just enough energy to boost him from here ...

Into the void.

A tangle of glowing umbilicals wrapped around him, greeting him, begging him to stay and play with them.

He pushed them aside, all except his own golden cord of life, Frank's uninteresting brown tinged with green, and Keerkin's muddy jumble of pale and undefined colors. Those he held close to his heart as he dropped them all ...

Onto the creaking floorboards of the upper room of the archives.

And almost into the laps of an astonished Lady Miri, Lady Chastet, and his two youngest half sisters.

Frank and Keerkin staggered backward, unbalanced in time and place, bodies working ahead of their minds, which were still back on Sacred Isle.

"Will you teach us that game, brother?" Princess Rossejosiline demanded, crowing with delight and clapping her hands.

"Not now, Josie." Glenndon reached out and ruffled her carefully groomed curls. "Um ... What are you all doing here?"

"Taking refuge from the coming flood," Lady Miri said, firmly closing her gaping jaw. "This seemed the only quiet and unoccupied space, so we commandeered it."

Frank and Keerkin each braced themselves against tall, freestanding bookcases and breathed deeply.

"Good idea. Um ... you might want to forget what you just saw."

The two ladies raised their eyebrows in speculation.

He wondered what kind of price they'd demand for silence. He hoped it would be as simple as a dance at the next court gathering. After the city had recovered.

"Where are the king and queen?" he asked, changing the subject to something more necessary.

The ladies shrugged in indecision. "They were still in the city rounding up refugees, last I knew," Lady Miri replied.

"I hope they have returned by now," Lady Chastet added.

"M'ma is in the formal salon," Josie said. Her eyes crossed and glazed as if looking into the far distance through a glass floating in water lit by a candle flame.

"P'pa is with her," Manda added. Her eyes remained focused, as if she didn't need to think about locating her parents. She was the quiet one. Almost as quiet as Glenndon had been before he learned to speak. He wondered if she read minds as easily as he did.

"Frank, Keerkin, you can stay here and help entertain the ladies. I must report to my father." Glenndon turned toward the trapdoor.

"You don't go anywhere without me," Frank said, following close on Glenndon's heels while looking over his shoulder at the girls with trepidation.

"Same here," Keerkin added. "We're all in this together."

Glenndon sighed. Was he never going to be left alone again?

Three minutes later he approached his harried-looking father in the salon. The king paced and prowled, shouting orders. Water still dripped from his tunic and boots, mud streaked his cheeks and his clothes. His golden hair looked dark and dull, escaped from his queue hours ago. Even the golden cord that normally held the four-strand braid in place was missing. Queen Mikka sat on the demi-throne, equally disheveled, one hand squeezing Mikk's shoulder tightly. The boy was as wet as Glenndon, filthy, and looked like he'd been crying.

Without thinking, Glenndon grabbed a memory from his cousin's mind. General Marcelle. He staggered in shock.

Frank caught him and eased him toward a chair. "Knew you shouldn't work such a strong spell on an empty stomach," the bodyguard growled into his ear.

The king nodded to Glenndon, acknowledging his presence and safety without disrupting his concern over water supplies, food, and barricades on all the lower entrances.

Glenndon steadied himself. He'd barely counted bodies in the room, thirty at least—he'd have a more accurate idea if they'd just stop moving—when the silver-rimmed circle of glass in his inside shirt pocket vibrated, nearly bouncing with energy.

He was still reaching for it when an image of Linda, his half sister in exile, closer to him than any of his siblings, came before his eyes. She looked a little transparent, but otherwise fully formed and three-dimensional, not the flat image he'd see in the glass.

"Come," she said and vanished, leaving in her wake a flood of awesome and terrible images.

"I've got to go home. Da is dying!" He stood and took three steps toward the door.

"No." King Darville, his father, stopped him with a word and a firm glance. "You are the heir. I need you here. You have a duty to me, to the people of our city, to all of Coronnan."

"But . . ."

"I am as sad and concerned as you. Lord Jaylor is my best friend, closer to me than a brother. I grieve with you and for you. But my duty is here. And so is yours. This is what both your Da and I have been training you for, leadership in a time of crisis. I can't imagine a greater crisis than the coming flood."

A new sound grabbed all of their attention, a vast roar that began in the depths of the Kardia and surged toward them from the east.

A wall of water a hundred feet high raced to engulf them all.

CHAPTER 33

SKELLER KEPT A wary eye on the black line writhing along the ridgeline running southwest. The other
caravan took the road parallel to that long steep hill. This
caravan needed to go around the end of the ridge to continue south. The slithering movement did not seem to
have a direction. Just back and forth, with forays down-
hill toward the animal bodies dead or dying on the slope.
Would the caravan have time to circumvent the hills and
get beyond the black mass?

What of the westbound caravan?

He'd heard of the black phenomenon, but never seen
it. It was one of those dark, nightmare tales that bards
sometimes whispered to each other when deep in their
cups, long after their audiences had gone to bed, but
never, ever, composed songs about or used as teaching
tales with the young.

Red and black eggs lying dormant in forgotten nests
covered with sand. King Lokeen offered a bounty for
them, unbroken. He watched in fascinated horror as
the nightmare of ancient times took form. Became
real. Threatened the lives of thousands of people as
well as the land itself. If left to their own devices, those
snakes would turn this lush land into sere desert in two
years.

And Lokeen exported them to his "allies."

"We have to get out of here and get help."

Champion and the few other animals who had managed to stay within the circle of sledges required his attention before he could begin to formulate plans. He hummed a soothing tune as he slid his shirt free of the steed's eyes. Champion shook his head and tried to rear in remembered fear. Skeller kept a firm hand on the bridle, continuing his hum while stroking the steed's long nose and letting him walk on a tight rein.

Lily chased after hens and drakes, trying to herd them toward cages—the few cages that hadn't been blown around and broken apart when they landed.

Champion reared his head up as he turned a tight circle and caught whiffs of the suspiciously tainted air. He knew that danger lay within that undulating mass to the south and west of them, even if the humans did not recognize it. His wariness came from there, not a holdover from the storm, though that left them all more than a bit bewildered and shaken.

Time to gather up whatever they could and get moving again. They needed to get past the tangle and as far away from it as possible. He didn't think the snakes could be killed with mundane weapons, even at night when they slept. Maybe magic had a use after all; if a magician could kill those snakes, then he'd thank them all.

Skeller looked around and caught Garg's gaze when he looked away from the black line. "Aye, boy, I see it. Don't understand it, but I knows it ain't friendly."

"We need to get out of here," Skeller said. "Quickly. It looks like they are feeding on the animals that died during the storm. I don't know how long before they decide to move on for fresh blood." Half-remembered bits and pieces of nightmare lore tumbled around his mind in no particular order.

"Agreed," Garg said as he cast his gaze around the mess of their hasty encampment. "Be a lot easier to stay here the night and get this all ordered and sorted."

"Not safer. We need to walk all night while they sleep off their feast."

Movement across the road at the tree line caught his attention. Lady Graciella drifted along a narrow game trail, seemingly unfazed by the disastrous storm. Her unfocused gaze drifted everywhere but toward the writhing black ridgeline.

Skeller wondered if any of the destruction registered with her.

Lily dropped two pieces of a crate that might fit together and dashed to the side of her charge. "Where have you been, Gracie?" she asked smoothing a lock of hair out of Graciella's eyes and tucking it behind an ear.

With a start, Graciella twitched and fixed her gaze on Lily. "Oh. Is something wrong?"

Skeller couldn't help rolling his eyes as he turned his attention back to calming and organizing the steeds. When Champion stopped prancing and sidling, Skeller took a moment to check Telynnia. He pulled the case around from his back and opened the latched flap. The harp looked undamaged. He ran his hand along frame and strings still inside the case. Nothing overtly wrong.

Nothing he could do to fix her now, if she were damaged. Just the changing air pressure and humidity could weaken her frame and destroy tension in the strings. At this point, not knowing meant he didn't have to worry.

Lily escorted Lady Graciella back within the circle of upturned and twisted sledges. "Gather what you can carry, my lady," she instructed. "We're moving on now."

"I need to sleep in the litter. Make sure they harness it to steady steeds." The lady's eyes glazed over again, almost as if reality was just too painful to remember.

Where had she been during the storm?

"Cat chased the weasel," Graciella sang to an old children's tune. "Up hill down dale. The weasel chased the cat." She swayed in the rhythm of the tune.

Lily looked toward Skeller in fright.

"What did you see, my lady?" Skeller asked gently, keeping a similar chant to the rhythm of his words.

"Cat chased the weasel. Spin, spin, twist in the wind with sparkling light. Weasel grew up and grew old. Cat hid behind him. Cat grew up and grew young. Weasel chased the cat. Not weasel and cat anymore. All gone."

"Stargods!" Lily gasped and swayed.

Skeller caught her before she collapsed.

"All the magic in the storm. Gobs and gobs of it. Even I could sense it, smell it. Feel the thickness of it. Krej tapped into it, even in his weasel form. He transformed them. I have to tell Da!"

"Can't go home. Don't want to go home." Graciella turned toward the ruins of her litter, swaying and singing, eyes not focusing.

Lily followed her. Skeller let go reluctantly.

A shimmer in the light made Champion shy and sidle again. Skeller searched the little hollow for signs of more danger.

Lily stopped short and held Graciella away from the shimmer. Within two heartbeats the distorted light coalesced into the outlines of two people. He had to look away from the intense glow of sparkling and swirling bits of matter.

What now? Hadn't the storm upset the natural balance of the elements enough?

When he looked back, Valeria and her lady stood in front of Lily. Valeria sagged with exhaustion, held half-upright by her companion.

"Val!" Lily dashed to aid her sister.

"Da is dying. We have to get home," Val gasped.

"You've overextended yourself, Valeria. You can take us no farther," Lady Ariiell said sharply, as if reprimanding a trying student.

"Da?" Lily wavered and nearly dropped to her knees.

Skeller forgot the steed and reached to hold Lily up. Graciella continued drifting in and out of awareness and ignored her companion.

"Da can't be dying!" Lily wailed. "He just can't. We need him too much. The king needs him too much."

"The summons was specific," Lady Ariiell said.

"We have to go to him," Val insisted. "I have enough energy for one more transport, if there is food and sleep at the other end . . ."

"We can't leave our ladies behind," Lily said softly, taking in Graciella's detachment. "They are our duty and responsibility."

Valeria eyed both women hesitantly and shook her head. "I can take you. No more."

"But . . . but . . ."

"Show me the spell, Val," Lady Ariiell said, grabbing Valeria by the shoulders and staring deeply into the girl's eyes. "Show me," she insisted louder.

"She can't. It's a secret. A big secret. We aren't supposed to know it," Lily replied, looking anywhere but at Ariiell.

"We haven't time to dither about duty and secrets," Val said. "Da is dying *now.*" She seemed to gather herself and fixed her gaze upon Ariiell.

The lady staggered a moment, shaken by whatever information passed between her and Valeria.

Skeller shook his head, amazed at the amount of trust these people put into magic. He felt like he should shield Lily from the manipulations of her sister and the lady, at the same time he couldn't keep her from seeing a beloved father one last time. He wouldn't care to go to his father in such a circumstance, but if his brother or his Aunt Maria needed him, he would do whatever he had to in order to return home at any cost.

All of Amazonia needed him if Lokeen had succumbed to the enscorcellement of the Krakatrice eggs.

"I have the strength to take Lady Graciella and Lily," Lady Ariiell said. "You just get yourself home. We'll be two heartbeats behind you, Valeria."

Valeria nodded and breathed deeply. Lillian and Ariiell matched the rhythm of intake and release.

Without realizing what he was doing, or why, Skeller grabbed hold of both Lily and Lady Graciella and closed his eyes. Intense cold enveloped him and would not let go. His bones ached with it. If he had bones to ache or teeth to chatter.

He opened his eyes a tiny slit and found himself in a vast pool of nothing, without being able to find his feet or any other part of his body.

Almost before he could register that something was not normal, the air around him warmed and a setting sun brightened his eyelids.

(Good-bye. Come again when we can linger and talk.)

He didn't really hear that faintly amused voice. No. He was certain he hadn't.

This little boat is as much a menace as the larger one. It bobs and drifts at the command of wind and waves. They have stolen my oars and the tiny mast and sail. I have not enough magic left to recall order to the ocean. Everything I have, everything I am, went into the storm and into the bone. I need help. There are those who will respond to my dream requests. There is one who will respond to my summons. He has no choice. The compulsion I planted in his mind overwhelms his feeble attempts at self-will. He owes me for his high position, for his secret education, for the training of what little magic he can command.

He left Coronnan City the moment he learned about the storm. I made certain he had no choice. He had time to steal a boat and follow the edge of the storm around the Bay while everyone else sought to go inland to higher ground. My control over his mind allowed nothing else.

I will manipulate my other tools. But my apprentice will come for me. He must divert his path from following the shore to my position. He has no choice.

CHAPTER 34

"**B**RACE YOURSELVES!" THE king cried, fling-ing himself atop the queen.

Mikk shook himself out of his self-imposed loop of misery and guilt over the death of General Marcelle. The deep-throated growl of water rushing forward faster than a fleet steed could run pounded against his ears. He looked around for a place to hide from the onslaught of sound and flood.

His gaze landed on Lady Miri standing near the door-way. She must have followed Glenndon down from the no-longer-secret room above the archives. She always followed Glenndon, seeking out Mikk only when she needed someone to talk to about Glenndon.

No time to wallow in that misery. If the water came this high, it would follow the corridors to open doors, or lash at the shuttered windows. He launched himself for-ward, taking her down with a body tackle, somehow catching the door latch on his way and pushing it closed. The back of his mind heard the latch click even as he did his best to cover the lady, protect her from the first gushes of water, if they came.

Stunned, Lady Miri lay quietly beneath him. When she roused enough to focus her eyes, her gaze landed on Mikk with a twitch of sarcastic humor masking darker emotions. "Couldn't get me in bed any other way?" she quipped.

"You wish." He kissed her nose and looked around at people hunkering in corners. And Glenndon standing alone in the middle of the room, head dropped in grief, eyes closed in concentration. His bodyguard and clerk tugged at him to join them against the inside wall, away from the windows. Away from whatever raced forward out there.

A walloping boom filled the room, reverberating and pounding at their sanity, shaking the stones within the walls, the planks of the floor. Mikk clamped his teeth shut, willing himself not to shudder and shake long after the assault passed.

At last Glenndon looked up and allowed his men to guide him to a less exposed place.

The building shook and groaned. Again. And again.

Mikk held on tight to Miri for many long moments while his heart beat too loud, too fast, in a nearly painful erratic rhythm.

He just held on, not knowing what else to do. Deep in his heart he knew that General Marcelle faced the same rush of water, naked, unprotected. No armor or weapons could deal with the unleashed fury of the storm surge.

He doubted even Glenndon's powerful magic could do anything to challenge that wall of water.

Glass shattered. A shutter splintered. The water laughed as it found entry, tearing at the stones around the narrow opening.

Mikk sprang up and hauled Miri with him. Urgently he pushed her toward a gaggle of royal retainers clinging to the interior wall.

Another boom and crash followed by a shaking of the floor.

"The doors," the king gasped. "Did anyone think to barricade the doors?" He tried to pull away from his wife and go to investigate. To stop that wall of water containing half the Bay.

Queen Mikka held him in place. "There is nothing you can do," she said loudly, firmly, holding his upper arms so he couldn't leave.

"I ordered the crossbars dropped," Mikk offered weakly. He hadn't looked back to make sure they were in place.

They all watched in horror as thick water filled the window opening, blotting out what little light the westering sun offered. It poured in by the tubful. It pounded at the other windows, seeking more openings.

The water spilled onto the floor, spreading out, deepening, reaching for them.

Miri clung to Mikk's hand as if to a lifeline. As if only he could save her. "I can't swim," she whispered.

"I can. I'll do what I can to save you."

"I know you will." She graced him with a smile, and he knew he could do anything. Anything at all.

And he knew what he had to do.

"Glenndon!" he called to his cousin.

The golden prince looked like a bedraggled stray dog at the moment, sunk deep in his grief, held upright only by the will and the iron grip of his companions.

"Glenndon," Mikk repeated more forcefully. "Is there a spell that will put a temporary wall between us and any more water crashing in?"

Glenndon blinked rapidly as he looked up.

"Well, is there?" Mikk demanded.

"Please, son, if there is anything you can do to protect the people sheltering from this unnatural storm, please do it," King Darville pleaded from his place on the demithrone beside the queen, where they should be, in command, leading by their calm example.

"I read something . . ." Mikk suggested.

"I'm sure you did," Glenndon replied, shrugging out of despair and into action.

"You'll need fire and Kardia. Stargods only know we've got more than enough water and air," Mikk added, somehow knowing he had to help Glenndon order his thoughts before they could do anything. His Da was dying.

Mikk knew he'd feel just as lost and frightened if something dire threatened Grand'Mere.

Glenndon sloshed over to a round table and started dragging it to the center of the room. Frank and Keerkin jumped to help him.

So did Mikk. He had no intention of being left out of this. He could only learn so much magic by reading. Now he had to do. He'd learned that much if nothing else from watching Master Aggelard.

"The water isn't coming in as fast as it was," Miri said, hope giving her voice a firmer lilt.

"The initial surge has passed," King Darville said, gaze fixed on the window. "It's settling into a level. It will go down again, very slowly though. Days probably before we see dry land beneath the hilltops. Weeks until we're rid of it all."

Glenndon paused, cocking his head as if listening. "The dragons say there are three more surges coming. Lesser than the first, still high enough to drown us if we don't do something."

"Can the dragons do anything? There are old tales of dragons being the harbingers of good weather. They are creatures of magic, this storm was born of magic . . . surely . . ." the king said, hopefully.

"If the dragons could do anything about it, they'd have done it! They have other concerns right now." Glenndon snapped. True pain haunted his eyes. His Da was dying!

With a sweep of his arm, Glenndon cleared the table of cloth, vases of flowers, all the elegant decorations that made the room— at normal times—welcoming. He left only a single candlestick with a ring of dried flowers adorning the base. A sharp snap of his fingers brought flame to candle.

"Kardia in the flowers and fire in the flame," Mikk said. He tried to follow Glenndon's motions, wondering if he thought through the spell the same way Mikk did, just faster, without having to concentrate a long time to bring forth the spark.

Water sloshed over the top of Mikk's half boots. He shook his foot, trying to discard the cloying sensation of impending doom. Outside another roar built, the deep growl gnawing at his belly. "We haven't much time. What do you need me to do?"

Glenndon placed the tip of his dripping staff on the tabletop and traced with wet lines a five-pointed star surrounded by a circle around the candlestick. Sparkles seemed to follow his tracings, quickly dying as he moved from here to there. The points of the star touched the rim of the round table, flaring at each point and continuing to glow faintly. The circle of the table rim defined the drawn circle, also retaining the fire of magic within the line, more than a reflection of the lit candle, less than a true fire. The symbolism struck Mikk as obvious now that he saw it and he understood the sympathetic elements Glenndon drew upon. He wondered how his cousin would bring them all together.

The magician prince didn't look up, concentrating deeply on his preparations, moving around the table, shoving people out of his way as he progressed. Sweat popped out on his brow. There was a cost to magic. Working a spell cost terribly in physical energy. He'd be hungry, near to starving before the end. Had anyone thought to bring food into the room?

Then he spotted Keerkin fumbling inside a pack and withdrawing bread, cheese, jerked meat, and dried fruit.

Mikk crept closer to his cousin following him, mimicking every move with his hands and inside his mind.

A half smile crept across Glenndon's face. *You are learning, little cousin. Your mother could probably do this without a thought.*

My mother is not here. I am, he replied, not realizing he hadn't spoken aloud until after the words were passed from his mind to Glenndon's.

Curiosity is a good thing, cousin. But sometimes it gets you into trouble.

"I need air. A lot of air all at once. You have learned to breathe. Can you empty your lungs completely all at once?"

Mikk shook his head. "I want to help. I just . . . I have experience . . . No training . . ."

"You want to be part of this spell?"

Mikk could only nod, eyes wide in wonder.

Then this is going to hurt, Glenndon said, looking him in the eye. Then without preamble or apology he grabbed Mikk by the shoulders and drove his knee into Mikk's gut.

All the air inside Mikk flew out in a long whoosh, emptying him of thought, of control. His vision narrowed to a dark tunnel as he gasped desperately trying to draw breath through pain.

Dimly he watched the candle flame flicker and hold as he doubled over, hands splayed on either side of the stick, well within the central pentagram of the star.

"Now the elements are complete and the water will not penetrate the wall of air around Palace Isle. Master Aggelard has directed a similar circle around University Isle." Glenndon proclaimed. "By the same token, if water cannot get in, nothing and no one can get out, by means magical or mundane. The water will remain at the current level within the bubble. We can't release it until the river recedes to near normal levels or it will swamp us. I hope you are happy, Father. Neither of us can go to Lord Jaylor in his last moments of life."

Mikk didn't really care. He just needed to breathe, and couldn't.

Miri waded over to him and gripped his shoulder hard. He concentrated on her touch rather than the pain.

CHAPTER 35

AN ANGUISHED BELLOW penetrated Jaylor's increasingly difficult attempts to breathe. His heart-beat sounded too rapid and shallow in his own ears.

Dragons keening in the darkness sounded louder.

Somewhere in the back of his mind, which seemed to be drifting away quite rapidly, he knew that a dragon grieved. He heard a great thunder as dozens of dragons took flight.

What had set them off? What crisis did he need to tend to now?

If only he could lift his eyelids and check the circle, see who had fallen. If only his chest and left arm didn't ache so abominably ... What had he been lifting to strain those muscles?

(You carried the entire circle on your back and in your heart,) Shayla said angrily. *(We await you in the void.)*

That made no sense at all. He'd never heard an angry dragon before. Where was the laughter and gentleness?

(In the void.)

"Easy now, roll him onto the blanket. Gently!" That was Maigret directing the care of the fallen, whoever it was.

Jaylor ceased fighting his own lethargy. Maigret would take care of it.

"He needs to go home," Marcus said more quietly.

His former student's breath crossed Jaylor's face, and he wondered why the master magician had come so close. Magicians respected the distance cast by another's aura and rarely crossed that boundary without invitation or reason.

"Easy now, Jaylor. Breathe easy. We'll take care of you," Marcus said.

I'm just tired. Need food and sleep. Suddenly he understood why Glenndon had taken so long to learn to speak. Telepathy was so much easier.

"Why'd he have to do it!" Lukan yelled, off in the distance somewhere. "Why'd he have to do it all alone? Never accepting help, never trusting anyone to know how to do it. Always taking control."

Jaylor struggled to go to the boy. Time he taught him some manners . . .

Who was Lukan complaining about? The only person who roared and insisted upon doing it himself . . . was himself. Jaylor . . . He'd been taking control of spells for so long he couldn't remember not doing it.

"Hush, boy. We'll take care of him," Maigret said.

Jaylor sensed that she gathered Lukan close in her motherly embrace. Strange, his strongest memories of Maigret were of a rebellious girl who couldn't stand to be confined by walls or rules. When had she become the nurturer of the apprentices?

A soft blanket of sleep enveloped Jaylor. He drifted easily, only partially aware that time passed. He thought that the pain in his chest and his inability to draw a full breath was all that kept him awake.

"No! No, it can't be. He can't be dying. I still need him!" Another scream jolted him out of his semisleep. Brevelan. He had to go to her. Keep her safe in her bed. He had to ease her mind. Make sure she . . .

Dying? Who was dying?

And then she was beside him, holding his hand to her wet face. Crying. Brevelan cried over him.

She should be in bed, taking care of herself and their unborn child. Her seventh child.

The dragon-dream long ago had promised her six. Dragon-dreams did not lie.

"Wh . . . who?" Jaylor croaked through swollen, nearly numb lips.

"Don't waste energy speaking," Maigret commanded. "Don't waste your strength trying to manage everything. You already did that and it nearly killed you." Her last words came out on a sob.

Then he felt the rim of a cup pressed to his mouth. "Just a sip, Master," Linda said quietly. "A few drops. Take a few drops, that's all we ask. 'Twill steady your heartbeat."

He tried. He really tried but he couldn't make his throat work. If only he could draw a full breath . . . half a breath would help. But the weight on his chest seemed to increase. Had one of the children climbed atop him?

"Let me try," Lillian said quietly. The position of the cup shifted as his daughter took command of it. "Drink, Da. You have to drink this."

Lily, where did you come from? Wasn't she weeks away with the caravan?

"Val and I transported in the moment we knew how ill you'd made yourself. Now *drink.*"

Jaylor tried. Lily sounded so much like her mother in that moment of command he felt compelled to taste the nasty smelling brew. Two drops bit into his tongue. He'd spit it out if he had the strength.

Brevelan's sobs increased.

I'm dying. Truth stabbed him behind the eyes. He'd tasked his heart beyond mending.

No one responded. Not even the dragons.

But he wasn't dead yet. He concentrated fiercely on what he had to say. What he had to do.

"Staff . . ."

"Your staff is here, Jaylor," Marcus said. "It will always be with you. You'll take it into the void with you."

The staff, an old friend and constant companion, glowed warmly beneath his hand. He clutched at it with weak hands, drawing a little strength from it. He needed a little help right now.

Jaylor fought to shake his head in the negative. The staff would have found him, even if he'd left it behind. "Lukan. Staff. Earned it tonight."

"Yes, yes. I'll see to it immediately," Marcus agreed.

One more thing. And then he could rest. Two more things. One after the other. Best to get it done before he ran out of time.

"Letter . . . Glenndon . . . desk."

"Yes, Master. I'll see that he gets it," Linda answered. Of course Linda would take care of it. She'd written the letter for him. Her blood and magical links to Glenndon . . . Jaylor was surprised the letter hadn't found its way to his son already.

"Brevelan." He could barely hear his own words. "Brevelan, I love you."

A wail of anguish. But he didn't care anymore. He was free of pain. Free of . . . free to soar with dragons into the void. As he had once before. This time his best friend and the love of his life would not be able to bring him back. His staff glowed brightly in his right hand. He reached behind him for the one thing he'd forgotten . . .

Lillian and Valeria reached for their mother at the same time. Desperately they drew her into their combined embrace, their tears mingling into a river of grief and disbelief.

"He . . . he can't be gone," Mama whispered. She broke free, flinging herself atop Da, pounding on his chest. "Come back to me, *S'murghit*. Don't you dare go without me!"

Lillian didn't need to exchange thoughts with her twin to convey her worry. Mama was too pale and shaky.

"Of course Glenndon gets a letter!" Lukan sneered.

He'd come to the scene late. "What do I get? Nothing. He never even thought of me, even after I saved the spell and grounded it properly when he couldn't finish the job." He turned and yanked open the front door of the cabin.

Lily needed to go after him. Needed to heal the gaping hole in his emotions that gnawed at his gut, had done so for a long time.

"Lukan, wait," Master Marcus called. "Your father told me to give you a staff. He said you earned it tonight."

"No, he didn't. That's just you trying to make up for his lack." Lukan said no more, yanking open the door and then slamming it shut behind him so hard it bent the latch and swung unevenly to and fro.

Mama's scream of pain was almost lost in the noise of her departing son.

Go to him, Val. I need to stay with Mama.

He won't listen to either of us right now. He won't listen to anyone, Val replied even as she knelt beside Lily, helping her draw Mama away from Da's bier of blankets laid before the hearth. Mama clutched her belly with tight fists.

If she could lose more color in her face she did so now.

"Lady Ariiell and I will see to Lukan," Graciella said softly. "We can be of no help here." She clutched her own belly protectively.

Part of Lily was relieved that her companion had not only come out of her horrified trance, but learned enough compassion for her own child—no matter how ill-conceived—to take care of herself, at least for a short time.

Most of Lily's attention turned to her mother. "Mistress Maigret, we're going to need some of your potions!" Val cried even as Mama doubled over gasping for breath.

A bright pool of blood dripped onto the floor beneath Mama's bedgown, spreading rapidly.

Without direction Marcus lifted Mama into his arms and carried her to the room at the back of the cabin. He laid her gently upon the bed and backed away. "Do your best, Maigret. Please. We can't lose her too. Together they were the heart and soul of the University, the Circle. With both of them gone . . ." He turned and fled.

Lily gathered clean rags from the bandage cupboard. Maigret and Linda rummaged around in a carved chest for herbs.

Val smoothed dull and sweat-darkened hair from their mother's brow with a damp cloth, murmuring soothing phrases.

Mama moaned.

Lily dashed back to her side, slitting Mama's gown from hem to hip with her utility knife.

"We're going to have to cut the babe out," Maigret whispered, crushing a bitter-smelling mixture in a ceramic mortar. "We don't have time to save them both. She's bleeding too heavily."

"The babe has not thrived," Lillian said. "It has troubled her for weeks."

"Thought as much. The babe should be much bigger."

Lily looked to her in question. She thought Mama looked huge, near to birthing a full term baby at five months.

"It's all swelling, water and blood. The babe's too small, probably died weeks ago. And . . ."

"And putrefied," Val completed the nasty sentence. No one else dared utter the words, lest saying them out loud made them true.

"My good girls," Mama murmured. She opened her eyes and fixed the twins with a fierce gaze, gripping their hands tightly. "You are the backbone of the family now. Take care of the little ones." Her grip grew slack as her lips turned blue.

Mama screamed, nearly sitting up in her agony. A gush of foul smelling blood flooded the bed linens.

She fell back. With a light smile she released.

In the far distance Lily thought she heard her mother say, *I thought you'd wait for me, my love.*

CHAPTER 36

NOT KNOWING QUITE what to do, Skeller stood outside the simple lopsided cabin with extensions up and down, out and back. He took up a guarding post just outside the door, watching the drama play itself out when the boy they'd called Lukan burst away from the grieving crowd. The door slammed behind him and bounced back open as he stalked—nearly ran—into the yard.

Five heartbeats later they both heard a woman scream in extreme pain.

Lukan paled even more. One look at his eyes, red-rimmed and deeply shadowed—almost bruised like Valeria's—mouth contorted, cheeks pale and hollow, and Skeller knew the boy grieved as much as his sisters. But he tried to hide it.

Skeller had felt like this boy looked the day his mother died. He'd run away two days later, before Queen Skalleria's funeral pyre had finished burning.

Skeller couldn't let Lukan repeat all the same mistakes that he had made.

"You need to stay." He grabbed Lukan's shoulders and spun him around to face the cabin.

"Don't tell me what to do," Lukan sneered back, trying to push Skeller out of the way. "Who are you anyway?"

Skeller held his position. Though not as tall as Lukan, he had a few years' maturity and muscle mass on the boy. "Skeller. I'm a bard, and Lily's friend. For her sake as well as your own, you need to stay. At least until the funeral. You'll regret it your entire life if you don't."

"How would you know?" Lukan pushed at him again.

Skeller braced for it and managed to stay upright, and in Lukan's path.

"Because I made the same mistake."

They glared at each other, weighing and assessing.

"For Lily. Please. She needs you right now."

"No one needs me. The twins have never needed anyone but each other. Glenndon's off being the grand prince in the city . . ."

"What about the two little ones huddling in the corner? They've just lost both their parents. Is anyone thinking about them?" He'd wanted to tightly hug the young boy and and girl, but was afraid he'd disrupt the attempts to save Lily's Da and her mother by getting in the way.

Lukan took half a step backward and chewed on his lip.

Marcus, the older man in a dark blue robe, stepped out of the crowded cabin, closing the door quietly behind him. A splotch of dark blood stained the front of the fine fabric. He looked up at the sky, screwed up his eyes and breathed in and out, trying for regularity. Each exhale came out more ragged than the previous one.

Lukan began easing around Skeller, obviously putting distance between himself and the older man.

"Ah, there you are, Lukan. I'm glad you didn't get very far," Marcus said. "There are decisions to make before you leave on your journey." He stepped closer, keeping his gaze fixed on Lukan.

"You and Maigret seem to have it all well in hand. Feel free to take over the family as well as the University."

"Lukan, it's not like that."

"Isn't it? Why should I stick around? No one will listen to me anyway. Da never did. Why should you?"

"Because I am your master and you are my responsibility!" Marcus yelled.

Taken aback, Lukan closed his mouth and dropped his eyes.

Skeller decided to change the subject, divert attention, and take some responsibility off his own shoulders—though he truly wanted only to dash to Lily's side and hold her close while she cried out her sorrow. She needed to do that before she could resume her duties.

"Sir," Skeller addressed Marcus. "I don't know who to report news to, but someone in authority needs to know . . ."

"I know about the storm."

"That too . . . but . . ."

"Do you know there is a tangle of Krakatrice feeding on the dead left behind by the storm?" Ariiell asked from the far side of the yard. She and Graciella sat together on a stump with deep ax slashes. A chopping block.

"What?" Marcus demanded, turning toward the two women, staff raised, eyes a-bulge.

"Krakatrice, ugly black snakes, females have six wings. Feed on blood, fresh if they can get it, meat will do in a pinch," Skeller supplied the missing information.

"I know what they are. I've killed my fair share of them too. Why are they in Coronnan? We turned the last matriarch to ash months ago."

"They are here because my father conspired with some magician named Samlan to bring Coronnan to its knees," Ariiell said, quite calm and sane. "King Lokeen was quite pleased to get rid of the eggs. Let them destroy Coronnan rather than Amazonia."

"Just who are you?" Marcus leaned forward, peering at the willowy blonde curiously.

"You won't remember me. I'm Lady Ariiell, Lord Laislac's insane daughter."

"I remember you," Marcus said.

Skeller and Lukan looked at each other, wondering when they'd become redundant to this conversation.

"I was there, in the old monastery, when ... when you ..."

"Brought down the Coven, twisted enough magic to turn Krej and Rejiia into their totem animals, and generally caused enough problems to upset the line of succession?" She quirked an eyebrow at him, then gracefully resumed her seat.

"Yes, that," Marcus agreed. "I was still a journeyman. But I was there and I remember it all."

"Fine. Now you seem to have more authority than you did sixteen years ago, go deal with the most recent crisis. I've had enough of being sane and coherent for one day. I think I'll throw a screaming fit until all those cats go away. I really don't like cats." She waved at the passel of furred creatures perched on the thatched roof of the cabin, watching the human activity closely.

Skeller remembered Lily's tale of Ariiell and Marcus' adventures. "Sir, another thing you need to know ..."

"What now? Don't I deserve a little time to grieve for the loss of my friend and mentor?"

"You wanted to be head of the University," Lukan mocked. "You want my Da's job, don't expect to go home to your family before next week." A little color came back into his face.

Good, Skeller thought. The boy was thinking again and not just reacting to strong emotions.

"A stray cat followed the caravan," Skeller said quietly. "Lily seemed to think it quite important."

"A stray cat? Lily and her mother always have ... had a dozen of them about."

"A black cat with one white ear. Thin and paw-sore but not ill, quite friendly for a stray."

Marcus' head reared up in alarm. "And was the cat alone?"

"No. There seemed to be a tin-colored weasel with golden yellow tips to its pelt waiting in the shadows."

"What was old is new again," Graciella sang. "Change is reversed. What was new is now old. Round and round. Change and change. Dance in a circle. Dance for life."

Ariiell picked up the tune and wove her fingers in a childish game. Both women seemed to pull a veil of forgetfulness across their faces and unfocus their eyes.

"Stargods," Marcus groaned. "I don't even want to ask what that means." He buried his face in his hands.

Skeller shrugged his shoulders, keeping his eyes on the two women, trying to see if either of them faked their sinking into insanity.

Lukan reached out and patted his master's shoulder.

"It means she saw the magic in the storm restore the cat and the weasel to their original forms," Lily said, appearing in the doorway, Valeria for once not semiattached to her. She dashed to Skeller's side, burying her face in his shoulder.

Gratefully, he wrapped his arms around her and held her tightly. It would all come around right again, as long as he could hold Lily and they could face the world and their problems together. He'd run away from home, seeking a life without violence—violence that Lokeen courted and encouraged among the people. Skeller needed a life without physical brawls to settle arguments, without executions for crimes committed and perceived. Lily represented everything he'd run toward. She was his new home.

"Oh." Lady Ariiell raised her head and fixed Skeller with a piercing gaze, as if she knew how important her next statement was to him and him alone. "My father, your precious Lord Laislac, has arranged for me to marry King Lokeen of Amazonia. From violence we come, to violence we go." Then she dropped her head and resumed singing nonsense nursery rhymes with Graciella.

The next morning, as dawn brightened the eastern sky and sent shafts of golden light atop the ugly mass of water that stretched from horizon to horizon—mere inches below the level trapped within the palace's magical protection—Glenndon paced the parapet of the highest spire of the palace. He stared malevolently at the thinning cloud layer as if it were the source of all his disappointments in life. As he watched, a freshening breeze from the interior shredded the pall, revealing tatters of brilliant blue sky.

He frowned at the omen and promise of better weather. It wouldn't do any good until the flood that swirled through the city up to the second-story windows of the palace dissipated and he could break the wall of magic that kept the water out of the building. Perhaps a week. Even with the force of tides and rain-swollen river currents pushing it back out to sea, it would take time to move all that water back to where it belonged.

Until then he could do nothing, go nowhere, help no one. And could not be with Jaylor, *his Da,* and his mother in this time of trial.

Not only could he not leave the palace by magical or mundane means, he could not throw magic through the wall for a proper summons spell. Even his unique mind link to Linda was broken.

He turned his attention away from the sluggish, muddy, debris-filled water that lapped at the palace walls, twenty feet above normal river levels, toward the rising north and west. He could see hilltops, far away, many miles away. To the south, well beyond the horizon, toward another chain of mountains, where he'd grown up, where his family lived, the land was flatter than to the north, stretching along the Bay coastline for many, many miles of farms and pastures. It was all underwater, with no relief in sight. Maps told him that the land rose quickly, three days' journey that way. Rolling grassland gave way to forests broken by small river settlements. He couldn't see that far. A FarSeer couldn't see that far with the magical wall in place.

Lily and Val had traveled in that direction over a week ago. He prayed they'd passed beyond the flood regions. His heart was full-to-breaking with grief and frustration already.

He gave up peering in that direction for any sign of life above the water.

To the west, he thought he saw tall trees poking above the flood. Surely Sacred Isle would be spared. If the Stargods ever thought to intervene they would save that one place from too much destruction. He had a particular fondness for one special Tambootie tree. Was that a gentle tug from the dragon bone embedded in his staff trying to reach out to the other dead dragons and host trees?

Bits of green and the tops of a few trees showed more clearly to the north on what he suspected was the second line of rolling hills. Cattle and steeds gathered there. Maybe he discerned a farmer's roof ridge. Hopefully city dwellers who could not get to the palace or University had managed to run that far.

He doubted it. As if to prove his statement, a body drifted by, facedown, arms and legs splayed. A man he guessed, since it wore trews. Another body, a woman this time, bobbed in hidden currents a few feet away.

"Stargods guide their souls to the void so that they may fly free of this life with the blessing of the dragons," he whispered, a prayer learned in childhood.

When this was all over, there would be many candles lit and prayers said for the dead. Father already planned a mourning service inside the palace for when the refugees sorted themselves out and counted heads to see who was missing.

One thousand people saved. Perhaps an equal number in the University. Two out of ten people from the city saved.

Among the dead General Marcelle, Glenndon's friend and mentor in the practice arena; his father's friend and loyal adviser. He'd sacrificed himself to save the cistern from damage. To save the city's water supply. They couldn't access the subterranean cavern now, but later, when the flood receded, they'd need fresh water more than anything. Mikk and General Marcelle had seen to that. At the cost of the general's life.

The boy had shown more initiative and responsibility than Glenndon had given him credit for. Perhaps he should spend some of the idle hours while waiting for the flood to go away teaching Mikk the basics of magic. Show him a few useful things like lighting a candle, purifying stale water, or turning nasty smells into more pleasant ones. They'd likely need that one a lot in the coming days with too many sweaty bodies crammed into too small a space for too long, without enough clean water for bathing. Even with spells, they'd only have enough water for drinking and cooking. The trapped floodwaters were just too tainted to hope for safety.

"And what of you, Da?" he asked the air, or the dragons, or whoever might be listening. "Did you survive? Is Mama well?"

No answer. Not even the dragons could break through his invisible wall of magic to give him news.

Glenndon pounded his staff onto the stone floor and screamed his defiance and dismay.

The flood swallowed the sound, not even giving him the satisfaction of a decent echo.

At last my apprentice approaches. I am nigh unto death with thirst and sunburn. His boat is not much bigger than mine, but it has an intact sail. Expertly he tacks and comes alongside my little dinghy. He has obeyed my compulsion to come for me, abandoning the young prince he was charged to guard. He took the position I found for him eagerly, hoping to learn something of magic. But he could not ignore my orders, even if he developed some loyalty to the boy. He has no loyalty to anyone but himself and his quest to become a magician. His obsession made him an easy target for my control over him.

Now, using his lifelong skills in a boat to circumvent

the storm along the Bay shore, he comes to me eagerly, hoping I will fulfill my promise to teach him magic.

He throws a rope ladder down to me without a word. I'd reprimand him for his lack of manners, for not greeting me. But that is his way. A silent observer who speaks only when required or ordered. He'd learn more magic if he asked questions rather than just watching.

"Could you find nothing better than this leaking tub?" I demand of him.

He shrugs and assists me aboard. Then he hands me a skin full of fresh water. I drink it down without hesitation.

As the last swallow sloshes around my mouth, moistening the delicate tissue I taste something. Something off. Something strange.

"Poison!" I gasp.

He merely lifts his eyebrows in that maddening way of his.

CHAPTER 37

"WHY?" I CROAK to my traitorous apprentice.
He shrugs again. "I do not like you. I do not like being a servant to the second heir of Coronnan. I do not like the destruction of my home you caused. I do not like being kept in ignorance. You promised to teach me magic. You didn't."

Quite a speech for the taciturn Geon.

"I have my reasons for keeping you uninformed and ignorant," I growl at him.

He watches my face for signs that the poison is taking effect on my body. I allow him to see a slight grimace of pain and slump my posture protectively over my cramping belly.

I do not allow him to see the packet of powder I draw from my belt script. I needed those few seconds of conversation to know which counteragent to use. I always carry several. I had the right ones. One for me. One for him. One never knows who one can trust.

As I straighten, I loosen the knots and drawstring with a tiny sliver of magic. Then I throw the caustic residue into his eyes.

He screams and covers his face with his arms. He screams again and again, rivaling the passing gulls in strident tones. When he drops to his knees and his voice *turns to moans I take the remaining powder from his hand.*

I have only minutes to act before the purgative begins its work of clearing my body of his feeble attempt at assassination. I use those moments to shove him overboard. He lands flat on his back in the dinghy. I cut it adrift and set the rudder of my sailboat toward Saria where I can be more certain of my welcome.

I should have expected Geon to try something like this. He was more adept at shutting me out of his dreams than my other tools.

As I contemplate how to draw my minions to my rescue I empty my guts back into the ocean and feed the fish the poisoned water.

❧

Val watched her parents' funeral pyre crumble to ashes and the last glowing ember cool and fade. Someone, probably Maigret or Marcus—Lord Marcus now— would gather the ashes into a lovely silver container. Soon Lord Jaylor and his Lady Brevelan would rest together, for all time, on a shelf in the ceremonial hall of the University. She hoped they stayed here in the Forest University Da had built and run for over fifteen years. The king, and probably Glenndon, would campaign to have them taken to the old University. They didn't truly belong there.

And she didn't belong here anymore.

Val stood there, watching and waiting—she didn't know for what—long after the rest of her family and the members of the University had drifted away to other tasks, other duties, other responsibilities.

What was her life to be like now?

Lily still had her journey to complete, escorting Lady Graciella to Castle Saria. The dark and gloomy castle was built into a mountainside hundreds of feet above the Bay, accessible only by a single road that climbed from a supporting village around the jagged cliffs. So it had probably survived the flood the master magicians had seen in their FarSeer spells.

Val suspected Skeller would choose to go with them—with Lily.

Lukan had a journey of his own to accomplish, first to gain a staff and then to complete whatever task Marcus determined for him—probably to find Master Robb.

Glenndon had his duty to the king and Coronnan. She knew he'd have to help with the aftermath of the flood. Lukan would take Da's letter to him once the land had drained.

The Circle of Master Magicians had elected Marcus their Senior Magician and Chancellor of the Universities. He in turn had decided to journey to the old University in the city and take up the reins of his responsibilities as Senior Magician and adviser to the king. His wife Vareena and their children would follow him shortly. The Circle had yet to elect a separate Chancellor of the Forest University, but conversations and votes tended to favor Maigret, simply because she worked well with everyone, generating no enemies, while the men tended to gather strong factions around themselves. None of them could command a majority of votes. And so by default, Maigret would step in and organize them, as she always did.

Linda had her work here with Mistress Maigret, an able and learned secretary and assistant.

With Lady Ariiell refusing to return to her father and an arranged marriage with a foreign king, Val had no responsibility to take her anywhere. The ugly knot of guilt and pain in Ariiell's mind had dissipated almost to a point where she didn't need The Forget anymore. The lady's fate must be decided by others now—or even by herself. An awe-inspiring thought that daunted Ariiell into her vague retreat from reality again.

So, what would Val do? What could she do?

Take care of the little ones, Mama had said with her dying breath.

That should be Lily's job. She was the nurturer, the one who enjoyed cooking and telling stories, and guiding lessons, and maintaining the kitchen garden and the herbs and ...

Val understood magic. She didn't understand or appreciate children.

A stick snapped behind her as someone trod carelessly along the path from the University to this mournful clearing.

"Valeria?" Ariiell asked tentatively.

"Yes?" Val didn't turn away from her contemplation of the ashes of life and death.

"I've had a vision."

Val came alert. Ariiell sounded quite sane at the moment. She still lapsed into periods of glazed indifference, but less often and for shorter periods of time than when they first started this journey together.

"What kind of vision?"

"More than a dream, less than reality."

"That sounds ... ominous."

"Yes, quite. I realize now, that some of my dreams on our journey were not true dreams, more like directions from outside myself."

Mama had talked about dragon-dreams, visions of the future, or warnings.

"Do the dragons talk to you?"

"No. I think this is a magician. A rogue magician who is trying to control me."

Valeria forgot to breathe for a moment.

"Why tell me? This sounds like something Lord Marcus should know about."

"He's so busy. And ... and I don't know ..."

"You don't know if you can trust him."

Ariiell nodded and swallowed heavily.

"I understand." Val knew how hard it was for Ariiell to trust anyone. She'd been betrayed by everyone: people she loved, people who should take care of her, but only used her. Val had built a small trust with her while enclosed in that litter that gave the illusion of blocking out a big, scary world outside. They'd formed an understanding through the letters that Val wrote for her then dispatched by magic transfer spells.

"This rogue magician is adrift in a small boat. He wants me to meet him in the cove below Saria with food and supplies and a means to take him to safety."

"Um . . . Is this rogue Samlan by any chance?"

"I think so. And if you are going to save Coronnan from him, we need to go soon and make sure he does not get to safety."

"I've had some troubling dreams of late," Lily confessed to her sister and Ariiell sitting on the ground across from her. Skeller sat slightly apart from them tuning his harp and humming a sad little tune with a hypnotic drone of a bass note beneath the melody. She suspected he composed a new ballad, possibly in honor of Mama and Da. Graciella half hid behind Lily. They had gathered for privacy near the little waterfall that tumbled into a broad plunge pool heated by a hot seep coming out of the core of the mountain. Too many people wandered in and out of the cabin and the home Clearing, wanting to help, needing to verify that Mama and Da had truly died and didn't still live there. At least Lukan had not run off on his own, or hidden up a tree, or in the thatch. His presence kept the most prying of the visitors away. He joined them in this semisecret discussion now.

Lily hadn't shared her dreams with anyone but Val and didn't want to trouble the others with a recounting of the latest nightmare of trying desperately to climb the broken cliff face below Castle Saria. The crashing waves towering above her, tugging at her, pulling her to her death felt too real, more real than the quiet loft room she shared with Val, Ariiell, and Graciella. Mistress Maigret had taken Jule and Sharl home with her.

Lady Graciella had described the cove to Lily and Val

in painful detail. She knew its wickedly sharp rocks pointing straight up above the tide and hiding below, waiting to shred living flesh from bone. She knew of the erratic tides and strong currents where ocean met bay at the solid outcrop of rock.

"I thought I was sharing some of Graciella's nightmares," Lily said, hanging her head, not willing to meet the all-too-knowing gaze of Lady Ariiell.

"I've had the same dream," Graciella admitted. "I woke up in a cold sweat of fear, almost saddened that I didn't drown and end the nightmare forever. I thought it came from the time Lucjemm showed me the cove and explained the ancient form of execution. He threatened me with the same fate if I didn't give in to his demands." The last came out as a bare whisper that Lily had to strain to hear.

"I thought he only threatened you with opening a vein and letting his snake feed on you," Val protested.

"That too."

"I dreamed I was adrift in a boat and in need of rescue," Linda said, stepping into the little clearing. "When I woke up I felt an unnatural compulsion to run off to this ragged coastline and rescue someone."

Graciella and Ariiell looked aghast, mouths slightly agape at the intrusion.

"I came looking for someone who might know why Jule won't eat his yampion pie. Mistress Maigret and I have tried everything to keep him happy but he misses his Mama and doesn't understand that she's not coming back." She stopped talking and looked everywhere but at the others gathered together. "I heard you talking," she rushed to explain her uninvited presence.

"Did you put a dash of nutmeg and an extra dollop of goat's milk in the vegetable mash?" Lily asked. How many times had she made the same dish with Mama? How many times had they talked through the process to discover the essence of each plant and what it needed to complement and complete it?

Never again. She was on her own with the cooking now. Val never helped because she didn't understand what to look for with nose and fingers and an open mind. She had no empathy with plants.

Not like Mama.

Oh! Mama. A wave of grief nearly swamped her heart and mind. She had to blink rapidly and swallow deeply to push away the sudden spate of tears.

"I'll try the nutmeg, but I think I need to know if what is troubling you is also troubling me." Linda swept aside the skirts of her pale blue robe and plunked down on the ground cross-legged. Just like any other apprentice. All traces of the former, haughty, fashion-conscious princess had vanished. Though she still maintained her upright posture and impeccable politeness and protocol.

"My dream is similar to yours, Linda," Lukan said, angrily clenching his fist and pounding it into his thigh. "I don't like being manipulated. Samlan left the Circle because he wouldn't bow to Da's authority—even though Da kept secrets from him when he shouldn't."

"So what are we going to do about it?" Val asked.

"We should tell Lord Marcus," Lily said.

"He won't do anything," Ariiell said on an indelicate snort. "I know him of old. He'll dither and delay until he has no choice but to take action, often too late."

"Maigret knows how to jump into action," Linda offered.

"But neither of them will allow any of us to go," Lukan reminded them. "We're supposed to hide here and grieve for the next year or two or whatever."

"We each have to grieve in our own way and our own time," Lily said. "Sitting and hiding from the world doesn't feel right."

"Got a bit of itchy feet?" Skeller asked. "Know how that feels. As long as we're leaving to complete an essential task and not just running away. I've done both often enough to know the difference. Running away doesn't accomplish anything other than delaying the inevitable."

He turned his head back to the harp, unwilling to meet the gaze of anyone. His deep thoughts remained hidden.

Val cocked her head and looked at her sister curiously. Lily felt her twin's mind seeking her thoughts. Deliberately she cut them off.

"I won't stay here any longer than I have to," Lukan said. Finally his angry clenching relaxed, as if making the decision sent his anger elsewhere.

"I have to stay," Linda said. "The University is where I belong at the moment. It is where I need to be. At least until Glenndon opens communications again. I don't know if my father will call me home to help rebuild or not."

"It's been five days . . ." Lily hesitated lest her constant worry over her brother's silence bleed over and divert her from this other task.

Linda shrugged. "All of you . . . go if you must. I won't say anything until after you're long gone. But I need to stay here. I also need an end to the nightmares. If this rogue magician taps into the mind of someone more vulnerable than any of us . . ." She stared long and hard at Graciella and Ariiell, knowing who was the most vulnerable among them. "Someone else might not realize they were being manipulated and do precisely what Samlan wants."

"We can't allow that," Val said.

Graciella and Ariiell nodded in agreement.

Linda rose gracefully and retreated, brushing leaf litter from her robe as she walked.

"That just leaves when and how we leave," Skeller said, putting his harp into its carrysack with gentle care, as if the instrument was the most precious thing in his life.

Lily doubted she could ever be more important to him than the harp. And that saddened her.

"Val, are you rested enough to transport yourself and one other?" Lukan asked.

"Stargods, yes! People have done nothing but stuff

food into me and make me lie down for another nap since we got home. I can take two if I have to." She looked around the gathering, fixing each of her companions with an assessing gaze, weighing mass and ability in each of them.

"I know the spell," Ariiell said.

"How did you . . ." Lukan protested. He looked ready to jump up and pound something, or someone. "That spell is the Circle's biggest secret."

"I had to show it to her to get Lily and me home," Val said defensively. "It was necessary."

"The dragons can make her forget it when we're done," Lily said.

"I can carry two," Ariiell continued as if she hadn't been interrupted. "But I'm not sure I'll be much use afterward. Sanity is hard work and I get tired of responsibility very quickly."

"Do you know the spell, Lukan?" Skeller asked, amusement coloring his voice. Had he learned that wry chuckle from the dragons?

"Of course! What kind of son of my father would I be if I didn't eavesdrop and learn things on my own? He'd never teach me anything so I learned to mimic everything and figure it out myself."

"When do we do this?" Lily asked. In her mind she organized her pack, and Val's, with a change of clothes, medicines, bandages, food, waterskins, a cook pot . . . all of the little things necessary for a long journey without a caravan full of supplies to rely on.

"Midnight," Val and Lukan said together.

"Betwixt and between, neither one day nor the other. The time when the world grows quiet and the dragons reign," Skeller said/sang, composing music as he spoke.

"The dragons . . . ?" Ariiell looked frightened.

"The dragons will know what we are doing. But they also know how to keep a secret if they approve," Lily replied, knowing in her heart that Indigo eavesdropped as they spoke.

"And will they approve?" Graciella asked, looking more frightened than usual.

(I am with you always,) Indigo said in the back of Lily's mind.

Lily and Val cocked their heads in identical listening poses. "They approve and will watch over us," they said together.

"Don't bet on it," Lukan grumbled.

CHAPTER 38

"S'MURGHIT, WHAT IS that smell?" Mikk gagged, burying his nose and mouth in his sleeve as he stepped into the palace forecourt for the first time in a week. Last night Glenndon and King Darville had agreed that the flood had receded below the base of the palace gates outside. This morning the protective wall of magic had shown signs of breaking down, as water inside the palace began leaking out slowly along the bottom of the bubble.

But there was still a foot or two of water in the courtyard.

"That smell is the dead, lingering to remind us of what we have lost," King Darville said sadly. He lifted his face toward the sky, but he kept his breathing shallow. A gesture sent a dozen men scattering around the walls of the palace and the old keep in search of ... an end to this disaster.

But the challenge of rebuilding was daunting. Coronnan would be a long time in recovering.

"It doesn't smell much better out here than in there," Glenndon said, pointing back toward the palace. He looked like he needed to cover his face, as Mikk did. One glance at his father and he endured without protection. But Mikk saw him weave his fingers in a now familiar pattern while his mouth moved, whispering a nonsense rhyme. Within a moment he'd balanced the acids in the air with a base scent similar to clean grass and fresh ocean breezes, achieving a faint smell of freshness in their immediate environs.

Mikk repeated the small ritual for himself and managed to come up with fresh baking bread. Not sweet like he wanted, but at least enticing rather than hideous.

The scent of yeast and flour made his stomach growl. Just that little spell ate up the small bit of fuel his scant breakfast of grains and boiled water granted.

"That smell can't be healthy and we can't keep it at bay forever," Mikk said, peering through a crack between the great double gates. The force of the water had pushed them out of alignment so they couldn't close completely.

That brought back the memory of struggling to close the gates between the river and the cistern. He bowed his head and grieved anew for General Marcelle. He wondered if the well had refilled with fresh water seeping through natural filters in the limestone. They could certainly use some fresh water in the palace, for drinking, and cooking. He didn't think there'd be enough to bathe a thousand people.

"No, leaving dead people, stranded fish, and rotting plants in the open is not healthy. And we have to do something about it before we can begin the rest of the cleanup," King Darville replied. He walked over to the gates and gave the sagging one a shove outward. It scraped and groaned against an accumulation of dirt and debris on the outside. "We'll have to clear this before we can do much of anything."

"Part of the obstruction is the remnants of my wall of magic," Glenndon grumbled. He scanned the walls. "The spell is eroding. But there's still enough of it intact to keep us from leaving, or communicating with the outside world."

"Can you take the remaining wall down now?" King

Darville asked, kicking at the debris sifting in through the small opening between the gates. "The river retreats. Much of the city should be accessible, if there's anything left. I doubt the bridges survived even after collapsing them."

Mikk looked at the mess with a bit of trepidation. He really did not want to have to inhale a vast quantity of this foul air tó reverse the spell.

"Mikk and I will take care of that right now, sir," Glenndon said, grinning wickedly at his cousin.

Mikk's heart sank to his belly.

"It won't be so bad," Glenndon slapped him on the back, hard enough to make him stumble.

"What do you need me to do?" he asked weakly, knowing he had no way out. Every bit of magic he'd read about seemed to demand a price—and he'd read a lot more this last week, combing the archives for reading material when there was not much else to do except wait for the water levels to return to normal.

"Bring me one cup of fresh water so I can wash the ceremonial table clean of my marks," Glenndon replied.

"I'll look in the cistern," Mikk replied and dashed in the direction of the kitchen courtyard and access to the city water supply. He stopped just short of the stout metal doors set deep into a stone shed sticking out from the exterior wall and still part of it. Stinking, squishy mud and rotting grasses and seaweed nearly covered the entire courtyard. He'd have to dig his way through half a foot of the stuff to get to the cistern, then hope none of it had seeped into the water.

He sighed in regret as he looked about for a tool. Nothing about magic was easy or provided a shortcut without cost.

"The pump in the kitchen draws water from the cistern," Glenndon said quietly, coming up behind him.

"Oh. I thought . . . I hoped . . ."

"You hoped you'd find General Marcelle alive and lurking down there, safe and sane." Glenndon clutched

Mikk's shoulder as they shared a moment of grief. "I hoped the same. But I know he couldn't stagger to the end of the tunnel and climb onto dry land from the river end. Not with a knee so badly damaged he couldn't climb the palace steps. Nor could he get back to this side of the doors, not if you latched them properly. I know you did. I shared your dream of that final thud of the crossbars dropping into place."

"How . . . how could you share my dream?"

"I'm not sure. As horrible as yours was, it was better than my own nightmare of climbing jagged cliffs with hungry waves lapping at my feet and making the rocks too slick to cling to." He swallowed deeply and looked up. His free hand trembled.

"I've had that same dream," Mikk admitted. "I've also dreamed of being set adrift in a small boat on a stormy sea and needing rescue. I thought perhaps I was reliving my fears that some of our people took to their boats, hoping to ride out the flood rather than flee."

Glenndon froze in place, barely breathing. Then he fixed his penetrating, golden gaze on Mikk. "Did you feel compelled to rush out to rescue one man set adrift?"

Mikk gulped, not liking the path his thoughts took. "Yes," he breathed.

"So did I. There is more going on than just our fears preying on our dreams. I need to talk to Da . . ." He stopped. "I don't know if Da survived."

This time Mikk pressed his cousin's shoulder in shared grief. "From what I know of dragons, I think they have more answers than we do."

"Yes. Let's get that cup of water and open the paths of communication. Da always told me that when all else seems hopeless, talk to the dragons. They may be able to help us clear off the dead bodies. Or at least bring us a few tons of salt to sanctify a mass grave."

"Where would we bury them all? There must be thousands!"

"The dragons will know. We can't just dump them all

into the ocean. Their remaining relatives need to know where they are, need to mourn, need a place to memorialize this event."

Mikk nodded glumly and trudged after Glenndon. They had a lot of hard work to do. Messy work. And he didn't know if Geon had survived to help.

Strange, this was the first he'd thought of his servant since running from the University to the palace over a week ago. He'd probably stayed at the University rather than take the risks Mikk needed to take.

Some bodyguard!

Inside the kitchen, three steps up from the courtyard, they found more stinking mud on the floor and small sticks and dead fish piled in the corners and along the walls. A flurry of frogs hopped quickly out the door the moment they spotted a path to freedom. This area had probably drained a day or two ago, trapping the frogs when they could no longer swim under the doors.

Nearly gagging, Mikk made his way to the pump in the scullery off the main workroom.

"Looks like they took your orders to heart and carried all the food and supplies up to the fourth story," Glenndon said, kicking at a knot of rotting green stuff, too slimy to tell what it had been originally.

The pump handle was dry. At its highest position it was about level with Mikk's shoulder. Right now it was frozen about halfway. He placed both hands on top of it and pushed down. It wouldn't budge.

"Let me try. I've got a bit more leverage in height and shoulder," Glenndon said, moving in front of Mikk.

Mikk stepped aside gratefully while his cousin leaned hard on the pump handle. It moved about two inches down and stayed there. Its own weight should have pulled it lower.

"It's stuck," Glenndon stated the obvious. "Probably got gunk in the pipes and it's too dry from not having worked in a week."

"The scullery lads pumped the cistern nearly dry, filling every bucket, tub, and cup with fresh water before the flood. I doubt any sludge could get into the pipes," Mikk replied, eyeing the contraption suspiciously. He tried to think through the method and mechanism for drawing up water.

"Maybe if we both put all our weight on it," Glenndon suggested.

Together they managed to push the handle all the way down. Mikk's feet dangled a few inches off the ground as he heaved himself up. Once down it stuck there.

"Under it. Put your shoulder into it," Glenndon ordered. They both crouched low with the handle resting on their shoulders and heaved upward. The handle moved a little easier.

"Again." Up and down. Up and down. Mikk pushed and pulled until he saw black spots before his eyes.

"One more time, I hear something gurgling," Glenndon shouted with glee.

Mikk couldn't hear anything over the pounding of his heart in his ears. He hadn't worked this hard since his first time in the practice arena with a sword that was too long and heavy for his ability. Glenndon broke a sweat but still looked strong and eager.

Three more pumps and a tiny trickle of lime-white water wandered out of the spout. Another five cleared the water of residue. At that point Mikk shoved a cup under the pump. Glenndon pushed down one more time and they had enough fresh clean water to reverse the spell.

Mikk fought the urge to drink it down. That would come later. When they all had enough to drink.

From the protection of tree branches ten feet off the ground, Lukan listened as Skeller plucked chords on his harp, matching his voice to the core note. Then he tried another, moving his voice up and around the scale expertly. Eventually he changed to single notes and he sang in a clear and pure baritone, "You can climb back to the Kardia in safety," he said, plainly, without a trace of a song. A smile tugged at the corner of his mouth.

Lukan dropped through a familiar pattern of hand- and footholds until he hung by his hands from the lowest branch and let go, falling only a few inches until his bare feet found purchase among the layers of moss and leaf litter.

"How'd you know I was up there?" Lukan asked, dusting off his callused hands. "No one thinks to look up."

"I do. Ever since your sister showed me my first dragon flying overhead. She taught me to sing with your friends." Skeller strummed a new tune that reminded Lukan of birds flying strong and free, accompanied by an odd chord that could have been a dragon screech sweetened up a bit.

"Lily." Lukan let his sister's name hang between them.

"Don't worry. My intentions are honorable toward Lily. If she'll have me."

"And if her family won't have you?" Lukan tried raising one eyebrow in skepticism, like Da.

He steeled his heart against the hurt of grief. He shouldn't feel this strongly about Da's passing. Except that Da had taken Mama with him. He'd never see his mother again. Never hear her gentle admonishment to stand straight, to wash his feet, to . . . to watch over his little sisters as they roamed the forest around the Clearing.

"The decision is Lily's, not yours," Skeller said flatly.

"Family is important to Lily." Lukan had to remind himself that he had a smaller stake in keeping all his siblings together, helping each other, advising each other. Loving each other.

Something stronger pulled him away from them. More than a yearning. A genuine need to be out in the world alone. Alone. The family would take care of themselves without him. As they had always done.

The family was scattering, like autumn leaves fleeing before a chill wind.

"Family should be important. I hope I can earn your trust, if not your love."

"You come from . . . elsewhere."

"Amazonia. Yes, our traditions are different. Our government is different. Our fashions are different." He flipped his fingers through the shoulder-length light brown hair. "But my people are not at war with your people. My own family is . . . less than loving and united. I have few reasons to return. Those reasons are weaker than my reasons for staying with Lily. Except . . ."

Lukan nodded abruptly, understanding, but not fully accepting the explanation. Now he needed more from the wandering bard who had traveled far and seen far too much.

"The other day, you said you ran away from your mother's funeral . . ."

"Yes." Skeller's face became a blank mask, hiding his true emotions. He was too good at that.

"I . . . I need to thank you for making me think before I ran. I'm glad now that I stayed, at least for the funeral."

"It seemed important. I was older than you when Mother passed. I'd been following caravans for a few years, singing my way around the continent. I thought I'd learned somethings about myself, and my family. I thought I needed to return to them and begin talking about all the reasons I needed to return. But I never thought about reasons to stay *with* them. Turns out I arrived mere hours before Mother stopped breathing after ten years of being an invalid. Ten years of barely having enough energy to talk to her sons, let alone hug us."

Something in Skeller's too-neutral tone stabbed Lukan in the gut. "At least you got to say goodbye," he said, not knowing what else to say.

"I'd said goodbye to the mother who loved me ten years before. I said goodbye to a wasted husk of humanity at the end. Something in me died that day too. It's taken me four, almost five years to bring it back to life. Lily helped. She helped a lot."

"She's like that."

"Take some time to talk to her on our journey. Val too. I have a feeling you all need to find closeness again. Find your childhood playmates again and cherish that."

"You said you had a brother . . ."

"He . . . he's taken refuge elsewhere, with . . . comrades who think and feel as he does."

Lukan remained silent. One of Mama's tricks. Forcing the other person to fill the gap with words.

"I'm not going to say anything else at the moment." Skeller stood up, carefully stowing his harp in its case and slinging it onto his back. "Come, your sisters are expecting us to help them pack for the journey."

"We don't need much," Lukan said, bewildered by Lily's need to sort and organize.

"We don't. But they do. Trust me. If we give in on this, they'll be a lot happier and easier to travel with, until they discover they've packed too much and discard half of what they brought."

"Why not discard it all now . . . ?"

"Because then they wouldn't be happy."

"Women!"

"Get used to it. We need them as much as we want to pretend we don't."

CHAPTER 39

A N HOUR AFTER clearing and grounding the protection spell, Glenndon took a deep breath and focused on his palm-sized piece of glass, floating in a bowl of fresh water barely large enough to contain it. He didn't dare ask for more clean water than that. They had so little to spare until the cistern refilled naturally and they got the pumps working full time. He was already tired from freeing up the kitchen pump and reversing the containment spell. A drink of cold fresh water would help a lot to revive him. Later. Others had more need than he. The first cup out of the pump, he and Mikk had used to wash away the spell that had saved them. They'd thrown the magic together; they needed to end it together. The second cup of precious water he'd confiscated to open communications again.

He knew he should contact the University first to find out who had survived and what damage they'd sustained.

He knew it in his head.

His heart and his gut rebelled. Some things were more important. He called into memory the unique shape and color of Jaylor's magical signature: a blue and red braid that twisted back on itself, knotting in an uneven pattern.

Nothing. No vibrations. No colors. Nothing but a milky swirl of nothingness.

Biting the insides of his cheeks in abject fear, he decided to go to the source. Linda had told him to come home. Linda must know Jaylor's fate.

Before he'd severed communications with the outside world, he hadn't needed a spell to find Linda. He kept the summons spell open anyway. Just in case. Resolutely he cleared his mind, breathed deeply of the fetid air inside his bedroom—the closest thing to privacy he could find even though he shared the space with Mikk, Keerkin, and Frank. Two families of merchants inhabited the outer rooms of his suite. Young mothers with two children each occupied Frank's and Keerkin's tiny alcoves. Every nook and cranny in the palace and the old keep was filled to overflowing with people.

People they'd saved from the flood.

Half in a trance, with his body firmly oriented to the magnetic pole, he stared into the glass and reached out with his mind to find his half sister.

Her face appeared in the glass and in his inner vision.

Linda, he said softly. He bypassed the glass and spoke directly mind-to-mind.

You're alive! she cried in the same intimate form. Tears streaked her face. But she smiled. *No one could reach you. We feared everyone in the city lost! My parents and sisters?*

Safe, Glenndon reassured her. *The flood is clearing. Many are dead. We don't know how many yet. We don't know if anything is left of the city other than the palace and the University.*

Glenndon, she said hesitantly.

My Da?

I am so sorry. We could not save him. His heart burst with the effort of breaking the storm.

Something stabbed Glenndon's heart. The explosion of light and popping air pressure just before the storm surge; his staff trying to merge with the eye of the storm . . . He knew there was more to that phenomenon than the creator of the storm releasing it to do its worst.

He realized that some part of him shied away from the truth. Da was always one to take the burden, to protect others from working beyond their ability. Each time he came back a little weaker. This time he'd tasked himself too much.

Say something, Glenndon.

Can't.

You just did.

He took a moment to teach his lungs to breathe again and his heart to pump. His world seemed dimmer, less vibrant. He nearly lost his anchor to the Kardia and the magnetic pole, set adrift in time and place.

Mama?

Oh, Glenndon, I am so sorry. The shock sent her into labor too early. She hemorrhaged, and we lost her too. This time Linda choked on unshed cheers.

The world came to a halt around Glenndon. He felt as if . . . as if he were alone in the void without the comfort of life umbilicals or dragon voices teaching him something important.

Nothing.

Glenndon, speak to me! Linda cried. *Glenndon, you're going transparent like a dragon with golden tips. Don't you dare fade to nothing. Don't you dare!*

(Be comforted,) Shayla said.

Glenndon had never heard the dragon matriarch sound so gentle and nurturing. The humor had left her mental voice; it was sad, but not prostrate with grief. As Glenndon was. He couldn't move, couldn't think straight. Did his heart and lungs work? Did he even blink?

His eyelids moved. Once. Twice. A third time brought forth tears, and he didn't bother blinking them away.

(Good. You are returning to life. Death is not yet your home. You have much to do before you can embrace the next stage of existence.)

Did Mama and Da embrace death? He couldn't imagine it. They both had so much to live for. They both attacked life with such enthusiasm. He saw them together at the end of the day, sitting opposite each other before the hearth, she with some mending, or knitting, or other small task. He with a text or some small piece of carpentry. A child asleep in each of their laps. Da would lift his head from whatever he was doing and smile. At the same moment Mama would look him squarely in the eye and return that smile. Then they'd tuck the little ones into their cribs and wander into their private bedroom holding hands. Not a word passing between them.

He sighed. *I hope they are together. I can't imagine them apart.*

That earned him a dragon chuckle. (*They wouldn't have it any other way. And neither would we.*)

Did you foresee this, Shayla? Did you know from your dragon-dreams that they must die together even as they lived together?

(*No. But they do not surprise me.*)

Glenndon let go of the breath he didn't realize he'd been holding, easier in his mind. *I will miss them.*

(*You have luck that you have a second set of parents. Your father and his wife love you, and need you. Now return to your chores. All of Coronnan needs your strength, your inventiveness, your courage, and your love.*)

Love. Will I find love as Mama and Da did?

(*That is beyond my knowledge at this time.*)

You gave Mama a dragon-dream when she first met my Da. You showed her happy and loving with six children and a loving husband. That made his breath catch a moment. Six children in the dragon-dream. The seventh had killed her. The birth order of the children came differently from the dream. But not the number. *Can you do the same for me? Give me a hint of my future?*

(*Later. When events sort themselves out. Trust yourself, my golden prince. Trust your father. Beware of small boats and rogue waves.*) The dragon withdrew from his mind, as gently as she had entered it.

"Glenndon!" Linda's voice came through the summons spell and into his mind, loud and demanding.

"I am returned to myself, little sister. I . . . I just need to grieve a moment."

"You looked like a dragon," she said, hiding her fear with a delicate snort of disgust. Linda would never do anything with less than royal subtlety and politeness.

"I needed to talk to them. Shayla is most comforting. What of my family? Did Val and Lily get home in time?" He had no doubt that Val knew the transport spell. She was too good at observing and mimicking from the shadows. "What's to become of the little ones?"

"Maigret and I have taken Jule and Sharl into her household. Maigret is missing Robb mightily. Filling their quarters to overflowing with lost ones seems to help. Lily and Val came home in time. Lukan was there as well. Your parents passed on surrounded by friends and family." For some reason she had withdrawn her mind from his and spoke only through the spell.

He gave a sigh of relief at her news. His other family here in the city demanded so much of his time and attention he doubted he could have left them without a great deal of guilt.

"Glenndon, Valeria and Ariiell say that I must warn you that Lord Laislaic is in league with the king of Amazonia—Lokeen by name. They planned for Ariiell to marry the king. Laislac was to receive a box of Krakatrice eggs to use as a weapon to bring Father down and become king himself. The eggs were hidden in a case of wine carried beneath Ariiell's litter. The crate broke during the storm and the eggs hatched . . ." She shuddered slightly in fear. He'd rescued her from a tangle of Krakatrice, and Lucjemm's obsessive need to own and control her, last spring. Then she drew a long restorative breath.

Glenndon braced himself, almost knowing what was to come. "The magic in the storm winds released the snakes from the eggs."

Linda nodded. "They feast on the carcasses of animals killed by the winds. Master . . . Lord Marcus has sent five masters and their journeymen and apprentices to deal with them. They carry bespelled obsidian blades. They know they have to use ley line magic to end that menace."

One problem Glenndon didn't have to deal with. Yet. Thankfully water was the bane of Krakatrice. They couldn't come near the capital and survive.

Pieces of information fell into place quite naturally, as if they needed Glenndon to not think about them in order for them to fit. Krakatrice eggs in a crate of wine from Amazonia. He gasped. "Was . . . was Master Samlan the ambassador from Amazonia?" What had become of the ambassador during the flood? If he was indeed Samlan, then he'd fled the city by boat before conjuring the storm.

"I . . . I don't know. I'll ask Skeller."

"Who?"

"A friend of Lily's. A bard from Amazonia."

"Oh." He thought he remembered a shorthaired bard wandering around the fringes of the caravans the day Val and Lily had left with their lady charges.

"Val also says to beware of a rogue magician."

"I know that Samlan created the storm with magic aided by a Krakatrice bone."

"He's coming ashore."

"When? Where?" Glenndon began a hurried accounting of the few magical tools in his possession. Nothing less than a gathering of master magicians could control Samlan if he still had the Krakatrice spine. Yanking control of the storm had killed his Da . . . and Mama. For that he must pay and pay dearly.

"We think he's headed for the cove below Castle Saria."

"A dangerous landing. Maybe the rocks will slice him to ribbons." Remembering nightmare tales of the place made him feel easier. Fishermen who knew the tides and currents and how they changed from moon phase to moon phase could negotiate the treacherous cove. Few others had survived.

"There's more." Linda looked like she was hiding something by diverting the topic. He knew her well. Knew intimately how her mind worked, because they worked alike. This was why she'd withdrawn from him and communicated only through the glass, flame, and water.

"Tell me the more, then tell me what you don't want me to know," he demanded.

She looked away briefly, as if consulting someone else. When she turned back to her own glass and candle flame, her face and mind were blank. "Samlan's spell centered around a need to restore order to the time before the Leaving."

"Logical. He never wanted Da to be Senior or Chancellor."

"Krej and Rejila were near Val's caravan, stalking Ariiell. They got caught up in the magic!"

"*S'murghit!* The storm restored them! I don't need two more rogue magicians on top of Samlan."

(One at a time. We will help,) Shayla reassured him.

"One at a time, Glenndon. Deal with one problem at a time. Have your FarSeers watch the Bay for signs of Samlan's boat while you help rebuild the city. That is your duty. Krej and Rejiia are the responsibility of the Circle," Linda reminded him. A bit of royal authority and hauteur crept into her expression and voice.

How could he disobey? "Yes, Your Highness. I will do my duty here. But please keep me informed how you and the Circle intend to deal with Samlan, and the Krakatrice, and . . . and everything."

"Very well. And Glenndon . . ."

"Yes?"

"Give my parents a hug from me and tell them I love them."

"Yes, ma'am." He cleared and grounded the spell, then sat staring into the distance wondering what to do next, when all he really wanted was to tear off in a boat and go hunting Samlan, the author of this destruction.

Shouts and bangs broke out above him. Two stories up, someone tried to break through his wards around the tightly rationed food stores. Loud footsteps pounded toward the trouble. One problem he could delegate. Making contact with the University he couldn't.

With a deep sigh he gathered his energy for the next summons.

CHAPTER 40

LILY SURVEYED THE contents of her knapsack one more time. She and the others had agreed to pack lightly for this trip to Castle Saria. None of them, not even Graciella, who was supposed to stay there until her baby was born, wanted to linger there. Lily thought about leaving the lady at home in the Clearing within the protection of the University. But Graciella jumped at every loud noise, was often distracted, and broke into tears frequently.

Perhaps Maigret and Linda could watch over her. But they had charge of Jule and Sharl, along with Maigret's two boys and the burden of missing Robb preying on them all. There was also the added responsibility of Maigret assuming the chancellorship of the Forest University when Marcus returned to the old University in the city. Lily couldn't ask them to take on more responsibility.

So, she checked Graciella's pack as well. Her fingers curved around a small, lumpy, cloth sack she didn't remember adding to the change of clothes, essential food and emergency medical herbs and bandages. Slowly she withdrew the unknown sack, fearing what she'd find.

One whiff of the contents told her. Rosehip candy. "I thought we got rid of all this," she muttered as she threw it all into the low burning fire in the cabin hearth. "Why does she still crave this if she's decided to keep the baby, protect and nurture it?"

"Because my lord husband is not the father of this brat," Graceilla said flatly, coming in from the Clearing. "The others are waiting for you. They sent me to find you," she said without any more expression than before.

"There are other ways to lose the baby. Safer ways," Lily said. She began spinning plots in her head to find a balance in the woman's mind and body.

Gracieella looked away.

"We'll talk about this later," Lily said gathering both knapsacks. "We'll decide if you stay at Castle Saria or come home with me after . . . after we complete this mission."

Graciella stared at the fire longingly for a moment.

Just as Lily was about to say something to break Graciella's absorption, something pale and flat fluttered to the ground in front of her. A quarter-fold piece of parchment sealed with a heavy blob of sea-green wax bearing an ornate impression, like a royal seal. "A letter?" She bent to retrieve it, reading the address on the front as she straightened.

"Skeller," she called.

He appeared almost immediately. His face lost color and his smile vanished as he spied the seal. Mutely he took the letter from her, turning it over and over without opening it. Finally he eased a finger under the wax and pried the missive open with only a little tearing of the parchment, like he knew how to do that from long practice.

"Is it important?" she asked, knowing it must be, for someone to take the trouble and cost of dispatching it with magic.

Skeller kept his eyes on the written words before him. "Nothing unusual," he said, refolding the parchment and slipping it into his harp case.

Lily's heart skipped a beat. He'd never lied to her before. At least she'd never caught him in a lie. "No one wastes the money and energy to dispatch a letter unless it is *very* important."

"My father thinks it is important. I don't."

"He wants you to come home and do your duty as a royal son." Why else would King Lokeen of Amazonia go to the trouble of finding a magician to dispatch the letter when few magicians lived on Mabastion and didn't hold the respect of kings and nobles as they did in Coronnan?

"Duty," he said flatly.

Lily flashed him a weak smile. They all seemed chained by duty of one sort or another. She reached to add a packet of flusterfoot powder to thicken Graciella's blood.

Skeller might dismiss the letter. But she couldn't. He might be a wandering bard now, but . . . What would he be when he stopped wandering and started heeding his father's demands?

He pulled her into a tight hug. "I have no intention of leaving you, my little love. My gentle Lily, who can't hurt anyone or anything. You calm violence just with your presence. My father and his followers incite it. I'll wait while you grow up a bit more in order to claim you. We were meant to find each other and be *together*." His words sounded defiant, fierce. Angry. "I can't live the way they want me to anymore. I need you and your gentle ways to guide me to a better life." He kissed the top of her head and released her.

She shied away from his banked temper.

Slowly, sensation returned to Skeller. He kept his eyes closed until his feet felt fully anchored on stone and his hands had a firm grip on Lukan's arm. Only then did he allow a sliver of light to penetrate beneath his eyelids.

"I really don't like that spell," he muttered, releasing Lukan.

"Gets easier with time." The young man grinned wickedly.

"Can't prove it by me." Skeller disengaged from Lukan, as if turning his attention elsewhere would settle his stomach and make the room stop spinning. They were in a room. That meant the interior of Castle Saria. He hoped they'd come to the right place anyway.

"I followed Lady Graciella's images to her private bower here in the castle," Lukan reassured him. He turned in place taking in the stark furnishings, a simple bedframe with a thin mattress and no draperies, a straight chair and table with a shielded candle stand, no candle. A small trunk on the bare stone floor beneath a high arrow-slit window.

"The lady's bower?" Skeller asked. "And where are the others?" He had trouble swallowing around the lump in his throat.

"Uh?" Lukan seemed surprised.

"You're in my maid's room," Graciella called to them from another room close by. "We are in the bower."

Skeller pushed his way past Lukan through the small doorway—he had to duck ungraciously and he wasn't overly tall—into a larger room, a little more luxurious with curtains and a wider, softer bed, but not much else.

"Life is rather primitive here in the wilds," Lady Ariiell sneered.

"We don't spend much time here." Graciella ducked her head as an embarrassed flush crept across her cheeks.

"I can see why. My prison tower room was more gracious than this." Ariiell picked at the threadbare coverlet, releasing a cloud of dust.

"They've been in the city since early spring," Lily defended her lady. "There should only be a few servants and guards here to maintain the buildings."

"They obviously weren't instructed to clean the place for your expected arrival." Ariiell continued a restless prowl. "But then you are only recently the lady of the castle and haven't established your authority over a bachelor household." She shrugged and perched on the long chest at the foot of the bed. It was well polished, if coated in a layer of dust, and covered in graceful flower carvings.

Lily shivered and wrapped her arms around herself. Skeller strode three long steps to her side and placeed his arm around her shoulder. "Cold?"

She nodded. "The sea breeze." She thrust her chin toward an unshuttered window, narrow by Amazonian standards but wider than the one in the maid's room.

Skeller didn't feel anything out of the ordinary.

Valeria lifted her head, also looking out that window. It faced northeast, toward where the high outcropping of rock marked the barrier between ocean and bay. Skeller had seen the shape of the place on maps. It didn't look inviting in a drawing. Less so in person. "He's coming," Val whispered. "I can feel him."

Ariiell's and Lukan's eyes widened as they nodded in agreement.

Lily buried her face in Skeller's chest. He took the opportunity to enfold her with both arms. "Do you feel him too?" he asked. She'd said that her talent was minor, but with so many strong magicians in her family he wondered if she hid her powers. There was so much about her and her family he didn't know; wanted to know; feared knowing.

At some point he had to accept that magic was an everyday part of life in Coronnan. Magic and ignorance powered their world instead of wheels, levers, and learning.

"Barely," she said into his tunic. "Mostly I share the tingling along Val's arms. She feels it as approaching magic. I just feel cold."

He held her tighter.

"What about Rejiia and Krej?" Val asked. "Would they come here first?"

Lukan shook his head. "I don't know for sure. But I thought the locals welcomed Jemmarc with open arms as a relief from Krej."

"Not the way I heard it," Ariiell said. As the oldest

among them, though not so very much older than Skeller, she alone had firsthand knowledge of the former Lord of Saria. "He talked big. Demanded control. But he was never cruel. Not like The Simeon and Rejiia. Krej felt he was doing Coronnan a favor by getting rid of Darville and his father, that he was the only person who knew what was best. Inside his province, and as regent of Coronnan, he only punished when there was a crime to punish. His people might still revere him."

They all stared at each other in indecision.

"We'll look for him later," Skeller said, taking control of the group when no one else would. "After we deal with Samlan."

"Let's get on with this," Ariiell said, decisively. "I'm tired of that man interrupting my dreams."

"I'm tired of him messing with storms and destruction," Lukan added.

"He killed our Mama, and our Da," Lily and Val said together.

Graciella bit her lip. "I don't know if my husband is alive or dead. What will become of me if he can't protect me?"

"He hasn't been doing such a good job of that this last week," Ariiell said. "How do we get down to the cove?"

"There's a track to the village," Val said leaning out the window and pointing. "I imagine we can make our way from there to the shore. I can see fishing boats out on the water on the bay side of the outcropping."

"That's a long walk," Skeller said. "He might make land on the ocean side before we can prepare for him."

"There . . . there's another way," Graciella said, still biting her lip. "I only know about it because Jemmarc told me how to find the secret door before I left the city. He said I needed to know in case of danger."

"Of course there are secret escape routes. There are always secret escape routes in every castle, palace, manor, and tower I've ever visited or heard about," Skeller said, mocking his own shortsighted plans.

"Get the women and children to safety first," Lukan mused, pressing his hands against various stones on the uncovered walls. "Give the women and children easy and immediate access." His circuit of the room took him back to the maid's alcove.

Graciella nodded to him. "Open the chest beneath the window."

"A trapdoor beneath a pile of ladies' underthings. Marauding soldiers would not think of looking deeper unless alerted ahead of time," Skeller said. Ingenious. He hadn't heard of that sort of entrance before. He'd have to suggest it to his fa ... to Aunt Maria.

If he ever went home again.

He had a duty. He seemed the only one willing to fix the problems Lokeen had created in Amazonia.

He could almost hear the latest letter from the King of Amazonia crackling inside his harp case.

CHAPTER 41

MIKK PUT HIS back into sliding his shovel into the layer of muck filling the kitchen courtyard, lifting the heavy load, and letting it fall into the waiting tub. Mud and slime oozed into the hollow he left behind in front of the low double doors that led to the cistern access. He cursed under his breath and dug in again, shoulders protesting more from this work than hours in the practice arena with a heavy sword and buckler.

Glenndon could do this better with his broad shoulders and strength. But Glenndon had his own job to do, clearing another portion of the palace grounds. Everyone worked today, including the king, his pampered daughters, and his frail wife.

Mikk could have chosen to supervise the raising of a collapsed bridge to restore foot traffic between Palace Isle and University Isle. He came here because he had to. He had to be the one to reopen the cistern. He had to be the one to determine how much clean water had returned, and if they should, or could, reopen the river doors to regulate the depth and flow.

He owed General Marcelle. Everyone did.

Not yet, though. He couldn't face the idea he'd find General Marcelle's drowned and mangled body. The river had not yet returned to normal levels below the runoff tunnel. No one could open those doors until it did. General Marcelle's body might be floating well out in the Great Bay by now.

He would not think of fish feasting on his flesh, or on any of the other bodies they hadn't found yet.

He dug in again. This time his back rebelled, sending lines of fire from his butt up to the base of his skull and along his arms. His hands shook as he dumped the latest load into the tub.

A kitchen lad dragged the tub away to the dumping grounds, wherever those were.

"Good silt will make a barren garden fertile again," Glenndon had said earlier.

Another lad shoved an empty washtub into place beside him. "I hope the city kitchen gardens flourish with all this muck," Mikk grumbled. He leaned on his shovel handle, trying to remember how to breathe.

"Sir?" the boy asked hesitantly.

"What?" Mikk tried not to sound surly, since he was grateful for the few moments of respite. "Sir, wouldn't it be easier to start by the kitchen door and work backward? That way the mud wouldn't slide in to fill the space you just cleared."

"The center of the courtyard is the lowest point and it drains out beneath the enclosing wall and into the river. The cistern access is actually higher than the kitchen steps to keep normal runoff from seeping under the doors and tainting the water." Actually, the ground behind the doors sloped upward another few feet until reaching the ladder that led down into the natural cavern. He hoped that the design had kept the water supply clean. At least clean enough that Glenndon could remove any taint with a quick spell.

Thinking about all that water made him thirsty. Again. Did he dare ask for a drink of the cloth-filtered and boiled water the queen rationed? She alone commanded the respect of all the refugees to obey her strictures.

Mikk returned his energy to the chore. One more tubful. Six more shovelfuls and he'd take a break. Then he'd feel he'd earned a few sips of water.

"Sir, I can see the bottom!" the lad cried in triumph. He knelt in the filth and began raking away the last few inches of accumulation with his hands.

Mikk sagged with relief. This truly would be his last tubful of muck for the day.

(A job well done is its own reward,) a voice announced in the back of his mind.

Shayla? Mikk here. He remembered naming protocols.

(Shayla here, and Baamin, and the entire nimbus at our king's disposal.)

An ear piercing bugling, like a deep-throated horn, echoed around the palace walls, bouncing and growing with each reverberation. The lad slapped his filthy hands over his ears and ducked his head.

Mikk searched the skies for a trace of a dragon. They were close. He could feel them in the back of his mind. Was that truly a glint of yellow, as sun struck around the edges of a crystalline dragon wing?

"Dragons!" he cried in relief. "The dragons have come to help."

"Where?" the nameless lad cringed against the stone shed that housed the cistern access.

"They won't hurt you. They've come to help."

"But . . . but what can they do? They're so big. Big as two sledge steeds across and two more high. My grandda says so. He saw a dragon once. Once when the king was new to the crown." He pressed himself harder against the stones, as if trying to merge with them.

"They won't harm you. I don't think they can. They are bound to the king by blood, tradition, and magic. They've come to help clean up after this disaster." Mikk shielded his eyes against the glare of the sun with one hand, still propping himself up with the shovel handle.

"Fat lot of help they'll be. They're just too damn big," the boy snorted.

"They can lift collapsed bridges off the river bottom, or rake a city street clean, or even retrieve a boat from a rooftop," Mikk chuckled.

"If you say so, sir."

Mikk returned to his work with a renewed sense of purpose. He could do this. He had to do this.

(Of course you can. And you will.)

Something tingled its way outward from behind Mikk's heart, filling his arms and legs with new strength. His feet stabilized against the slippery courtyard with refreshed balance. Details of dirt and plant life and of tiny rotting fish jumped to the front of his awareness.

Suddenly he felt as if he could accomplish anything. *Shayla, what is this?*

(A gift to help you learn what you must more quickly than most.)

"Magic," he breathed.

A low chuckle echoed around the back of his skull like the dragon call had echoed around the courtyard.

He pushed his shovel into the ground and cleared a few more inches of muck.

"We are not alone," Valeria whispered. Her small sound echoed off the slimy walls encasing an iron spiral staircase. She hated gripping the cold metal that sent chills through her entire body. Lukan descended in front of her, keeping close enough so she could clasp his shoulder for balance. Skeller did the same for Lily. The iron didn't seem to bother them.

"Servants," Graciella dismissed her worries. She led the way, walking with a surety that led Val to believe she'd been here before. Possibly Lucjemm had led her this way when threatening her with the razor-sharp rocks in the cove.

Unspoken fear lodged in Val's throat. Was it all echoes of the past? She knew criminals had been led this way to their executions upon the rocks.

No, this was something newer. *Lily, what do you feel? Graciella is trembling inside.*

Maybe that was it.

Ariiell stopped short behind Val. The ball of witchlight she carried on her open palm wavered and nearly blew out. It shouldn't. Only withdrawing the spell would extinguish witchlight. She grabbed Val by the shoulder and held her back. "They are here," she whispered. Her words did not echo or carry ahead to the others.

"Who?" Val asked, holding Lukan back as well. Had it been wise to place the three strongest magicians at the back of the line? Lily and Graciella had little magic to defend themselves with. Skeller had a long knife. Would that be enough if their enemy awaited them below?

Darkness pressed close against them, rapidly filling the gap between Lukan and Lily. Graciella's candle lantern flickered and disappeared around yet another curve. Its light did not penetrate the shadows between them.

"The weasel and the cat," Ariiell said.

"Didn't Graciella see them transform?" Lukan asked. He kept a wary lookout, peering over the inside railing for signs of the others.

"They are still a weasel and a cat inside their human bodies," Ariiell spat.

"Were they animals trapped inside human bodies before the spells? Then humans trapped inside animals . . ." Val had to ask. How else could she explain the longevity of two wild animals that should have succumbed to starvation or predators long ago. Sixteen years they'd lived wild.

"Which part of them dominates now is what we need to know," Lukan said. "Are they cunning magicians or wild animals?"

"Both," Ariiell insisted.

They continued downward more cautiously until they reached a broad landing where the others awaited them. A heavy door leading inward to the lower levels of the castle filled most of the wall. The stairs spiraled downward into the murky darkness. Graciella's candle did little to alleviate the gloom. Val wondered if even witch-light would push aside the shadows down there.

"Listen," Skeller whispered, turning toward the continuing stairs. "I can hear the boom of surf crashing onto land."

Val picked up the sound more as a thud against her belly than noise tickling her ears.

"I have to leave you here," Ariiell said. "I'll guard your backs, make sure the cat and the weasel do not follow or interfere. Help me with the door, Lukan."

"If you stay, I have to stay," Val said hesitantly. "It is my duty . . ."

"I discharge you of your duty. I am sane now. I have acknowledged the sins of others against me as their sins, not mine. As for my own sins? I know what I did and why. I'm learning to cope with my guilt. Go, Val. Go to your other duty." Ariiell turned her back on them and shot a hot, white stream of magic into the lock.

Before Val could follow Ariiell, Lukan hauled the door open. The massive panel nearly filled the landing. Graciella, Skeller, and Lily had to retreat down the stairs to make room for it.

"I can't let you go alone," Val protested. "You have not kept up your magic . . ."

"Neither have they," Ariiell said.

"I'll go with her, Val," Lukan reassured his sister. "Lily needs you beside her. We'll meet you back in the bower. Keep your mind open for our messages." He stepped through the portal after Ariiell and pulled the heavy door closed behind him him.

That left Val the only true magician facing Samlan, a ruthless master in full command of his power.

I long to feel the Kardia beneath my feet once more. This endless rock and sloshing works against what little healing I can manage. Geon's poison has left me weak.

I can barely force myself to eat and drink to replenish myself.

Solid ground will heal me more than time or remedies.

There is little dragon magic for me to gather. I used too much in my spell to conjure the storm. This reminds me of the days right after Shayla and her consorts flew away, nigh on twenty years ago. Jaylor forced us to learn to use ley lines in order to survive as magicians. I learned, but I hated every moment of every spell. My voice rejoiced the loudest when the dragons returned.

Now I am forced once again to seek out elusive bits of magical energy that drift through the ocean. I use it to cleanse water and catch fish so that I may survive. There is barely enough magic left over to cook the fish.

But the end of my ordeal is near. Yesterday I spotted land on the horizon. Today I can make out the ragged headland that marks the opening of the cove that will shelter me. My minions await. They have been most agreeably vulnerable to my dream probes since the end of the storm. They have no choice but to serve me so that I may restore Coronnan to greatness. They will learn the necessity of my cleansing the land of the corruption brought on by Jaylor. They will worship and obey me as their savior.

Now I must watch and wait for the precise moment just after the slack tide when the currents will carry me forward. The worst of the rocks will submerge and the rest will be exposed enough for me to steer around. Fishermen have used this technique for centuries. I shall be perfectly safe if I am patient and wait just offshore for the right moment.

I have infinite patience. I have waited twenty years for Jaylor's death and my elevation to his position so that I may guide the king along the proper path.

CHAPTER 42

LUKAN WOUND HIS way through a cluttered storeroom. Nothing neat and organized here, a clear sign of neglect by the lord and lady. He kept his glowball small, illuminating only a small puddle of light around his feet so he didn't trip over a sack of tubers or a leaning barrel of salted meat.

His nose itched. He swiped at it with his shirtsleeve.

"The flour is rotting," Ariiell whispered, half a step behind him. "What kind of reception do they expect to put on for Lady Graciella's return?" She seemed angry, not just annoyed.

"More than rotting flour and overripe red fruit," he whispered back. "Magic." Ley line magic that smelled faintly of earth and ocean, flowers, and tall trees. Dragon magic smelled sharp and aromatic, exotic in comparison. He looked around for a source of the power.

Tiny trickles of silvery blue led inward. They combined into a barely solid line against a wall. A glimmer of light showed around a doorway. The line crept under it. Losing potency in an effort to follow the stones rather than sink through them into the land beneath.

A trapped line, then, not a natural one.

Lukan doused his glowball and pressed his ear against

the wooden panels. Ariiell did the same, pressing her body close to him from behind.

He gulped as her musky scent filled his senses and blotted out all thought.

"Concentrate, you idiot. I'm not going to seduce you here and now. Though I might consider it later." The latter came out on a chuckle.

Lukan's face heated almost to burning the roots of his hair. He was grateful for the darkness so she couldn't see his embarrassment.

"Listen!" she hissed.

"We need another day of dry before you bring in the first hay," a man said in educated tones.

"In time for the Solstice celebration. We'll erect a Festival Pylon and dance, as we did in ancient times." A woman's husky tones sent enticing shivers up Lukan's spine.

Behind him, Ariiell went rigid.

Her wary alertness told Lukan more than he wanted to know. Krej and Rejiia spoke in the next room.

"Who else is with them?"

"Kitchen staff of three, and five villagers," Ariiell whispered directly into his ear. "Elder retainers who remember him from the old times."

How did she know? She must have counted heartbeats. That was something journeymen learned in the first few weeks after promotion.

Lukan forced his hearing deeper, consciously blocking the everyday sounds of words, clothing rustling, fire crackling, scuffing of restless feet. Deeper yet.

Ka-thump thump. One heart. Strong and confident. Krej. He found its rhythm and banished it from his mind. Three more hearts sounded in his mind, pounding different beats. One too fast—he thought that was excitable Rejiia—another slow and steady, listening and noncommittal, the other faint, as if it was somehow muffled or the owner stood apart from the others across the room.

He had to fight to find the rest. But find them he did, and agreed with Ariiell's assessment.

Now what? he asked.

We wait. And listen. Until they are alone.

Sound advice. Mama and Da would have said the same.

Krej issued a few more orders about the crops. Then a stool scraped across the stone floor. More foot shuffles.

Lukan felt a lessening of the pressure against his deep hearing before he heard doors opening and closing.

At last.

"Now, my dear, we have rested, eaten our fill, bathed, and attired ourselves in appropriate clothes. The time has come to plan our next move," Krej said.

"And what is that, dear Papa?" Rejiia spat.

Trouble between them? he asked Ariiell.

Always. We can take advantage of that.

Graciella led Skeller, Lily, and Val through six cellars, each a step lower than the previous one. Skeller recognized casks and barrels bearing the seals of Amazonia, Venez, and SeLennicca burned into the staves. The first room contained dry goods, flour, salt, and sugar. The next held barrels of dried fruit, then hanging meat, heavily salted to preserve it, then wine casks. The last two rooms remained empty, too damp to store anything without risking heavy mold and rot.

Amazonia didn't have tall mountains and jagged cliffs near the sea. His mother's castle sat atop an artificial hill overlooking the vast plains to the east and the seaport to the west, so tunnels were not common to him. Fascinating. He wanted to linger and examine the stonework and chisel marks. He couldn't. A mission awaited him. One he didn't want to think about, but had to.

He fingered the long knife sheathed at his belt. Would killing a man *feel* different from hunting animals for food? He'd given up the latter as he'd given up so much inherent to daily life in Amazonia. He gratefully joined Lily in her meatless diet because the thought of killing anything turned his stomach now.

He'd never taken the life of another *person*.

He pondered the various strengths of his companions. Graciella appeared vague and incapable of making a decision. But she harbored a lot of anger and fear. Val, though slight of build and often sickly, revealed whipcord-lean muscle and fierce determination. She also had a formidable magical talent, or so everyone told him. Then there was Lily. His gentle, nurturing, empathic Lily.

She had to know his trepidation. She had to feel his determination to do what had to be done.

Skeller lifted a heavy crossbar from the last door in their path. Sound and the scent of the sea washed over him the moment he pushed the door outward. He followed the muted boom of the surf, magnified by the twisted natural cavern. His nose told him that salt air awaited them only a few yards away. One more turn and they would face the enemy.

The man he had to kill.

Lily reached for his hand and squeezed. She gave him a weak smile of encouragement. He was a prince, trained for battle long before he cast away his heritage and embraced music. He could do this. He had to do this. It was his duty to the world, to himself, and to Lily.

The dragons have deserted me. I see them flying between large white clouds toward the city. I hear their belling calls. But their magic stops short of me and my little boat. I can no longer gather their magic.

I feel as if the special organ behind my heart, where I store the energy I gather from them, has shriveled into a desiccated, hard-shelled nut. Did I use too much of myself in creating the storm?

I do not think so. I am offended that the dragons give their magic to my enemies but not to me. They do not understand and appreciate what I have done for them. I have brought the Circle of Master Magicians back to the glory days without the manipulation and interference and changes implemented by Jaylor.

Women at the University! Legalizing ley line magic! Younger men ruling when older, more experienced masters are cast aside, ignored, and kept in ignorance of facts. That is what Jaylor brought.

I will restore the Circle to the basics of the covenant with dragons. I have restored Coronnan by wiping away the corruption of my enemy.

And still the dragons withhold their magic from me.

Very well. I can survive without their blessing. In time they will recognize the rightness of my actions. For now I will use the ley lines I espy on the strand to bring me and my boat to safety.

I can see a nice one running parallel to the shore. I pull on it through the medium of the water and the boat. The soles of my feet tingle with power. The energy moves upward to my heart and my mind.

The magic gives me full vision above and below the water. I see the route through the deadly rocks. The land and my minions await my return.

CHAPTER 43

"I NEED TO flex my magical muscle," Krej said as he left the kitchen area. "A summoning spell I believe is what we need."

"What we need is to grab Jaylor's daughters and find out what is happening in the capital," Rejiia insisted.

Lukan put his hand on the door latch to follow them.

"Wait," Ariiell whispered, placing a hand on top of his. Then she waved an intricate design with her fingers and touched the doorjamb, the hinges, the iron strips binding the door planks together, and then finally the latch. Her face paled, and she bit her lip. Sweat dotted her brow.

She had little magical stamina after sixteen years alone in her tower.

How much strength had Krej regained after those same sixteen years locked in the body of a tin weasel?

A plan began to form in the back of Lukan's brain. If he could push the two rogue magicians to overextend their strength, become vulnerable . . . he could . . . What? What could he do? He wasn't even an official journeyman yet. What skills and spells could he bring to the battle?

Ariiell cut short his musing by pushing gently on the door. It eased open silently even though a bit of rust tinged the hinges.

A quick assessment showed the kitchen empty. The hearth had been banked, and the workers had gone off to other tasks. The room was huge, taking up the entire undercroft of the hall above. A cook could roast an entire ox over the hearth. A leather treadmill on wheels would turn the spit when two boys walked on it.

Wheels! Lukan had never actually seen one, though he'd read about them in some of the oldest writings in the library. He wanted to kneel down and examine them minutely, figure out why the Stargods forbade them.

But he didn't have time. Not now anyway. Later maybe.

His mind turned to the task at hand. "If Krej used wheels in the kitchen, what other things did he do within the castle that the Stargods forbade?"

"He turned living creatures into statues," Ariiell said hesitantly. Then her words gained steadiness and verve as she let her anger build. "The creatures lived inside their frozen sculptures, still aware, but unable to move. More than once he bragged how he held Shayla, the dragon matriarch, captive."

"That is why the dragons left Coronnan," Lukan affirmed. He turned toward the narrow staircase that twisted upward into the hall, Ariiell close on his heels.

Twenty steps up, without a landing, the air grew fresher, his sense of space around him opened. He encountered a leather curtain. Beyond he heard nothing.

Ariiell stopped short. *Heartbeats,* she reminded him.

Lukan focused his hearing once more. *Two,* he mouthed, holding up two fingers.

Ariiell nodded. Then she pointed straight forward with one finger. Her other hand fluttered around.

Krej was still, Rejiia pacing.

"The ley lines are disrupted. I can't get the candle to reflect in the water," Krej complained.

A summoning spell. Lukan's gut grew cold. He couldn't allow Krej to find out yet about the chaos in the city and the disruption at the University. He'd take advantage of the crisis to regain control of the government and the Circle.

They needed time to recover.

"What about the dragons?" Rejiia asked. Her voice faded as she moved farther away.

"Nothing! Are you certain this glass is pure?" He kicked something, perhaps a chair or table leg.

"It was your spare glass, hidden in the secret recess in the inglenook. You took it out yourself and examined it." Her voice rose again, with strong emotion as well as proximity.

She's still ruled by the cat, Lukan thought.

Dangerous. Cats are unpredictable, Ariiell agreed.

Lukan smiled as he readied an old trick. A prank he used to play on Glenndon when they were little.

A pump in the kitchen below. He found the mass of metal in his mind and followed it. Iron pipes led down into a cistern. And *up*. He had water in the alcove on the exterior wall, across from the massive fireplace on the interior wall.

I need to see where she is.

Ariiell pushed the leather curtain aside three finger-widths without disturbing the rings and rod that sus-pended it.

Lukan prepared himself, watched and waited . . . waited . . . He had to be as patient as when he watched and waited for Glenndon to tread across the right part of the path near the creek.

Rejiia, tall and proud, with a fabulous mane of black hair streaked with blazing white from left temple to the ends near her knees, looked . . . far too young to have spent sixteen years trapped in a cat body. Twenty-five, he guessed. No more. How?

Krej, though, looked old, stooped and slowed by a joint disease that twisted his fingers. Older than he should look; ancient instead of late middle age.

Something had gone amiss during the restoration

spell. As if Rejiia had shoved some of her real age onto her father.

If she could do that, then . . . a truly formidable sorceress stalked across the far side of the hall, came to the center to peer over Krej's shoulder, then marched toward the mantel. "Your candle is too short," she said succinctly. "It's not reflecting properly. You are rusty, old man."

. She moved again, unable to sit still. Like a cat twitching its tail. Two more steps. He needed her to move two more steps . . .

And he pulled.

Water responded, spouting out of a gilded faucet into a shallow basin. He pulled harder. More water. It moved too fast to settle into the bowl and bounced up, showering Rejiia with a steady stream.

She screamed and ran toward the main entrance as if fire burned her. She had to escape. Now! She covered her head with her hands, dodging drops that became streams seeking her specifically.

Lukan pulled more water through the pipes and sent it showering across the room to drench Krej's white hair.

Rejiia's emotions flooded the room, nearly sending Lukan scurrying back to the kitchen.

Krej paused only half a heartbeat before following her, ducking and hunching his shoulders against the assault of water.

"They aren't too separate from their animal selves," Ariiell chuckled.

"I'm guessing they learned to react together for self-preservation," Lukan admitted. He walked cautiously toward the tall table in the center of the room, keeping an eye on the main entrance. The door remained open and untended, creaking in the constant sea breeze.

Resolutely, he picked up the palm-sized glass circle edged in silver from the basin of water. A journeyman's tool. "I'm a journeyman now. I claim this as my right."

Deftly he wiped it dry on the cloth clumped nearby, then wrapped it in a neatly folded square of silk.

"Can we go back to your sisters now?" Ariiell asked anxiously. "I'm feeling a need to stomp and throw things and screech uncontrollably."

"Hang onto your sanity a few more moments. I think we need to walk out the front entrance and around by the village, make sure Krej and Rejiia aren't coming back for a bit. They need to run until panic gives way to logic again. The old Krej would never have left the room. How long now?" He offered her his arm and escorted her from the ancient and gloomy castle.

"There is no other way?" Lily asked her companions. She watched the waves beyond the treacherous jutting rocks in the cove. Just after low tide, the rocky strand was bigger than she had envisioned, stretching a mile or more between headlands. The mouth of the natural cave that led to the castle cellars was well above normal high tide lines. On the ocean side of the promontory, she saw little evidence of the storm and flood.

All of the rain and surging waves had gone directly into the Bay and up the River Coronnan.

Just beyond the tallest of the jagged spires a sailboat tacked back and forth, waiting for the tide to turn and begin to fill the cove once more.

She saw a single man sitting at the tiller, manipulating both rudder and sails with magic instead of hands.

Samlan. The man who had destroyed a large portion of Coronnan with his vengeful ambition. The man who had caused both of her parents to die.

"We agreed," Val replied.

"This is something the Circle of Masters should be doing," Lily replied, trying to find a different path.

Only one path remained, and Samlan turned his boat onto it.

"The Circle has other tasks," Skeller said gently,

squeezing her shoulder. His other hand fingered the pommel of his dagger.

Lily knew the keenness of that blade. When she'd first met Skeller she'd watched him skin a rabbit with it in a few quick slashes; as efficient as Mistress Maigret or Val.

Since that time, Skeller had given up eating meat. He'd shared her distaste for taking a life. Any life. Val still ate meat. Val didn't share the pain and terror of the victim—large or small—that Lily did. That was a talent, or a curse, she'd inherited from their mother.

But Skeller's knife remained sharp, the blade straight and true.

"Samlan sent the Krakatrice eggs to Ariiell's father, knowing they would wreak more destruction when they hatched," Graciella said, coming out of her vacant state for a moment. "He restored Krej and Rejiia to their natural forms. This castle once belonged to them. They used this cove for executions. Horrible executions." She shuddered, then set her chin in determination.

"The Circle uses every magician they can find to fight off the Krakatrice and to rebuild the city," Val continued. "We are the only ones left."

"Lukan . . . ?"

"Is searching the castle, making sure Krej and Rejiia don't sneak up on us," Val reminded her.

The sailboat wove a convoluted path among the rocks. As Lily watched, the boat keeled over, mast almost touching the waves to avoid a rock that would rip the hull to shreds. Then it righted and continued forward. Samlan seemed calm and assured. He touched the waves and rocks with the tip of his staff to aid his navigation through the maze of obstacles, both obvious and submerged.

"He's powerful," Val stated. "Can you feel the magic he's using to guide him in?"

"I don't have to," Lily said flatly.

"He's exhausting himself," Graciella added. "See how he falters beside Traitor's Rock?"

"I see." Val raised her hands, fingers pointing directly

at the boat. She walked toward the incoming waves and adjusted her feet for better contact with the ley lines within the Kardia. Her eyes closed and her brow furrowed in a deep frown as she pushed her magic out toward the boat, the water, and that viciously sharp rock.

Her aura spiked bright purple slashed with red. She used a huge amount of energy.

Samlan responded with a stronger push with his staff against the rock, forcing his boat away from the knifelike protrusions. But he overcompensated into another rock, just as sharp above and below the water.

They all heard the crash and boom of the surf, the groan of sundered wood as the hull scraped stone.

The boat rocked violently, sinking rapidly.

Samlan scrambled to keep it afloat as long as possible, shedding mast and sail, using his staff to fend off more rocks. He lost his balance and toppled into the water, still holding his staff.

He bobbed to the surface, gasped and sank again. The staff floated. He clutched it desperately.

"Is the staff straightening back to its original grain?" Lily asked no one in particular.

Beside her, Skeller shrugged. Graciella didn't seem to hear and Val was too engrossed in her repulsion spell to pay attention.

Lily held her breath, hoping, praying that the relentless tide and the punishing rocks would do their work.

Val kept pushing, crashing the boat, pulling the ferocious waves inward. She sagged with fatigue. Color drained from her face while her aura deepened.

Lily reached to hold her twin upright and feed her strength. Graciella and Skeller beat her to it.

Val dropped her hands, unable to sustain her battle with wind and waves.

Samlan rode a wave ashore. He landed on the pebblestrewn beach facedown, feet still in the water. The next wave tugged at his shirt and trews, but did not reach far enough to drag him backward, or drown him.

Slowly he lifted his body, bracing on hands and knees, head hanging lower.

He crawled forward three paces and collapsed again. "Help me!" He reached forward a plaintive hand, lifting his head, and stared sharply at the companions. His gaze burned deep inside, compelling Lily . . . to come to him, to carry him to safety.

She had to obey. Her hands and feet moved without her willing them. And yet . . .

CHAPTER 44

TIME STRETCHED AND thickened. Val saw each breath, each eye blink, each move of her companions in slow motion. The air became difficult to breathe.

Samlan lay across a ley line, all of its magical energy available to him.

Val had used so much magic she had no strength left to even tap that line. If she could get to it.

She watched Lily deftly grab Skeller's dagger from its sheath. Val doubted he even noticed the loss of its weight against his hip.

I'm sorry, Lily mouthed. Then she withdrew her mind from Val's. The emptiness where her twin had always been, even when separated by many miles, left Val sagging and inert.

Skeller's hands on her rib cage tightened. Still trapped in the sludge of slowed time.

Lily withdrew farther, breaking the time manipulation. Then she turned back toward Samlan and dashed across the rocks. They cut her bare feet, leaving a trail of blood. Val could not follow or stop her.

Skeller blinked, too startled to move.

Graciella dropped to her knees, gasping in horror.

They all saw Lily twist her fist in Samlan's shirt and hoist him to his feet.

"Good girl. You know your true master," he said on a weak smile, gaining strength and magic with every heartbeat where his feet shuffled for contact with the ley line.

Too much magic. Val didn't have the strength or the mastery to counter him again. She'd given all her energy to wrecking his boat.

"Yes, I do know my true master," Lily repeated back to him. "I am my own master. My dreams are my own. My life is my own. My magic, such as it is, is my own. And this choice is my own."

One strong thrust and the dagger impaled the man, driving straight for his heart.

Blood gushed across Lily's hand and from the man's mouth. "The trouble with magicians is that they expect only magical attack. They don't prepare for anything else." Lily slowly withdrew the blade, staring at it as if she didn't know what she held. What she had done.

Val pushed through Lily's defenses and rejoined her mind to her twin, giving her love and reassurance. Horror rushed back to her.

Samlan's eyes glazed over and his body sagged. And still Lily held him up by his shirt, a part of that terrible tableau, bound to him in death as she refused to be in life.

A wave, much bigger than previous ones, poured over Lily and her victim, washing away some of the spilled blood. But not all of it. It left behind a dark stain on Lily's gown and a stout, straight branch of hawthorn on the strand, just the right size for a staff. Samlan's gnarled staff of sturdy oak rolled back to sea and split in two on impact with the first rock.

Lily dropped Samlan and picked up the perfectly smooth and straight stick, stripped of bark, ready to use and twist into her magical signature, whatever it became.

Then Lily's empathy joined with her enemy and his death invaded her soul. And Val's.

The world grew dark, and a roaring of dragon anger filled their ears.

❧

"You aren't the woman I thought you were," Skeller staggered to hold Lily upright. They both sagged to their knees. The full weight of Samlan's death weighed them down. He felt the sharp stab in his heart just as Samlan had, just as Lily did.

Her empathy had forced her to share the awful moment when the man's eyes glazed and life drained away from him. Her bond with Skeller, their growing love, had pulled him into that intimate moment of sharing death.

Skeller had to fight his own bond with Lily to keep from following into the enticing darkness.

(Not yet,) a dragon reassured him/them. *(The realm of death is not yet yours to claim.)*

He blinked rapidly. The wash of another big wave dragged him back to awareness.

The ache in his gut and in his soul remained.

How much worse was it for Lily?

She'd done what he didn't have the courage to do.

"D . . . don't touch me. My deeds will taint you," she stammered.

They already had.

"Lily, dear heart, you must live. You cannot allow that man's evil to take you from me."

"He already has."

"No. I won't allow it." He dragged her and himself upright and away from the compelling grip of the tide. He thought to entrust Lily to her twin. But Val was exhausted, in dire need of strength. Strength and renewal she would draw from her twin by instinct, even though Lily had nothing left to give.

So he held Lily close, wondering what to do next. How to . . . continue living with that horrible pain in his heart and his soul.

"We need time," he whispered. "Time to heal our minds and our bodies from this."

Lily nodded. A little color returned to her face but her eyes continued to stare hollowly at nothing.

A sense of crowding pressed him closer to her. Ethereal pain, and aloneness.

The cove had seen so many other bloody deaths, natural and not. The screech of dragons and gulls overhead sounded like so many ghosts haunting the place. Haunting them all.

She'd killed a man.

She couldn't swat a fly.

She drove the long knife straight and true deep into Samlan's heart.

"You were prepared to do the same," Graciella reminded him. "I saw how you worried at the grip of your knife."

"'Twas my duty . . ."

"I think we all had the same idea. The same perverted sense of duty," Ariiell said, appearing at the head of the path toward the village and to the castle's main entrance. Lukan was not at her side.

Skeller didn't care. His chest felt as if Lily had ripped it open, the same as she had Samlan's. His head hurt with confusion and unshed tears.

"I murdered him. Murder," Lily whispered, still caught in the loop of her own empathy. How many times must she relive that moment of becoming the instrument of death?

"Not murder. Execution," Val snarled.

"Execution," he agreed. His father had brought executions back to Amazonia in place of exile. Veneza held public executions. He'd run away from that to find . . .

Something better.

"The land groans and mourns the loss of life," Lily stammered. "Not just his life—all the lives lost to the storm and the aftermath. All the lives he was responsible for. The land is as wounded as the kingdom." She seemed to be talking more to herself than to their companions. But Skeller felt every word drive into him as if his own.

"If you help heal the land, can you heal yourself?" he asked gently. "If you help restore the lost crops, the downed trees, the despairing people, will you heal within yourself?"

"I . . . I think so." She looked up at him, eyes clearing. "The people and the land need seeds and cuttings. I can take them from unaffected places and plant them where they are needed. I can bring life back to Coronnan."

"And back to yourself."

She nodded mutely.

"You will need time. I need time to accept what we have done here this day."

Questions appeared on all of their faces.

"Lily may have wielded the dagger. But I carried the dagger. Graciella led the way. Val crashed his boat, made him vulnerable. Samlan called us to gather here. We are all responsible." He drew a long shuddering breath.

So did Lily. She bent low, as a new wave circled their feet. Something rolled and bobbed . . . The hawthorn bit of driftwood. She claimed it as her own, planting the broad base of it firmly in the gravel shoreline.

"I have to go back to Amazonia," he said, coming to a decision that had nagged him since the first letter from his father. A letter that reminded him of his duty elsewhere. "I hope not forever, but for a time."

"I know," Lily said, raising her eyes from her study of the staff, learning every line of the wood grain.

Skeller touched the letters in his script. "My father calls me home. He has corrupted Amazonia in partnership with Samlan. There are others who could end his tyranny, bring peace and compromise back to my homeland. But I seem to be the only one who will do it. I have to go. It is my duty." Deliberately he released his hands from her and took a step toward the path away from this awful place of carnage.

"Skeller!" Lily reached out toward him. When he made no move to capture her hand with his own, an extreme effort, she dropped her hand to her sister's shoulder. She leaned heavily on the bit of driftwood. No, it was her staff, highly prized among magicians. "I did it for you, Skeller. So you would not have to live with that man's death on your hands."

"I was prepared. I could deal with it because it was necessary."

"Exactly," Val said for her sister. "It was necessary. Lily did by mundane means what Samlan least expected and could not defend himself against."

"I have no magic. I could have done the same," Skeller said softly.

"Could you?" Lily captured his gaze with her own. All he saw was pain.

"Or would Samlan have expected a mundane attack from a bard, the son of King Lokeen?" Val continued for her sister. "He wouldn't expect a mere woman to deal the death blow. My memories of him at the University taught me that he had little respect or use for women. He wouldn't consider Lily capable, and so dismissed her as a threat. You, Skeller, could not get close to him."

They all stood in silence a long moment, instinctively edging away from the incoming tide, but not toward the natural cavern that led to the castle. No, they moved toward the village, toward mundane life.

"So, you are returning to Amazonia," Ariiell summed up the conversation. "I'm taking Valeria back to the Clearing in the mountains so that she can heal and regain strength. We'll look after Jule and Sharl."

Val didn't look too happy about that. Then she sighed and nodded acceptance. "It's what I need."

"Where do I belong?" Graciella asked, looking up toward the forbidding walls of Castle Saria. "Not here."

"Then return to your husband in the city, or to your mother. Or go back to the Forest University. The choice is yours, my lady," Lily said.

Graciella looked frightened at the need to make a decision. A choice.

She hugged herself and looked at nothing.

Ariiell rolled her eyes in near disgust and wrapped an arm around her shoulders. "I'll help you sort through your choices. The University for now, I think. But only for so long. I'm having trouble holding to my own decisions."

"Where's Lukan?" Skeller asked, drawing his awareness to the larger group and away from his own hurt and emptiness. The time had come to travel again. His feet itched to start the journey he didn't want to take, though he knew he must. Just like the first time he'd run away from home—wishing to stay, knowing he couldn't. Shouldn't.

Great Mother, he wanted to hold Lily close and kiss away their hurts. But if he did that, he'd never do what he must. Go home.

"Lukan is following Krej and Rejiia," Ariiell said. Briefly she recounted their encounter with the infamous rogue magicians.

They all found a bit of humor in Rejiia's reaction to a drenching. Skeller heard the chords of the rousing chorus of that tale in his head, felt it in his fingers.

"They are still a threat, Ariiell," Lukan said, stumbling down the steep path to join them. "When Rejiia stopped running just beyond the curtain wall, I threw my knife. She's bleeding from the upper left arm. Maybe she was already wounded and running opened it again. I don't know. They are running again, out beyond the fields. Even if they return, they won't find Krej's glass. His magic is crippled without it."

He held up a wad of silk with near-reverence. "Coronnan has a bit more time to heal before those two are ready to gather forces and launch an attack. I was promised a staff and a journey. I'm taking it."

Lily straightened enough to pull him into a hug. "Where?" she gulped.

"I'll deliver Da's letter to Glenndon. Then I'll find a staff and go in search of Master Robb and his apprentices. I'm thinking Amazonia. The scrying spell sent the pendulum swinging across the map from Lake Apor to Amazonia. We know Lord Laislac was in league with Samlan and Lokeen. That's the connection. If Robb isn't in Aporia, then he's across the ocean. Do you need a traveling companion, Your Highness?" He bowed slightly toward Skeller.

Skeller could only nod acceptance. Sadness at separating from Lily choked him beyond speech. Realization of all he was leaving in Coronnan dug deeper into his gut. He wanted to double over in physical pain.

"Coronnan needs nurturing. The land needs seeds and a gentle touch. The people need healing." Lily looked off into the distance. "I need time alone with my grief and pain."

"You can't leave me," Val protested, holding her sister tighter.

"You and I will never be totally alone." Lily returned the hug with a weak smile. "I'm only a thought away. The sea gifted me with a staff. I'll take my own journey." She held up the smooth stick and examined the wood grain closely, committing it to memory. It was a constant reminder for her of why she would wander the land. Alone.

Perhaps more alone than Skeller would ever be. "Someday . . . when we all have grown away from this terrible day, I will come back for you," he whispered.

If duty and family and arranged marriages didn't interfere.

"You were happy here, Skeller. You had the carefree life of a wandering bard," Lily reminded him. "Hold those memories close and let them sustain you on your journey."

"You too." He turned and walked away while he still could.

CHAPTER 45

"*INDIGO, BANK TO your left!*" Glenndon called with voice and mind to the purple-tip dragon. He rode the dragon's lower neck, carefully braced between two jutting spinal horns, gripping the dragon body with his knees. Wind whipped at his face and hair, playing joyfully with him, taunting him with reminders of the freedom of his youth. For two brief moments he breathed deeply of the fresh cleanness of the air, luxuriating in the raw sensations and his own uncensored response.

A wail of despair pierced his brief reverie. He repeated the silent signal to go left with his body and his heels, as General Marcelle had taught him to do with a steed.

Indigo dipped his left wing and curved gracefully into a new direction. Glenndon didn't know if he responded to the verbal or the tactile command.

(What do you sense?) Indigo asked, raising his snout to sniff the air two hundred feet above the maze of river branches and islands peeking out from the murky waters.

Someone alive and pleading for rescue.

(Not a magical mind,) Indigo excused his own lack of sensitivity to normal humans.

"That's why we work together. We make a good

team." Glenndon patted the soft fur of the dragon's neck. Hardly any silver left in the fine hairs. His friend matured by the day. But he hadn't grown to full dragon size. He wondered if Indigo would ever achieve the mass of older dragons, or if being a very special, rare, and asexual purple-tip meant he was also destined to be a runt.

No matter. Today, his reduced bulk made him an excellent partner in negotiating the remnants of Coronnan City for signs of life.

Or dead bodies that needed to be removed.

Indigo had already lifted a dozen corpses, with reverence and delicacy, and delivered them to the mass grave at Battle Mound, an hour's steed ride outside the city.

"Can you see that long roof, slightly to your left?"

Indigo flashed an image of the dark apex and slanting sides with three chimneys that seemed to float in the river but did not move downstream.

"Must be a Temple or meeting house," Glenndon mused, wishing he'd taken the time to memorize the city before the flood, when he didn't really need to know every building on every island.

(Something moves beside the center chimney.)

"Yes, indeed. Can you hover?"

A moment of reflection. *(Easier to grip the chimney top as if landing.)*

"Try not to damage the bricks and mortar." Glenndon knew how much work went into repairing a chimney. He'd done it for his mother. Twice. If she'd just banished the mice and bats and other critters that clawed at the mortar and loosened the stones . . . Or if Lukan had chosen a different hiding place.

He'd never get to fix something for his mother again . . . And Lukan?

He bit his lip and concentrated on the three figures cowering against the roof, hiding in the shadow of Indigo's wings.

(Better to save a life than worry about a replaceable

chimney.) The dragon circled the building three times in a tight downward spiral.

Waves of fear flooded Glenndon's mind and tightened his chest. "Empathy. Their fear of the dragon, not mine," he reminded himself. Blanking his mind, he uncoiled a rope ladder from the spinal horns behind him and threw it toward the tallest of the family sheltering on the roof.

The woman, holding a babe in her arms while a toddler clung to her skirts, ignored the lifeline. She looked up toward Glenndon, too terrified to move.

"Indigo will not hurt you," he reassured the woman. Her hair lay in a tangled mat down her back, an indeterminate color, matching the mud smeared on one cheek. Fatigue and hunger wove deep shadows on her gaunt face and haunted eyes.

"The little ones . . ."

"Indigo does not eat people."

(They taste bad.) Indigo injected some dragon humor. Good thing the refugees couldn't hear him.

"On my honor as a prince and heir to King Darville, we have come to rescue you. I promise no harm will come to you." Glenndon wondered if he'd have to climb down and carry the woman and her children aboard.

(I cannot balance here much longer,) Indigo warned him.

Biting her lip, the woman urged the toddler to climb the ladder. The little boy scrambled up easily. He hadn't learned to fear dragons yet.

The woman held up the baby to Glenndon. He cradled it gently against his chest with one arm while reaching his other to assist her in the awkward climb.

"Keep moving," he encouraged her. "If you stop, the ladder will twist and throw you off."

Mutely she nodded and continued up, more slowly than Glenndon liked. Indigo fluttered his wings, striving for balance. The woman cried out in fear.

Glenndon hauled her the rest of the way up with one

arm. His muscles trembled and strained. The shoulder seam of his once-elegant tunic ripped. He kept pulling until at last she straddled the dragon back, skirt hiked up above her knees, exposing her filthy legs and shoeless feet.

Embarrassed, she fiddled to push her skirt down.

"Don't worry. My mama never wore shoes either, except in deep winter if she had to go outside. I think I was four before I had a pair of my own." He handed the baby back to her, concerned that it seemed too still and pale.

Next stop would be the University and a healer.

Indigo thrust his wings down once and released his grip on the chimney. Six bricks bounced down the sloping roof into the river.

Squealing with glee, the little boy gripped Glenndon's tunic and peered all around at the wonder of flying after days of being trapped by the flood.

"You're sure this dragon isn't hungry?" the woman asked.

(*I'm always hungry.*)

Glenndon gave the dragon a light tap as a reminder that dragon humor wasn't always funny to humans.

"Indigo is our friend. He is dedicated to *helping* people and Coronnan today."

(*And always.*)

So am I, my friend. Thus is our duty.

Coronnan heals, but slowly. The dragons enter into the chore with strength. The people face their grim future with courage. The king and queen are in the midst of it all, winning back the hearts and loyalty of their people after years of distancing themselves from them.

Things have changed greatly since I last looked hard at people and politics. My dream of restoring myself to my own body is complete. But it is a hollow victory, won by chance and not by my own skill and determination.

I merely grabbed the magic flung wildly about and

held on. Another magician's carelessness did the rest. Though I did manipulate things a bit, sheltering behind my companion and letting him take the brunt of conflicting magics. He is old beyond old now. I am not.

I will accept my restored body for what it is. While chaos lies just beneath the surface, ready to attack Coronnan, I shall watch and wait and pounce when I am ready.

But I won't allow too much peace and order to return, to banish my dearest friend, Chaos.

Irene Radford
The Pixie Chronicles

Dusty Carrick lived in the small town of Skene Falls, Oregon, her entire life. And, like many of the local children, she played with "imaginary" Pixie friends in Ten Acre Woods.

But the Pixies are not imaginary at all, and Ten Acre Woods is their home. Now, the woods are in danger, and if it falls, the Pixies too will die. Only Thistle Down, exiled from her tribe and trapped inside a mortal woman's body, can save her people—as long as she can convince Dusty Carrick to help her before it's too late.

THISTLE DOWN
978-0-7564-0670-7

CHICORY UP
978-0-7564-0724-7

"Enjoyable romantic urban fantasy." —*Alternative Worlds*

To Order Call: 1-800-788-6262
www.dawbooks.com

S.L. Farrell

The Nessantico Cycle

"[Farrell's] best yet, a delicious melange of politics, war,
sorcery, and religion in a richly imagined world."
—George R. R. Martin,
#1 *New York Times* bestselling author

"Readers who appreciate intricate world building,
intrigue, and action will immerse themselves effortlessly
in this rich and complex story."
—*Publishers Weekly*

A MAGIC OF TWILIGHT
978-0-7564-0536-6

A MAGIC OF NIGHTFALL
978-0-7564-0599-1

A MAGIC OF DAWN
978-0-7564-0646-2

To Order Call: 1-800-788-6262
www.dawbooks.com

DAW 119

Violette Malan

The Novels of Dhulyn and Parno:
"Believable characters and graceful storytelling."
—*Library Journal*

"Fantasy fans should brace themselves:
the world is about to discover Violette Malan."
—*The Barnes & Noble Review*

THE SLEEPING GOD
978-0-7564-0484-0

THE SOLDIER KING
978-0-7564-0569-4

THE STORM WITCH
978-0-7564-0574-8

and

PATH OF THE SUN
978-0-7564-0680-6

To Order Call: 1-800-788-6262
www.dawbooks.com

Kari Sperring

Living with Ghosts

978-0-7564-0675-2

Finalist for the Crawford Award for First Novel

A Tiptree Award Honor Book

Locus Recommended First Novel

"This is an enthralling fantasy that contains horror elements interwoven into the story line. This reviewer predicts Kari Sperring will have quite a future as a renowned fantasist."

—*Midwest Book Review*

"A satisfying blend of well-developed characters and intriguing worldbuilding. The richly realized Renaissance style city is a perfect backdrop for the blend of ghostly magic and intrigue. The characters are wonderfully flawed, complex and multi-dimensional. Highly recommended!"

—*Patricia Bray, author of The Sword of Change Trilogy*

And now available:

The Grass King's Concubine

978-0-7564-0755-1

To Order Call: 1-800-788-6262
www.dawbooks.com

MICHELLE WEST
The House War

"Fans will be delighted with this return to the vivid and detailed universe of the *Sacred Hunt* and the *Sun Sword* series.... In a richly woven world, West pulls no punches as she hooks readers in with her bold and descriptive narrative."
                                        —*Quill & Quire*

To Order Call: 1-800-788-6262
www.dawbooks.com